ETERNITY

BITES

ETERNITY BITES

An Eternal Novel

Book 11

K.G. INGLIS

Also by K.G. Inglis

The Eternal Series:

Eternity Begins (Prequel)

Eternal Covenant

Eternal Possession

Waking The Eternal Dragon (short story)

Heart Of Eternity

Eternal Temptation

Eternal Craving

Eternity Is Forever

Eternal Youth

Hunt For Eternity

Eternity Unveiled

Eternity Unbound

Eternally Entangled (novella)

Eternity Bites

Coming Soon:

Glimpse Eternity

ISBN:
Softcover: 978-1-7635061-2-1
eBook: 978-1-7635061-3-8

Published by: K.G. Inglis
Covers by: Eerilyfair Design.

ACKNOWLEDGEMENTS

I would like to say a huge thank you to my family for all your support. The last eighteen months have been very difficult at times, and I'm very grateful for everything you've done to help make things easier and much more enjoyable.

And, as always, I would like to thank you, my reader, for continuing to read this series. I hope you enjoy this next instalment.

Darkened hordes shall seek the one,

Through whose touch truth is revealed,

The mark of a dragon on a lycan son,

By blood and fate, their future is sealed.

When hearts collide, the storm shall rise,

Then both dragon and wolf will unify,

Together alive, apart they die,

He must defend her from the sky.

Wyvern Prophecy

1

Brin stood inside the forest, only metres from the back gate to Doran and Zoe's modest cottage in Dunn Turidd, Fey. Her sharp green eyes scanning her surroundings as the nephilim portal began to close behind her and Seth with a faint shimmer of golden light. She ran her fingers through her thick, wavy red locks, slightly frizzed from the static energy of the portal travel, exhaling deeply on a sigh.

While the instant convenience of portal travel had its perks, Brin still favoured the exhilaration of riding on the back of a dragon. There was something incomparable about the freedom of flight, soaring through boundless skies and the raw power surging through the dragon beneath her. She loved watching the landscape shift far below, tiny villages, rivers, and forests all rolling by, dwarfed by the immense shadow of the dragon stretching across the land like a passing cloud. The wind whipping through her hair made her feel alive, although she could do without the inevitable battle to untangle the knots afterward. So, when taking that into consideration, instant travel through a nephilim portal with only a bit of frizz to deal with, wasn't so bad.

She breathed in deeply, filling her lungs with the fresh forest air. The air here was cool, carrying with it a faint, earthy scent that felt ancient, timeless, like it had never known the taint of pollution or modernity, which in fact, it hadn't. Nothing in Fey had. Brin had often compared it to living in a bubble, perpetually the same, never changing or evolving. Although, that wasn't entirely true. Over the past decade or so, they had acquired a few new residents from Earth, like Zoe, and her two sisters-in-law, Kaitlyn and Jasmin. And with them came a few trinkets of technology like watches and laptops and solar power to run them. Even Gwynn ap Nudd, the Nephilim High Lord, had installed solar power to his own home. And, looking at Doran's home, Zoe had insisted on it too.

Brin loved her home in Avengard, but it seemed so backward compared to all the wonderful advantages of modern advancement that Earth had to offer. And now here too, Dunn Turidd seemed to be evolving, albeit at a snail's pace, but the first steps toward embracing a more advanced way of life had begun.

This was far from Brin's first time in Dunn Turidd. In fact, she'd been coming here throughout her life, for the past two centuries, but it was times like this that she wondered why she didn't come more often. The Nephilim's woodlands radiated a unique stillness that had a way of relaxing her far more easily than the forests near her home in Avengard ever did.

"Well," Seth said, hitching the satchel on his shoulder a little higher. Her older brother's tone was neutral, though Brin caught the way his sharp green eyes darted around. Ever the protective brother, he was already calculating escape routes and potential threats. "We're here."

They walked side by side toward the house, her own gaze continuing to drift over the manicured garden and shady lawn. "It's different from what I expected," Brin admitted, her voice lilting with approval as she took in the scene before her. The home itself was unassuming, with weathered stone walls, a thatched roof, and ivy creeping up its sides.

Brin looked about the yard she was standing in, with Seth less than an arm's length away. In the three years Zoe had lived here in Dunn Turidd, this was the first time she had paid her a visit. It wasn't that she hadn't wanted to, she just hadn't had any reason to come sooner. It was a poor excuse really, but in the past, whenever she and Zoe had met, it had usually been at Havenswood Manor, in Cadley, England, a place Brin had come to think of as her second home.

Despite Zoe's home here in Dunn Turidd and Havenswood manor being vastly different in size, and situated in separate realms, there were two very distinct similarities between them. That being that both homes were located on the edge of an angelically protected forest. The forest here in Dunn Turidd, Fey, was called the *Coed Caer Ffin* (Border

Fortress), and in Cadley it was Savernake Forest. The most important similarity being that both forests contain the same tree, the Elder tree. A sacred, angelic bridge inhabiting the triad of realms simultaneously: Earth, Fey, and the Angelic realm, its height reaching one hundred feet, and width large enough to encompass a house.

The Elder tree was one of a kind. On Earth, its presence remained hidden from humans and supernaturals alike, with only a select few being granted the privilege of laying eyes on it. In Fey, however, anyone permitted entry to the forest could see its immense, radiant form. Even so, very few who lived in Fey outside of Dunn Turidd, had ever ventured to the forest to view it.

Brin and her four brothers were among an even smaller number who had seen it both here in Fey and on Earth. Its awe-inspiring presence never failed to leave her humbled. Even now, standing on Dunn Turidd soil, she could feel the tree's energy resonating through *Coed Caer Ffin*, ancient and unyielding.

The sound of a door opening caught Brin's attention, looking up in time to see Zoe step out of the cozy cottage, her expression lighting up as soon as she recognised Brin and Seth. A wide smile spread across her face as she walked briskly toward them, her arms outstretched.

"Brin! Seth! It's so good to see you!" she exclaimed, pulling Brin in to give her a warm hug before turning to embrace Seth as well.

"Come on in," she said, gesturing toward the door. "Can I offer you a drink?"

As they stepped inside the cottage, Zoe led them into a quaint kitchen that was neat and welcoming, soft sunlight streaming through the window to cast golden patterns on the wooden countertops. The air smelled faintly of herbs and something sweet, like baked apples. Zoe moved toward the kitchen cabinet with an easy grace and began retrieving glasses.

"I'd offer you coffee or tea," she said with a rueful smile. "But I haven't quite adjusted to life here without my electric kettle. It's ridiculous how much I miss that thing. I can cope without my hairdryer and even my phone, but waiting for water to boil on the stove feels like it takes an eternity, and I'm not exactly known for my patience."

Brin laughed softly. "I think you're doing great. It's a huge adjustment moving from the modern conveniences of Earth to Fey."

"True," Zoe said, pouring chilled water from a ceramic pitcher into the glasses. "Although I was raised in Far North Queensland, so I got used to this kind of life at a very young age, since every second storm knocked out our power and communications for days on end. The only difference is, now the power never comes back on," she laughed. "Don't get me wrong, I love it here, I really do, and this is where Doran lives and works. The leader of the Wildings can't exactly do his job from Far North Queensland, or even England for that matter, could he?" she said with a casual shrug of her shoulder. "Really though, Fey should look into inventing a magical version of an electric kettle. I'd be first in line to buy one."

"You're the one with magic, why don't you invent it yourself?" Seth suggested.

Zoe thought on that for a moment and nodded. "You know what, I just might do that. Sometimes I forget I'm still a druid, now that I'm also a vampire, that side of my life seems to take precedence, plus there aren't any other druids between here and your place in Avengard, to practice the craft with," she said with a shrug.

"We saw solar panels on your roof, why aren't you using that for power?" Brin asked.

Clearly that was a sore point by the way Zoe's brow pulled together, and she pursed her lips tightly.

"Yeah, we have the solar panels and the battery to store power. What we don't have is an electrician to wire up the house." She huffed, quickly changing the subject. "How is everyone at home by the way?"

"Good. Everyone's good, thanks for asking." Seth replied.

Zoe handed Brin and Seth their drinks with a smile and leaned casually against the counter. "I'm glad to hear that."

There was a brief moment of silence before Zoe broached a new question, looking at each of them in turn.

"So, as much as I'm happy to see you, what brings you here? It's not every day my favourite wyvern healer and her chick magnet brother comes to Dunn Turidd," she added, her tone curious. "Is this a social visit or do you have Alliance business to discuss with Doran?"

Seth suddenly looked uncomfortable, clearing his throat he took a large gulp from his glass. While he enjoyed flouting his Cassanova prowess with his brothers and friends, who were all happily mated, it felt less like a proud achievement and more like a personality defect to have a woman in his extended family circle, commenting on his romantic escapades and reputation for seducing anything in a skirt.

"A bit of both really," Brin replied. "I'm here for a social visit and Seth wants to talk to Doran and his uncle, Gwynn, about what's been happening recently with the healers in Fey."

"Ahh, yeah, I've heard about that. I'm surprised you left the citadel, let alone come all the way here, under the circumstances," Zoe said, wrapping Brin in a supportive hug. "If you want to see Doran and Gwynn, you'll probably find them at the Archons Hall. I believe the nephilim council are meeting today to discuss that very issue," she told Seth.

"Thanks. In that case, I'll see you both later. Brin, if there are any problems, send someone to fetch me. Otherwise, I'll be back as soon as I can, and don't go anywhere, okay?" he added.

Brin smiled at her brother, pent-up frustration backlighting her eyes. "Nothing's going to happen while I'm here, stop your worrying."

"I mean it Brin, don't go anywhere until I get back," he told her, uncomfortable to let her out of his sight, even for a couple of hours.

"Seriously, I'm here with Zoe, a vampiric druid. Not to burst your macho bubble, but she can probably protect me better than you can. So, just go to the meeting. Don't worry about me."

Seth's brow furrowed, his ego having taken a lashing twice in as many minutes. "Fine. But you know where to find me if you need, yeah?"

Brin's response was to lift her glass to him in salute and take a sip of the fruity liquid, offering him a mildly obstinate smile. Seth turned on his heel with a huff and left the cottage shaking his head in dismay, hoping but not expecting her to obey him.

The two women watched him leave, staring toward the kitchen door as they listened to his heavy boots walk the length of the corridor and the creak and click of the front door.

"So, what do you want to do for the next couple of hours?" Zoe asked excitedly.

"Have you ever gone into the heart of *Coed Caer Ffin,* to see the Elder tree?" Brin asked her.

"Once. I was completely gobsmacked. I've never seen anything like it. If anyone had told me three years ago that such a tree existed, I would've asked them to lay off the weed or whatever drug they were on."

Brin nodded, chuckling. "I know what you mean. I grew up here in Fey, I've seen the tree here in *Coed Caer Ffin* several times, but I still have the same reaction whenever I get near it."

Brin closed her eyes, envisioning the Elder tree with its massive form stretching high above, standing out among the other ancient giants of the forest, dwarfing them in comparison. Its trunk's span was akin to the size of Zoe's cottage, and its roots sprawled out like a network of veins, connecting it to every part of the forest. Its leaves shimmered with a silvery, ethereal energy, casting a faint glow in the dim light of the densely canopied forest surrounding it.

She'd seen it only once back in Savernake Forest on Earth, but here in Fey, the tree seemed more vibrant, more alive.

"It's beautiful," she said softly, more to herself than to Zoe. "Umm, I wonder, would you be interested in coming with me to see it?" Brin asked.

"What, now?"

"Yes."

"Why? Would it be safe for you, that is?" Zoe asked.

"Sure." Brin replied. "Besides, I'm safer in *Coed Caer Ffin,* than I am here, with you. Nothing can pass the forest border that has evil intensions, the same can't be said for the village borders."

That was true enough, Zoe thought. "What about Seth? He was quite adamant that you stay here until he gets back."

Brin rolled her eyes. "He's my brother, not my keeper. So, what do you say?"

Zoe tilted her head, her brow creasing and lips pressing together as she pondered the implications. "Hmm, you know what? Right or wrong, fuck it! I'd love to see that tree again."

"Great! Let's go."

"Hang on, wait up a second. No doubt you're right about the forest being safe, but we're not going anywhere until I let Doran know where we've gone, just in case."

Brin let out a frustrated sigh, although she didn't bother arguing. Her irritation, however, had less to do with their delay in leaving, and more to do with an inexplicable pull toward the tree, a pull she couldn't quite understand. It had gnawed at her for days, like an itch just beneath her skin, impossible to reach and unable to ignore. The resulting sensation leaving her feeling restless, a simmering unease paired with a strange, jittery anticipation, as though there was something important about going to the Elder tree, but she couldn't put her finger on what it was, or why it even mattered. All she knew was, if she didn't go, she'd probably develop a nervous twitch, or worse, start compulsively counting tree rings on every piece of furniture she owned, convinced they were trying to send her coded messages, or something else equally as insane.

"Is this really why you chose to come for a visit?" Zoe asked, her tone curious with just a hint of disapproval.

"I'm sorry. Yes. I really did want to visit earlier, honestly. It just seemed that life kept getting in the way and other things took up my time." Brin looked down, unable to meet Zoe's gaze. Those words felt like a lie, she could have found the time for a visit, but she hadn't.

"Not to worry, I understand. I haven't visited you at Avengard, either. What I really want to know, is why didn't you ask one of your brothers to take you to see the tree?"

Brin's relief at Zoe's understanding, coupled with the question, caused her to inadvertently snort.

"Are you kidding? You've met my brothers, haven't you? With what's happening to healers in Fey, my family wants to wrap me up in cotton wool and lock me in my room to protect me. I'm going stir crazy at home. I needed to get out…and I *really* need to see the Elder tree. Don't ask me why, I don't have an answer to that, it's just a feeling that I need to go. Does that make sense, at all?"

Zoe studied her for a moment, her expression softening. Then, with a slight nod, she said, "Wait here. I'm going to leave Doran a note on his desk, letting him know where we're going." She slipped out of the kitchen, leaving Brin alone.

Brin took the opportunity to glance around their neat and cozy kitchen. It was small but thoughtfully arranged, with a lived-in warmth that spoke of care and comfort. The wooden shelves were lined with jars of herbs, teas, along with magical ingredients, all meticulously labelled in Zoe's neat handwriting, and separated into two sections according to use, the blue ones labelled, *"To put on chicken"*, while the red ones were labelled, *"To turn someone into a chicken",* delineating which ones were for potions and which ones were for food. No doubt the labels were designed for Doran's benefit, to avoid any possible magical catastrophes.

On another shelf, nestled between a stack of well used cookbooks, stood a collection of framed photos. Brin stepped closer, her curiosity piqued.

They were photos of Zoe and Doran together, their faces glowing with happiness. A candid shot of Zoe laughing, her head tipped back as Doran looked at her with unmistakable adoration. And another with them sitting cozily by a fire, wrapped in each other's arms.

Brin felt a sharp pang in her chest, an ache she couldn't quite name but recognized all too well. Was it regret? Self-pity? Jealousy? In truth, it was all of them tangled together, a knot of emotions she hated acknowledging. She truly was happy for Zoe and Doran, but there was no denying the shadow of her own loneliness that lingered constantly just beneath the surface. Being around happy couples had a way of reminding her of what she didn't have, but so dearly longed for, and she couldn't help feeling a flicker of self-pity. Deep down, she doubted she would ever know that kind of unshakable happiness.

With her thoughts unchecked, her mind shifted toward Marcus, the infuriating lycan who had spent more than a decade making her life more complicated than it needed to be. Every time they crossed paths, it was like a spark ignited between them, but not the pleasant kind. They bickered, argued, and generally got under each other's skin. She'd never figured out why he seemed to dislike her so much, not that she'd ever bothered to ask. Worst of all was her own maddening attraction to him. No matter how hard she tried, she couldn't turn it off. It was a slow-burning torture which she couldn't escape, even when he wasn't around.

Shaking her head, Brin forced herself to look away from the photos. She wouldn't let her own romantic trainwreck of a life, overshadow her happiness for Zoe. Her friend had found her *mate*, and deserved the wonderful bond which that entailed, and Brin wasn't about to let her own insecurities and disappointment tarnish that.

The sound of footsteps brought her attention back to the doorway. Zoe returned, now dressed in comfortable hiking boots, sturdy leggings, and a light jacket, clearly ready for the "leisurely" two-hour walk to the Elder tree.

"Alright," Zoe said, grabbing a small satchel and slinging it over her shoulder. "Let's get going. I think a walk will be good to stretch our legs." She shot Brin a quick smile.

Brin returned a wry smile, following Zoe toward the door. "Just keep in mind I'm not a vampire like you, my legs don't move as fast as yours, and I may need to rest once or twice along the way."

"I've got that covered," Zoe replied, tapping the backpack she'd slung over her shoulder. "I've got a couple of bottles of water and a bag of scroggin."

"A bag of what?" Brin asked, although she wasn't too sure she really wanted to know the answer.

"Scroggin. It's a trail mix. It's made up of nuts, seeds like pepitas and sunflower seeds, dried fruit and chocolate. It's to help you keep up your energy. I don't particularly need the extra energy these days, but I still love eating the stuff. I used to love eating it in front of the TV, but since we have no electricity, or a TV in Fey, I just eat it." She confessed happily.

"You had me at chocolate," Brin told her with a grin. "Okay, lead the way."

As they stepped out into the fresh air, Brin couldn't help but feel a renewed sense of anticipation. Whatever awaited her at the Elder tree, she hoped it would bring some clarity, or at least a distraction from the tangle of emotions twisting inside her.

Coed Caer Ffin forest stretched out in front of them, an endless expanse of towering hardwood trees that seemed to touch the sky. Their trunks were massive, some so wide their girth measured nearly ninety feet, more than three times the length of a dragon from nose to the barbs at the end of their tail. The trees rough bark varied from deep hues of red to dark brown, soft moss clinging to their roots in vibrant shades of green, while ferns and wildflowers bloomed in small clusters along the forest floor. The air was alive with the faint pulse of energy from their ancient life force, muted only slightly by the dappled sunlight filtering through the canopy. High above, bird songs mingled with the rustling of leaves in the gentle breeze.

Brin stepped from the yard, back into the forest she'd recently arrived in, dried leaves crunching softly under her sandals along the path that wound its way through the trees. Light fluctuated as they walked, sheltered by the canopy above, thick enough to filter out most of the sun, producing a cool, soft breeze. Shafts of golden light pierced through here and there, illuminating the forest floor in shifting patches to make the dew-covered foliage sparkle like gems.

The air grew cooler with each mile they travelled deeper into the forest, and the faint hum of energy grew stronger, almost like a pulse, and their conversation became less frequent and more subdued.

"Do you want to talk about what's been happening, to the healers, I mean? I would've thought you'd want to stay close to home," Zoe said when she stopped under one of the large shady trees to give Brin another short break, handing her the water and the bag of scroggin.

"There's not much to say really. No one seems to know very much."

The truth was, Brin hadn't left her home at all recently, not since Kendra, another Wyvern healer like herself, had been found dead two weeks ago. Kendra's death wasn't an isolated incident, it was just the latest in what felt like a growing epidemic of healers dying under mysterious circumstances. Were these deaths connected, or was it just some cruel coincidence? The uncertainty of being on some kind of healer hit list gnawed at her, leaving her torn between fear and fury…and more vulnerable than she cared to admit.

More than anything, it was that feeling of vulnerability that bothered her the most. Staying in the safety of her family's sprawling citadel in Avengard, guarded by a hundred soldiers and surrounded by her fiercely protective family, had its appeal, she couldn't deny it. But even Brin, for all her love of the familiar, had to admit it was suffocating. Being with Zoe, at least, her friend didn't hover over her like she was some fragile flower in need of constant care. That alone made this visit worthwhile.

Maybe she was vulnerable, but she wasn't helpless. Brin had learned a few fighting techniques over the past few years, she reminded herself, defiantly at first…then, with a flicker of doubt, realizing she might be overselling her resilience, trying a little too hard to convince herself.

As Brin and Zoe rounded a bend in the path, Brin dropped another handful of scroggin into her mouth and chewed, only now realizing how little was left of the once-full bag. Glancing down at the empty water bottle in her hand, she frowned.

"Well, this is unfortunate," she muttered.

Zoe, walking beside her, licking the last bit of chocolate from her fingers. "What is?"

Brin waved the bottle in the air. "It'll be another two hour walk back with no water. I really should've thought to ration it."

Zoe gave a lazy, apologetic shrug. "I did bring an emergency flask for myself, I'd offer you some, but, you know, vampire."

Brin wrinkled her nose. "Yeah, I think I'll pass on the plasma cocktail, thanks."

Their conversation fell away as they stepped into a wide clearing, and all thoughts of food and thirst vanished. Before them, standing at the very heart of the open space, was the Elder Tree.

Brin stopped in her tracks, once again awe struck by the sight. The tree was impossibly vast, its silvery-white bark appearing to glow with an inner light. Its roots stretched out like veins through the earth, thick and sprawling, while its branches arched wide and high into the sky, their canopy stretching so far it felt like they'd stepped beneath a green sky. The leaves shimmered faintly, catching the light and refracting it in strange, shifting colours. The entire tree radiated something ancient, something both comforting and unsettling, a living entity aware of their presence.

Brin inhaled deeply, the very air around the tree carried an electric charge, buzzing faintly beneath her skin. The itch that had been gnawing at her for days flared sharply, making her tense. She needed to be here. But why?

Zoe stood silently beside her, letting out a slow breath. "I'm not sure whether to feel like I should kneel or run for my life."

Brin's hands fidgeted nervously in front of her. "Yeah, I know what you mean."

Then, without warning, a section of the trunk at the base of the tree shimmered, the bark rippling like water. Light pulsed outward, and from the shifting glow a figure stepped forward.

Brin's breath hitched. The man was tall, his presence commanding. His great wings, feathered and vast, bore hues of violet at their base, shifting seamlessly into deep blue, then burning orange and gold at the edges, just like the heart of a living flame. He stepped forward with deliberate grace, his gaze piercing as he regarded them.

Zoe sucked in a sharp breath beside Brin, her body rigid, her mouth falling open but no words came out.

Brin, however, merely narrowed her eyes, crossing her arms as she regarded the celestial being. "Hello, Grandfather."

2

The heavy thud of Marcus' rucksack hitting his bunk was a sound he'd grown accustomed to. He'd never been the most meticulous guy. After the month-long mission, his back and shoulders ached, and his chest felt tight from the repeated, almost constant bouts of adrenaline. He couldn't be bothered putting his pack away neatly, or at all. Instead, he left the ruck right where it landed.

The door to the barracks creaked open. Without looking up, he knew from the footsteps that it was Callum, his best friend since childhood and constant companion, and he was also his total opposite in thinking and behaviour. While Marcus was short tempered and tended to act or speak before his brain connected with his mouth, Callum considered everything he did carefully and spoke with diplomacy, just like his father Oliver, the alpha of their lycan clan. How the two of them had stayed friends all these years was anyone's guess.

"Callum," he said casually.

"Marcus," he replied, giving Marcus a sideways glance, his lips curling into a lopsided grin. "You're really just going to leave that there, again?" Callum chuckled, a hint of mockery in his voice as he started emptying his own pack on the bunk beside his, sorting everything into piles of clean and dirty as he went.

"Yeah, why not? I can unpack later," Marcus said, his voice rough from the dust and dirt of the mission. His eyes flicked to his phone, checking the time. His date with Candy was scheduled for a few hours time. A sense of unease settled in his stomach at the thought.

Callum shook his head, continuing his task. "You know, it's amazing how you manage to make even your rucksack look like a disaster zone."

"Thanks, it's an art I've spent decades perfecting," Marcus answered proudly, booting the pack onto the floor haphazardly and throwing himself onto the bed, letting out a groan as his aching muscles released under protest. His mind drifted back to the mission and he quickly shut those thoughts down again. They would have their official debriefing soon enough, no point stressing over it until then.

"So, plans with um…what's her name again?" Callum asked as he neatly placed a t-shirt in a drawer, his voice casual but with a hint of humour.

"It's…it's Candy. My girlfriend's name is Candy," Marcus said, trying to sound nonchalant, though there was a tightness in his chest that made the words feel hollow.

"You sure about that, because you don't sound too sure. You can barely remember her name."

"Of course I'm sure."

Callum's eyebrows shot up. "Huh! That's a surprise. You've barely said two words about her since we left for the mission. If you're really keen on her, shouldn't you be counting the hours until you see her again?"

"She's been blowing up my phone for the past few days. It pisses me off. I hate needy, clingy women. And…Yeah, well..." Marcus' words trailed off. He sat up, scrubbing his face with his hands. "I'm not really feeling it, to be honest."

Callum paused, glancing over at him. "You're telling me you're thinking about breaking up with her?"

Marcus' lips tugged into a bitter smile. "I don't know, bro. It's not like I don't care. It's just...I'm not...I don't know. You ever feel like things don't line up the way they're supposed to?"

Callum set his folded clothes aside, frowning at Marcus. "You're going to have to elaborate, because I don't get what you mean. You've been together for what, six months? Shouldn't it be easy? Fun?"

"Yeah, you'd think. But...I don't know. It feels like I'm pretending to be someone I'm not," Marcus said, his voice quieter now, rawer. His eyes wandered to the window, where the afternoon sun was starting to dip toward the horizon. "Like...like I'm just going through the motions. A part of me feels like I should be...I don't know, somewhere else."

Callum watched him closely. "Somewhere else, or with someone else?"

"It's strange, but sometimes I have a feeling I'm not the person I'm supposed to be. I know that doesn't make any sense, but there it is." Marcus motioned vaguely to himself. "I don't feel like I fit in this life anymore."

Callum gave a half-laugh, scratching the back of his neck. "In what way, you live for travelling around the world, searching for the missing artefacts, hunting down Guild members and killing demons."

Marcus cracked a grin, but it didn't reach his eyes. "Yeah, I do. But…I can't explain it, it's a feeling that there's something more I'm supposed to do. Like I said, it doesn't make sense. I don't expect you to understand when I don't understand myself."

There was a long pause before Callum spoke again, quieter this time. "If you're really not into this girl, you're going to have to tell her, and soon. It's not fair to string her along."

"I hear you, and I plan to tell her tonight at dinner. I've booked a nice restaurant and I'm hoping that if I tell her in a crowded place, she won't make a big emotional scene about it. But, before that, I need a few glasses of Dutch courage. Want to join me?"

"I would but I have to see my parents. I'll walk with you over there though." *There,* being the Drunken Duck Pub, the lycan's go-to place to drink, play pool, have a meal and generally socialise. And, since Callum's family owns the pub, and live in the apartment beneath it, the two men were heading to the same place.

Marcus stood up and looked down. His bed was a mess, just like his life in general.

"Hey George." Marcus said as he took a seat at the bar.

"Marcus. I figured I'd see you in here this afternoon."

"Am I that predictable?"

The barman didn't answer, he just pulled a bottle of Glenfiddich single malt from behind the bar and placed it in front of him with a glass.

Marcus sighed. It seemed he was.

"Thanks. You might as well…"

"Leave the bottle? Yeah, I know." George finished his sentence, a knowing smirk tipping up one corner of his mouth, humour in his gaze. "I'll put it on your tab, will I?"

"I'm surprised you haven't already done it." Marcus grinned.

"Actually, I have," he said, pulling the ledger from under the bar to show Marcus the entry.

Marcus snorted out a laugh as he filled his glass.

"I heard the mission didn't go as smooth as you'd hoped."

"You could say that." Marcus hesitated whether to elaborate or not. But this was George, he probably knew all the details already. Being both the alpha's confidant, as well as every patron who took a seat at the bar, there wasn't much that happened without him knowing. So, Marcus continued. "We ran into a team of Guild operatives working in the same area as us."

"Coincidence, or do you think there was a problem with your intel? It's not too often your team is caught off guard like that."

Marcus shrugged and downed the glass of Scotch. "It's hard to say. There's something about what happened that just doesn't sit right. I know the Guild is still looking for the same artefacts as us, there's nothing new about that, so it could be just co-incidence that we came across them. On the other hand, I have no doubt they still have one or two spies in the Alliance, just like we have in the Guild, so them knowing where our team would be isn't a shock either. Yet, in the past, when we've come across each other, there's always been a pretty intense battle. This time…"

"There wasn't any battle?"

Marcus thought back to the skirmish from just days before, where Marcus' team had nearly lost one of their own. The Guild had ambushed them, fast and silent like shadows. They'd gotten lucky, but it hadn't been luck that had saved them.

That moment had been burned into Marcus' memory. One of their men, Sergeant Finch, had been shot with a paralysing dart. The temporary paralysis worked fast, but the team was trained for this. They'd reacted quickly, administering the antidote before Finch's body froze completely. And then, the Guild had retreated as quickly as they'd appeared, leaving Marcus and his team confused and wary.

The Guild had caught them off guard, but it was the way they retreated that bugged him. They were known for their ruthlessness. Yet, they'd disappeared into the shadows as quickly as they'd struck.

"There was, although instead of coming at us with everything they had, they seemed to make a show of attacking, there was no true aggression, it was like they had some other agenda. Their focus was calculated, they were shooting at us at random, and once Finch was shot with one of their paralysing darts, they retreated. Just like that. Which is weird too, they rarely use those darts anymore, they know all lycan and wyvern military carry an injectable with the antidote. We can reverse the drug before it takes effect. Something about the attack doesn't sit right."

"Well laddy, you're all home safe, so why don't you give your brain a temporary reprieve and not think on it too hard, hey? I'm sure there will be plenty of time for that later." With that, George poured another glass of Scotch and placed it in front of Marcus. "Besides, here comes your boss, ahhh…brother-in-law, and he looks like his mood is even blacker than yours. I'd drink up if I was you, and quickly or you might end up in *his* firing line."

Marcus did just that, downed the glass in one swallow and poured himself another. Not because he was afraid of Sanders, not in the least, he just really wanted the extra emotional buffer.

"You're in a good mood," Marcus commented dryly.

"I've just arrived back from a *pleasure* trip," Sanders replied, his top lip curling in a snarl.

"Where'd you go?"

"I had to pick your mother up from the airport."

"Fuck! My mother's here? Fuck! For how long?" he asked, slurring his words slightly.

"She hasn't given a time frame," Sanders replied. *Unfortunately.*

"Fuck! Hopefully she thinks I'm still off on a mission somewhere."

Sanders chuckled. He sympathised with Marcus' desire to avoid any mother-son bonding, but he was more than happy to throw him under the bus if it meant that he didn't have to spend any more time with her himself.

"I'm afraid not. You're a member of my team, where I go, you go. So, she's expecting to see us both at the manor tonight for a family dinner."

"Fuck that shit! I've got other plans."

"To get to the bottom of that bottle?" Sanders queried.

Marcus looked from his glass to the half empty bottle and considered the option as a viable possibility before answering. "No, I'm seeing Candy tonight…I'll be outta here just as soon as I finish this drink," he replied, lifting his glass to salute him before downing the contents.

"Hell no. If I have to sit at a table with your mother, then so do you. That's an order soldier." Satisfied with Marcus' groan of compliance. Being married to his sister meant that Marcus often got away with liberties that other soldiers under his command didn't, but he still loved to pull the senior officer card when necessary.

Marcus had been in the pub for a little over an hour. What was supposed to be one glass had turned into a serious drinking session. Now that all those hefty shots of Scotch were reaching his blood stream, Marcus was feeling the effects, and he wasn't at all sure he would be able to remain upright without a stumble or two, let alone get his middle leg into the upright position to please his girlfriend.

His long legged, big breasted, gorgeous girlfriend.

His extremely demanding girlfriend.

Whom he was planning on breaking up with tonight at dinner.

Marcus sighed, staring into his empty glass. Even so, he still didn't feel it was enough and was now considering graduating to the mind-altering bliss that was found at the bottom of a bottle of Absinthe. Especially if he was expected to tolerate a meal with his mother.

Truthfully, he wasn't sure which of the two women he dreaded spending the evening with more.

While he'd loved the sex he had with Candy, she bored the shit out of him, always yapping on about something trivial. In fact, he was grateful he was a soldier in the lycan military, which kept him away from home sometimes for months at a time. He doubted he could have kept his relationship with her going this long, any other way.

"Here's an idea. Bring her to dinner too."

"What, are you serious, bring her to the manor? Nope. I think not. For one thing, she'll never be able to find the place. In case you've forgotten, it has a protection spell on it. Plus, she doesn't drive, and I think I'm one or two drinks past being able to drive myself." *And I was planning on breaking up with her at dinner tonight!*

"She doesn't drive?"

"Nope. She's a model, she doesn't need to. She gets chauffeured everywhere."

"Okay, we can work around that. Call her and let her know to be ready in an hour. I'll have a car there to pick her up."

With that, Sanders turned on his heel and left the bar, leaving Marcus floundering, caught somewhere between; *What the fuck just happened?* And, *Is there time to skip the country?*

Marcus sighed, staring into his empty glass, his fingers idly tracing the rim, debating whether to go for that drink of Absinthe after all. It wasn't that he was deliberately trying to get drunk, it was more that he needed something, *anything*, to dull the restless irritation clawing at the back of his mind. A nameless feeling he'd come to recognise as his constant companion over the last decade, just as his inner wolf was, dimmed only by copious amounts of alcohol. However, anticipating it was likely going to be an eventful evening, in one way or another, he figured it was best to avoid dosing himself with another shot of *medicine*, and keep his head as clear as possible.

One thing was for sure, he wasn't likely to get an opportunity to have *the talk,* with Candy tonight. The prospect had been stewing in his mind for days, and he'd reached a point where he didn't relish having to break up with her, but he was looking forward to being single again, and he planned on staying that way. It would have to wait until tomorrow. *Fuck it!*

3

Nathaniel, Angel of Fire, let out a low chuckle, the sound was warm, yet edged with something unreadable. "My dearest granddaughter. You don't seem particularly surprised to see me."

Brin lifted a brow and tilted her head. "I suppose I'm not. What brings you down from the Higher Realms? I know it's not just for a friendly family chat."

Nathaniel smiled faintly, though there was weight behind it, something solemn. "No. I'm sorry, it's not. I've come with a message."

"At least now I know why I've had an uncontrollable urge to come here. I assume that was your doing?"

Nathaniel nodded in acknowledgement. "I apologise, but as you know I'm forbidden to help unless the balance has been disrupted. Even then, I walk a fine line between helping you and influencing your free will."

Beside her, Zoe finally seemed to find her voice. "Brin, your grandfather is an angel?"

Brin smirked. "Yep."

Zoe's gaze darted between them. "And you didn't think to mention that before?"

Brin shrugged. "It never came up."

Zoe exhaled, rubbing her temples. "Unbelievable," she mumbled to herself.

Nathaniel cleared his throat, drawing their attention back to him. "We have little time," he said. His eyes locked onto Brin's, burning with the intensity of urgency. "You need to listen carefully."

Brin shivered as the sense of uneasiness which had been nagging at her recently, suddenly intensified into an ice-cold knot in the pit of her stomach. Whatever his news was, it wasn't good. And judging by the look in her grandfather's eyes, it was something she wasn't prepared for.

"The Guild has modified the paralysing toxin which, until now, they've used to temporarily paralyse lycans and wyverns. Now, it's much worse."

Brin's arms tightened across her chest as she listened to what Nathaniel told them. Standing rigidly beside her, Zoe was the first to break the heavy silence.

"Wait, are you saying the Guild has weaponized the toxin? In what way?" Zoe's voice was edged with anger.

Nathaniel nodded, his sharp eyes dark with concern. "Yes. It now carries a virus designed to attack the bond between the man and the beast within him, similar to the spell Morganna struck your brother Raif with, severing the bond between his two halves."

Brin stiffened at the mention of her brother. She remembered those terrifying weeks when Raif had been stuck in a coma, his body unresponsive, his dragon half severed from his human self. They had been helpless to do anything but wait and hope. It had been sheer luck that Kaitlyn's physical touch, his *mate*, had broken the spell.

But, if this new toxin now contained a virus…

Brin's voice came out hoarse. "Are you saying they'll be stuck? That once the virus takes hold, they can never shift again?"

Nathaniel nodded, his wings shifting slightly, the movement giving the illusion of the faint glow of fire along the edges. "As the virus progresses, it fractures the connection between man and beast. But they won't just be stuck in their human form…" He hesitated.

Zoe finished grimly, "They'll lose control?"

Nathaniel gave a single nod. "Completely. Their humanity will regress, leaving only the primal instincts of their beast. They will become mindless, unable to recognize friend from foe. They will attack anything in their path."

Brin swallowed hard. "Will it kill them?"

"Yes. And not just the person who's injected with the virus, it will spread, and quickly. Every wyvern and lycan is susceptible to it."

Zoe let out a low curse, pacing a few steps before turning back to Nathaniel. "How fast does it spread?"

"Too fast." Nathaniel admitted. "After the paralysis toxin wears off, the infection will take hold quickly. Within days."

Brin exhaled sharply. "If the wyvern and lycans injected become the initial hosts of the virus, how is it spread?"

"I'm not permitted to tell you that, I'm afraid. That's something you'll have to figure out yourselves."

"This could spiral out of control fast."

Nathaniel's expression darkened. "Which is exactly what Morganna intends."

"Okay, we need a plan. How are we going to stop this from happening?" Zoe asked, although she was met with silence.

Brin frowned, "I don't understand. Why are you telling me this? Wouldn't it be better to go straight to Raif or Alaric? They're the ones in charge of the Alliance, not me."

Nathaniel sighed, his violet-tinged wings shifting slightly as he studied her. "Because there is something else you need to know, something that concerns you directly, Brin."

A cold shiver ran down her spine at the grim tone in his voice. "More?"

Nathaniel's golden eyes softened with sadness. "The reason the other healers have been killed…it isn't random. Morganna and Scorpion believe the healers pose a threat to their plans. They fear that a healer might find a way to cure those infected, and that would unravel everything they are working toward."

Brin's breath hitched. The deaths of the other healers had been disturbing enough, but to hear that they were being systematically eliminated, it sent a new wave of dread through her.

"Wait," Zoe interjected, her brows furrowed in concern. "If they've been targeting healers...then that means…"

"Brin is on their list. Yes." Nathaniel nodded gravely, turning his attention toward Brin. "Although, unlike the others, there is some debate as to whether they should eliminate you outright or capture you first."

Brin let out a humourless laugh, her stomach churning enough that she wondered if she might lose its contents. This was bigger than just another cruel experiment by the Guild. This was a calculated attempt to throw the Alliance into chaos, eliminating lycans and wyverns. And worse, it was now confirmed, without a doubt in her mind, that she was on their hit list?

The weight of her grandfather's words settled over Brin like a suffocating blanket. She exchanged a stunned glance with Zoe, who looked equally shaken.

Drawing in a long deep breath, she let it out again slowly, in an attempt to steady herself.

"Why would they want to capture me?" Brin asked, swallowing hard, although silently, she suspected she already knew the answer to that question too.

Nathaniel's expression grew even more serious. "Because of your unique gift. Your ability to heal those you touch with a good soul, and destroy those who are corrupt. The Guild and Morganna see you as both a threat and a curiosity they'd like to study."

Brin's stomach twisted into knots. She had known that her dual ability was rare, and she'd always been cautious about using her gift, yet until now, she had never considered it might make her an object for study. Brin let out a shaky breath, trying to supress a sudden wave of nausea.

"Great," she muttered, "So, I'm either going to be hunted down and killed, or kidnapped and used as a lab rat in some torturous experiment. Really loving my odds right now. Not!"

Zoe turned to Brin, her expression hardening. "They're not getting to you. Not while I'm around."

Nathaniel stepped forward, his gaze softening just slightly. "You're not alone in this, Brin. But you must be careful. They will come for you, one way or another, so you'll need to be ready."

Brin forced herself to straighten her spine, ignoring the icy dread still coiled in her gut. "I guess I'd better start preparing then, huh," she replied in a sarcastic tone.

"Yes, but there is something else you need to prepare for too," he told her.

"More!? Are you serious? I don't know if I can take any more news right now." Brin blinked at her grandfather, her mind still reeling from the revelations he'd already shared. "I hope it's good news," she said.

"Well, that depends on your perspective," Nathanial replied, one corner of his mouth tipping up into a cautious smile.

"What exactly, does that mean?" Brin asked warily.

"The Alliance is close to finding the next missing artifact."

"Well, that's not good, but what does that have to do with me?" She queried, narrowing her eyes at him.

Nathaniel's expression was calm, patient. "Because Brin, you are essential in retrieving it," he said.

"Hold on, you're not making sense. How am I supposed to be involved?"

"Only a female descendant of its original owner can touch it safely."

Brin let out a short, incredulous laugh. "Oh, come on. That sounds way too convenient."

Nathaniel arched a brow. "And yet, it's the truth."

Zoe, who had been listening intently, tilted her head. "I'm lost, what artifact are we talking about?"

Nathaniel shifted his gaze toward her. "The Serpent Armband."

Brin frowned. The name sounded vaguely familiar, but she couldn't place it. "And that is…?"

"A relic with immense power," Nathaniel explained. "Its magic was bound to the bloodline of our family by a healer who once wielded it eons ago. And you, Brin, are the last direct female descendant, and the only one who can handle it safely."

Brin's stomach twisted. Of course she was. Fate just loved throwing curve balls like this at her.

"So, let me get this straight," she said, rubbing at her temple. "The only way to retrieve this thing, is if I go along with an expedition and grab it myself, otherwise…what? It explodes? It curses whoever touches it? Sucks out their souls?"

Nathaniel's lips twitched in amusement. "Let's just say, that if the wrong person touches it or tries to grab it, it wouldn't be pleasant."

Zoe snorted. "That's angel-speak for, *'It'll kill them horribly,'* isn't it?"

Nathaniel inclined his head slightly. "A painful fate, yes, but not *necessarily* death. At least, not for everyone."

Brin groaned into her hands. "And where exactly is this armband?"

"In the northern region of Canada."

"Northern, as in the cold region?" Brin scrunched her nose in disgust. "How far north?"

"That," Nathaniel admitted, "is something you'll need to discuss with your brothers and the Alliance."

"Well, that's just great! Not that it really matters though, have you met my brothers?" she said to her grandfather sarcastically. "They won't let me leave my bedroom without supervision lately, how am I supposed to get them to let me go trapsing off to who knows where?"

Nathaniel's gaze softened. "I know this is a lot to take in, but have a little faith that everything will work out the way it's supposed to. The Alliance needs that artifact, and you are the only one who can claim it without risk."

Brin studied him for a long moment. She knew better than to think he was telling her everything. There was something he was holding back, and judging by the faint, knowing smile on his lips, whatever it was, it was likely going to be something unpleasant for her.

Exhaling sharply, Brin rolled her eyes upward toward the Elder Tree.

Nathaniel chuckled softly. "You can handle this," he reassured.

Brin blew out a long breath, shaking her head. "You sound way too confident in me. You do know that the most adventurous thing I've done in my life was pat a hellhound."

Nathaniel only smiled, a glimmer of something unreadable in his eyes. "And yet, you still have your hand. I'm confident you'll survive this too."

"Survive!? Great. Just great! Couldn't you have chosen another word like…I don't know…excel, or maybe proficient?"

Nathanial knew this mission would change everything for her. But he dared not tell her what destiny had in store for her, there were some things she had to learn for herself.

"I should be going, I've already stayed too long."

"Just once couldn't you visit without some earth-shattering news?" Brin asked, her tone as hopeful as her eyes were sad.

"One day." He promised, taking her hand to draw her in for a hug, which she eagerly returned.

Taking a step away from her grandfather, she offered him a half-hearted smile.

"It was a pleasure to meet you, ahh…Nathaniel" Zoe said, unsure how to address the angel.

"And you," he replied, his eyes twinkling with amusement.

"What's so funny?" Zoe asked, perplexed.

"I was just wondering how you will fare on the back of a dragon."

"Huh?"

"I believe Seth will be taking you home." Nathaniel looked to the sky above the trees just as a large shadow blocked the light in the clearing.

Brin and Zoe watched as the enormous emerald coloured dragon came to land in the clearing, changing back into Seth's human form in a flash of shimmering light.

"Brin, what the hell are you doing out here? I told you to stay at Zoe's house" Seth chastised the instant he shifted back to human form.

"Seth, I can explain. I…"

"Was that grandfather?" Seth interrupted, his sharp gaze flicking toward the Elder Tree, a furrow forming between his brows. His grandfather never made an appearance without good reason.

Both Brin and Zoe turned back to the massive tree just as the shimmering doorway faded from sight, sealing the portal he'd stepped through, back to the higher realms.

Brin exhaled heavily, running a hand through her hair. "I think I'm going to need a stiff drink first, I'm still trying to process it myself," she told her brother.

"Um, I know you've just met with the Nephilim High Council, but I think you'll need to call another meeting, and not just with them. *Every* leader of the Alliance needs to hear this." Zoe added solemnly.

Seth's unreadable expression slowly darkened, his jaw clenching as a cold shiver ran up his spine and a sinking feeling settled in his gut. He *knew* he should have left Brin at home. If he had, then maybe…just maybe, whatever disaster was about to unfold could have been avoided.

He knew it was a foolish thought, a desperate attempt to grasp at control of a situation that he sensed was already beyond his reach.

Brin's presence here at the Elder Tree wasn't the cause of whatever storm was brewing, it was merely a piece of the puzzle, a thread already woven into the fabric of destiny. And yet, his instinct to protect his sister, to shield her from the danger that seemed to be pressing in around them, was impossible to silence.

His fists tightened at his sides as he took a steadying breath, forcing down the frustration clawing at his chest. What the hell had their grandfather just set into motion?

He cast a glance at Brin, studying her carefully. She looked tense, but not afraid. If anything, there was a quiet determination in her eyes that sent another uneasy ripple through him. She wasn't backing down from whatever this was.

And that, more than anything, worried him.

4

"Grace. Hi, what are you doing down here?" Holly asked as she placed the fifth load of dirty clothes for the day in the washing machine, curious why Grace was sitting on the bench in the laundry, playing on her iPad. Especially since there were so many other choices for rooms to hide out in, in a mansion of this size.

"I figured this was the last room in the house your mum would go."

"Ahh, right. I know my mother can be a bit overbearing." Holly winced in apology.

"Ya think?"

"Occasionally she likes to remind me that I'm her only daughter, and she had such a hard time giving birth to me that she marks my birthday on her calendar as her 'painiversary'," Holly said, using air quotes. "But, she's not so bad."

"Really." Grace answered, drawing out the word with dry sarcasm.

"Sure," Holly replied assuredly, though her facial expression was in complete contradiction.

"You keep telling yourself that and one day you might start believing it. Although, I'm sure she's really good at keeping food chilled if you have a dinner party on a hot day, all you'd need to do is stand her next to the buffet table, or she could keep an ice sculpture from melting." Grace suggested.

Holly laughed. And then laughed some more. "That's probably not far from the truth. I wish I'd thought of that," she laughed again.

"For a fourteen-year old, you're wise beyond your years, you know that?"

"What can I say, you grow up fast in this family."

"Yeah, you do at that," she answered wistfully.

Grace punched Holly in the arm. "Sometimes I forget you grew up in this house too."

"Ouch! Yeah, I did." Holly answered, rubbing her upper arm. "For as long as I can remember, my mum used to fob Marcus and I off to Gran for weekends and holidays, as often as possible. Then, when I was sixteen and Marcus was eleven, she decided we were cramping her style with her new husband and sent us here to live permanently."

"And did my dad enforce a curfew on you too?" Grace asked.

Holly chuckled. "He did. And while I didn't exactly appreciate it at the time, I'm grateful for it now. Back then, I probably would've gone off the rails if he hadn't. I was a bit of a teenage delinquent back then."

"I find that hard to believe. Wait, nope, I take that back. I can totally see that. You're still a bit of a delinquent. Where do you think I've learnt all my bad habits lately?" Grace quipped.

"If you want my opinion, I'd say your uncle Alex probably corrupted you long before I moved back to this house," Holly said.

"Okay yeah, that's fair. Hey, did you know Marcus' girlfriend is coming for dinner tonight?"

"I heard. I feel sorry for the poor girl. She has no idea what she's walking into. My mother is going to bombard her with a thousand personal, very invasive questions that'll leave her feeling both embarrassed and guilty about things she probably doesn't even have any knowledge of."

"Don't forget the backhanded compliments your mother's an Olympic-level expert in."

Holly rolled her eyes and groaned. "How could I forget. She was barely out of the car this afternoon when she told me how good I was looking, that being married obviously suited me. Since I've put on a few kilos, I clearly no longer feel any need to make an effort with my appearance."

Grace let out a snort that was half a laugh and half a gasp of disbelief. "Ouch. I have to give your mother credit for one thing, she never holds back what she's thinking, does she?"

"Never. Not even when you really, really wish she would. The woman has no filter."

Grace shook her head sadly, thinking of someone else who has no filter between their brain and mouth. "I think Marcus' girlfriend's in for a very rough night. She might survive your mother, but what are the chances that before the end of the night Uncle Alex will ask her if he can use her as a guinea pig in some kind of experiment that's likely to leave her either maimed or dead?" Grace grimaced.

"My mother and Alex in the same room, with a fresh victim to play with? It's hard to know which of them will traumatise the poor girl more. Not that it really matters, it's not likely she'll be allowed to remember her night here anyway. It's too risky to have a regular human exposed to our secrets."

Grace nodded. "But what if she's the *One*, Marcus' true *mate*? At some point she'd recall all the memories that have been suppressed."

Holly's gaze held a knowing, a truth that Grace was unaware of. "She's not. Trust me."

"How can you be so sure, do you know who is?" Grace asked, intrigued.

"I'm pretty sure, but since Marcus seems completely oblivious, I can't say anything."

"You can tell me, I promise not to tell anyone."

"Nope, sorry kid. Not yet."

"Well, that sucks." Crossing her arms in disappointment, Grace sat further back on the bench, into the corner.

"If I'm right, it won't take him too much longer to figure it out for himself, but there is still the complication of his current girlfriend," Holly sighed, shaking her head regretfully.

Grace checked the time on her iPad. "It's 6:00 o'clock". Nearly time for dinner, and it had all the right ingredients for a very interesting evening. She couldn't wait! This was likely to be the most entertaining night she'd had in months.

"I'd better finish up here and get changed. I suppose I should introduce myself and rescue her from my mother before she gets her claws into her." What was her name again? Cindy? Carly? Umm…Candy?

"Marcus is here." Candy exclaimed to Alex with relief, who looked casually around her at the object of her attention as he appeared in the doorway.

Marcus practically staggered into the dining room. To be honest, Candy was amazed he was walking at all, considering he appeared to have consumed half the bar beforehand.

Maybe she'd mistaken her sunglasses for a pair of rose-coloured glasses, but Marcus looked good. His jeans hugged his muscular thighs, and that t-shirt highlighted, rather than concealed his wide chest and six-pack stomach, not to mention his bulging biceps, tanned from his recent deployment to somewhere sunny. He looked like the poster boy from the pages of a Bad Ideas catalogue, which was why she found him so irresistible.

"Last time Marcus was this drunk, he got his head stuck in the steam press."

"What? How did he manage that?"

"With my help." Alex grinned.

Candy looked at him sceptically, unsure quite how to take Alex's sense of humour. It didn't occur to her that he might actually be telling the truth, it was just too farfetched. But then again, in the hour she'd been at the manor, there had been many unusual comments bantered about the room, things that just didn't make sense: Hellhounds roaming around in the forest. An eleven year-old boy, Riley, accidentally stabbing Alex with a sword when they were sparring in the pleasure dungeon. Alaric deliberately stabbing Alex with the same sword for letting Riley in the pleasure dungeon. And they spoke about these things as though it was everyday conversation.

Spotting the latest arrival, Alaric tapped his glass with a spoon to get everyone's attention.

"Now that we're all here, please take your seats for dinner," he said.

Marcus took a deep breath before stepping into the grand dining hall, bracing himself for the chaos that was inevitable when sixteen of his loud and opinionated, immediate and extended family members were gathered together in one place. The long oak table was already laden with platters of food, half eaten plates of hors d'oeuvres, and a selection of beverages. And right in the middle of it all, as expected, was his mother.

"Marcus, darling," Jocelyn called the moment she saw him, her voice smooth and saccharine. "You're late. But I suppose that's to be expected. Punctuality has never been your strong suit, has it?"

Marcus sighed, forcing a smile. "Good to see you too, Mother."

Candy, making a B-line for him from the other side of the room, beamed at him. "Babe! You made it." She leaned in, placing a kiss on his cheek. He returned the gesture out of habit, already regretting everything to come.

"So," Jocelyn continued, her eyes gliding over Candy with thinly veiled disdain, "This is your…companion for the evening?"

"Girlfriend. Candy is my girlfriend." Marcus corrected.

"Oh, of course," Jocelyn said with a delicate laugh, as if the term was subjective. "How…refreshing."

Candy, oblivious to the insult, smiled. "Nice to meet you, Mrs. Thorne!"

Jocelyn blinked slowly. "It's Jocelyn, dear. 'Mrs. Thorne makes me sound old."

Mrs. Philpot, who had just entered with a tray of steaming dishes, muttered, "Sorry love, that ship has sailed."

Marcus bit his lip to keep from smirking, while his sister Holly snorted into her wine.

"Why don't you two come and sit here with us," Holly told her brother, who quickly ushered Candy away from his mother and toward his sister. However, to his surprise, the moment he pushed in Candy's chair, about to take the seat beside her, his mother got there before him, seating herself between them.

Oddly, he felt almost relieved that his mother sat between them. No doubt he'd likely feel differently later, especially since he'd planned on breaking up with her tonight. However, for now at least, he was saved from any awkward, meaningless conversation with Candy. His mother would take care of that for him. For now, he had to focus on pretending to play happy families with his mother, he'd worry about Candy later.

Across the table, Alex was deep in a heated debate with his wife, Abby. "I'm just saying, if we genetically enhanced chickens to have four drumsticks, we could solve a lot of problems at dinner."

Abby groaned. "That's a terrible idea."

Candy tilted her head, trying to keep up. "Wouldn't that make it harder for them to walk?"

Alex pointed at her enthusiastically. "Not at all! We'd breed out the wings altogether, they don't use them anyway."

Marcus pinched the bridge of his nose. "Can we not discuss mutant chickens at the dinner table?"

Alaric, at the head of the table, smirked. "Considering some of the other things we've discussed, this is actually rather tame," he said, looking at Candy.

Grace, who had been quietly sipping her soda, added, "Remember the time Riley asked what happened if a vampire tried to transform a werewolf?"

"It was a valid question," Riley piped up from his seat between Narayan and Paige.

Candy turned to Marcus, her expression bewildered. "Is this a Sci-fi convention or a family dinner?"

Marcus took a long sip from his wine glass before answering. "Honestly, it depends on the night."

"Candy, isn't it?" Jocelyn said, swivelling toward her in her seat.

"Yes," she smiled.

"I was just wondering if you had plans after dinner tonight."

"No. Why?" Candy replied, still smiling.

"Oh, no reason. I just thought you might have been working this evening."

"No, why would you think that?"

"Mother. Candy is a model, *not* a hooker." Marcus growled.

"I didn't mean any offense, I just assumed with a name like Candy, and the way she's dressed…"

"Seriously!"

"Well, nobody ever tells me anything, so I have to ask questions myself. There's nothing rude about that."

"Candy, ignore our mother, everyone else does. She has foot in mouth disease. She has a habit of removing one foot only to put the other one in." Holly told her, leaning around her mother.

Candy's smile had lost its lustre, her eyes beginning to look a little glassy from welling tears. Looking way from the table to compose herself again, she focussed her attention on the two very large dogs curled up in front of the fireplace. The larger suddenly lifted his head, his ears twitching as though he was engaged in listening to the conversation. Candy watched as his eyes glowed an eerie red before he let out a small, rumbling growl and lowered his huge head back to the floor.

"Aw, what a cute doggie," Candy cooed. "Does he have, special eyes or something?"

"He's a special breed, his eyes reflect the fire light," Marcus said smoothly, before anyone else could answer.

"Like…night goggles?"

"Sure," he replied, although to be honest, he didn't really know what she meant by *night goggles*.

The rest of the dinner went relatively smoothly with general, *normal* conversation about the kids at school, the price of groceries these days and which phone plan was best. And every time Jocelyn looked like she was about the speak to Candy, Marcus discretely growled in her ear, a low guttural sound that rumbled from the depths of his chest. She wasn't happy that he was shushing her, but she understood the warning and kept her mouth shut for the rest of the evening.

Just as dessert was finishing, Marcus' inner tension began to rise. While dinner with his mother had been tense, it was equally as torturous sitting at a table with Candy, knowing he was going to break up with her just as soon as he could excuse himself from dinner. He'd prefer to get it over and done with as quickly as possible, instead of dragging out the evening any longer.

Marcus pushed back his chair with a quiet scrape against the hardwood floor, standing slowly. His movements were practiced and polite, yet there was a subtle urgency in the way he gathered the dessert plates, his and Candy's stacked neatly in his hands. She looked up at him with a soft smile, her body already turning slightly in her seat as if preparing to rise as well.

"I should get Candy home," Marcus began, glancing at the room more than addressing it. "It's a long drive, and it's been…"

He didn't get to finish his sentence.

At the other end of the table, Alaric turned toward the doorway. "We have company," he said, urgency in his tone.

Marcus exchanged a glance with Sanders, who pushed his chair back and stood, clearly ready to deal with whatever new crisis was about to unfold.

"I agree Marcus, now might be a good time to take Candy home."

"No. Marcus, you're staying." the deep, authoritative voice cut through the air like a blade only a moment before Oliver himself, the lycan's alpha, appeared in the doorway. Behind him was a full entourage of Alliance members, from both Earth and Fey.

"Sorry to interrupt dinner, but we have something very important to discuss." Raif added, Seth and his other two brothers entering the room behind him, followed by the entire nephilim high council, the Lemurian high council….And Brin.

Marcus' gaze fell immediately to Brin, her downcast eyes hiding her feelings, but he could see by her fidgeting that she was nervous about something other than the wall of seven-foot men accompanying her. She was born and raised as a princess of Dunn Turidd, she wasn't intimidated by them in the least.

Marcus shivered, not from cold but from something he couldn't describe. A feeling of dread that somehow his future was about to change. Which, of course made no sense, and so he quickly squashed the unwarranted feeling, burying it deep inside, just as he did every other emotion he'd ever felt.

"It's no interruption, we're just finishing up dinner. Would you like to join us?" Alaric asked.

"No, thank you. I wouldn't mind raiding your bar though," Raif told him.

"Sure. You know where to find it." His face remained relaxed, although a subtle twitch of his hand conveyed his distress, with a ripple effect through the rest of the family seated at the table, as the tension in the room once again began to rise.

Alex looked to his wife Abby, her expression also unreadable as she conveyed the new arrivals news to Alaric, which she read straight from their minds.

One by one, everyone stood from the table, crossing the room to greet their visitors with hugs and kisses. After all, family was never unwelcome, even if they were bringing bad tidings.

"I really think I should take Candy home," Marcus stated emphatically.

"No. Sebastian or Philippe can drive her. I believe you're needed here," Alaric told him, his tone leaving no room for negotiation.

"Yes, Sir."

"Marcus? What's going on?"

"Sorry Candy, it looks like I'm going to be on duty tonight. Can we take a raincheck?"

"I suppose we'll have to. Will you call me tomorrow?"

"Absolutely," he told her, leaning in to give her a peck on the cheek, but she shifted her head at the last moment, landing the kiss squarely on her lips.

Marcus' stomach rolled with a sudden onset of nausea. Why? He wasn't certain, but he assumed it was just his conscience getting the better of him. He was just feeling guilty because he was planning to break up with her the first moment he could get her alone. Unfortunately, it wasn't looking like that would be tonight.

Without conscious thought, his eyes shot across the room toward Brin, wondering if she'd seen the kiss. Once again, he found himself warring with his feelings. Why did it matter if she did? Brin meant nothing to him, she was just a painful thorn in his side, there wasn't a time they'd shared the same space when they hadn't argued, so why would it matter if she saw him kiss his girlfriend. Soon to be ex-girlfriend. It shouldn't matter. It *didn't* matter!

Brin finally looked up, her vibrant green eyes locking directly onto Marcus. Her long wavy red hair, still slightly tousled from the wind outside, framed her pale, lightly freckled face, and though she held herself with her usual confident posture, Marcus caught the way her fingers twitched at her sides nervously.

The moment their gazes met, his body tensed, his senses sharpening as if every cell in his body was suddenly on high alert. And that damned irritation started up again, low and insistent under his skin, like an itch he couldn't scratch. His inner wolf stirred, prowling just beneath the surface, agitated and restless.

Brin, for her part, visibly stiffened, her lips pressing into a thin line as if she had just caught the scent of something particularly unpleasant. Being in the same room as Marcus always made her uneasy, not entirely in an unpleasant way, but in a way that was still deeply annoying.

Standing beside Marcus, Candy noticed the shift in him immediately. Her sharp, heavily mascaraed eyes darting between him and Brin, her expression tightening into an unimpressed frown. Crossing her arms, she drummed her fingers against her upper arm in irritation. "Oh, don't let me interrupt," she said, voice laced with forced sweetness. "Clearly, you two are having a *moment*."

Marcus exhaled sharply, dragging a hand through his short hair. "I'll see you out," he muttered, ushering her toward the kitchen door, at the opposite end of the room from Brin, eager to escape the stifling tension pressing in around him.

"Marcus, you're staying right where you are." Oliver told him.

"Can't I at least walk her out?" he protested.

Marcus turned his head, his expression already darkening as his Alpha strode further into the room, his son Callum at his side. Behind them followed Gustav, the Northern European lycan leader, and the druid sisters father, his imposing presence unmistakable.

Oliver's gaze remained firm, leaving no room for argument. "You need to be present for this meeting."

Marcus clenched his jaw, debating whether to argue, but he knew better. Oliver didn't make commands lightly.

"I'll take Candy home. I'll see to it that she's well taken care of," Philippe announced. The latter part of his statement wasn't meant for Marcus' reassurance, but to let it be known to everyone else present that Candy will arrive home blissfully unaware that she'd even been out this evening.

Candy let out a breathy scoff, flipping her hair over one shoulder. "So, what, I'll see you again in another month I suppose?" She shot Marcus a pointed look, her tone saccharine, laced with irritation.

Marcus barely suppressed an eye roll. He wasn't looking forward to that.

"I'll call you tomorrow and we'll talk then, okay?" he told her. Feeling every eye in the room on him as he woodenly placed a brief kiss on her cheek.

"We certainly will," she replied curtly, stepping past him with pursed lips and a heavy scowl.

The moment she left the room he released a breath he hadn't realised he'd been holding, only to suck in another one just as tensely. They were all still staring at him.

Alaric, who had been quietly assessing the room, pulled out his phone. "Saladin and Dray will arrive from Oxford in the hour," he informed the group. "Until then, why don't we all head to the lounge room, grab a drink and get comfortable. I suspect this might be a long night."

The lounge room he was referring to, decorated with a beautifully painted fresco ceiling, was once called the ballroom, although it had never been used for the occasion, was now the family's lounge room - entertainment room, complete with a fully stocked bar, pool table, a one hundred inch flat screen TV and impressive sound system, several sofas and recliner lounges, along with two huge fireplaces.

Marcus' shoulders slumped, his stomach rolling. Maybe he should have kept drinking through dinner, he thought to himself. Whatever news was about to be delivered, he had a sinking feeling it wasn't going to be pleasant.

Just how unpleasant?

He would find out soon enough.

5

Sanders surveyed the room, feeling the weight of expectation pressing in as heavily as the crowd itself. Alaric's study was packed tight with nearly every Alliance leader and high ranking member from Britain, Northern Europe and Fey, along with several of the women, their voices low as they talked amongst themselves. It wasn't often so many of them gathered at the same place, at the same time, except for matters of great importance. The last time had been for Wade and Yasmin's wedding, three years prior. And, by the pensive moods and unexpected arrival of the newcomers, it was not difficult to discern that this gathering was not one of celebration.

"Callum, you might want to repack, and Marcus, I wouldn't bother unpacking your gear. I have a feeling we won't be home for long." Sanders told them quietly.

Callum nodded in acknowledgement. "Yes, Sir."

Marcus on the other hand, turned to face him, "What makes you think I wouldn't have unpacked my stuff already too?" he asked, his tone tainted with offended indignation.

"Am I wrong?"

"No. But what makes you assume I'm not as organised as Callum?"

Sanders raised an eyebrow offering him his best incredulous glare. "Organised, is that what you call it?"

"I'm a free spirit and my environment reflects that," he replied.

Once again Sanders just stared at him, his brow lifting even higher.

"Okay, I'm a slob, so sue me. At least I don't have to re-pack my gear," Marcus declared, shifting his eyes toward Callum. "What do you think this is all about anyway?"

"Fucked if I know, but looking at how edgy the wyvern brothers are, I have a feeling we have a few sleepless nights ahead of us."

Marcus studied each face in the room intently, gauging their mood and steeling himself for whatever was coming. What unsettled him most was Oliver and Gustav, each appearing equally as pensive as the wyvern brothers, when neither of the lycan leaders were easily rattled. In fact, they were usually the calm influencers in any situation.

Then Marcus' eyes fell toward Brin, lingering there far longer than they had on anyone else in the room. It puzzled him, she looked withdrawn and anxious, nothing like the confident woman he was used to encountering. Nor was she joining the other women's conversation as they huddled together in the far corner of the room. She seemed almost oblivious of their presence, her focus lost somewhere in her thoughts. He almost felt concern for her. Almost.

By the fireplace, the Irish Wolfhound Tilly, shifted uneasily on the rug beside her mate Cujo, the imposing alpha hellhound who now claimed Havenswood Manor as his den. Cujo too seemed agitated by the gathering, but it was hard to tell whether it was the general mood of the room he was reacting to, or simply that there were far more people in his vicinity, and he didn't like it. The fire crackled and spat, its glow casting restless shadows across the walls, as if feeding on the tension in the room.

As they waited, the minutes passed, stretching just shy of half an hour before the front doors to the manor finally opened with the arrival of Saladin and Teagan, along with Dray, his mate Shani and their eight year-old daughter Anjuli.

"Sorry we're late, we tried getting a babysitter but it's impossible on a Friday night at short notice," Dray told them apologetically.

"You're not late, but now that we're all here, we'd best get down to business. I've organised a video conference with Emil Wagstaff at 10 pm," Alaric announced, looking at his watch which read 9.30pm. "So, if no one has any objections I'll hand things over to Raif to fill us in on what's been happening in Fey recently."

The room fell silent apart from the sound of shuffling feet on the hardwood floor, and the muffled murmur as each person present made themselves more comfortable.

Raif stepped forward, the firelight highlighting his auburn hair and deepening the worry lines of his face.

He didn't waste words on pleasantries, his voice carrying the kind of clipped urgency that commanded immediate attention.

"This morning, Brin and Zoe ventured into the Nephilim forest, *Coed Caer Ffin*. Against better judgement," he added with a pointed glance at his sister, though there was no true rebuke in his tone. "They went to the Elder Tree, and there, they met with our grandfather, Nathaniel."

A ripple of murmurs ran through the room. The angel of fire's name alone carried weight. Few people could command the presence of an angel, and even fewer had the privilege of one paying them a visit voluntarily, and those who had seldom left the encounter unchanged. Regardless of the fact that the particular angel in question, was also a relative.

Raif continued, his tone taking on a harder edge. "Nathaniel confirmed what we'd already suspected. The death of our healers has not been random or coincidence. Morganna and Scorpion have been targeting them deliberately to ensure we have no one left to reverse the effects of the paralysing toxin, which the Guild has apparently re-engineered into something potentially more deadly."

Angry curses and growls reverberated around the room.

This was not good news. Raif's words struck a heavy blow that left the group reeling from the implications. Even seasoned warriors like Sanders and Gustav stiffened, their jaws clenching. A faint growl rumbled from Cujo by the fire's hearth.

"But there's more." Raif's gaze swept the room, before finally settling on Brin. "Nathaniel warned us that the Guild is close to finding one of the sacred relics. The Serpent Armband."

"Obviously we can't let that happen. We need to get to it first." Dray stated flatly.

Brin's shoulders tensed, and Marcus caught the slight tremor of her hands which fidgeted in front of her. Raif's next words explained why.

"Nathaniel was clear, the armband cannot be handled by just anyone. It's harmful to anyone who's not of the rightful bloodline. My family's bloodline…And, only a female can touch it."

Marcus inhaled sharply, a sudden cold knot forming in the pit of his stomach. He knew where this conversation was headed, Raif didn't need to fill in the blanks. There was only one female left in their bloodline.

The room seemed to shrink around Brin. Dozens of eyes turned her way. She kept her gaze steady, though Marcus saw the flicker of nerves beneath the surface. For once, her usual fiery affect was muted by the weight of responsibility.

"What would happen to a male if they touched it?" Dray asked.

Brin lifted her face and spoke clearly, even if a little timidly. "Grandfather didn't say, although from his expression, I don't think it would be a pleasant experience."

Alaric checked the time, 9:55pm.

"Alex, could you get the link set up to Emil?"

"Already done. Just waiting for him to join the conversation," he answered with a sly grin.

"Alex? Is there something else you'd like to share?" Alaric asked suspiciously.

"Nope." Alex pursed his lips together and frowned, shaking his head in the negative.

Less than a minute later, the laptop chimed, notifying them that Emil had logged on, his face looking a little flustered.

"Everything alright Emil?" Alaric asked, concerned that the impromptu meeting may have placed him in an awkward position with the Guild. Working as a double agent, gathering Guild secrets for the Alliance, in the hope that what he funnelled their way might one day bring down the evil organisation, was not without its challenges, or risk.

"Yes, everything's fine. I just wasn't prepared for the link that was set up."

Alaric looked toward Alex, his glare darkening. "Oh, did you have a problem logging in?" he asked Emil.

"No. No. It was however, the first time I've had to follow prompts to a video link that instructed me to click on a man on the screen, who then walked across the screen to bury his face into a woman's nether regions, accompanied by audible cries of her orgasm, whereby the picture faded to become the link to join the meeting."

"What?" Alex asked innocently. "It wasn't explicit, it was animated." He added, as though it was nothing out of the ordinary.

Alex's idea of fun never failed to exasperate Alaric, even if the majority of people in the room discretely tried to cover up their snorts of laughter and snickers.

"I'm sorry Emil. I promise it won't happen again." Alaric told him.

"No problem. It was entertaining, much like the last time when a cartoon tongue had the words: *"LICK HERE TO PROCEED,"* making a *slurp* sound effect as it licked the rear end of a donkey before launching to the video link."

Emil's favourite however, was the caricature of Alaric wearing speedo bathers and a cape. When he clicked on it, the figure turned around and bent over, farting loudly. Not that Emil was going to mention that now, Alaric wasn't known for his good humour most of the time. He'd probably feel the snap freeze in temperature from where he was in London, from Alaric's resulting hissy fit at Alex.

Not that Alex would care. As an immortal vampire with no conscience and an IQ higher than Einstein's, along with a preference for BDSM and little requirement for sleep, Alex could be annoying and was definitely an acquired taste. Even so, Emil couldn't help liking him.

"Emil, no doubt Alaric's already filled you in on our news. We were hoping you might have some information you can add." Oliver prompted, changing the conversation before Alaric decided to rip Alex a new hole, literally…again!

"I'm afraid I don't have much to offer. I haven't been involved with many of the senior Guild members lately, they've been keeping their circle pretty tight."

"Emil, do you think they suspect you've been passing on information?" Dray asked, concern edging his tone.

"It's the Guild. They suspect everyone and trust no one. I don't think I've been singled out, they're just being extra cautious lately."

"You know you only need to say the word and we'll pull you out." Alaric told him.

"Yes, thank you. But, for now I'd prefer to stay where I am and take my chances."

"Fair enough. For the record though, we really appreciate everything you pass on to us." Saladin told him.

"Which is why I'm still here," he replied with a sigh. Emil was in a unique position within the Guild. As the son of the former UK leader within the organisation, although he'd been estranged from his father whilst growing up, Emil was groomed as a spy for them before his father's death several years earlier. As a Psychiatrist specialising in techniques like hypnotherapy, he's adept at acquiring information without his clients ever being aware they're over sharing. Unfortunately for the Guild, Dr Emil Wagstaff despised his father and the organisation he stood for, and in recent years he'd been working for the Alliance, more than happy to breach his client confidentiality ethics, if it meant bringing down the Guild.

"I can tell you that there is a specialist team that's being dispatched sometime in the next 24 to 48 hours. I would assume they're being sent to find the armband."

Oliver's voice cut through the silence in the room, calm but firm. "Then it's settled. We'll send our own team out first thing in the morning. Sanders, I know you and your team only arrived back this afternoon, but yours is the best and most seasoned team we've got. Brin will be accompanying you for the retrieval."

"Where are we going?" Sanders asked, his military tone short and sharp.

Raif's mouth tightened. "Canada. Nathaniel believes it's close to the Arctic Circle." He slid a look of sympathy toward his sister, a woman who was used to the mild climates of Fey, and positively hated any cold weather.

"Yes, Northern Canada. That's where the Guild's headed too." Emil told them.

Marcus blew out a long breath. "Craptastic! We're going to the fucking Arctic," he muttered under his breath. "Today just keeps getting better and better."

Brin's head snapped toward him, a spark of her usual biting glare returning. "If you're worried about frostbite, Marcus, you're welcome to stay behind."

"Don't tempt me," he shot back, though the growl in his voice carried more unease than humour. "Although, I'm likely to get frostbite just by being in the same room as you."

"Enough!" Oliver snapped in exasperation, his tolerance of the pair having frayed to breaking point. His hard glare pinned them both with anger. "You'll work together, whether you like it or not. There's more at stake here than your pride and petty squabbles."

The verbal smackdown effectively quashing the pair's heated banter.

"Yes, Sir." Marcus replied, penitence in his voice, but his eyes still blazed with indignation.

"Sorry." Brin added contritely, casting her eyes downward toward her fidgeting hands.

The fire cracked violently in the silence that followed, sending sparks up the chimney. Every man and woman present felt the gravity of what lay before them. This was no ordinary mission. Failure meant handing Morganna and the Guild a weapon of power, one which they still had no clear idea of what it actually did…besides harming everyone, except Brin.

Brin drew in a long breath, squaring her shoulders. "Fine. I guess it's settled."

Marcus and Brin locked eyes in a silent battle of wills, neither willing to give in first. In the end, it was Marcus who looked away with a sharp pang of frustration twisting in his chest.

"Emil, I don't suppose you know how many men they're sending or where in Northern Canada they're headed? That's a lot of territory up there," Dray asked.

"No. Sorry." Emil thought for a moment, his face lighting up as a new thought occurred to him. "I don't know if this is of any value, but I overheard a couple of the regional leaders discussing the need for C4. One of them joked about whether they'd need it for the cave or whether to save it to use on themselves if they failed to find it." Dying at their own hand quickly was a far better option than the alternative, being flayed one layer of skin at a time by Scorpion or Morganna. "From what they were saying, I got the impression they were talking about a cave that's recently been uncovered from a shifting glacier. I'm assuming they were talking about Canada. I hope that's of help."

"More than you know. Thanks. We'll get back to you soon." Dray told him, disconnecting the link.

"What is it about a shifting glacier that helps us?" Oliver asked.

"We already know from Nathaniel that the armband is in Northern Canada somewhere, but now we can narrow it down to Auyuittuq National Park, on Baffin Island's Cumberland Peninsula. It's in a remote region with an excess of fjords, glaciers and ice fields that are constantly on the move. This is also the only region where one of its glaciers has recently broken away and opened up a large crevice. It's certainly large enough to be concealing a cave."

"It sounds promising but as you say, glaciers are constantly moving, what's to say this is the right place?"

Dray moved around the other side of Alaric's desk, dragging the laptop with him. A few keystrokes later and he turned the screen to face the group.

"Here." He pointed to an area on a satellite image. "Going by the current images and geological records, this region was free of glaciers back in the early 1300's, when the Knights Templar were hiding all the relics. This particular glacier," he pointed on the screen, "While already in existence back then, was located several miles north. This region was still covered in vegetation." Dray explained.

"Okay, so tell me this. How is it that if we can use satellites and all manner of other technology to find things, why is it that the Guild still seem to locate the artefact hiding places before us?" Gustav asked in his broken English.

Dray shrugged a shoulder. "I can only speculate, but I suspect Morganna is either using dark magic to locate them, or the demons she's been resurrecting from the Underworld have a method of sensing them. Fortunately though, we have Emil, and we have angels like Nathaniel who are willing to stick their necks out to help us get to them first."

Of the thirteen artefacts they'd been tasked to find thirteen years ago, so far only six had been found, and of those they only had five in their possession, the Seraph Blade, Tyrfing Sword, Book of Thoth, the Aegis and the Cintamani Stone. The sixth, the Ring of Gyges, an invisibility ring, had been stolen by Philippe's brother Nicholas, a few years earlier, when he betrayed the Alliance and joined with Scorpion, the vampire who, as it turned out, had sired him.

That left seven artefacts still missing. Finding the Serpent Armband was essential. They couldn't afford for the Guild to get their hands on any more powerful items. Besides the Ring of Gyges, Morganna also had in her possession the Thunderstone. A stone, cut from the Higher Realms by the Elders, and placed in a cave in the Valley of Vardin, Fey, imprisoning Morganna and her followers for one and a half millennia. The Thunderstone contained the power of the Higher Realms, which she was now using to power the portal device which was created, unwillingly by Alex, to free demons from the Underworld, building an army in preparation for Mephistopheles return.

Marcus listened to the conversation as they debated and speculated where his team would be deployed. Not that it really mattered to him, he was just a soldier. He went where they told him to go, did what they told him to do. Okay, so maybe he wasn't so good at doing what he was told, he tended to question his orders on a regular basis. But, if he was given a direct order, he always obeyed.

The question was, was he willing to follow orders that would put him in close proximity to Brin? Somehow, he doubted he would. He was no doubt going to be the recipient of several 'dressing-down' reproachments from Sanders over the coming days, and most likely have his pay docked…again. And maybe even be confined to quarters for an extended period once they returned.

He was fine with all that. He didn't care if his pride was at risk by being around Brin, but he was determined that his independence wouldn't be. Yet, something in his gut told him otherwise. It was just over thirteen years ago, during the battle against Bordan in Fey, that Marcus had been mortally wounded by a dragon, and Brin had saved him. The thing was, in the process of saving him, something happened between them. Something that terrified him enough he has made a point of avoiding her at all costs ever since.

As Brin worked to save him, a connection between them seemed to emerge. A momentary bond between their souls, which on its own, he could have discarded as a side effect of the healing. What he couldn't disregard however, was what happened when blood from his wounds, covering her hands, was absorbed into her palms. It was freaky, although again, he might have ignored it, except for a prophecy which also involved her.

Marcus knew the wording of the prophecy, it was one which was passed down to every lycan as a child as a fairytale. Essentially, it said: *A lycan male wearing the mark of a dragon will become the guardian and protector to a wyvern princess. Immortal in his own right as long as she lived, the two would be bonded together for eternity.*

Marcus had believed it to be just another fairytale, until it was confirmed by her grandfather, Nathaniel, to be very real. In fact, it had been foretold by Nathaniel himself several millennia earlier, when he was still a flesh and blood wyvern and renowned sear.

Surely though, he was overreacting. The prophecy related to some other poor sucker who was destined to be sidled with Brin. Not him. After all, he didn't have any dragon markings on him. He didn't have so much as a freckle. Besides that, neither of them had ever had a single kind word to say to each other, and their mutual loathing suited him just fine.

Despite his sound logic, he still couldn't shake the nagging feeling that if he wasn't careful, in some awful twist of fate, he could very well end up being her prophesied *mate*. Hence his *'Avoid Brin at all costs'*, policy.

Sanders stepped forward, concern creviced in his forehead. "As you're no doubt aware, on our recon mission to Peru, we were ambushed by Guild operatives. They hit us hard and fast. After they shot one of my team with a dart laced with the toxin, they were gone. He seemed to recover from the paralytic effect quickly, but developed a mild temperature. As soon as we arrived back this afternoon, I arranged for him to be transferred to the medical facility at the Ukraine base." He said, addressing the group in general, before directing a question to Gustav. "Has there been any improvement in his condition?"

Gustav's hands clenched and unclenched at his sides, the only outward sign of his agitation. "I'm sorry to say that, unfortunately he seems to have deteriorated in the past few hours. We're still running tests, but the best we can determine at this stage, it's looking like the toxin does indeed contain a virus."

"Are you certain? A virus?" Oliver asked.

"Unfortunately, yes. What's more, he seems to have lost the ability to shift. It's too early to tell if it's only a temporary issue, or permanent." However, after learning all the details about Brin's conversation with Nathaniel, he suspected it was the latter, or would be if they didn't find a cure quickly.

"Hell's hairy balls!" Raif cursed.

"Needless to say, he's now in strict quarantine in one of the holding cells." Gustav added.

Varying renditions of the sentiment, *"Fuck!"* reverberated about the room.

"A virus. Are you absolutely certain? I didn't think it was possible for lycans nor wyvern to carry viruses, their beastly halves irradicate anything before it can take hold," Alex stated, scratching his head in a quandary. "Is it contagious, or is it only contracted when injected from a dart? And for that matter, if it is contagious, is it spread by air or contact? And is it transmittable to regular humans?" He didn't bother including vampires, they may look human, but for all intents and purposes, they no longer had a functioning nervous system that might be susceptible to viruses or bacteria.

"That's what we need you to determine, Alex." Gustav turned his body to face him directly, his large frame wired tightly, seemingly increasing his already imposing stature as his biceps muscles rolled visibly beneath his thin shirt.

"I'm your man." Alex grinned. He was the only person whose enthusiasm and excitement increased in dangerous and even deadly situations. "Gustav, I'll need to relocate my lab to your base, temporarily."

"Whatever you need. All our resources are at your disposal. We need an antidote to this thing as quickly as possible."

The room fell silent for a moment as everyone absorbed and processed this new unsettling news, until Sanders cleared his throat.

"Considering the urgency of our mission tomorrow, the fact that we're a man down in our team, and the high likelihood that we'll encounter more Guild operatives out there, who no doubt carry more of those darts, I'd like to enlist someone who might come in very handy for just such an occasion."

"Do you have someone specific in mind?" Oliver asked.

"Yes, I do."

"Owen, the Aussie druid whose been tagging around with the lycan military in Australia. His gift is immunity to all toxins, yeah?"

"That's true. That's not to say he'll be immune to this new Guild concoction. But, if you feel he'd be of value to your team, sure. I'll have someone retrieve him this evening from wherever he is."

"That would be great. I guess all we need now is a map of the terrain we're heading into."

"I'll make sure you have it within the hour.

Brin and Marcus locked eyes once again as everyone began to file out of the room.

It seemed that not only were they heading into what was likely to be a dangerous region of wilderness in search of an artefact that only Brin could touch, but he was now responsible for her wellbeing, as her protector and escort. Living in close quarters together until the mission was over. He almost hoped that he'd be the next Guild target for a poisoned dart. Anything would be better than being around her.

What a fucking shit show his day had turned out to be.

Life definitely wasn't a unicorn shitting rainbows of candy. At least, not his life, Marcus grumbled to himself.

Marcus returned to the barracks dormitory, unsure of what he was supposed to think, how to feel. Logic told him that this was just going to be a run-of-the-mill mission. Sleep under the stars, eat crappy military rations, lots of hiking through inhospitable terrain, kill a few bad guys, find the missing artefact and return home. No biggy. He was good with all that, especially the part that involved killing a few bad guys, he really needed to blow off some steam after the fucked-up day he'd had.

What he wasn't sure about was how to feel about having Brin along. Clearly, she was a necessary tag-along, but surely there must be a way to just bring her in at the last minute after they'd found the armband, have her collect it and then send her home again straight after. Maybe have one of her brothers fly her in on their dragon's back or a Nephilim could open a portal just long enough for her to get in and out without needing to spend any unnecessary time amongst their team. Not only was she a distraction for the other men, but she really got under his skin.

He honestly didn't think he would cope one whole day being near her, let alone three or four days…maybe longer!

Yet again however, the universe seemed to be conspiring against him. With all the unrest in Fey at the moment, none of her brothers can afford to spend any extra time on Earth, to wait around for a call to swoop in and out again with Brin. Whilst the Nephilim had issues with the terrain they were heading into being rather barren of vegetation, except for a lot of ice, since they could only open a portal into heavily tree covered areas.

His day seemed to have gone from one shit storm to another. First, they returned home this morning after being gone for a month, to discover his mother was paying an extended visit, which led to having to endure a family dinner where Candy was 'invited'. That really sucked because he had intended to break up with her over a private dinner, and now he'll have to wait probably another week. And finally, worst of all, he's been informed that he's going to have to share the same breathing space as Brin for the next few days.

Sometimes life really sucks.

Marcus pushed his rucksack off his bed and onto the floor with a heavy thud, collapsing onto his back to stare up at the ceiling, a hand resting beneath his neck on the pillow. His dark eyes fixed and unblinking, although seeing nothing as his mind continued to mull over his troubled thoughts.

"How you doing?" Callum asked, his voice catching Marcus by surprise in the silence, breaking him out of his stupor.

Marcus looked across to the next bed where Callum was meticulously sorting the contents of his rucksack, dirty clothes in his washing bag, clean jocks, socks and uniform in the rucksack, along with his usual arsenal of weapons. Silently, Marcus made a mental note to do the same before they headed out. Realistically however, the only things he was likely to change over in his pack were his weapons. There was no way he would ever leave his guns uncleaned or his ammunition unstocked. His uniform however, was another matter. Even if his jocks had major brown stains or his socks were water sodden, or his fatigues were covered in grass stains and dirt, he wouldn't care. Yeah, Sanders was definitely right. He was a slob.

"Yeah, it's cool." Marcus replied.

"Can you deal with the fact that Brin's coming with us?"

Marcus sat up to face him, his hands gripping the mattress on either side of him. "Of course, what makes you think I can't?"

"Maybe because you've been staring at the ceiling and growling for the last half hour," he told him, his look of concern pissing Marcus off further.

"Fuck off!" Yeah, he wasn't just a slob, he was an arsehole too. No surprise there either.

"Very mature response. Don't get me wrong, I'm totally sympathetic with your predicament, but if you don't get your head out of your arse quickly, Sanders is going to sideline you. You get away with a lot of shit with him because he's your brother-in-law and anything he does to you, Holly gives him hell for later. But, we're all going to have to bring our A-game on this mission, and you know it."

Fuck! As much as he hated to admit it, Callum was right. And being sidelined wasn't an option. Not only would he be forced to remain here in Cadley and have to endure the shame of being booted off the team for such a critical mission, but he would most likely be forced to spend more time with his mother. That thought put his situation into a clearer perspective. And while he could cope with a few days in Brin's company, he couldn't say the same about his mother. Besides, there would be a dozen men all itching for her attention, surely he could easily avoid her for at least 90% of the time.

"Sorry. I've got a lot on my mind. Seriously bro, I'm fine. I promise I'll be on my best behaviour."

"If it makes you feel any better, I'm pretty certain that Brin's as unhappy about being stuck with you for the next few days too." Callum smirked.

That was probably true, which in a twisted way, did make him feel better. As they say, misery loves company.

"I know you probably don't want to talk about the prophecy, even though I know you think about it, a lot, and I can't help wondering if you truly are *the one*. I'm not saying that to scare you, but think about what happened between you two when she healed you in the battle against Bordan. In all the years since, I've never seen or even heard about anyone else's blood being absorbed into Brin's hands, and I've never heard of it happening to any other healer either. Besides that, you've admitted it to me yourself, that you feel a strong attraction to her, despite your antagonism toward her."

Marcus didn't reply, however his glare hardened enough to freeze the midday sun in summer. Not that Callum was perturbed, he'd known Marcus his whole life, and there wasn't anything his best friend could say or do that he hadn't encountered before.

"Marcus, you go out with women who look very similar to Brin, but whose personalities are very different. It's almost as though you deliberately choose women who you know you're not compatible with, but remind you of her, giving you noncommittal companionship and a legitimate excuse to avoid Brin, avoiding the possibility that she might be your true *mate*. You repeatedly do things to push her away and drive a wedge between you." Callum said.

Again, Marcus didn't answer, though his eyes glinted with a hint of acknowledgement, even if he wasn't willing to verbalise any credence that what Callum was saying held some measure of truth. Even so, he hated when Callum talked logic to him, he much preferred his own irrational point of view.

"If she is your *mate*, you could be torturing yourself needlessly with years of disappointing shallow relationships. That's just my opinion, you don't have to give it any thought, and I know you'll do your best not to, but…"

"I have three words for you bro. Pot. Kettle. Black."

"What's that supposed to mean?"

"You and Elise. She might have had a crush on you when she was a kid, but you've been avoiding telling her how you really feel about her, for just as long as I've been avoiding Brin. You think about that!" Marcus told him, lifting his legs back up onto the bed and turning on his side, placing his back to Callum.

Not surprisingly, Callum made no further attempt to share his opinion, having a dose of his own reality delivered to him.

Several hours passed and the first glow of light began to show through the window above Marcus' bed. He hadn't slept a wink, but he had managed to clean every bit of equipment in his kit in the intervening hours and even swapped out his dirty clothes for clean ones in his rucksack.

Callum too hadn't fared much better. The two of them sat on the end of their beds, side by side, scrolling through Tik-Tok and YouTube on their phones, just waiting for the call to roll out.

6

Well, that went pretty much as she expected, Brin thought. Except, for some reason she'd assumed that the team to lead the expedition wouldn't include Marcus. She'd been almost ready to accept the fact that she had no choice about going. Now? Now, she was praying for a meteor to fall out of the sky and land on top of her. Anything to avoid being stuck in close quarters with him for who knows how long. A few days? A week? Longer?

Brin's heart began to pound beneath her ribs. Anything longer than five minutes in the same room as Marcus was too long for her liking. What the hell was she going to do?

As the meeting broke up everyone began to scatter throughout the house, some like Alaric, Saladin and Dray remained in the study to discuss matters further. The men from Fey headed for the forest and back to their homes in Fey, whilst the lycans returned to Cadley to make preparations for an early departure in the morning. That left the women to pursue their own goals for the evening.

Leaving Alaric's study, Brin barely had time to gather her thoughts before Cassie intercepted her in the hallway, flanked by the other women in the house, Abby, Teagan, Paige, Kaitlyn, Holly, and Megan. With an unspoken air of purpose, the women herded her toward the kitchen.

"Sit," Cassie ordered, pulling a chair out from the kitchen counter. "You look like you could use a coffee."

Brin slumped into the chair, exhaling through her nose. "Coffee? Hell, no. I need something stronger?"

"Not today," Teagan replied.

Brin scowled dejectedly at the group surrounding her, each shaking their heads in agreement with Teagan. They were a wall of female authority, and she didn't have enough remaining energy to argue with them.

Abby leaned against the counter, crossing her arms. "The last thing you need is to be hungover in the morning, not with where you're going. You need to keep your wits about you at all times."

"Pfft. I have no intention of being hungover," Brin shot back, waving away their concerns, her green eyes glinting with mischief. "What I'd prefer to do is to start drinking now and not stop, stay drunk for the entire time we're in that frozen wasteland. It might make the whole ordeal more tolerable."

There was a beat of silence as the women stared at her. Then Paige arched a brow. "You're joking, yeah?"

Brin shrugged. "Mostly."

Kaitlyn shook her head with a laugh. "I don't deny the occasion warrants something stronger than coffee, but..."

"Yeah, I know the *'but'* you're concerned about. BUT, right now I'm not interested in any sensible logic. I want to wallow in self-pity, and I'd really appreciate it if you could all be my enablers instead of my well-meaning buzzkill babysitters."

Snickers and chuckles rippled about the kitchen from the other women, equal parts sympathy and amusement. Although, none would have traded places with her if given the opportunity.

Well, actually, that wasn't strictly true. Megan would give her right arm to go, for no other reason than just to leave the manor for a short while. She was so tired of being sequestered inside the manor's grounds. Of course, if Megan left the manor, she wouldn't be any safter than Brin currently was. They were both marked women, hunted by the Guild for their abilities. Brin was on their hit list because of her healing abilities. Megan on the other hand, was valued for her ability to communicate with the angels themselves, not just animals. The Guild would gladly torture her for information about the higher realms, get inside knowledge of what the Elders and angels might be planning against The Guild and their bosses, Morganna, Scorpion, and of course, the biggest of all evil baddies, Mephistopheles. The fact that the angels rarely communicated with her with anything of importance, was irrelevant to the Guild.

If it wasn't for the fact that Brin had been ordered by her grandfather to go on the expedition, there was no doubt that she wouldn't be allowed to leave the secure confines of her own fortress home for the foreseeable future. Sometimes it really sucked to be *special*.

The moment of levity eased the heavy weight of the situation, but the reprieve was short-lived.

The kitchen door banged open and in marched Grace, her moody teenage demeanour oozing more angst than usual, with Tilly padding faithfully at her side, and Cujo lumbering behind like a great dark shadow. Grace's expression was thunderous.

"I swear, I can't get five minutes to myself anymore!" she groaned, dropping into a chair opposite Brin. "Tilly, I understand. She's stuck to me like glue since I was a baby. But Cujo? What's his deal? He's *everywhere!*" she cried, her eyes rolling to the ceiling with wide, frustrated arm gestures. "If I so much as go to the bathroom, he's sitting outside the door growling and pacing like some deranged creepy babysitter. And lately, he's started sleeping in my room. He used to give me some space by sleeping outside my door. Now, he's been pushing his way into my room and sleeping beside my bed. It's bad enough having Tilly farting all night, but having two of them…I need a gas mask." Grace pinched her nose in disgust.

Brin chuckled softly at the girl's theatrics, but she noticed the way Cujo positioned himself, broad shoulders tense and eyes alert, following every movement in the room. Watchful. Protective.

"Have you considered changing the brand of food you feed them?" Teagan suggested.

"Maybe he just likes your company," Holly told her with a grin.

"Or," Paige teased, "Maybe he's worried you're going to get into trouble, Grace. Fourteen is a dangerous age."

Grace scowled, throwing her hands in the air. "Thanks for the vote of confidence Aunt Paige, but unlike you at my age, I don't go looking for trouble, I couldn't find any even if I wanted to. I have too many people watching my every move," she huffed, her hard gaze skimming over each person in the room with annoyance. "I just need some *personal space*! Is there anything wrong with that?"

Cassie looked at her daughter. She wasn't going to apologise for wanting to keep her safe, although she did understand her need for more space.

"Mum, can't you do something?"

"Sorry love, I don't know what I can do. Tilly will never leave your side, you know that. And Cujo? The only one he seems to listen to, is Megan," Cassie told her.

Every eye turned toward the Scottish woman.

Looking suddenly uncomfortable under everyone's expectant gaze, Megan tilted her head, eyes narrowing on the hellhound. "Okay…why don't I ask him why he's behaving so oddly, aye?"

"Please." Grace encouraged desperately.

The room fell silent as Megan looked at the hellhound. "Okay, so what's yer problem? Why are yer being so protective of Grace?" she asked him.

Cujo's massive head dipped and responded with a few growls and whiny barks rumbling from his throat. Megan's brow furrowed in concentration as her gift bridged the language gap.

Megan gasped, clasping her hands over her mouth, and before she could speak, Abby let out an uncharacteristic high-pitched squeal and snort of laughter, catching everyone off guard, the group turning toward her, confused.

"What?" Cassie demanded impatiently.

Abby clutched her side, laughing harder. "Oh, Alaric is going to lose his mind over this!"

"What the hell are you talking about?" Holly pressed, glancing between her and Megan.

Megan's own laughter spilled out from behind her hand, her shoulders shaking as she tried to contain her outburst, and eyes bright with amusement.

"For heaven's sake," Teagan snapped. "Would one of you just spit it out already?"

Megan finally straightened, wiping at her eyes. "Tilly's pregnant."

The kitchen erupted in stunned silence as they processed the news. Brin blinked, her mouth falling open a fraction in astonishment.

"Pregnant?" Kaitlyn repeated.

Megan nodded. "She has been fur some time apparently. Cujo's been shadowing her because she's nearing full-term. He won't leave her side. Not now."

As her words sank in, the women looked from one to another, then at Tilly, who tilted her head innocently, tail giving a soft thump against the floor as though she knew exactly what they were talking about.

"Pregnant?" Grace echoed faintly, then burst out laughing.

At that precise moment, the kitchen's external door from the garden opened, and Philippe strolled in, brushing a few drops of rain from his shoulders. "Alright, ladies, what did I miss? The meeting's over, yes? Fill me in."

Everyone in the room turned to him and spoke in chaotic unison.

"Tilly's pregnant!"

Philippe froze, blinking at them, utterly wrong-footed. "I, ahh…come again…what?"

From the distant study came Alaric's unmistakable bellow, the news having carried easily to his superhuman hearing through the stone walls and corridors.

"*Fuck!*" he roared.

That did it. The room collapsed into complete hysterics, the women all doubling over with laughter. Grace slid from her chair to the floor, clutching her stomach, while Brin found herself laughing harder than she had in months, the tension of the evening dissolving in riotous laughter.

Philippe glanced between them all, baffled by their behaviour, muttering under his breath, "I should have used another door."

The laughter only grew louder.

Philippe gave his wife Nadia, a brief kiss hello and excused himself, heading for Alaric's study where the sound of cursing continued.

It took the women a few minutes for their chortles of amusement to subside, replaced by semi composed curious chatter.

"That explains why Tilly's been off her food lately, I guess, and it's had nothing to do with eating that highly processed, round balls of sadness," Holly commented.

"Tilly's going to be a mother?" Teagan asked rhetorically, shaking her head.

"We're going to have pups in the house? I wonder how soon?" Grace asked eagerly.

"Too soon for Alaric's liking," Kaitlyn smirked, grateful it was their home that was about to be overrun with more destructive, but no doubt very cute, hellhounds, and not hers.

"I wonder how many pups she'll have?" Grace asked, looking at Megan.

"Don't look at me. Yer guess is as good as mine. I didn't know she was pregnant until now either."

"I guess we'll have to take her to the vets tomorrow and get her checked," Cassie told them.

"In the meantime, we have other matters to take care of," Paige announced," turning her attention toward Brin.

"What do you have in mind?" Cassie asked.

"Brin's going to the arctic circle in the morning. I think she needs a wardrobe makeover, don't you girls?" she stated.

"What? No. My wardrobe is just fine, thanks anyway." Brin countered quickly. If she was being given the option to go shopping and choose her own clothes, she'd be all for it. But, she knew every one of these women well enough to know they meant to dress her up to be the very picture of a succulent lamb chop ready for tasting, amongst a military team of hungry wolves. No thanks. She didn't need that complication.

"You might want to reconsider, unless you're keen on wearing military clothes." Paige told her. "I'm assuming you didn't pack any winter woollies or snow gear."

"Um, no. I hadn't thought about that. Besides my underwear, I've only packed light weight tops and pants. I don't own anything suitable for snow. I think I've only seen snow once, when I went to your dad's base in Ukraine," Brin told them, looking between the druid sisters. "No, I tell a lie. It snowed here once when I came to visit, but I remember I refused to go outside, it was too cold."

"Well, lucky for you, we live in a much colder climate than you, and have more than enough clothes between us to keep you toasty warm, without having to resort to any of those itchy and uncomfortable khaki and cammo uniforms the men will be wearing."

"They wouldn't really make me wear that stuff, would they?"

No one answered her, but their raised brows and incredulous glares spoke volumes. These were practical minded, battle-hardened men, used to doing, wearing and eating things that would make her stomach churn.

Brin plonked her fists on her hips and huffed out a resigned sigh. "Fine. But I really hate it when you all gang up on me."

"We love you too." Paige grinned.

"Do I get a say in what I can borrow?"

"No!" Was the unanimous reply.

"Great." Brin mumbled under her breath.

"Oh, stop sulking," Holly teased, tossing a folded jumper at her from the washing basket on the floor at the far end of the kitchen bench, just waiting to be folded. "You'll thank us when you're not freezing your tits off in sub-zero temperatures."

"Speaking of which," Teagan said, setting her mug down with a clink, "We also need to talk about your footwear. You're going to be trudging through snow, not strolling through Fey gardens. Do you even own a pair of boots?"

"Define *boots*," Brin replied cautiously.

"Ones that have flat soles, and don't have heels higher than two inches," Abby answered.

Brin sighed. "Then no. Not unless we're counting the furry ones with pompoms."

The room erupted into snickers again.

"Right," Paige said decisively, rolling up her sleeves. "Operation *'Keep Brin Alive and Cute in the Arctic',* commences now."

Over the next hour, the kitchen transformed into a flurry of fabrics and feminine authority. Jackets, jumpers, thermals, gloves and scarves appeared from all directions, landing in untidy heaps on the counter. Brin was pushed, prodded and spun around like a reluctant mannequin as each woman took turns sizing her up, muttering about layers, warmth retention and colour coordination.

"Try this one," Teagan said, holding up a navy waterproof jacket that looked capable of withstanding a hurricane.

"I'll drown in that," Brin protested.

"Good. That means it'll actually fit over your ego," Holly quipped.

"Ha ha," Brin muttered. "Remind me again why I let you lot dress me?"

"Because if we don't, someone like Marcus will probably shove you into a snowbank and call it camouflage," Paige replied sweetly.

That earned another round of laughter. Even Brin couldn't help but smile at that one, though it faded quickly. "He's got Buckley's chance of ever getting that close to me."

As the chaos continued around her, the teasing, the talk of layering and heated socks, the sound of mugs clinking and Tilly's gentle thump of a tail on the floor, her mind drifted elsewhere.

Tomorrow. The Arctic. A cave. A relic that could kill anyone not of her bloodline.

And Marcus. Always Marcus. Why did he always manage to weave his way into her thoughts and conversation.

Her heart gave an uninvited jolt at the thought of him, which in turn irritated her. Everything about him irritated her. His smug smirk, his clipped tone, the way he looked at her like she was both a burden and a problem he couldn't quite escape from.

And yet, under all that aggravation, there was something else, something she couldn't name without hating herself for it.

Being trapped with him, in close quarters, surrounded by his pack of surly, overprotective lycans, was a recipe for madness and most likely disaster. She could already picture it, all of them looming, barking orders, insisting she stay behind them, treating her like some fragile porcelain doll. She'd have to fight twice as hard just to prove she wasn't a liability. And Marcus? He'd hover the most, not out of care, but out of stubborn pride and some ridiculous sense of duty. The whole time making snide remarks and making her life miserable.

Maybe, she thought, maybe being forced into the same space with him would finally give her the chance to confront him. To ask him why he was so determined to dislike her. To find out what it was that turned his every glance into a wall of hostility.

Part of her longed for the answer. Part of her dreaded it.

"Earth to Brin," Cassie's voice broke through her thoughts. "You still with us?"

Brin blinked, realising she was holding a pair of snow pants upside down. "Yeah. Sorry. Zoned out."

"Understandable," Paige said softly, handing her a pair of fleece-lined gloves. "You've got a lot on your plate."

"Understatement of the year," Holly muttered.

"Just remember," Abby added, her tone warm but firm, "You're not alone out there. Even if you think you are."

Brin forced a small smile and nodded. "Thanks. I'll try not to freeze or die. Promise."

"Good girl," Teagan said, giving her shoulder a squeeze. "Now, let's see about hats. You'll need something that covers those ears. No point looking like an elegant icicle."

By the time they were finished, Brin felt less like a warrior preparing for battle and more like a child bundled up for a snow day. Layers of borrowed warmth cocooned her, and yet none of it touched the chill that had settled in her chest.

At last, Cassie yawned and declared it was time for everyone to get some sleep. "Big day tomorrow," she said, ushering the others toward the hall. "Brin, try to get some rest. I have a feeling you're going to need every ounce of energy tomorrow."

Left alone in the quiet kitchen, Brin stared at the pile of winter gear on the counter, a mountain of borrowed faith from women who believed she could do what needed to be done.

She wished she had the same faith in herself. Nevertheless, she was committed to the expedition, whether she wanted to go or not. Collecting the horde of clothes in a basket she headed upstairs.

Closing the door to her bedroom, a quiet peace enveloped her. In fact, the whole manor seemed to have fallen into the kind of silence that only arrived after midnight, deep and still, broken only by the low whistle of the wind outside. Brin sat on the edge of her bed, tugging at the laces of her boots before giving up entirely. The room smelled faintly of lavender and firewood. The curtains were drawn back, framing the window like open arms letting in the pale moonlight.

She lay back against the pillows, her body exhausted but her mind spinning.

Tomorrow, she would step into a frozen wilderness. Tomorrow, she would need to prove herself worthy of the huge responsibility she's been handed. And tomorrow, she would face unknown challenges, danger and…Marcus.

Her gaze shifted toward the dark sky beyond the window. Clouds drifted lazily across the half-moon, smothering the stars one by one until only thin streaks of silver light remained. The world outside looked cold, vast, and uncaring, a mirror to the uncertainty inside her chest.

Somewhere out there, on the other side of the forest, Marcus was no doubt sprawled across his bunk in Cadley, probably snoring, probably dreaming about how much she annoyed him. The thought made her lips twitch. She hated that he occupied so much space in her head. But maybe tomorrow, in the middle of all that ice and danger, she'd finally make him tell her why.

Her eyes shifted to the small clock beside the bed. The glowing red digits read 4:00a.m. Brin exhaled, long and heavy, her breath fogging faintly in the cool air.

"Enough," she whispered to herself.

There was no point dwelling on what was to come. Morning would arrive soon enough, bringing with it whatever destiny had planned for her.

That thought struck a chord deep within her soul. Destiny. Underlying all her anxiety lay one simple truth. She felt as though her destiny was racing toward her, and there was nothing she could do to stop it.

She turned her face toward the window again, watching as the last wisp of moonlight faded behind a bank of clouds.

Whatever happens, good or bad, she'd deal with it.

She always did.

7

Denial, anger, bargaining, depression, acceptance. The five stages of waking up. Currently, Brin was only at number three.

Go back to sleep, just for one more hour, she begged silently.

Her pillow, traitorous and unsympathetic, offered no comfort. Her mind, already awake, hummed with anxiety. Nope, it really wasn't happening, no matter how much she wanted it to.

With a groaning huff, she pushed back the covers and flopped one leg out, her foot dangling mid-air for a moment before she forced herself upright. Her toes touched the cold floorboards, and she hissed at the icy sting.

"My life sucks," she muttered.

The dim morning light filtered through the window, the curtains stirring faintly in a draft that carried the scent of damp earth and wood smoke, probably from one of the many fires no doubt already burning within the manor. England's chill was nothing like what awaited her in Canada, but it was still cold enough to make her teeth chatter if she lingered too long in her thin cotton pyjamas.

Brin crossed the cold floor quickly on the balls of her feet, heading toward the sofa, eyeing the pile of clothes the women bestowed upon her the night before. She half expected the mish-mash of personal styles would tally up to a major fashion disaster. Cassie's floral thermals, Holly's vibrantly coloured tops and jumpers, Abby's leather everything, and Paige's idea of "practical but cute." Instead, the collection was surprisingly useful. Thick leggings, fleece-lined pants, a soft merino undershirt, a padded vest, and a wonderfully warm, waterproof snow jacket.

She pulled on the layers one by one, each adding a bit more warmth and a bit less mobility. By the time she zipped up the jacket, she felt somewhere between adventurer and overstuffed burrito.

"At least I'll look the part," she muttered dryly at her reflection in the full-length mirror by the wardrobe.

She tied her hair up into a messy knot, the long red strands refusing to behave, and glanced back at the rucksack Sanders had delivered sometime through the night, military grade, big enough to fit a small person in if necessary.

Brin crouched beside it and began stuffing it with the horde of borrowed clothes. Each layer was neatly folded at first, then shoved in when she realized the bag wasn't quite as bottomless as she'd hoped. Still, she had to admit, the girls had outdone themselves. Between the gloves, scarves, and insulated trousers, she could probably survive the next ice age.

Her hands paused when she spotted something silky tucked between a wool jumper and thermal socks. She pulled it free, a silky wisp of midnight blue fabric. A negligee. Very sheer. Very sexy. *Not* at all survival gear.

"Oh, for the love of..." she groaned, holding it up by the straps. "Really, Abby?"

The tag still had a little bow on it, along with a note scrawled in looping handwriting: *Just in case you need to feel sexy in sub-zero temperatures. Love, A.*

"As if," Brin muttered, rolling her eyes. "What would I even do with that? Seduce a grizzly bear?"

Still, she stuffed it into the bottom of the bag. Mostly out of spite. The telepathic vampire would know if she chose not to pack it, and would no doubt slip it into her bag anyway.

When she finally finished packing, Brin sat back on her heels, surveying her work. The rucksack bulged, the zippers stretched to their limits, but at least she was ready for whatever the frozen north had to throw at her. She hoped.

She rubbed at her face, exhaling through her nose.
At this point, she'd take almost any alternative to this mission, even being locked away in her family's citadel for the next decade.

"Yeah," she muttered under her breath. "Even solitary confinement sounds better than having a pack of overgrown, bossy wolves, babysitting me."

Her gaze drifted toward the window again. The faint light of dawn had started to break through the mist, turning the frost on the glass into silver streaks. In just a few hours, she'd be standing in snow up to her knees, halfway around the world.

Her stomach clenched. She swallowed hard. "Brilliant," she said flatly. "Absolutely bloody brilliant."

At least, if this was going to be the worst day of her life, and she had a sinking feeling it might be, she was at least going to face it dressed like she had a fighting chance.

Brin stood, grabbed the rucksack strap and attempted to lift it over her shoulder. Holy crap that was heavy. She tried again, lifting it almost to shoulder level, but she just wasn't quite able to hitch it over her shoulder. So, instead, she grabbed both straps and she forced one foot in front of the other toward the door, dragging the overstuffed pack behind her.

By the time she made it downstairs, the manor had begun stirring to life. Yet, in the kitchen only the hum of the refrigerator and the soft whistle of wind through the eaves outside broke the silence. Brin made herself a coffee, convinced it was going to be her last *decent* cup for the foreseeable future, and wrapped her hands around it, letting its warmth seep into her palms, grateful for the small window of peace and personal space before the manor erupted with its usual clamour of noise and activity.

The toast she made sat neglected beside her, only one bite missing. Her stomach was too busy performing backflips to consider food.

She stared out the kitchen's window at the grey dawn. A misty fog clung low to the ground, swallowing the spacious lawns and garden in a silvery haze, blocking out the forest beyond. For a fleeting second, she considered sneaking back upstairs and pretending she'd come down with a serious case of something, maybe frostbite *in advance*. But she knew there was no escaping her fate. Of all the people going on this trip, she was the only one who *wasn't* replaceable.

Over the next twenty minutes, the kitchen filled up with every member of the household, all twenty of them, one by one, plus two enormous canines.

So much for peace and quiet.

Brin's haven was transformed into a whirlwind of voices, footsteps and overlapping conversations. Mrs P. was first, firing up the frying pan and topping up the coffee maker. Tilly waddled in, nails clicking on the tiles, Cujo lumbering behind her like a hulking shadow. Grace followed close behind, taking a seat beside Brin at the bench, clutching her phone in one hand and a piece of toast in the other.

Cassie and Megan entered next, already deep in discussion about whether to get Tilly to see the vet or not. Paige and Nadia filled mugs and a large thermos with coffee, while Abby and Holly debated whether Brin had packed enough thermal layers…and other necessities.

Fortunately, the industrial sized kitchen was designed for large-scale chaos. Even so, it was just barely keeping up. Chairs scraped, cupboards banged, and the sink filled up with dishes, leaving a lingering smell of fresh coffee, toast and wet dog to mingle in the air.

The men weren't far behind, Alaric, Narayan, Sebastian, Sanders, Alex, and Philippe, though most of them, after taking one look at the crowded room, made a hasty retreat, grabbing food on the go, disappearing again quickly to do whatever it was they needed to do.

"Cowards," Holly muttered with a grin as the last of them slipped out the door.

Brin couldn't blame them. Nine women, and two oversized dogs before breakfast was enough to make even the bravest man question his life choices. Then again, maybe they were just trying to avoid the ninth female currently in the house. Jocelyn, Mrs P's daughter, Holly's mother, Brin thought as the sour faced woman entered the kitchen only a moment after the last of the men disappeared.

"Mmm, something smells delicious." She announced loudly, looking for a seat at the kitchen bench and seeing none free, she approached Grace swatting the air with her hand until she gave up her seat begrudgingly for the older woman.

"Would you like toast, cereal or bacon and eggs?" Mrs Philpot asked her daughter.

"Yes." She replied, expecting a selection of each. "But make sure you don't overcook the eggs, and ensure the bacon is nice and crispy. There's nothing worse than eating half cooked bacon, wouldn't you agree?" she asked, turning her attention to Grace who was now on the opposite side of the bench glaring at her.

"Actually, I'm happy to take whatever comes. I'm just grateful that Gran is willing to make my breakfast at all, maybe you should be too," she bit out in response. Grace shot her mother a covert glance expecting to be chastised for her rude outburst, or at least deliver a disapproving scowl in her direction, but instead Cassie offered her a proud smirk.

Holly stepped up beside her mother. "Grace is right, mum. If you want something, the cereal boxes are there on that counter, the coffee maker is next to them, and you know where to find the dishes and cutlery. If you want bacon and eggs, I'll make it for you, but you'll take them as they come. We're not here at your beck and call and this isn't a restaurant." Holly told her. She may have been her mother, but the woman infuriated her, always had. She'd been at the manor less than a day and already they were winding up for another argument.

"Fine." Jocelyn huffed. Climbing down from her seat she made a point of banging the cupboards, fridge and drawers as noisily as possible, as she fixed herself some breakfast. The whole time muttering loudly about her ungrateful family.

Brin was almost glad to be getting out of there shortly as the tension in the room began to rise. It amazed her how just one person could change the mood of everyone around them. Jocelyn was certainly one of those people.

Then her mind shifted to another very annoying person. Marcus. He may not affect the mood of everyone around him, but he certainly altered her mood, and not for the better, she thought with a sigh.

Ignoring Jocelyn, who continued to complain about anything and everything, the women flocked around Brin like mother hens as she finished what passed for her breakfast, i.e. two cups of coffee and half a piece of toast, stood and began putting on the last layers of clothing, readying to leave. Someone adjusted her scarf, another tightened the strap on her jacket, and someone else shoved a wrapped snack into her pocket, a block of chocolate if she wasn't mistaken.

"Eat that later," Cassie ordered. "You'll need the energy."

"Make sure you layer properly," Teagan added, tugging on Brin's sleeve.

"Don't lose your gloves," Kaitlyn said. "Or your fingers."

"I'll… do my best," Brin managed, trying not to laugh.

She didn't have the heart to tell them to back off, their fussing came from love, not condescension, and besides, arguing would just make them double down and fuss over her all the more. So, she stood there and endured it, half-amused and half-overwhelmed, until they unanimously declared that she looked *"battle-ready and adorable."*

The flurry of activity began to ebb as they realized the time. Grace glanced at her phone, thumb scrolling, and frowned.

"Brin? There's a storm warning," she said. "Heavy snow and possible blizzard conditions later today. Right over where you guys are going."

The mood in the room shifted, the laughter thinning into quiet concern.

"Well," Brin said, forcing a smile she didn't quite feel, "I knew this trip would take me out of my comfort zone. I guess if there's a blizzard coming, that'll probably include having a bad hair day, but look at me, I think I'm ready. Bring it on." she joked.

She moved around the kitchen, hugging each of them in turn. Each person a member of her extended family.

When she reached Grace, she gave the girl a proper squeeze. "Keep me posted on Tilly. Let me know if she has her pups while I'm gone, yeah?"

Grace smirked. "I'm pretty sure you'll hear my dad cursing all the way in Canada when she does."

Brin laughed softly and scratched Tilly and Cujo behind the ears. Tilly's tail thumped happily. Cujo, ever the stoic, only blinked and leaned into her hand. The simple act sent a pang of anxiety through her chest. For a fleeting moment, an irrational thought crossed her mind. *What if this was the last time she saw them all?*

Sucking in a sharp breath, Brin mentally scolded herself. *Don't go there. Not today.*

"Alright," she said, voice steadier than she felt. "Let's get this over with."

Her gaze fell to the rucksack propped against the doorframe. She bent down to pick it up, but before she could, Grace grabbed it.

"I've got it," the girl said, effortlessly hefting the pack onto her shoulder as if it weighed nothing.

"Show off," Brin muttered, grinning despite herself.

Grace just smirked over her shoulder and started walking down the hall toward the front doors. "Someone's got to make sure you actually leave." She called back with a laugh.

Brin followed, shaking her head with a soft chuckle. Sometimes it was easy to forget that Grace was half vampire, and twice as strong as anyone her age had a right to be.

The scent of coffee and toast trailed after them as the kitchen noise faded behind her. The closer they drew to the front of the manor, the louder the sounds of the outside world became, masculine voices, engines, the low thud of boots on gravel.

Brin exhaled slowly.

Showtime, she thought grimly.

Outside, the gravel driveway was a bustle of activity. The lycan militia had already gathered, their breath visible in the crisp morning air. The rumble of engines mixed with low voices and the clatter of weapons being checked and re-checked.

Brin hesitated on the manor steps, clutching her thermos of coffee like it was her lifeline. Every one of them looked carved from stone, broad shoulders, grim faces, disciplined movements. Soldiers through and through.

She spotted Sanders near the front, barking last-minute orders. Callum was beside him, adjusting his gear. And there, leaning against a jeep with his infuriatingly smug posture, was Marcus.

His family had come out to see him off, his mother Jocelyn, his grandmother Mrs P, and Holly his sister. Although, Holly didn't so much as give him a fond farewell, as she gave him a clip across the back of the head, telling him not to be a total bastard toward Brin. It seemed she was on a roll, dishing out good advice to her family this morning, Brin thought with a smile.

When Brin approached, Marcus' eyes flicked toward her with his usual guarded indifference. She was determined not to take his sourness personally, nor was she going to start the trip pretending to ignore him. She was an adult, and she was determined to act like one.

"I just heard the news," she said, as way of a conversation breaker.

He didn't even blink. "Why don't you run along then, make a friend and tell them all about it."

Brin folded her arms with a huff. "You're an arsehole, Marcus, you know that?"

"Yep," he said easily, a smirk tugging at his mouth. "And proud of it."

She tipped her chin up a little higher, planting her feet in deliberate defiance of Marcus' typical default mode…steely, immovable, infuriating.

"I can only assume you've managed to unlock your sphincter and discovered what a smile looks like," she said sweetly, lifting a brow.

A low rumble of laughter came from Callum behind her. Marcus' lips twitched, not quite a smile, but close enough to irritate her.

Marcus walked away.

Okay, so maybe acting like an adult wasn't going to work out very well. Fine. She was happy to go back to ignoring him.

"What's the news?" Callum asked casually, slinging his pack over his shoulder.

"The weather," she said. "Apparently there's likely to be blizzard conditions later today where we're headed."

Callum nodded. "Yeah, I heard that too. Don't worry though, it shouldn't affect us much." He looked her over approvingly. "Looks like the women have kitted you out pretty well."

Brin looked down at herself. Layer upon layer of borrowed warmth, thermal gear, snow pants, insulated jacket, scarf, gloves, hat. She felt less like an adventurer and more like a stuffed sausage.

"Yeah, well… I'm pretty sure if I fall over, I'll just roll until someone stops me."

Callum laughed. "It's better than freezing."

Brin watched Marcus return to the group of soldiers. Bulging muscle wrapped around every inch of them, each man a wall of power, standing shoulder to shoulder like carved granite.

Brin stood by the manor's front steps, fidgeting under the weight of so many eyes.

It seemed everyone was there to see them off. Not just his family, but hers too, and every member of the family at the manor. Each person wanting to hug her for luck and wish her well. She appreciated the sentiment, but it only made her feel like none of them expected her to come back alive. At least, she really hoped that wasn't what they were thinking. It would really put a crinkle in her day if she was to die out there in the wilderness.

Some were checking gear, others lifted crates, but all of them, she was certain, were sizing her up. A healer among soldiers. A wyvern woman among wolves. She wasn't sure if they thought of her as a hinderance or a novelty.

Brin bent to grab her pack from where Grace had dropped it beside her. Determined not to look like a frail and useless female, she pooled her strength into lifting it, her arms shaking with the effort. "Bloody hell," she muttered, trying to heave it onto her shoulder, the bag barely reaching halfway, dropping it back to the ground.

Despite his outward appearance, Marcus watched Brin intently from the corner of his eye. For a moment, he actually felt sorry for her.

"Here, let me," Marcus said, stepping forward, his voice low, almost kind, taking her off guard.

"What?" Her eyes narrowed like he'd asked her to donate a kidney. "Umm, okay. I guess you'll do. No one better seems to be available."

Marcus paused. "Was that a compliment, or an insult?"

"Honestly, I'm not sure," Brin muttered, then added, "Thanks."

Marcus' answering closed lip smile confused her. "You're welcome."

He hoisted the pack over one shoulder as though it weighed nothing and carried it toward the forest trail leading into Savernake, where Doran waited to open the portal.

Brin followed, muttering curses under her breath. How was it that someone so infuriating, someone who brought out the worst in her temper, could also liquefy her bones with a single look? His presence always stirred something inside her, mostly fury, but also something she didn't dare name.

As Brin reached the border between Havenswood Manor and Savernake Forest, she stopped for a moment and turned to take in the crowd of people gathered, watching each of them disappear in turn as they approached the mist shrouded forest.

At the forest edge, the morning mist shimmered with an eery light as dappled sunlight filtered through the trees. Doran stood beside Brin's brothers, each one standing intensely stoic waiting to offer her their own version of encouragement.

Brin's stomach twisted.

Before she could step closer, Paige and Nadia approached, both looking far too pleased with themselves.

"Wait! We almost forgot to give this to you," Paige said, pressing something into Brin's palm, "We made this gift for you."

Brin looked down to find a sleek smartwatch, its dark face glinting faintly in the filtered light. "What's this? Is this so I can track my steps or monitor my heart rate when I have a panic attack?" she jibed.

"Umm, yes and no," Nadia said, sharing a conspiratorial smile with her sister. "It's also got a GPS tracker, so if anything happens, hopefully we can find you."

"And," Paige added, lowering her voice, "We placed a forgettable charm on it. If you need a bit of privacy," she mouthed the words *toilet*, "Just change the setting in 'Activities' to 'Yoga', and it will activate the charm. Then just deactivate the activity and it will become just a normal watch again."

Brin blinked. "Wait, *really*? That's…actually brilliant. Thanks."

"Just use it when you have to, okay?" Paige said, waggling a finger. "You can't use the charm all the time. Only use it if you need privacy or if you're in danger. Remember though, if you are in trouble and the charm is switched on, no one will know."

Brin chuckled softly despite the tension knotting in her chest. "Right. Got it."

"You're welcome," Nadia said cheerfully. "And for heaven's sake, try not to lose it."

Brin strapped it on and smiled. “Thanks. I owe you one for this. I think I’m ready.”

“That’s the spirit,” Paige said, pulling her into a quick hug. “Now go show them you’re not just a pretty face.”

Rejoining the others at the clearing, Brin’s heart thudded as the sound of Sanders’ sharp whistle pierced the quiet surroundings.

“Hey sis, you’ve got this, yeah?” Seth said, giving her a hug.

“Of course.” She answered with far more certainty than she felt.

“You know grandfather wouldn’t send you on this mission if he thought it would put you in danger.” Raif told her, seconded by each of her brothers.

“Yeah, I know.”

Saying goodbye to them was far harder than she’d expected. Maybe they weren’t going to encounter any danger, but that didn’t negate the gnawing feeling in her gut that somehow by the end of this trip, she wasn’t going to be the same person she was right now.

“It’ll be fine. I’ll see you all again in a few days. Don’t worry.”

Wade and Ky both hugged her tightly before stepping back, ushering her toward the portal that Doran had just opened. The enormous vortex of pale blue and silver, its surface rippling like water suspended in mid-air. The cold emanating from it already hinted at the icy world beyond.

Sanders gave a sharp whistle again, gaining everyone’s attention. “Let’s move out.”

Before them, Doran opened a portal, the swirling vortex wide enough for two men walking side by side to fit through, and high enough that a nephilim like Doran, could step through with height to spare.

This was it, Brin thought nervously.

“Alright, let’s move out.” Sanders called again.

The air shimmered as Doran stabilised the opening of the portal, the swirling curtain stretching high enough to envelop the men and the equipment they carried.

Brin swallowed hard, the taste of nerves sharp on her tongue. She could feel the hum of power vibrating through the air, brushing against her skin like static.

This was it.

She glanced once more at the gathered group, every face full of encouragement and worry.

"Good luck!" Nadia shouted.

Brin lifted her gloved hand in reply, forcing a smile. "Yeah. I'm going to need it." She mumbled to herself under her breath when she turned away again.

She drew in a long breath, straightened her shoulders, and stepped toward the portal.

It was time to put her big girl pants on and deal with whatever waited on the other side of that portal, face it head-on, good or bad.

What choice did she have.

And with that, Brin stepped through the portal, light engulfing her, a cold chill rippled up her spine as the world around her dissolved into a swirling vortex of white and blue.

8

The transition through the portal was instantaneous, but the change in temperature hit Brin like a brick wall of ice. One moment she was in the cool damp air of Savernake Forest, the next, she was standing in a dense, snow-laden forest on the outskirts of Fort MacKenzie in northern Quebec. The cold here wasn't just sharp, it *bit* into her flesh and straight through to her bones. She gasped, her breath forming a cloud of white vapor that froze almost as quickly as it appeared.

"Bloody hell," she muttered, gripping her cheeks, fearing they might be frozen solid in under a minute, along with her ears and the tip of her nose. With more effort than anticipated, hindered by the thickness of her jacket, she reached behind her head to pull the fur-edged hood as far down over her face as possible.

The world around her was a blur of snow-dusted pines and dappled light filtering through from the overcast sky. Every inhale felt like she was sucking in shards of glass.

Her jacket, covering two jumpers and a long-sleeved top, kept her upper body reasonably warm, but her legs were another story. The thin thermal-lined ski pants she'd chosen were already failing her. She silently cursed herself for not wearing the extra thermals the girls had insisted on packing.

Next time, listen to them, idiot, she chastised herself silently.

Snow crunched beneath heavy boots as Marcus walked toward her. His breath came out in a cloud, his dark hair dusted with flakes, jaw set in that familiar perpetually irritated line.

Without a word, he dropped her pack at her feet with a heavy thud, in the one and only puddle of water.

Brin glared up at him as she bent to grab the handle, barely lifting it more than a few inches before dropping it back down with a huff.

"I'd pick that up quickly if I was you, or you'll find yourself wearing nothing but wet clothes for the next few days."

Yeah, that would suck. "You'd like that, wouldn't you? Me, freezing to death out here. Would that make you feel like a *big* man?" she retorted.

Marcus' brows lifted. "Get over yourself, princess," a hint of something wicked glinting in his eyes.

"Excuse me?!"

"Fortunately for me," he went on, unbothered, "I'm *big*, no matter what the situation. Candy loves what I have to offer...Every long, thick inch." He told her, gripping his crotch suggestively. "Plus, she has the biggest norks and a hot, tight pussy. Everything a man wants in a woman." Marcus grinned, demonstrating his girlfriend's breast size with cupped hands against his chest.

Brin froze, half in outrage, half in disbelief. "Arrgh, do you have to be so crass all the time?" she groaned.

"What can I say? You bring out the best in me," he replied, absently brushing snow from his sleeve.

"*Best?* You mean worst," she shot back, pulling a face of complete and utter disgust before spinning on her heel and stomping away, boots crunching through the thin layer of snow.

Although the moment she was out of his sight, she couldn't help glancing down at her own chest, purely for *research purposes*, of course, to assess how hers compared to Marcus' *girlfriend.*

"Don't let him get under your skin," Callum said, appearing at her side with an amused smirk.

Brin jumped in surprise, embarrassed that she'd been caught in the act of cupping her own breasts.

"That's easier said than done, I'm afraid," Brin huffed out bitterly, tugging her gloves on tighter.

"Maybe this trip would be a good time for you two to sort things out? It doesn't achieve anything being at each other's throats all the time."

"Sort out what? I have no clue why he hates me so much. You're his friend, Callum, do you know?"

Callum shifted uncomfortably on the spot, clearly regretting saying anything. "That's something you need to discuss with him."

Brin barked out a humourless laugh. "Yeah, right. That's easier said than done, too."

Callum chuckled, clapping her lightly on the shoulder. "You never know. Sometimes being stuck in close quarters with someone makes you see them differently."

Brin rolled her eyes. "Or makes you want to kill them all the more."

Snow swirled around their boots as the rest of the team gathered, the wind howling low through the trees. Sanders called for formation, his voice cutting clean through the cold air.

As Brin slung her pack onto her back, with Callum's help, she caught Marcus watching her again, not with mockery this time, but something unreadable. The look vanished as quickly as it came, leaving her wondering if she'd imagined it.

If the biting wind didn't kill her, Marcus' attitude just might, or she'd be crushed under the weight of her pack, she thought sulkily.

Most of the men were already moving toward the edge of the forest, scanning the tree line. Sanders marched toward her, his face a mask of efficiency and combat readiness.

"You ready, Brin?"

"As I'll ever be." She was disappointed to hear a slight tremor in her own voice. Being the only woman on the team, she was loathe to show any weakness, despite how unprepared she felt. She especially didn't want Marcus to see her falter.

"When you're ready, call Alaric and I'll return to open the portal to get you back home. Yeah?" Doran told Sanders, leaning down to hug Brin.

"See you back here in a couple of days," he told her, his crystal blue eyes looking at her with a mixture of concern and pity. The pity part, she assumed related to Marcus, sparing a brief look in his direction.

"Tell Zoe to put the kettle on for a coffee," she replied, forcing a smile. Not that he could see it, after zipping up her jacket to the top, it covered the bottom half of her face.

Doran stepped back through the portal only seconds before its energy began dissipating, folding back on itself and vanished.

The moment the portal closed behind him, the fleeting warmth of England disappeared, leaving her lungs aching from the shock of the cold.

There really was no backing out now.

"Okay Brin, let's go." Sanders told her, the same look on his face as Doran's.

Brin huffed, pulling down the zipper of her jacket so she could speak to him more clearly.

"I'm ready. I just wish everyone would stop looking at me with pity. I'm here and I'm doing this, and I'm going to do it on my own, without anyone's help." She told him resolutely. Although, she suspected she was going to regret her words. She'd had the pack on her back for only ten minutes, and already it felt like the circulation to her arms was being cut off and her spine was going to break in two.

"One question. How many hours will we be trekking before we stop to make camp?"

"About four."

"I thought you'd say something like that," she groaned, her shoulders slumping a little further from the weight of her pack.

"Don't worry. We'll do this in stages. It's only a fifteen minute walk to the airfield, then it'll be a three and a half hour helicopter trip to the Auyuittuq National Park. From there we'll take plenty of breaks throughout the afternoon and stop to make camp somewhere around 16:00 hours."

16:00 hours, what's that 4pm, she thought. Pulling the watch from her pocket the druid sisters gave her, she checked the time. It was only a few minutes past 7am. Assuming the helicopter took off by around 7:30am, calculating the flight and time to break camp, she estimated she only had to endure an hour of walking between breaks. Once again, she sighed.

"Great. This is going to be a very long day." She tried to smile, but it came off more like a pained grimace.

The trek through the snow-laden forest led them to a moderate sized clearing which she assumed passed for the airfield, although the herd of Caribou lazily grazing at patches of grass across it, suggested it wasn't used very often. The wildlife didn't seem at all interested in the Chinook helicopter perched in the centre of the clearing, its twin rotors slicing through the air with a deafening rhythmic thud that vibrated through Brin's bones as they approached. The back ramp yawned open like the mouth of a great metal beast, and Sanders motioned for them to board. Brin hesitated at the threshold, squinting against the stinging snow that whipped about the clearing, before stepping inside.

The noise hit her first, as noisy inside as it was out, maybe even more so. An all-encompassing roar that swallowed every other sound.

So, *this* was what a Chinook helicopter looked like. It was big, certainly big enough to fit everyone and the mountain of gear they were hauling.

Inside, the cargo bay was dimly lit by narrow strips of red light running along the ceiling, bathing everything in an eerie glow, but comfort clearly hadn't been on the designer's mind. Rows of webbed seats lined either side, bolted to the ribbed aluminium walls. Thick cables, harnesses, and gear hooks dangled overhead, clattering with each shift of the rotor blades. The air reeked faintly of fuel and cold metal, mixed with the musk of leather and dampness. Every vibration of the floor thrummed up through her boots and into her legs, a constant reminder of just how far from solid ground she was.

Brin dropped her pack with a grateful thud and rubbed her aching shoulders, silently thanking whatever deity was listening that she wouldn't have to carry it again for the next few hours. She eyed the narrow webbed seat warily before lowering herself onto it. No doubt it was sturdy, but if they hit turbulence, she suspected she'd be one jolt away from needing a spinal realignment.

Marcus grabbed her discarded pack, securing it with their equipment and the other packs, before taking a seat opposite her with his usual brooding ease, one knee bouncing restlessly. The rest of the team filed in, a wall of heavy coats, rifles, and stoic faces illuminated by the dull red light. Brin couldn't help feeling absurdly out of place among them, too small, too fragile…too female, surrounded by soldiers who seemed carved from the same piece of iron as the aircraft itself.

The ramp groaned, shutting behind them, sealing away the wind and daylight. Red safety lights cast everything in a murky glow, making the men's faces look sharper, harder.

In the gloom, the Chinook shuddered and lifted, a hollow pressure filling her ears as gravity loosened its grip. Brin's gloved hand gripped her seat, hoping and praying that the quivering bolts and rivets of the fuselage held fast, trying to ignore the anxious drumbeat of her own heart. This was definitely not like riding the back of a dragon. She much preferred that any day over this. If she vibrated any harder, her teeth were going to rattle free of her head.

Three and a half hours later they touched down in another clearing, a few miles from Mountt Odin, and she couldn't get out of the helicopter any faster if her pants had been on fire. In fact, she was almost looking forward to the next four hours of trekking through the wilderness. Almost.

Their new location was even colder than the last, the air felt thinner, sharper, every breath a blade of ice in her lungs. They were definitely into the Arctic Circle now. Still, stepping out of the helicopter brought one small mercy…distance. At least out here, she didn't have to feel Marcus' eyes on her quite so much.

Throughout the flight, she'd been painfully aware of him. His gaze had burned across the dim, red-lit cabin like a touch she couldn't shake. Every time she dared glance his way, she caught him watching her, steady, unreadable, infuriatingly calm. It made her pulse trip over itself, made warmth pool in places she'd rather not acknowledge. And yet, beneath that heat, a knot of unease twisted in her stomach. Was it desire? Dislike? Or just nerves from the endless vibration of the aircraft and the mission ahead? She didn't know, and that uncertainty unsettled her more than she liked.

There had been something in his eyes, something primal, dark and volatile, glittering with an emotion she couldn't name. It wasn't simple anger, nor was it attraction. Whatever it was, it made her feel exposed, as though she were pinned beneath a magnifying glass, her every reaction laid bare for him to dissect.

Out here, in the biting cold, she finally had space to breathe. But the echo of that stare lingered, a phantom heat against her skin that no Arctic wind could quite erase.

The wind from the helicopter's rotors whipped at Brin's hood and sent snow swirling around their boots as they disembarked. The cold here was brutal, no longer the crisp bite of winter, but a full-bodied, merciless chill that seemed to slice straight through to her soul. Their surroundings were stark and silent, a stretch of snow-blanketed tundra fringed by a skeletal forest, the low sun hanging like a pale golden coin above the horizon.

The Chinook's engines finally wound down, leaving behind a heavy, almost eerie quiet. The two pilots stepped out, a man and a woman, both bundled in thick arctic flight gear. The woman, a tall brunette with wind-chafed cheeks and a bright red toque pulled low over her ears, greeted them with an easy grin.

"Alright, folks, before you head out, a little parting gift from the Great White North," she said, her accent pure Québecois warmth. From a side compartment she hauled out a crate of large orange canisters, handing them out one by one. "This, is bear mace. Industrial strength. Trust me, you'll thank me later if you meet a grizzly or a polar."

Brin blinked. "Wait, *polar*? As in *polar bear*? As in big, white, and hungry?"

"Yup," the woman replied cheerfully. "Don't worry though, they don't usually come this far inland. *Usually*. The grizzlies on the other hand, well, there's a few hundred of those roaming this region."

"Okay, would it be asking too much to get two of those cans?" Brin asked.

The woman let out a hearty laugh. "With any luck you won't need any, but surc. You can havc two."

"Thanks."

The woman threw Brin a second cannister and proceeded to give a quick demonstration, unclipping the safety pin and miming a spray into the wind. "If you see a bear and it's just watching you, *don't run.* Talk calmly, back away slow. If it charges, spray the mace. And if that doesn't work, hit the ground."

"Hit the ground?" Callum asked, incredulous.

"Flat on your stomach," she said, dropping down onto the snow to show them, unfazed by the cold. "Hands behind your neck, legs apart, stay still. Basically, play dead and pray it loses interest."

Brin stared, wide-eyed. "That's your survival plan?"

The woman climbed back to her feet and dusted off her knees. "Welcome to Canada, sweetheart."

A few nervous chuckles rippled through the group, but Marcus stepped forward, extending a gloved hand. "Thanks for the demo, ma'am. I have to say, you've got nerves of steel. I admire that."

She smiled, shaking his hand firmly. "Just doing my duty. And hey, keep your food sealed tight. Bears love careless tourists."

"Noted," Marcus replied with a grin that was uncharacteristically charming, his voice smooth enough to make even Sanders glance sideways.

Brin watched the exchange, unable to ignore the ease in his tone, the polite smile, the respectful posture. He was warm, attentive, even a little flirtatious. And it grated on her nerves.

As the pilots waved farewell and trudged back toward the aircraft, Brin folded her arms. "You were great with her," she said, trying, and failing, to sound casual. "I always knew you could be charming if you wanted to. Why can't you ever be like that with me?"

Marcus didn't even hesitate. "I can fake being a nice guy when the occasion calls for it. I didn't think I needed to with you," he said flatly.

Brin huffed, her breath misting in the frigid air. "I appreciate you being *real* with me, but that doesn't mean you have to be an arsehole either."

"Arsehole," he echoed with a low chuckle, as though she'd just given him a compliment.

They trudged through the snow toward the frozen river, winding a stagnant path between sheer cliffs, Marcus stepped ahead with a sweep of his arm and an exaggerated bow. "After you, milady."

Brin arched a brow, her expression dripping with scepticism as she brushed past him. "You know what? I've decided I prefer the bad-mannered, uncivilised you. This nice version just doesn't feel right."

Behind her, Marcus' grin broadened, his voice a low murmur almost lost to the wind. "I was hoping you'd say that."

She turned just long enough to give him a glare. "You're impossible."

"You're just jealous. You want a piece of this." He swished his hands down the length of his body with mock arrogance. "And you know there's no way in Hell, I'll ever let you near it."

"Oh, please," Brin groaned, rolling her eyes skyward. "You're so superficial. Get over yourself." She waved him off and began to walk away, boots crunching in the snow. Then she stopped, glancing back over her shoulder. "No, you know what? If you want to go through life emotionally constipated and alone, then suit yourself. I won't lose a night's sleep over it."

Marcus barked a short laugh. "I might be emotionally constipated, as you put it, but I'll never be alone. I can have my pick of any female I want. In fact, I already have one."

"Congratulations," Brin said sweetly. "Maybe you can flirt with the next polar bear you meet too."

She strode ahead toward the front of the group before he could reply, though the sound of his growl and snickers from the other men followed her across the snow. And didn't that make her smile, just a little.

Stepping up beside Marcus, the other odd one in the group, Owen, the human druid, easily matched Marcus' pace.

"Have you got a thing for redheads or just that one in particular?" Owen asked Marcus.

"What?"

"The ginge, Brin. You haven't stopped staring at her. You know, they say redheads are supposedly crazy."

"Pfft, you might be right about the crazy part, but you're way off base if you think I have the hots for her."

"So, you're not currently, or planning on tapping that arse in the future?"

Marcus pulled a face of disgust. "Absolutely not."

"Great. Coz redheads might be crazy, but they're amazing shags," Owen replied, waggling his eyebrows with a lopsided semi-stifled grin.

"Oh, I didn't realise your right palm was a redhead," Marcus retorted testily.

Owen laughed, slapping him on the back. "I like you. I don't care what anyone else thinks," he said, walking away before Marcus finished processing what he'd said.

"Wait…What?" But it was too late.

For the next few hours, they trekked in single file through the narrow corridor of ice, moving with the instinctive precision of a wolf pack. Brin at the front with one of the soldiers, being the weakest in the group, she set the pace. Next in line were the strongest in the group, Marcus, Callum and Owen, followed by the other lycans, and lastly Sanders took up the rear. Being the leader wasn't about being out in front, it was about taking care of his team.

They paused every half hour to let Brin rest. She knew she was slowing them down and the guilt gnawed at her. Even so, after the second stop, she forced herself to let it go. They wouldn't even be on this mission without her, she was the only one who could retrieve the Serpent Armband. So, if she needed to stop, then they could all damn well wait. And they did, without complaint.

By the time they reached the rocky rise chosen for their camp, the weak Arctic sun was already crossing the horizon, painting an orange hue against the landscape. The temperature was plummeting fast, the air heavy with the stillness that warned of an approaching storm. Sanders yelled out orders with urgency, the set of his jaw confirming what they all already knew, the blizzard forecast earlier in the day was rapidly closing in.

Brin barely made it to a boulder before collapsing against it, her legs trembling, lungs burning. The men moved around her with efficiency, pitching tents, unpacking supplies, securing gear before the wind could snatch it away. The air had grown thick, muffled, as if the whole world was holding its breath.

Whether they cooked a hot meal on a fire or they tore open cold military rations, she couldn't say. Nor did she care. She was too exhausted to have an appetite. As soon as her tent was erected, she dragged herself inside and collapsed.

By the time darkness fell, the first howls of the storm had begun. The wind came in fits at first, gusts that tugged at guy ropes and flapped loose tent corners, but before long it had become a relentless, deafening roar. The blizzard hit with full force, shrieking across the ice like a living thing, tearing at the world outside. Snow and sleet battered the tents in violent waves, and the sound was like a freight train passing inches from her head.

Brin lay cocooned in her sleeping bag, too exhausted to move but too restless to sleep, the cold seeping in despite the layers. Every time the wind screamed, her tent shuddered violently, the thin canvas bowing inward as if trying to breathe.

She wasn't sure if the others were awake, although she suspected none of them were sleeping much. Somewhere outside, she thought she heard Marcus' voice shouting something over the wind, followed by the muffled thud of heavy boots and the snap of a rope being tightened. Then, nothing but the endless, roaring blizzard.

By the time the storm eased in the early hours of the morning, she had long since succumbed to her exhaustion. Crawling deeper into her sleeping bag, she let the rhythmic howl of the wind pull her into a fitful sleep.

9

Brin woke feeling as if her limbs had been welded into place, a combination of the cold and being cocooned inside her sleeping bag without any wriggle room. Every joint mutinied as she stretched, the recent storm still alive in her memory. She may have achieved a modicum of rest, but no restful slumber. When she did manage to fall asleep, it was plagued by disturbing dreams of caves and serpents…and irritating lycan males, i.e. Marcus. Needless to say, she woke feeling sore, moody and hungry. Heaven help anyone who crossed her today.

She shoved aside the stiffened tent flap and stepped out into a world freshly reshaped from the powdery white snow. She expected to find half buried tents, the camp snow locked from the overnight blizzard and sluggish men going about their business, just as it would be back in her home, in Fey. Instead, there was motion everywhere she looked. The men had already dug the tents free, reinforced guy lines, created new paths, repaired what the night had torn loose and prepared breakfast. No fuss. No orders shouted twice. Just discipline moving like a well-oiled machine.

Brin stood quietly, watching with a newfound respect for these men.

Callum caught her eye and tipped his chin. "Morning, Brin. How'd you sleep?"

"Let's just say I now know what a popsicle feels like," she said, scrunching her nose.

Callum laughed softly, nodding in agreement.

"Looks like you've all been busy." There was a stark comparison between their camp, which was mostly snow free and the surrounding landscape, now blanketed in an extra half a metre of snow for as far as the eye could see.

"We've been at it for a while." He paused, then added lightly, "I'd avoid Marcus as much as you can today, if I was you. He didn't sleep at all."

She blinked. "Not even a little? Why?"

Callum's mouth curled, sparing a look in Marcus' direction. "Parked himself outside your tent. All night."

Hmm, that explains why she was so sure she'd heard him throughout the night, it hadn't been her imagination. It also probably explained why he featured so prominently in her dreams too, because it definitely had nothing to do with attraction. She thought on that a little more, lifting a brow. "Why would he do that?"

Callum shrugged, a maddeningly neutral response. "That's something you'll have to ask him, I'm afraid."

Like that was going to happen. "Didn't you just say to stay away from him today?"

"I did. But…"

"Don't fill in the *but,* I'd prefer not to know…I think." Brin shut down the idea of any kind of discussion with Marcus. If he wanted to sit outside her tent all night, that was his choice. It was probably only one of those dutiful soldier things, following orders and protect the helpless female in the group. Beyond that, she intended to file the matter under, *irrelevant,* and move on. Even so, she couldn't help searching the campsite for him, spying him by a small campfire, pushing something around in a pan.

Breakfast.

Brin's stomach growled loudly just from the thought of food. She hadn't eaten in nearly a full twenty-four hours, she realised. And after all the noncustomary walking she'd done, and no doubt burned quite a few calories just trying to stay warm, she was famished. Dammit, if she wanted any of that food, she was going to have to go and talk to him.

Some days it really sucked to get out of bed, she thought. Nevertheless, in this moment in time, curing her hunger was more compelling than having to endure a conversation with Marcus, so she put one foot in front of the other toward the fire.

"Marcus." She greeted in a neutral tone.

"Brin." He grated back, more irritably.

Okay, so I'll just grab some breakfast and move at least ten paces away from him, she told herself.

"Is that food just for you, or for anyone?" she asked hesitantly.

"Here, I saved you some." Slapping some bacon and cheese onto a muffin, he handed it to her. Actually, it was a little more like shoving it at her, but she was hungry, so she chose not to complain.

"Umm, thanks."

She wanted to walk away, she really did, but her feet were noncompliant. She took one step and stopped, then another disjointed step, her eyes locked onto him in an unerring gaze of curiosity. She just couldn't figure him out. On one hand, he spoke to her as though he truly hated her, but on the other, he guarded her tent all night, in a blizzard of all things, and then saved her some breakfast. It was enough to make her head spin.

Don't go there, she told herself, once again shutting down her wayward thoughts.

Just turn around and walk away.

So, she did. A full twelve paces away to sit on a snow free, but freezing cold boulder. With the number of cold surfaces she was likely to sit on over the next day or so, she'd be lucky if she left there without a case of haemorrhoids.

That jolted a thought about something else unpleasant. She quickly checked the inner jacket pocket for one of the orange cans of bear mace which the pilot had given her. Still there. Good.

Please don't let this be the day when I need to repel a bear.

Satisfied everything was in order, she focused her attention on the muffin, which she ate in record time. It tasted good, really good. So much so, she was tempted to ask Marcus for a second. Of course, that would mean talking to him again and so opted against it.

Marcus watched Brin walk away, his head cast downward, watching her from the periphery of his vision as he continued to push food around in the pan.

"Ouch! Fuck!" he cursed, dropping the tongs in favour of rubbing the burn at the base of his thumb. *Dammit!* He really needed to pay more attention to what he was doing.

Marcus' mood barometer flipped another notch higher into the 'foul mood' parameters. It had oscillated between irritable to stormy all night, just like the weather. Right now, he was in a mood that could curdle milk.

It was Brin's fault.

She was the bane of his life.

He had so many reasons for disliking her. For one, she was stubborn. She had a talent for arguing in circles, always needing to get the last word in. She had a hoity-toity, prissy, princess-like attitude that had a way of getting under his skin, like ground glass. And that was just the tip of the iceberg of his issues with her.

What baffled him was his behaviour toward her. Despite the fact that he detested the woman, he couldn't help feeling overprotective of her. Nor could he shake the need to be close to her even though her nearness and scent caused the rod in his pants to harden to tensile strength.

Likewise, his wolf paced irritably just beneath his skin whenever she was around, forcing him to behave in ways that were illogical.

It had been his wolf who'd forced him to sit outside her tent all night, despite his aversion to being there. Even now, his wolf still clawed at him to be free, leaving his skin feeling itchy and hot. His wolf's heightened presence must be because of the importance of their mission, maybe sensing a possible hidden danger. At least, that's how he chose to interpret it. There wasn't any other explanation, his wolf wouldn't be this close to the surface for no good reason.

Marcus caught himself glancing at her again, that long red hair of hers spilling over the rim of her jacket, the steamy vapor of her breath wafting on the cool air as she closed her eyes and lips around the muffin, as though indulging in a moment of ecstasy.

Taking the pan off the fire, he pushed himself up from the camp stool he'd been sitting on, to pace back and forth in an attempt to work off some of the nervous energy juicing through his veins.

Warmth stirred in his groin with a fresh flood of blood, twitching and throbbing his manhood. Cursing under his breath, he picked up a handful of snow and dumped it on the fire, quashing it immediately. If only his own fire could be dowsed so easily, he thought, discretely rearranging the package within his pants to relieve the building pressure. The last thing he needed was to have the circulation cut off to his favourite pleasure stick.

Enough. Get your head back in the game!

Within the hour they broke camp. Sanders' brief was short and to the point. "Five miles northeast is the base of Mount Odin. The cave entrance should be near the base of the slope. Visibility's bad, so Marcus and Brin, you're on point. Callum, Owen, you're behind them. The rest fall in, in front of me. Let's move out."

Across the clearing, Brin's eyes met Marcus', disappointment and irritation colliding in the frozen air, adding another layer of chill to the morning. Regardless, neither objected.

"You sure you want them together?" Callum asked Sanders quietly when the group broke to collect packs and supplies.

"Nope. But, if I put him at the back, he's only likely to mow down every man in front of him to get close to her anyway."

The two men looked toward Marcus, their gazes a matching blend of pity and worry. In his current state Marcus was unpredictable and possibly even a liability to the group. But, since there was no way to send him home until the mission was over, it was probably best to keep the pair close together.

"I've never seen him so off his game. Callum, you know Marcus pretty well, does he share his personal shit with you?" Sanders asked him.

"Sometimes. Why?"

"Clearly he's having woman issues, and I'm guessing that having a girlfriend whilst being so close to his true *mate,* is messing with his head."

Callum nodded his agreement.

"I get it if he wants to postpone the inevitable, but he seems totally clueless about Brin's importance to him and treats her like shit. What's his story?"

"Let's just say he's in denial out of fear of a prophecy." Callum told him.

"What prophecy?"

"The one about the lycan with a serpent mark." Callum had never shared Marcus' secret ever, even though he'd known about it for several years. Now however, it seemed Marcus himself couldn't hide his predicament, so what was the harm in adding a little more context to his situation with his brother-in-law.

Sanders was quiet for a moment as he replayed the verse in his head that he'd learned as a child, his brow rising sharply as the pieces fell into place. "Fuck me. And here we are on a quest to find a serpent armband with Brin. This must be his worst nightmare coming true."

"You could say that."

"Does he have a serpent mark though?"

"No. But we all know that the universe has a way of changing the rules of the game and moving the playing field to suit the occasion. Marcus is certain that somehow this will be that time for him."

"Fuck, I love it," Sanders chuckled. "He's so screwed."

"Yeah. Better him than me," Callum smirked.

They trudged through fog and snow, the world reduced to laboured breathing, exhaling puffs of steam and the squeak of soft powder beneath their boots. Each step sinking them shin deep. Brin's lashes gathered frost, the cold slowly leaching through the seams of her clothes. Twice she slipped, and twice Marcus steadied her with a quick, aggravatingly gentle grasp.

"Careful," he said quietly, his mood improving marginally as his wolf slipped further into the background contentedly.

"Thanks. If I faceplant, just leave me. The snow looks comfy."

"Not a chance. You're my problem until we get the artefact."

"Your concern is so touching," she deadpanned.

He gave her a sidelong glare. "You talk too much."

"I only talk because you don't. Someone has to fill the awkward silence."

His jaw worked, but nothing came out. A minute later, she lobbed a small, compact snowball into his shoulder without looking. It thunked and exploded. Satisfying.

He stared at her, incredulous. She lifted an eyebrow.

He let loose a shocked gasp.

"You're enjoying this, aren't you? You've got one of those weird fetishes where you can only get turned on by the sound of a woman yelling at you while pelting you with…snowballs."

Marcus' jaw hung a fraction too slack for a timely comeback. "Shit. Until this moment I would have said you were dead wrong. But now…?"

Brin snorted despite herself and pushed on.

The banter between them continued, either unaware or they didn't care, that the other men were listening and snickering only a few paces behind them.

As the sun rose higher, the fog thinned by degrees until the cliff rose out of it, a dark rib of stone veined with frost. Sanders checked his data. "This is it. The entrance should be just up there," he said, and all heads tipped upward.

Brin craned. The opening yawned fifteen feet above the drift. "Of course it is."

Owen stepped forward, ready to scale the cliff and pull Brin up, but Sanders put an arm out to block him.

"Trust me, if you want to keep your hands attached to your body, you need to let Marcus help her up," he muttered quietly to him.

Wisely, Owen stepped back again. He wasn't a lycan and wasn't familiar with all the unspoken rules, but he was smart enough to know when to give the male some space…and keep his body parts attached.

"Alright, princess," Marcus said, stepping close. "Up you go."

"What's your plan, toss me?" There was no way she could climb up there. It may only be fifteen feet, but it was still more than double her height and the cliff wall was almost vertical, save for a few craggy rocks to grip onto.

He let an annoyed breath slip through his lips, then stepped up behind her, gripping Brin's arse with both hands.

Thrilling? Yes. Appropriate? Not on your life.

Brin slapped his hands away, heat flaring across her cheeks. "What the hell are you doing?"

"I'm giving you a boost."

"A *boost*. Great. A cheap thrill? No thanks. You didn't need to go for the grope. For the record I didn't appreciate it one bit. Your technique is all wrong."

He paused, looking down at her for a long, unblinking moment. "You didn't give me a chance to finish." His voice took on a deep gravelly timbre that sent a shiver of heat through every cell of her body, which pissed her off all the more.

Her lips twitched into a humourless smile. "I don't care," she assured him, anger straightening her spine. His smarmy grin said he could read her like an open book, and she hated how naked that made her feel. "Cup your hands," she ordered, before the dark glint in his eyes talked him into another butt grope.

Reluctantly, he laced one hand over the other and bent. Brin planted a boot in his palms and surged upward, fingers scraping stone until she reached the rim of the ledge. "Don't you dare…"

"I'm not touching you," he said, holding her boot to steady her.

"I was going to say, don't you dare let go. Dumbass." She retorted. Levering herself up, she swung a knee and rolled onto the ledge, then turned and reached down. "Your turn."

"I appreciate the offer princess, but I've got this," he told her, that smarmy smirk still on his face.

He flowed up the wall like he owned it.

For a moment she wished they were in a warmer climate with fewer layers of clothes, imagining all the well-honed muscles rippling and tightening under the strain of the manoeuvre. She hated being this close to him, she really did, it set her off kilter and played havoc with her hormones.

Bad hormones!

Behind him, each of the men followed suit, each making the effort look just as easy.

Inside the cave's entrance, the air felt different. Not quite still, with a slightly musty odour to it, and a whistling sound could be heard deeper within its depths.

"Here. Looks like we've got the right place." Callum said, scratching away dirt from a symbol, carved near the mouth of the cave. A circle and cross, the Knights Templar mark.

Sanders' mouth tightened. "We're in the right place alright. Now, to get this armband and get home."

That was going to be easier said than done.

Heavy footsteps thudded up behind them, a soldier slid to a stop. "Guild forces are on our trail. Half a mile. Moving fast."

"Positions," Sanders snapped. Then, to Brin he said, "You'll have to go in there alone, can you do that?"

Holy hell! Brin gulped, her eyes widening in fear as her heartbeat doubled its pace.

"Right. Umm…Yep. I can." She doubted she sounded any more convinced than she felt, but this was what she was here for. Realistically, she may be the only one able to enter that cave anyway.

Suck it up. You can do this! She told herself, desperate to believe it.

"Hurry." Sanders said, handing her a torch. "Take your time and be careful, but hurry, yeah?"

Right. Go slow, but hurry. Got it. *Holy Crap!*

Seriously, what was she worried about, she was only going into a dark, damp, scary cave. They were all staying outside to battle to the death with the Guild. In this case, she was getting the better deal.

That thought had her feet moving toward the heart of the mountain, one nervous step at a time. As she turned the corner, her ears tuned into the sounds of weapons being drawn, gruff voices and heavy boots on the floor at the cave's entrance.

And one low growl, guttural, inhuman, filled with the promise of pain and dismemberment.

Brin walked quickly, the corridor dipped, widening for a short distance before the path abruptly reduced to a narrow ledge, descending at a sharp angle along the wall of a huge cavern. Brin shuffled to the edge and dared a look over its threshold.

She could see nothing inside the dark pit below, she shuddered and gripped the wall behind her for stability. Picking up a stone, she tossed it over the edge and counted…one-one-thousand, two-one-thousand, three-one-thousand…until she heard it hit the bottom. That was a long way down and she didn't have much time for messing around.

Swallowing her nerves she put one foot in front of the other and continued the descent. It wasn't as bad as she'd first expected, the ledge remained roughly two feet wide, winding a path all the way around the wall in a helical fashion. Still, as her torch only illuminated a few feet ahead, she had to take each step carefully. The farther she descended, the less she could hear of the men far above at the entrance of the cave, and she couldn't help wondering if the Guild had reached them yet. She really hoped they hadn't.

Then, after what seemed like an eternity, she found herself perched on another ledge, this one however, was only about five feet from the cavern floor.

Shining her torch onto the cavern floor, she jumped back abruptly with a start.

"You've got to be freaking kidding me!" She cursed. The Templars were nothing if not thorough with their efforts to protect the artefacts they hid.

It was like a scene out of an *Indiana Jones* movie. An ancient crypt with musty smelling air, a dusty floor…covered with snakes. Yes, snakes, hundreds of them, rippling in slow, sinuous waves.

She didn't *dislike* snakes. How could she? She was wyvern. That didn't mean the sight of a living carpet of serpents was all that appealing.

Do I dare step into that? Which one is the one I'm supposed to find? And how many of them will bite me before I do?

Brin drew a shuddering breath, braced herself on the ledge and closed her eyes tightly as she lowered herself down.

Her boots met solid rock, not scales. The pit blurred, shimmered, and evaporated away.

It was only an illusion. Thank the Elders.

Not that it improved matters, the illusion might've vanished, but her luck hadn't improved. The "floor" still looked like a dragon's dental nightmare, filled with jagged rocky teeth just waiting to bite and tear at her flesh.

Picking her way across, she struggled to gain a sure footing. Brin caught her shin on a ragged spur and felt a trickle of blood run down her leg. A couple of metres further, she slipped again, catching the side of her thigh on another rock.

"Shit."

The treacherous rocky minefield was proving more difficult than she'd anticipated, opting to remove her gloves, shoving them into her pockets to steady herself more efficiently.

Finally reaching the far side, Brin came to a halt and groaned. The grazes on her legs and her hands looked like she'd been in a fight with a cheese grater and lost. Not much she could do about it now though. Unfortunately, she couldn't heal herself. Her gift was only useful on others.

At the back of the cavern, a small stone niche had been carved into the wall, an ancient altar in the centre, its smooth surface etched with faded symbols. On top stood a shoe box sized wooden box, covered with hoarfrost lacing along its seams, adding an ethereal, enchanted chill to the setting.

"Do I open it, or not?" she asked herself, examining the box from every angle. If she broke the seal, what would happen?

She picked it up. It was heavier than it looked. It wouldn't be easy carrying it back across those ragged rocks, she barely made it intact when she could use both hands to help steady herself.

"Okay. Here goes nothing."

Flipping up the old metal latch, she eased the lid open with numb, bleeding fingers.

The torchlight illuminated a beautiful golden serpent armband, its coiled body so finely detailed it looked real.

The tail end of the armband moved.

Did she just imagine that? She wondered.

"Oh no!" she gasped.

Before she could flinch, it sprang, curling about her wrist in a flash, cold and lithe…and alive. Brin gasped as it slithered beneath her sleeve, racing up her arm like a live wire.

"Off. Get off me!" She screamed, shedding layers in a panic, her jacket, jumper and top, until she stood there bare skinned down to her bra, completely oblivious to the cold in her panic.

The serpent climbed to her upper arm, coiling snuggly, head settling to face her wrist. Then it froze, returning to its solid gold state once more.

She tugged. It didn't budge.

Gunfire cracked above, ricochets ringing through the cavern. The Guild had arrived.

Crap! Crap! Crap!

What was she going to do? Nothing, that's what. Right now, her best option was to just get out of there. Deal with the armband later. Hopefully the druid sisters would know how to get it off.

Brin hurriedly redressed, cramming her arms back into her jacket, she snatched up her torch and scrambled back toward the ledge and the path out. Halfway up, she heard it, the scuffle of boots too light to be lycan. And then a man appeared at the top of the tunnel, rifle sweeping. She was on the ledge directly opposite him, about fifty feet down.

Looking up, she watched him.

Quickly switching off her torch, Brin's breath stopped, locked in her lungs and she stood as still as a statue.

Marcus hit him from the side like a storm, slamming him into stone, his weapon skittering from his grip, tumbling down to the cavern floor with a clatter. The man's terrified cries echoed loudly through the cavern, ending with a pitiful gurgling sound, his lifeless body following his rifle down to the bottom of the cavern with a loud thud.

"Brin?"

"I'm here. I've got it."

"Where are you?"

"I'm coming." She called back, flipping on her torch once again.

Marcus followed the movement of light as she wove her way along the ascending ledge toward the top.

He grabbed Brin's hand to haul her through the opening and lifted her over another fallen Guild agent.

In her relief, Brin didn't notice the armband shift form again, slithering quickly down her arm, its head peaked out beneath her jacket's cuff, latching onto Marcus.

The serpent *bit him.*

Marcus swore, jerking back as twin pinpricks burned into his wrist. The serpent on Brin's arm flared, heat and light pulsing through gold like something alive and *listening.* For one dizzy heartbeat, a thread tugged through her chest, two rhythms syncing, the world narrowing to the hot thud of his pulse under her fingers.

Then it faded. Awareness rushing back with a snap of frosted breath.

Marcus stared at the faint marks beading on his wrist. "What the hell was *that*?"

"I…I don't know. The armband, I think it's alive." Brin's voice sounded far away in her own ears, her eyes wide with surprise.

But it wasn't random, she thought to herself silently as the armband returned to snake about her upper arm and become solid once more.

Sanders' barked orders over the last sounds of gunfire and battle.

"Brin. You okay? Did you get it?" he asked.

Brin's mind was reeling. She couldn't get her mouth to move to answer him, she just nodded. There was far too much happening for her brain to process it all at once. The armband, Marcus, dead and dying Guild men everywhere and her inner worry for the lycan men she couldn't see within view inside the cave.

One by one, the men each reappeared as the last Guild fighters either died or retreated. Blood coated the floor of the cave around the bodies and splashed like a modernistic painting against the snowscape outside. Fortunately, none of their group were severely injured.

Brin's hands hovered over a soldier's cut shoulder. "Let me heal it."

"I'm good," he replied, already reloading his rifle, his fierce eyes scanning their surroundings.

"Let's get moving before they come back with reinforcements." Sanders ordered.

Brin couldn't agree more. Despite the fatigue she'd felt, adrenaline pumped through her veins motivating her to move at a clipped pace. In fact, for once she had no trouble keeping up with the men at all.

10

The fog thickened as they neared their camp, wind combing the drifts into low curls. The clouds above blending seamlessly with the landscape, except in sparse patches where they thinned enough to allow the sun to peak through, displaying that sideways look which occurred in such high latitudes, its passage limited to a shallow curve over the land beneath.

They topped the last rise, and stopped.

Smoke feathered up from the basin where their camp had been. Figures moved below among the torn tents and destroyed supplies. Some were regular men, others were too tall, too thin and an unnaturally grey colour.

"Demons," Marcus said, his voice hard and cold.

Sanders lifted a fist. The line knelt as one. "Go wide," he murmured. "Brin, stay between us." He considered leaving her behind but there wasn't enough cover, and he'd be leaving her unprotected. That was never going to happen. Despite the fact they were walking into an ambush, she'd still be safer with them.

Brin swallowed and nodded. Her fingers brushed her jacket pocket, reassured by the curve of the can of bear mace. It might be useless against demons, but if anyone got up close and personal, she had no problem in using it anyway. If nothing else, it might give her the element of surprise and buy her enough time to run like hell.

Drawing in a deep breath, the air tasted of smoke.

"You okay?" Owen whispered at her shoulder.

"Absolutely." Brin answered, keeping her eyes on the camp below. "I have a plan B. Panic, die dramatically, and then haunt whoever survives."

He swallowed a laugh. "I'm glad to see your sense of humour isn't affected by stress. But don't worry, we've got your back. You won't be needing your Plan B, today," he replied.

They began to move again.

Up ahead, the enemy split into two kinds of nightmare. The Guild men, bundled in winter whites, rifles at the ready, picking their way through the camp. And among them, four demons stalked the parameters, six feet of hairless, slate-grey menace with long, razor sharp nails and mouths filled with needle-like teeth. Their eyes were pits of polished onyx. These weren't creatures they'd seen before, so there was no telling what they were capable of. What they knew for certain…They were trouble with a capital T.

The group moved stealthily, quickly but silently through the frozen landscape, taking advantage of the banks of snow drifts and scattering of larger boulders. Careful not to leave footprints where they could be easily seen from the camp.

"Targets marked," Sanders said. "On my mark…three, two, one."

The clearing detonated into motion.

Brin dropped low as the first shots cracked. The demons moved too fast, blurring sideways in wrong, lurching strides. Bullets slowed them, drawing black ichor from shoulders and thighs, but didn't drop them. One snarled, the sound was like a wasp-nest of static, then bounded for the nearest enemy, Callum.

"Shift!" Sanders roared, and three lycans did just that, mid-stride. Their bodies breaking and reforming into muscle, fangs, and fur. They hit the grey shapes like sledgehammers. Claws tore and teeth found purchase in their smooth grey flesh. One demon shrieked, a high pitched sound. It staggered, then backhanded a wolf hard enough to send him cartwheeling through a collapsed tent.

Marcus remained human, staying close to Brin, firing short, sharp bursts. His wolf hovered close beneath his skin like hot wire, begging for release.

A Guild rifleman caught the splash of auburn hair under Brin's hood, his gaze and rifle locking onto her as she ran with the soldiers. He pivoted smoothly, breath fogging, steadying his aim.

Marcus caught the glint of the muzzle a moment before it was fired.

"Down!" he snapped, pushing Brin behind him, he moved on instinct before the word was fully formed.

The shot punched him in the chest. For a heartbeat, he remained on his feet, surprise widening his eyes. Then his knees buckled and he toppled sideways into the snow.

"Marcus!" Brin's scream tore her throat raw.

She dropped to the ground beside him, hands already glowing with that warm, low hum of healing light. Her world tunnelled into stark focus, the colour draining from his face as rapidly as his blood was draining from his wound.

Something nearby hissed.

She looked up in time to see a demon running at her, black eyes fixed on the easy target kneeling in the snow. Thinking fast despite her fear, Brin yanked the orange can from her pocket, thumbed off the safety, and blasted a furious stream into its face.

The thing reared back with a sound like tearing metal, claws windmilling at the capsicum stream in its eyes. It stumbled and backed up a few paces, shook his head, then came at her again, even angrier.

Dammit. Looks like I'm going with Plan B. Brin threw her forearm up to shield her face, closing her eyes she waited for the inevitable.

The demon took full advantage of her vulnerability, seizing her wrist. The feel of those long cold fingers on her skin sent a shiver of revulsion through to her core. The evil rolling off it made her stomach churn violently.

This was it, she thought desperately. The end!

None too soon, and to her surprise, the serpent armband woke once again.

It uncoiled with a flash of heat and motion, sliding down her arm, beneath her cuff, and struck, its fangs burying themselves into the demon's hand. Black blood welled and smoked where the gold bit deeply. The grey creature recoiled, but it was too late. Dark veins laddered up its arm, across its chest. Brin's hands were already primed to heal Marcus, only now she felt the power twist. The same channel that carried her healing, turned inside-out, reversing on this creature, not healing it, but unmaking it. The demon convulsed, it's skin blistered, peeling away to sinew and skeleton, and then collapsed into ash that was swept away on the wind.

Brin stared, breathing hard, her heart hammering. Her wrist throbbed with a stinging pain where the creature had gripped tightly. Her other hand hadn't left Marcus' chest.

"Come on," she whispered. "Stay with me."

Across the clearing, Owen tackled the Guild rifleman who'd taken the shot. They went down in a tangle, each scrambling back to their feet in the slippery snow. Taking aim at Owen, the man's pistol misfired. Tossing it aside he reached for a dart gun. Owen grunted as a dart sank through his jacket above the ribs. He didn't even slow. His Bowie knife flashed once, and the man's head separated from his shoulders before he had a chance to process the danger, landing with a thud in a snow drift.

"Bloody hell," Owen breathed, yanking the dart free and flicking it aside. "That's rude."

"Finish them!" Sanders shouted. The wolves obliged, swiftly dispatching the remaining Guild men, and driving two wounded demons from the campsite. The things scrambled out of reach with that insect jerkiness, then fled.

The gunfire thinned and finally stopped.

Brin pressed both palms to Marcus' chest, the way she had years ago on a different battlefield. Heat surged out of her and into him, a clean burn that found the torn lung and sealed it. Gritting his teeth, the bullet began reversing out of the wound, rolling to the ground beneath. She felt the blood in his chest recede, the jagged edges knit and the furious haemorrhage slowing to a stop. Finally, his pain subsided.

Marcus sighed in relief. Even so, he couldn't thank her. Having Brin's healing touch wasn't something he wanted. Not after the last time. Sitting up, he grabbed her hands to look at them, relieved when he saw his blood still covering them, it hadn't been absorbed into her skin like the last time. Once had been enough to haunt him forever.

"Look, I don't need your charity," he bit out irritably.

"Arsehole," Brin snapped. "You think I enjoy putting my hands on you? I saved your hairy butt, you ungrateful jerk." She informed him, her eyebrows coming together in a dark scowl. "Keep up this attitude and the next time you're lying dying at my feet, you just might find yourself neutered too."

She yanked her hands back and glanced, almost against her will, at his wrist. No trace of the armband serpent's bite from earlier in the cavern either. His skin was smooth, unmarked. Good. Whatever the armband had done to him back there, seemed to have healed too. She flexed her fingers, relieved, even if she was still a little shaken.

"Report!" Sanders barked.

"All the Guild men have been neutralised," Callum called, wiping his blade on a dead man's coat. "One demon has been sent back to the Underworld, thanks to Brin," Owen announced, "Two were wounded but still mobile, they headed north beyond the rocks."

Sanders' mouth flattened. "Which means they'll report back to their puppet master. And we still don't know how to kill them outright."

His gaze cut to Brin. "How did you kill it?"

"I'm not sure. He grabbed my hand, and the armband bit him. Then his veins started to bulge with lots of black lines, then he just…disintegrated. To be honest, I don't know if it was the fact that he was touching me that caused it, or the armband's bite."

"What do you mean, *the armband bit him*?"

"Just that." She shrugged off her jacket and slipped her arm from her jumper sleeve so they could see the armband for themselves. The solid gold, life-like serpent, coiled about Brin's upper arm. "When I first opened the box it was in, it came alive and climbed up my arm before becoming solid again. Then, when I reached the entrance of the cave…" She looked toward Marcus, whose brow furrowed and he shook his head, pleading for her not to tell what had happened with him.

"Umm…then when the demon grabbed me, it came to life again, slithered down my arm and bit him." She told them uncomfortably, not at all sure why it was such a secret that it had also bitten Marcus. Considering what happened to the demon, the bite might have some kind of delayed effect on Marcus they needed to be looking for. But, she did as he wished and remained silent on the matter…For now.

Several of the men took a wary step away, all eyes glued to the harmless looking golden armband.

"I guess we now know why only a female wyvern can touch it," Callum commented dryly.

"If you would like to see which was the effective method of killing the demon, we may have a…creative way of testing it." Sanders told her.

Brin swallowed. "How, exactly?"

"I mean your touch. We still have one of those demons secured on the far side of the camp. It's injured and couldn't escape. I cut off both its legs at the knees." He told them matter-of-factly. "If your armband can fry one when it's stupid enough to grab you, maybe your hands can eliminate this one without the jewellery. We can't leave it to regenerate."

Every instinct screamed no. Touching those things felt like volunteering to stick her hand into a nest of live wires. But the men were watching, and time was in short supply.

"Fine," she said, her voice thin. "But the armband doesn't come off, and I can't will it to life. It just seems to happen on its own. If you want me to put my hands on the demon, okay, but I can't guarantee what'll happen."

They approached it as a group, every rifle trained on its evil body, Brin's heart pounding hard enough to break a rib.

Why am I doing this again, for scientific study or to satisfy the men's morbid curiosity? She wondered to herself. Not that it mattered, she was doing this one way or another. She just wasn't comfortable acknowledging that she was as curious about the outcome as they were.

Tentatively she reached out a hand toward the snarling, hissing creature that thrashed within its restraints.

"Oh, wait! Let me get a selfie with him so we have a record of what he looks like before he goes, *poof*!" Owen said, whipping out his phone to take a photo with the demon in the background.

"Brin, are you ready?" Sanders asked in a calm, even tone.

No. I'm not ready. I'll never be ready. Brin nodded, swallowing hard against the lump in her throat.

Brin touched the demon's forearm. This time though, the armband didn't flare to life. Regardless, the reaction was immediate and awful. Her healing power met whatever animated the thing and inverted, locking onto the thread that anchored it here. The demon stiffened, its mouth yawning wide in a silent cry. It convulsed and began oozing black blood from every orifice in its body…then died. However, it didn't disintegrate into ash as the other one had.

How interesting. Clearly her touch would kill it regardless, but it seemed that the venom from the serpent armband added an extra *oomph*, to the creature's demise.

Silence followed, stunned, grateful, their amazed gazes filled with more than a little admiration for Brin.

"Right," Sanders said at last, scratching his head. "I guess we have our answer. Pack up the gear lads, it's time to go home."

Pulling the satellite phone from his pack, he called the Chinook pilot. They spoke quietly for a couple of minutes before ending the call. Sanders returned to the group, his face lined with concern.

"We have a problem. The Chinook's hundreds of miles out," he said, covering the mouthpiece. It's busy on a rescue mission from that storm last night. Eight hours minimum before it can reach us."

"We don't have eight hours. If those demons share a hive mind like others we've come across, those two that got away will no doubt be spreading the word about where to find us. We've seen it before. Plus, they know Brin's with us, and they know we've got the armband." Callum said, verbalising what everyone else was thinking.

"No, you're right." Sanders agreed. "Here's the catch. They're sending in another chopper that's only about four hours out, but it can only take three passengers, tops. They'll send the Chinook for the rest of us when it's available."

"You're on the first chopper, Brin. Marcus, you're going with her."

"Go fuck yourself." Marcus told him flatly.

Sanders stepped closer toward Marcus with an expectant look. He made a 'come-on' gesture with his fingers. "Finish the sentence."

Marcus rolled his eyes. "Go fuck yourself…Sir."

Sanders was silent for the longest second, his eyes glowing with anger.

"Who the fucking cock-sucking twinkle-toes do you think you are? You mangy fucknut! You'd better unfuck yourself real fast or I will unscrew your fucking head from your shoulders and shit down your fucking neck. Do you understand me, soldier?"

"Fuck!" Marcus cursed under his breath.

Sanders got up close in his face and raised an eyebrow.

"Fuck…Sir."

"And?"

"And, it would be my greatest honour to escort Brin back home." Marcus bit out between clenched teeth.

"Better."

"So, this is what it's like to get screwed with your pants on," Marcus grumbled.

Sanders walked away quickly before Marcus could see his smirk. He liked the guy, he really did. But there were times, like now, when being his superior was so much fun…at Marcus' expense.

Brin and Marcus were going on the first chopper. That left one available seat.

"Anyone hit with one of the Guild's injectors?" Sanders asked.

Owen nodded. "For the record, I'm not affected by the toxin."

One of the lycans, Farrell, also nodded, his expression tight. He held up a spent injector. "I took a hit. I administered the antidote fast, but…"

"We're not taking the risk that they've injected you with the virus," Sanders finished. "You're on the chopper with them. Get yourself to isolation as soon as they land."

Owen frowned. "You sure you don't want me to go as escort and leave Marcus with you?"

"You're immune to whatever they cooked up," Sanders said. "You're staying."

"Yes, Sir."

Brin approached, her jaw set with determination. "Why can't I stay with you and the rest of the group? I can heal everyone's injuries, and we can all go home together."

"Sorry Brin, the answer is, no. The Guild knows who you are, and where you are. We can't let them get their hands on you. You're too important."

"Wow, I'm both flattered and freaked out."

"Good," Sanders said. "Fear keeps people alive. Eat something, hydrate. We'll move out in one hour to the pickup point."

The next few short hours crawled and raced away at the same time. They cleaned what they could, burned what they couldn't, and left the rest for the snow to bury…or the bears to eat. Every distant crack of ice, every shift of wind, made heads turn and fingers find triggers. Brin kept her hood up and her gaze low and tried very hard not to tremble.

"How you doing?" Callum asked her once they reached the pickup point.

"Great. Never better," she replied, adding a smile she hoped looked genuine.

Just once I'd like to see a liar's pants catch on fire, she thought wearily, a.k.a. her own, at least then she might be warm.

When the chopper finally beat its way through the low ceiling of cloud, it looked small and fragile against the iron sky. One pilot. No door gun. A civilian frame with no military upgrades.

It landed smoothly on a scoured patch of ice. The pilot, in his late twenties, short beard and glasses rimmed with frost, gave them the thumbs up that said both, *let's go and please hurry.*

Crouching low to avoid the spinning rotor blades, Brin climbed in first, Farrell climbed in behind her, taking a seat opposite her, with Marcus climbing in last, slamming the door. The chopper lurched skyward before he'd even yanked his belt across his chest.

"Easy," he barked, bracing

"Not a lot of easy today," the pilot replied over his shoulder, in a thick eastern Canadian accent. "We'll be threading the needle to make it back to Fort MacKenzie. There's another storm coming in faster than forecast. If we're lucky, we can skirt the worst of it. If not…"

"We're in for a bumpy ride." Brin finished.

"Yes ma'am. I suggest you keep your seatbelts on tight."

Brin swallowed and stared at her gloved hands. The armband lay warm and heavy under her sleeve, a sleeping snake that wasn't truly asleep, just dormant. She leaned back into her seat and let out a shudder, releasing a small amount of the fear she didn't realise had gripped her so tightly. At least, they were out of the reach of the Guild and demons.

Below, the rest of their group slipped away, becoming smaller and smaller, until they were no more than dots against the snow. Further in the distance, remnants of their camp smouldered, ash blowing like dirty confetti across a white backdrop, until it too disappeared behind them.

Brin looked down through her window and let relief loosen her lungs a little more. Home. Heat. Coffee. And several thousand miles between her and their enemy. She closed her eyes for three breaths, the first easy ones she'd taken all day.

Across the cabin, Marcus stared out his own window, his jaw locked and eyes hard as obsidian. He should have felt the same relief, their mission objective had been met, his team was still breathing, and an exit achieved despite the obstacles. Instead, fury gnawed at him with small, impatient teeth. Fury that two demons managed to escape, and fury at himself for moving before thinking, and taking a bullet meant for Brin. He didn't regret saving her, but he regretted leaving himself open to the attack and needing her healing…again!

He also felt fury at the serpent armband. He could still feel heat coiling beneath the skin of his wrist where it had bitten him. He was also furious at the way his wolf lay smugly just beneath the surface, like a dog that had finally herded its sheep where it wanted. Marcus flexed his hand and the phantom ache answered.

He didn't look at Brin. He didn't need to. He could feel her in the cabin the way you feel a storm rolling over a plain, the air pressure, taste and hum of electricity under the skin.

The helicopter pitched its nose into the weather and kept climbing.

11

Cassie shouldered the study door with her hip while coaxing Tilly through with a gentle nudge. Grace followed, clutching a folded printout from the vet's ultrasound scan like it was a royal decree.

Alaric looked up from a stack of documents and satellite photos, pen paused mid annotation. "What's the verdict?" he asked grimly.

Grace couldn't keep the grin off her face. "She's only having four pups. The vet says she could deliver them anytime within the next week."

"So soon?"

Cassie nodded. "He says she's doing pretty well despite being off her food a bit and sore in the hips, but considering she's carrying hellhound pups, that's probably normal."

Alaric exhaled through his nose, the picture of stoic resignation. "That's good news."

He set the pen down and steepled his fingers, gaze drifting, inevitably, toward the mother-to-be now making herself comfortable on the hearth rug.

Alaric's mouth twitched in a long-suffering line. It wasn't any secret that Alaric had never wanted a dog, but circumstance hadn't given them any option. The day she found the holy cup under the sofa and drank what was left of Cassie's blood in it, had sealed the deal, so to speak. They couldn't exactly re-home a mutt that transformed into an enormous hellhound whenever she became upset.

Alaric rubbed at his temples in slow circles. *Let Cujo stay in the house, they said. It will be fun, they said,* he repeated in his mind.

Cujo, the enormous, battle scarred alpha hellhound wouldn't have been his first choice for a second pet…Nor his last, or anything in between for that matter. Regardless, he didn't have any say in the decision. With Tilly as his *mate*, he'd been outvoted by biology…and his family, and now he was stuck with both the beasts.

If it had been just Cujo who had come to live in his home, Alaric would probably have learned to live with that, eventually. However, since Cujo was the alpha of his pack, where he went, so did the pack. In the beginning, he'd set some strict ground rules regarding the hounds not being allowed inside the manor or on the grounds, restricting them to Savernake Forest, rules including not hunting within the forest's borders. Not surprisingly however, since the hounds had never lived within restrictions before, they had trouble conforming to Alaric's rules. After a great deal of discussion with Megan as the go-between, a few ruined floor rugs, destroyed furniture and a little bloodshed, mostly Alaric's, they finally came to a compromise.

Now, only Cujo was allowed inside the house with Tilly. As for the rest of the pack, half remained within Savernake Forest and roamed the manor grounds, while the other half roamed *Coed Caer Ffin forest*, in Fey. Those who came across to Havenswood manor wore magical collars, thanks to the druid sisters, which gave them the appearance of only being very large dogs, not the terrifying hellhounds they actually were. That way they didn't terrify any humans who might choose to take a stroll through the forest, which was after all, technically public property.

Grace crouched down to scratch behind Tilly's ears. The hound pressed closer to the fire and released a tired, contented huff.

"Four pups, you say." Alaric pinched the bridge of his nose. "Once they're weaned and old enough, we'll find homes for all of them."

Cassie nodded easily. "I agree."

Grace said nothing, her face the portrait of teenage neutrality, i.e., plotting. There was no universe in which she didn't keep at least one pup. To derail the topic, she pivoted hard.

"So, Dad, if I were to get a second ear piercing, which is, like, totally normal and not a big deal, do you think silver or gold hoops would go better with my school uniform?"

Alaric blinked. "What?"

"Uncle Alex says I should go all out and get a belly piercing too," Grace breezed on.

"Well, that's not happening," he told her adamantly.

"What about a tattoo? A couple of my friends at school have tattoos, just the name of their favourite bands, nothing fancy."

"Absolutely not! At least not before you're twenty-one."

"Seriously dad, you're so out of touch," she huffed indolently.

Alaric recovered. "I'm not old. Look at me, I look like I'm still twenty-eight." He told her, looking to Cassie to back him up, to which she waggled her eyebrows suggestively with approval of just how good he looked.

Grace rolled her eyes and sighed loudly, hip jutting in maximum haughtiness. "Oh please. That's like saying you're the youngest dinosaur. You're still old," she told him.

Cassie snorted out a laugh, kissed Alaric's cheek, and steered Grace toward the door. "She's right you know."

"I don't care what you two think, I think I look pretty good for someone over two thousand years old," he frowned peevishly.

"I can't argue with you there, love. And, I'm looking forward to getting a closer view of your perfect pecs and glorious glutes later," Cassie grinned.

"Oh, for God's sake, get a room already. If I have to hear any more, I'll need therapy." Grace yelled out from halfway down the corridor.

Both Cassie and Alaric laughed. There was no easier accomplishment than tormenting a teenage daughter.

"I'll leave you to your work. The others are no doubt dying to hear about Tilly, and I need coffee."

"Kill two birds with one stone?"

"You know me so well," she chuckled, waggling her eyebrows at him again, a cheeky glint in her eye, which he knew meant there'd be playtime tonight.

Suddenly his mood brightened, looking toward the mutt who remained in his study.

Tilly didn't follow Grace, which was unusual. She stood, then circled once and curled tighter by the fire, eyelids drooping, tail thumping twice before settling. Near-term and tired, Cassie had said. Alaric let out a long sigh before returning to his work.

The flames stretched and shrank, pulsated and crackled within the hearth, and for a rare minute the house was almost quiet.

Almost.

Alex sauntered in without knocking, hands in his pockets and trouble in his lopsided smile. Narayan followed with his usual calm demeanour, and Sebastian closed the door behind them, already frowning at some offensive remark that Alex had made.

Narayan inclined his head. "Any word from Canada?"

"Not since yesterday's check-in when they set up camp," Alaric said. "They should be somewhere near the cave's location by now. With any luck they might already have the armband and they're on their way back." He paused, the quiet stretching. "Hopefully we'll know more soon."

The door pushed open once again and a shadow padded his way across the room, blotting out the hearth's light with his huge presence. On all fours, Cujo stood the same height as a rhinoceros, his gaze almost meeting Alaric's six foot six frame, eye to eye. Long muscular legs ended in dinner plate sized paws, and claws the length of a finger, tipped each toe, tapping lightly across the timber floorboards as he walked. There was more muscle on his frame than a WFC wrestler on steroids. Curling up on the rug in front of the open fire next to Tilly, his elongated canines protruded past his bottom lip. His thick snout, made all the more prominent by the threatening curl of his top lip and black eyes, narrowed warily, his triangular ears flattening slightly in agitation.

Tilly's eyes drifted closed again. Cujo took up silent guard beside her, his vast head on his paws, black gaze tracking each speaker like a chess player considering the board.

Narayan broke the silence. "Gustav confirmed the darted lycan has been moved to quarantine at the Ukraine base. He's stable but starting to show flu-like symptoms."

Alaric nodded once. "That's not the news I was hoping for, but at least he's stable. Alex, you'll need to relocate your lab to Gustav's bunker in the next day or so. We need to find an antidote as fast as possible and travelling back and forth is time we can't afford to waste."

Alex didn't argue. "Sure. I'll organise it right away."

Alaric Blinked, sitting back in his chair. "Did you just say, yes?"

"I did. What of it?"

"You're being reasonable. Where's the snide remark or derogatory comment? Is there something wrong with you?"

"Is that a rhetorical question?" Alex queried, tipping his chin in thought.

It was a valid question. For anyone else, polite acquiescence was normal. For Alex? Well, he had his own definition of normal.

Not wishing to invite an argument, Alaric moved on. "I'm just glad we're on the same page with this."

"Of course. Until we know more about this so-called virus, we can't create the vaccine. By chance, Dr Wagstaff hasn't managed to find out any more about it, has he?"

"Not yet. He's looking into it."

Sebastian scrunched his nose, tipping it into the air. He began prowling the study, sniffing out the origin of the offensive odour. "What is that God-awful smell?" he asked.

"Tilly," Alex said without looking up. "I think she must have rolled in something dead in the forest."

Everyone looked at Alex.

"What? Don't look at me. I haven't buried any bodies out there." *Recently*, he tacked on silently.

Alaric levelled a long, sceptical look. "I know you, Alex. You wouldn't care if disposing of a decaying corpse in Savernake pissed off the angels," he growled.

"That's true, but it would piss you off, and as you know, I live to annoy you," Alex told him theatrically, laying it on so thick even Cujo huffed.

Alaric rolled his eyes as though bored.

"It wasn't me. Scouts' honour. Cross my heart and hope to die, stick a needle in my eye," Alex said, performing all the accompanying hand actions and finishing with his middle finger at his brother-in-law.

"I might just do that anyway," Alaric said mildly. "I don't think it's Tilly, she's been at the vets most of the afternoon."

"Hey, guys," Sebastian called from the hearth, sniffing again. "It's definitely not Tilly."

"What's not Tilly?" Philippe asked as he slipped into the study, bringing with him a gust of cold corridor air.

"That smell. It's not coming from Tilly. It's coming from Cujo."

All eyes slid to the alpha hellhound. Cujo stared back, unblinking. If Alaric wasn't mistaken, the beast was…smiling.

"I'm not washing him," Alaric said emphatically.

"Me neither," Sebastian seconded.

"Thanks for volunteering, Alex," Philippe said without missing a beat, slapping him on the shoulder.

"Fuck off. Last time I tried to bathe the crazy beast he pissed on me and then bit my hand off."

Alaric couldn't hold back a low chuckle. "Come on, Alex, you love to live dangerously. Besides, I'm sure Abby would love to soothe over any *boo-boo* you suffer."

Alex actually considered it for a full second, eyes narrowing as if doing complex maths. "Nope. Fuck it. It's still not worth it."

"Okay, so what do we do with him? We can't let him run around stinking the way he does," Narayan said, ever practical.

"The duck pond," Philippe suggested. "If we throw a tree trunk in for him to chase, make him swim a bit, hopefully the stink will wash off."

Alex brightened. "And I'll film it."

"Of course you will," Sebastian muttered. "Because nothing says, 'Freaky Friday', like posting 'Hellhound bath time' on your socials."

"Exactly!"

Cujo's ears pricked at the word 'chase.' His tail thumped once, twice. Tilly, unbothered, exhaled a long warm breath and curled up closer to the blaze.

Alaric looked from the hounds to the men, then to the frost rimmed windows. Somewhere far north, family and friends were risking everything in the freezing Arctic conditions, while here at home, life ticked mundanely on, fires to stoke, a home to manage, hellhounds to deodorize.

He reached for his pen again. "Fine. The duck pond it is. And someone had better warn the ducks."

The kitchen was a symphony of chopping, simmering and clattering pots and pans when Cassie and Grace walked in, the scent of rosemary and roast chicken mingling with something sweet, Megan's peach crumble, judging by the bubbling dish cooling on the benchtop.

Holly stood washing dishes at the sink. Megan was at one end of the bench rolling pastry with paced determination, not satisfied with only one dessert with dinner, and at the other end, Mrs P, chopped vegetables with practiced ease.

Cassie paused in the doorway, inhaling the warmth. "You know, it almost feels too quiet in here, any coffee made?"

"Shhh. Don't jinx it," Mrs P warned without looking up, her knife working in brisk efficiency. "And no, the pot is empty I'm afraid, you'll need to put another one on, love."

Cassie laughed softly, thinking she was kidding, then instantly regretted the mocking thought. Not only was the coffee pot truly empty, as if by some cosmic irony, a familiar voice pierced the air.

"Oh, for heaven's sake, *who* leaves hiking equipment in the hallway?!" Jocelyn stormed in, brandishing a chain cabled sling, like a weapon.

The peaceful bubble popped. Holly winced. Megan turned her head away to hide a grin. Grace, quick on the uptake, leaned toward her mother and whispered, "You did this. You summoned her."

Cassie sighed. "Yeah, I think I did. I didn't even need to say her name three times." Like they did in every evil urban legend, ever!

Jocelyn, mid-rant, didn't even pause for breath. "And another thing, someone's taken my Dior face cream. The *very expensive* one. Do you people *not* understand boundaries?"

"Hello, to you too, dear." Mrs Philpot said to her daughter, her tone clipped short with frustration.

"Mum. I think you might find that you left your face cream by your nightstand. And *that*, isn't hiking equipment. It's Alex and Abby's sex swing. It was just delivered an hour ago after being fixed," Holly happily told her.

The colour from Jocelyn's face suddenly drained. "Well, I never!"

"Well, maybe you should, it might loosen you up a bit." Holly retorted, although her meaning was totally lost on her mother, who stormed from the kitchen holding out her hands as though she'd just touched a leper.

"Not to be rude, but I'm just wondering how long Jocelyn is planning to stay?" Cassie asked.

Holly huffed out a forced laugh. "She hasn't said, but I'm sure if we leave a few more of Alex and Abby's toys lying about, she might not want to stay very long at all. At least, we can hope so."

Mrs Philpot heaved a heavy sigh with a seconding nod. "She's my daughter and I love her, but…But she has a way of outstaying her welcome even if she only turns up for dinner."

There were lots of agreeing mumbles and nodding heads about the room.

"What happened at the vet with Tilly?" Megan asked, changing the topic.

"The vet says she's having *four* pups, and they're due any day now."

All the women began talking at once.

"Four?" Holly repeated. "That's wonderful!"

"Four?" Mrs P echoed, hands flying to her cheeks. "Bless her heart!"

Megan beamed. "She'll be such a good mum."

Opening the back door, Paige entered the kitchen from the garden, straightening her long hair, blown about in the wind, her eight year-old son Riley, close on her heels. "What's all the excitement about?" she asked.

"The vet says Tilly's having four pups!" Grace blurted before anyone else could.

Riley's eyes lit up like a Christmas tree. "*Four?* Can I have one, Mum? Please? I'll feed it and train it and everything!"

Paige blinked at the bombardment of enthusiasm, then turned to Cassie for backup. Cassie mirrored her look, the universal one that says, *absolutely not, over my dead body.*

Riley wilted.

Grace caught his eye, waited for a moment until the adults were distracted, and gave him a conspiratorial grin that clearly meant, *Don't worry. We're totally keeping one each,* turning his pout into a sly grin.

Paige noticed the exchange, but wisely said nothing.

Moments later Abby strolled in, fresh from the gym, towel slung around her neck. "Oh, I see our swing is back, all fixed I hope?" she said, picking it up from the counter to check it over to snickering chuckles from Riley and Grace.

"What's this about hiking equipment? Did I miss something?" she asked bemused, adding her own chuckles to the mix after reading a couple of their minds.

"You just missed my mother, the drama queen," Holly announced.

"And the coffee maker is empty," Cassie sighed.

"Tilly's having four pups," Riley finished with excitement.

Abby grabbed an apple and bit into it. "So…it's business as usual."

"Pretty much."

"Hey kids, if you want to watch your Uncle Alex try to bathe *Cujo*, I'd head to the duck pond."

Grace's head snapped up. "You're kidding!"

"Nope." Abby grinned. "He's already out there with a bone the size of a cricket bat trying to lure him to the water."

They didn't need further encouragement. "Come on!" Grace grabbed Riley's hand and they bolted for the kitchen's back door, disappearing down the garden path.

"Oh, I want to see this too," Cassie muttered.

It seemed everyone had the same idea, abandoning what they'd been doing to follow the kids to the duck pond.

The household gathered by the pond, which in reality was a two hundred by four hundred foot lake.

Cujo sat at the water's edge, massive and unmoving, his dark eyes locked on Alex and the bone in his hand. His smell was appalling, like wet leather, old socks and the smell of death all rolled into one. Not even being outside in the fresh air did anything to lessen the stench.

Alex stood a cautious few metres back, holding up the enormous bone. "Go on, good boy. Get in the water."

Cujo's head tilted. Then he sat on his haunches, tail flicking once, twice. His mouth curved, just slightly, into what could only be described as a grin.

"Why do I feel like he's laughing at me?" Alex muttered.

"Because he *is*," Philippe said.

"Megan, could you ask him what he rolled in?" Alaric asked her, pinching the bridge of his nose. "Before my eyes start watering."

Megan knelt a safe distance away, closing her eyes briefly to tap into her ability. "Uhh ohh," she said, wrinkling her nose at Cujo's reply. "He found a leaking sewage pipe somewhere around the far side of the manor…and he rolled in it."

The entire group groaned.

"Why?" Abby demanded.

Megan paused, listening again, then translated flatly, "Because he wasn't allowed to go to the vet with Tilly. This was payback."

Alex gaped at the hulking hound. "You rolled in *shit* because you were jealous?"

Cujo's tail wagged proudly.

"He's very proud of himself," Megan confirmed.

Sebastian gagged. "Shit! And I mean that literally and figuratively."

There was a mix of gasps of horror and peals of laughter.

"Alright," Alaric grumbled, "Enough of this. Time for a bath, Cujo."

"Fetch!" Alex threw the bone into the water.

Cujo looked at the ripple on the water and then looked back at Alex, otherwise he didn't move a muscle.

Next, Alex took two bold steps forward and smacked the hound's backside. "In you go, you mangy mutt!"

Nothing. Cujo didn't even twitch.

"Maybe you need to motivate him a bit more," Sebastian offered dryly.

Alex cracked his knuckles. "Fine. Motivation it is." He raised one hand, gathering a flicker of electromagnetic energy, blue static shimmering between his fingers a moment before zapping Cujo right on the rump.

The hellhound yelped, spun with a snarl, and lunged.

Alex leapt back, laughing nervously. "Oh, don't be like that! It was a *gentle…*"

Cujo's growl deepened to flash a full set of pearly white fangs.

"Alright, alright," Alex said, eyes darting about for a quick escape. "Last resort!"

Before anyone could stop him, he darted behind the hound, and sunk his own fangs deep into the soft flesh on the inside of his thigh.

The sound Cujo made was half bark, half demonic roar. He bounded forward, straight into the pond, with Alex sprinting ahead of him.

"Run, Uncle Alex!" Grace shrieked, laughing.

"I'm running!" Alex shouted back as the enormous beast thundered after him, sending up waves of water and pond weed.

Cujo's splashdown was titanic. Alex barely avoided being flattened as he dove into the water, soaked to the bone but grinning. "Ha! You didn't see that coming, did you, huh?" he gloated.

The rest of the pack appeared on cue, another five gigantic shapes galloping out of the tree line of the forest, answering their alpha's roar.

Alex froze mid-boast. *Craptastic! This is going to hurt.*

The pack plunged into the pond, water exploding in all directions.

From the bank, Grace, Riley, and half the manor household doubled over with laughter.

A heartbeat later, water erupted as all six hellhounds pounced on Alex.

"Do you think we should help him?" Narayan asked nonchalantly.

"Nah, they'll get bored with him soon enough and he'll be fine. Besides, if we try to pull them off him now, Cujo won't stay in there long enough to get clean, and I'm not volunteering to wash him again." Alaric told him.

"Me neither."

12

The helicopter pitched and rolled through the storm like a tin can in a washing machine. The small craft shuddered under the strain, the engine whining in protest as the pilot fought to keep it level. Outside, the world was a maelstrom of snow and flashing light. Lightning struck so close that the occupants were momentarily blinded by a brilliant flash, and thunder cracked and rolled through the cabin in a deafening explosion. That one was far too close for comfort.

Brin tightened her belt and gripped the edge of her seat, her white knuckled fingers biting deep into the soft padding. Her nervous breath fogged the cool air, shallow and fast, intermittently holding it for long seconds when the helicopter struck another severe patch of turbulence.

Across from her, Marcus sat braced against the opposite bulkhead, his eyes sharp and alert, his jaw set in the same stoic way she'd seen in battle. He looked carved out of iron, though the pulse in his neck betrayed his tension. The wolf inside him paced restlessly, close to the surface, wary. He could feel it, coiled under his skin, agitated and strange, as though the static of the exterior atmosphere had somehow leached into his bones. He blamed the feeling on the storm…or maybe it was the nearness of the woman sitting only a foot away, her terrified scent setting his teeth on edge with a need to protect her. A natural response, since protecting her was his mission's primary objective and responsibility.

The helicopter flew lower than it should have, Marcus knew that even before he glanced at the altimeter. The pilot was skimming the valleys, trying to use the mountains themselves as a buffer against the worst of the wind. Beneath them, jagged peaks glinted with snow and ice, ghostly white ridges vanishing into the swirling grey. The landscape below was vast and merciless, and damn near impossible to distinguish land from sky in this weather. It was a risky move, but there wasn't much option.

Then, through the haze, Marcus caught sight of something no more than a hundred metres below, a large timber cabin positioned near a frozen river, smoke-black roof half-buried beneath snow. He noted its location, maybe a mile past the tree line, locking the information in his memory vault.

A flash, brighter than any before, lit up the cockpit. The world turned white and the helicopter jolted violently, spinning half a turn before the pilot wrenched the controls. A crack like the splitting of metal echoed through the fuselage.

"Lightning strike! The tail rotor's been hit!" the pilot shouted, voice almost drowned out by the noise. Warning alarms blared, red lights strobed in the confined space.

The craft lurched sideways. Gravity tilted. Marcus' shoulder slammed into the wall. Brin screamed as her seatbelt bit deep.

"Hold on!" the pilot barked as he fought with all his strength to regain control. "We're losing stabilisation! I can't..."

The rest was swallowed by another crack of thunder. Not that he needed to finish that sentence, they all knew what came next.

They were going down!

Brin's stomach dropped as the helicopter careened into a sickening spin. The horizon vanished in a blur of grey and white. She clamped her lips shut to hold back a moan of despair. Dread felt like a lead weight on her chest, eroding away the last threads of confidence she had that they would get out of this alive. If she was going to die, she was going to go with dignity and not let Marcus have the satisfaction of knowing how scared she really was.

Marcus unbuckled, half-crawling toward her against the centrifugal pull, refastening his belt as he sidled himself up against her, wrapping his body around hers, shielding her instinctively as the aircraft screamed in protest. His warmth, his steady breathing, pressed so close, somehow managed to drive away the worst of the terror clenched in her lungs, as though crashing to earth in a helicopter was just another day for him.

"Brace!" the pilot yelled.

The world became noise, metal twisting, wind howling with the gut-churning drop. Brin buried her face against Marcus' chest, holding onto him for dear life. He locked his arms around her.

The last thing either of them heard was the deafening crack of rotor blades snapping on their jarring impact, and the world around them went dark.

When awareness returned, it came in fragments, cold wind sifting through a broken window with a quiet whistle, the tickling of snow against their faces, and the acrid tang of leaking fuel, and the salty taste of blood.

It was cold. So damn cold.

Marcus opened his eyes, but he saw…nothing. Groaning, he shifted, he seemed to be face-down. Yeah…he was doing a face-plant alright. But where was he? All he could see was snow. No, that wasn't true, in the distance he could see trees laden with snow. And snowbanks laden with snow. And snow laden with more fucking snow.

So, he was in middle of fucking nowhere…with snow. But where? Why?

Brin coughed, tasting blood. "Marcus?"

A groan answered her. He was slumped beside her, blood streaking down one side of his face, already healing. He opened one eye, met hers, and exhaled. "Still breathing. You?"

"I think so." She looked around the wreckage. The pilot was slumped forward, motionless. Farrell, the lycan soldier, was pinned by the crumpled bulkhead, his skin already pallid grey, his forward gaze, fixed and unblinking. The same bulkhead that Marcus had been sitting against only moments earlier.

Marcus unlatched Brin's belt and looked her over. Only a few cuts and bruises, nothing life threatening he surmised with relief.

"We have to get out of here. Can you walk?"

"I…I think so." She replied tentatively. She didn't think she had any broken bones, but her body was shaking so violently, she wasn't at all certain her legs would hold her weight.

Marcus crawled out through the broken side door with Brin close behind, snow whipping into the cabin in angry gusts. He grabbed his rifle and the emergency kit from a wall compartment, tossing Brin a flare pack and first-aid box. "We take only what we can carry," he said, voice low and tight.

Brin nodded numbly. Her mind buzzed in that empty way created by shock, where thought and emotion wouldn't connect. She looked at the bright red flares in her hands, so carefully stored for emergencies like this. No one ever thought they'd ever need them…until they did.

Marcus tested the radio, nothing. It was completely dead. He looked toward the horizon. The snow was coming in harder now, already burying the downed helicopter into a pale mound. "We have to move. It's getting late and once the sun dips past the horizon, the temperature's going to plummet even further. We'll freeze to death if we stay here."

"Move, where?" she asked, her teeth chattering loudly.

"I saw a cabin before we went down. Maybe two miles east, near a frozen river. That's our best shot. With any luck, someone might be home."

Brin glanced back toward the wreckage, at the two still figures. "We should…bury them so bears and wolves won't find them."

Marcus shook his head, regret shadowing his eyes. "We don't have time. Besides, the snow will cover them soon enough and with any luck the smell of aviation fuel will deter any predators from taking too close a look. When a rescue team arrives, we'll come back for them, okay?"

"How will they find us?" Brin asked.

"They will." He gave no further explanation, how could he, he had none. He had no idea where they were, he suspected the helicopter had been blown several miles off course in the storm, and with the severity of damage to the aircraft, he knew there was no functioning GPS beacon to help rescuers locate them. It was a miracle that he and Brin had survived. However, if they didn't reach that cabin within the next few hours, he couldn't guarantee they would survive the night.

"Wait! I have that watch the sisters gave me. The one they put the forgettable charm on, they said it has GPS." She told him excitedly, searching the various pockets of her jacket, pulling it from an inner pocket.

Marcus' gaze was sympathetic but held no encouragement. "Unfortunately, that won't do us any good unless a plane with a tracking device happens to fly nearby, its signal is very limited." They were back to where they started, up shit creek without a paddle. "Put it away, we might be able to find a use for it later." Doubtful, he thought, but he wasn't going to dowse all her hopes entirely. Not unless he had to.

Searching the immediate area around the wreckage, they collected their packs which had been thrown clear, along with enough rations to see them through the evening. If they didn't find shelter before nightfall, he doubted they'd need any more food or water.

They started walking. The landscape stretched endlessly around them, a wilderness of snow covered boulders and a forest of pine trees looming darkly in the distance. The wind keened between the peaks, cutting through every layer of fabric like it sought their bones.

Brin tried to keep up, her boots crunching in snow drifts that swallowed her calves. Each step was a small act of willpower. Marcus walked ahead, breaking the trail, every muscle cramping painfully in the cold. He'd been shot less than five hours ago, and even with Brin's healing, his body wasn't fully recovered. Each breath scraped his lungs, each step felt heavier than it should have, weighted further by their situation and his duty to keep Brin alive and safe. And beneath it all, his wolf still felt…wrong. Altered somehow. Quiet, but too aware.

After an hour, they stopped beneath a ridge of rock to catch their breath. The forest loomed just beyond, the tree branches bent low under the weight of snow. Marcus scanned the horizon while Brin slumped beside him, chest heaving.

"You doing okay?" he asked.

"Define okay," she managed in reply. Her voice was a whisper from exhaustion, but her eyes lifted to meet his, backlit with stubborn determination.

He grunted something that might've been a chuckle. "We'll rest five minutes, then keep moving. The cabin can't be too far now. I'd rather get there before the temperature hits minus twenty."

She nodded, leaning back against the rock. "If you say so."

The weather had once again begun to clear and the subsequent silence that enveloped them was a strange contrast to that of the cacophony of their flight through the storm…and crash landing. Here, only the creaking of tree branches under the heavy load of snow, offered relief of the deafening quiet.

For once, Marcus had no snide words to throw at her, and he didn't try to fill the empty silence with sarcasm. He simply sat beside her, close enough that their shoulders brushed, the faint warmth of him soaking through their layers. There was comfort just knowing that neither of them was out there alone, an only survivor.

Brin's breath slowed, heartbeat syncing with his. The world felt narrowed to this small pocket of stillness, their shared heat, the rise and fall of their chests. She didn't mean to close her eyes, but exhaustion blurred the edges of everything.

Her thoughts drifted where they shouldn't. She imagined what it would feel like to rest her palm against his bare chest, to feel the steady thrum of his heart beneath his muscled pecs, to trace their lines which she'd only glimpsed through the snug fit of his shirt. The thought of his body, solid, powerful, alive, pressed unbidden in her mind, stirred something she had no energy to fight. She swallowed hard, forcing her eyes open.

Marcus, for his part, stared straight ahead, jaw clenched, every sense too aware of her beside him, the faint hitch in her breathing, the honeyed scent of her hair despite the cold, the accidental brush of her thigh against his. He told himself it was proximity, adrenaline, exhaustion. Nothing more. But when her head slipped sideways to rest lightly against his shoulder, he didn't move.

For a long moment they sat like that, two survivors in a sea of white, their body language that of weary contentment and reluctant trust.

The wind had eased a little more, the snow softening to a light drift. Marcus rose, offering his hand. "Come on. The cabin's that way."

She took it, his grip, strong and steady, she was reluctant to let go of his hand, holding onto it for a few seconds longer. Together, they pushed on through the snow, toward the dark line of the forest and the glimmer of the frozen river beyond, their breaths merging in the air like ghosts.

Survive first. Everything else could wait.

Breaking through the tree line, they followed the meandering curve of the river. It wasn't long before the last streak of daylight bled from the horizon, but they weren't left completely without light. A low, greenish shimmer to the north, the Northern Lights, the Aurora Borealis, faintly pulsed through cloud gaps, ghostly and surreal, illuminating the landscape just enough to make out the shape of the cabin.

He slowed, eyes narrowing, double-checking that what he saw wasn't an illusion of exhaustion. No, the angular shape was real, a wide log building huddled against the slope, its roof heavy with snow.

Brin stumbled the last few steps beside him, her breath forming shaky clouds. "Please tell me that's it."

"That's it."

Relief softened her knees. From above, it had looked small, a modest hunting shack. Up close, it was far larger, two stories, a wide veranda with double front doors framed between rough-hewn beams.

No light glowed from within. No curl of smoke rose from the chimney. The place was silent. Empty.

Marcus approached first, testing the porch boards beneath his boots. They held. He tried the handle.

Unlocked. In fact, on closer inspection, the door had no lock. "They must feel pretty safe out here. They probably don't get many visitors," he muttered.

The hinges groaned as he pushed the door open. The air that spilled out was musty and still, carrying the faint scent of old wood and time.

He flicked a switch by the door out of habit. Nothing.

"Power's out," he said. "Stay here, I'll see if I can find the generator."

In the semi-darkness shadows shrouded the corners of the room, making it difficult to discern its size.

Brin nodded, hugging her arms to her chest as he disappeared through a hallway to her right, his flashlight beam cutting through the gloom until it vanished down a stairwell.

For a long moment she didn't move, just stood there letting her eyes adjust to the dim wash of moonlight slipping through frosted windows. Then she stepped cautiously forward, fingers trailing along the wall until they met leather.

The couch was old and cracked, the leather rough beneath her fingertips, cold and creased with age. She followed its back to the corner, then winced as her shin collided with a low table. "Ouch, dammit," she muttered, nudging it aside with her boot and rubbed the smarting spot. Not that she gave it much thought, it was just one more bruise. With everything that had happened in the last twenty-four hours, she felt like she was nothing but one large walking bruise. Nearly every inch of her body hurt, and those few that didn't, were frozen. She suspected that when her hands and feet thawed, they would probably hurt too.

Stepping around the coffee table, the faint outline of a hearth took shape at the far end of the room. Brin crossed to it, guided by touch. Her hands found the cool, uneven stone of the fireplace, smooth in some places, rough in others, shaped by hand tools and time, not machines. Above it, a thick railway plank served as a mantel. Her fingers brushed across it and found a small cardboard box. Matches.

"Thank God," she breathed, smiling faintly. Fire! Now *that* she understood. Electricity was a novelty she enjoyed on Earth, but this, wood, spark and flame, was elemental and familiar to her home.

She crouched by the hearth, feeling along its edges until she found a copper bin with wood and kindling. Removing her gloves she stacked the logs in the hearth, striking a match with numb fingers. She built the fire by instinct, thin kindling first, then heavier logs. The first flames caught, licking upward with soft, crackling life. She leaned closer, feeding it until the glow brightened and warmth began to spread.

And then, suddenly the room blazed with light.

Brin blinked, half-blinded. The lamps overhead flickered on, humming softly.

"Found it!" Marcus' voice echoed from down the hall, triumphant.

He emerged a few seconds later, hair damp from melted snow, an armful of food and a bottle of wine balanced against his chest, and a grin that made him look…kissable. And what that thought did to her nether region, heat pooled in her belly, sending minor shockwaves of excitement straight to her clit.

"There's a working generator downstairs. Two of them, actually. One was still running, keeping a freezer going." He paused for dramatic effect. "Did you know freezers in the middle of nowhere are creepy as hell? I was fully expecting to find body parts in there. Fortunately though, it's full of moose steaks, caribou, and a tonne of frozen vegetables. There's also a pantry down there with enough canned food to last a whole winter. And get this…there's even bacon and other cured meats."

Brin gave him a tired but genuine smile, the firelight reflecting in her eyes. "You found bacon? Then this might actually qualify as heaven."

"Yeah. If heaven smells like diesel and frozen meat." He dumped his haul on the kitchen counter, producing the wine bottle with a flourish. "And this. It's vintage *something*, I don't know much about wine, but I'm sure it'll help warm us up."

As the fire roared to life, the chill began to recede. They explored the place together, their footsteps echoing softly through the hallways.

Downstairs, on the ground level, a bathroom tiled in slate and pine gleamed faintly under new light, a stocked cabinet, clean towels, even soap and shampoo. Upstairs, three bedrooms branched off a narrow landing, two with neatly made beds, the third stacked with boxes of spare gear, snowshoes, coats, ammunition, and hunting rifles carefully racked on the wall.

"This isn't a holiday cabin," Marcus said, scanning the room. "It's a lodge. Someone who's serious about surviving winters out here."

"Lucky for us," Brin murmured, tugging the heavy drapes shut against the night.

Back in the living room, they settled cross-legged by the fire with their meagre feast. Tinned beans, spaghetti, eaten with two mismatched forks. They ate straight from the cans, laughing softly at how absurdly good it tasted. The wine, dark and decadent, burned a comforting trail down to their stomachs.

When the last of the bottle was empty, they sat in companionable silence, watching the flames curl and fall.

"The day could've ended worse," Brin said at last.

Marcus' gaze lingered on her profile, soft in the glow. "You can say that again. If we have to be stranded in the middle of nowhere, at least it's somewhere with heat, food, and wine."

"Hmm," she agreed, stretching her legs toward the fire, propping her feet on the coffee table beside Marcus'. "You know something, you're not such bad company."

He smiled faintly. "Don't tell anyone. It'd ruin my reputation."

They both laughed, quietly, tiredly. The sound felt like a release valve, letting out the pressure that had been building throughout the last couple of days.

After a moment, Brin pushed herself up, swaying slightly. “I think I’m officially done. My body’s plotting mutiny.”

“Go on,” Marcus said. “Pick whichever bed looks least haunted.”

She managed a small smile. “Thanks, Marcus. For…everything today.”

“Don’t mention it.”

She hesitated a second longer, exhaustion and adrenaline warring, and then leaned forward. The kiss was brief, soft, almost absent-minded, but it landed squarely on his lips. Warm. Real. Then she blinked as if waking from a trance. “Umm, Goodnight.”

He didn’t answer right away, just watched her climb the stairs, boots dragging, until she vanished into the shadows above.

Only when the silence returned did Marcus finally exhale. The faint taste of wine lingered, mingled with something more dangerous he didn’t dare name. His mind tried to replay it, but fatigue drowned the thought before it could form.

He pulled a blanket from the back of the couch, laid back onto the cracked leather, and stared into the fire. His wolf was quiet again, watchful, content…unnervingly so.

Maybe tomorrow, he’d think about what that kiss meant. But not tonight.

Tonight, survival had given them some fragile peace, and the warmth of the fire was all the comfort he needed.

As the flames crackled low and the wind moaned beyond the windows, Marcus drifted off to sleep on the couch, the echo of Brin’s lips still haunting the edge of his dreams.

13

Brin woke sluggishly, her mind hazy from sleep. For a few extra minutes she lay still beneath the thick doona, having created a warm spot on the soft mattress.

Reluctantly she stretched, feeling muscles protest, but not aching as they had the night before. The air smelled faintly of ash and timber polish, a comforting, domestic scent that belonged to a life far removed from the Arctic wilderness she found herself in.

Rubbing the sleep from her eyes, she realised she'd slept more soundly than she had in weeks. She told herself it was purely from exhaustion, her body having had nothing left to give. It definitely had *nothing* to do with the man sleeping downstairs. None at all. The fact that she felt safe with him nearby, was irrelevant.

Rolling out of bed, she found her rucksack where she'd left it on a chair in the corner of the room, changing quickly into yoga pants and a soft long-sleeved top. There wasn't any need for half a dozen layers today, not when the fire had done its work, taking the chill from the air and leaving the cabin with the kind of cozy warmth that made her toes curl in contentment.

The first thing on her to-do list for the day was find some food, real food, not another tin of beans.

After quickly tying her hair into a ponytail, she padded down the stairs in woollen socks, her footfalls silent on the solidly built staircase.

The lodge retained its residual warmth, the thick log walls and stone fireplace having trapped in the heat, even though the fire itself had died sometime during the night.

Marcus remained where she'd left him, sprawled on the couch, one arm thrown over his head, the other resting near the rifle, which he'd left propped against the chair beside him. Had it had been his intention to stay awake, on watch all night, she wondered. Even if it was, it seemed exhaustion had gotten the better of him.

Tip-toeing closer to check on him, Marcus looked tense, even in his sleep, she thought. His jaw shadowed with stubble, brows drawn as if wrestling unseen enemies, even as his chest rose and fell in the steady rhythm.

Brin hesitated, a flicker of something uninvited tightening her chest. She told herself it was pity. Deciding he'd earned the rest, she covered him with the multicoloured crocheted blanket which looked like it had been well loved with its yarn balled from use. Then, continued tiptoeing past him toward the kitchen.

The pantry smelled faintly of flour and oil, and to her delight, was fully stocked. She found flour, butter, bottled water, powdered milk, and miracle of miracles, several dozen eggs.

And coffee.

Real coffee.

"Oh, there is a God, and she loves me," she whispered reverently, clutching the packet to her chest.

Moving quickly, and as quietly as she could manage, she boiled water on the stove, adding a few spoonfuls of coffee into the percolator. As the rich aroma began to fill the air, she sighed audibly, her shoulders relaxing in pleasure. While the coffee brewed, she whisked batter for pancakes and laid bacon in the pan. Within minutes, the cabin was alive with the comforting sizzle of frying meat and the smell of breakfast that belonged in a home, not a survival scenario.

The scent reached Marcus before consciousness fully did. He stirred, grimacing at the stiffness in his shoulders and neck. Sleep had been anything but restful. He'd been plagued by strange dreams of wolves and dragons and serpents. No doubt a result of the events over the last few days, and the fact that his wolf remained restless. Not agitated, exactly. He had no words to describe it.

Something just felt…wrong.

Swinging his legs off the couch to stand, Marcus stretched until his spine cracked, the rifle clattering to the floor when he bumped it with his foot. Picking it up, he set it against the wall beside the front door and followed his nose toward the kitchen, the scent of bacon and coffee teasing his sensitive nose, bringing him fully awake like nothing else could.

Leaning his shoulder against the door frame, he stood there for a moment, watching her with a smile.

Brin was at the stove, humming softly, a strand of hair slipping free to brush her cheek. She moved with an ease that made the simple act of cooking look graceful.

"I didn't realise you knew how to cook," Marcus said, his voice still rough with sleep, a cocky half-smile tugging at his mouth.

"There are a lot of things you don't know about me," she replied readily, the twitch of her lips betraying her amusement.

"I'm sure there are."

"Here," she said, turning and holding out a steaming mug. "I also know how to make coffee."

Marcus chuckled, accepting it like it was the elixir of life. "Thanks," he murmured, inhaling deeply before taking a cautious sip. The bitter warmth hit his stomach like salvation.

Brin arched a brow, waiting for one of his trademark smart-arse comments. None came. For once, he just drank it quietly, appreciation written across his face.

She blinked, almost disappointed. "Who are you and what have you done with Marcus?"

"What do you mean?"

"No snide remark or derogatory comment?"

He smirked faintly. "Don't get used to it."

A few minutes later she set two plates of food on the table, pancakes stacked beside crisp bacon, glistening with melted butter and maple syrup. They sat opposite each other, the tension that had haunted them since the mission began, slowly loosening its grip. The combination of warmth, food, and coffee worked a kind of magic neither wanted to acknowledge.

Conversation came easier than expected. They spoke about the crash, the odds of rescue, and whether anyone had realised they were missing yet.

The morning light leaking through the windows suggested that the sky might clear soon.

As Marcus spoke about his team, Sanders, Callum, and the others, his eyes brightened. For those few minutes, it felt as though they were two old friends rather than reluctant allies stranded at the end of the world. Brin found herself laughing softly, teasing him over the way he referred to Callum's "Zen patience" like it was a personal affront.

When they'd finished eating, Marcus leaned back, more relaxed than he had been in days.

However, the peace didn't last.

"I'll check the perimeter later," he said, matter-of-factly. "See what's around, if there's any sign of a road or trail. You stay here."

Her brows lifted. "Excuse me? You're not my commanding officer."

"This isn't a debate, Brin. You're safer inside."

"I can take care of myself, and I'll go outside if and when I choose, thank you very much," she snapped. She wasn't helpless. Not totally. She still had a can of bear mace, and frankly, her patience for being told what to do had expired with the helicopter crash.

Marcus snorted. "You're not going outside, and don't argue with me."

"Sometimes I don't think you take me seriously," she huffed.

"Really?" He rose from his chair, towering over her. "There are times you think I do?"

Her jaw dropped. "You're such an…"

"Arsehole. Yeah, yeah. Blah, blah blah. I've heard that one before," he interrupted, stepping toward the door.

"Where are you going?" she demanded hotly.

"To punish the porcelain. You're welcome to come and watch, but I don't want to scare you with the impressive sight of my huge cock," he tossed over his shoulder, smirking.

Brin snorted derisively, her eyes flicking pointedly toward his groin. "I wouldn't go boasting about your package. You're forgetting I've already seen what you have to offer, and that bone of yours is hardly enough to tempt me."

His grin widened. "I get it. You're jealous someone else gets to play with my 'bone', and not you."

"Jealous?" she scoffed. "Hardly."

As she bent to pick up the fork she'd dropped, the argument hit a pause that neither of them had planned for.

Marcus' breath caught.

Without meaning to, she gave him an excellent view of her rear, the material shrink wrapping to her backside so precisely, the space inside his own pants began tightening painfully from his growing turgid length, and for one insane heartbeat, the wolf inside him stirred, not with agitation, but with heat.

Marcus swore under his breath, turning away quickly before instinct betrayed him further.

Without another word, he stalked down the hall and into the bathroom, slamming the door behind him.

Relieving himself wasn't his immediate concern. The truth was simpler and far more frustrating. Being near Brin calmed the strange agitation in his wolf, yet her nearness also ignited something far more primal in *him.* He didn't understand it, nor did he want to.

All he knew was that if he didn't put a door, and maybe a few feet of solid wall between them right now, he might make an even bigger mistake than that inadvertent kiss between them last night.

Marcus stayed in the bathroom for nearly an hour.

He wasn't hiding. Not exactly. He told himself he was just trying to get his head straight, and failing miserably.

He paced the narrow space, hands on his hips and jaw tight, the mirror reflecting a man he barely recognised. His wolf was restless again, prowling just beneath his skin, claws raking at his insides demandingly for something he didn't understand. It wasn't pain, but a strange agitation, a pressure that made his pulse hammer and his thoughts short-circuit.

It didn't help that every time he closed his eyes, he saw *her*. Brin.

The way she'd looked, eyes bright with mischief, the delicate curve of her smile when she handed him the mug of coffee. Their easy conversation over breakfast, and the way her pants hugged her arse, had made the world tilt sideways.

He braced his hands on the vanity basin and glared at his reflection. "Pull yourself together," he muttered. "She's your responsibility, nothing more."

But saying the words out loud didn't necessarily make them true.

Then there was Candy. The woman who, technically, was still his girlfriend. The thought made him scowl harder. She'd been a distraction, nothing more. A warm body and easy company, no strings. He'd intended to end things before the mission, or at least as soon as he got back. Now? He was stranded in the middle of nowhere with a woman who infuriated him, fascinated him, and made him feel more alive than he had in years.

He exhaled sharply, raking his fingers through his hair. "Brilliant, Marcus. You're so screwed. Royally, fucking screwed."

And while he also acknowledged that he was also an arsehole, he wasn't a cheating arsehole. That was one rule he had no intention of breaking, especially not with Brin. So, why was there a tiny voice in the back of his mind laughing at him?

He glared at himself in the mirror as he ran a hand through his short hair, something catching his attention on his wrist. The same wrist the serpent armband had bitten. The skin there still burned and had now begun to itch. So too, an angry rash had begun to spread over a ten centimetre square area. Under the fluorescent light, a faint dark line seemed to shift and move beneath the skin.

His stomach tightened. He ran cold water over it, but the sting only deepened. The mark wasn't infected, it felt *connected.* To what, he didn't know. But the thought unsettled him more than he wanted to admit.

A shower would help, he decided. Stripping off he stepped beneath the steaming hot jets, hoping the blast of water would wash away more than just sweat and irritation. It didn't. The heat seemed to rouse his body further, his mind spinning between Brin's soft but stubborn voice, her laugh, and the memory of her pressed against him in the helicopter.

By the time he stepped out of the shower and towelled off, his frustrations hadn't subsided, if anything they had increased. The rash hadn't lessened, nor had his steely hard erection.

A sharp rap on the door had him jumping with a start.

Outside, Brin crossed her arms and glared at the closed door. He'd been in there for nearly an hour and while she'd tried to be patient, her bladder and her temper, were nearing their limits.

"Marcus," she called, knocking sharply. "You've been in there forever. Unless you've decided to stay in there permanently, I need to use the bathroom."

No answer.

She tried again, louder this time. "I mean it. If you don't open this door in the next ten seconds, I'm going outside to find a nice tree, or maybe I'll just fill one of your boots while I'm at it."

A pause. Then, the faint sound of him chuckling. "You wouldn't."

"Try me."

The door clicked. Brin braced herself to lecture him within an inch of his life, only her words vanished the second the door swung open.

Marcus chuckled as he unlocked the door, opening it a crack to let her in and turned back to face the basin and waited for her reaction.

Brin was ready with a lengthy tongue lashing, but all she could manage was a gasp of surprise.

His naked body took her breath away. Flawless skin, marked only by his military tattoo on his upper arm, and a couple of minor battle scars on his torso, thanks to the healing power of his wolf…and her own healing power. His butt cheeks were twin globes of perfection that would make a Greek God envious, and his athletic thighs looked like they were sculpted from marble.

Just when she was about to back silently out of the bathroom, Marcus turned around, his grin was infuriatingly smug. Damp hair clung to his temples, droplets of water still tracing a lazy path down his chest.

Brin's eyes dropped lower, over his six pack abs to his...

Holy Moly, his package was big. Not just big, it was huge, especially now, fully erect, his fist wrapped around its girth, pumping it at a leisurely pace. There had been only one other time she'd seen his manhood. The day they first met. It wasn't the best of introductions, and while she thought seeing his hard erection then had left a memorable impression, she was surprised to see just how badly her memory had failed her.

"Holy shit!" Was that thing real, or some kind of realistic looking strap-on?

Brin froze mid-breath, her mouth dropping open on its hinges. All she could do was stand and stare at him for the longest moment, before her brain finally kicked back into grinding motion, blinking a couple times.

A shiver gripped her, rooting her to the spot with desire. A desperate, suffocating urge tightened around her lungs as she inhaled his musky wolf scent. Butterflies swarmed her stomach and tipped her mood meter to become horny and annoyed simultaneously.

She opened her mouth. Closed it. Opened it again.

"You…I…" Her face flamed scarlet. "Aren't you the least bit ashamed of yourself?"

"Ashamed of what, exactly?" he asked innocently, his slow hand action gliding from base to tip on each upward pass, adding a twist over the flushed head.

She gestured wildly, trying not to look directly at him.

"Opening the door naked, and…and...." she couldn't finish the sentence, her brain had turned into to a puddle of hormonal mush. She may have even licked her lips.

"Not one bit." He flashed her that grin he seemed so damned proud of. Mischief practically oozed from him, along with arrogance and a healthy dose of over confidence. She wanted to ignore him, but unfortunately his bad-boy charm drew her like a magnet.

"I wouldn't flatter yourself. Your junk is just that...Junk. Piteous, poorly developed, ugly junk," she sputtered, though her pulse betrayed her. Her eyes betrayed her too, drawn against her will to the trail of water glinting on his perfect body and the heavy erection between his legs. She snapped her gaze upward before she did something truly stupid, like start drooling. She tried to sound bored and uninterested, and to her ears she actually sounded pretty convincing.

Marcus grinned and her panties dampened.

"You're impossible. I'm not one of your military buddies. I don't want to see all your dangly bits." That was a flat out lie. She didn't want to just see them, she wanted to fondle, lick and suck every inch of them…and the rest of that muscle bound eye candy he had to offer, of which there seemed to be a mouthwatering supply.

She quickly tried to shut down her wayward thoughts. These were not normal thoughts. She hated Marcus, she reminded herself. Didn't she?

"Then maybe don't look," he replied unrepentantly. You wanted to use the toilet, there it is," he pointed with his free hand at the porcelain amenity in the far corner. "I'll just be here…doing my thing." He told her matter-of-factly, as though his behaviour was an everyday occurrence. "Unless you'd prefer to finish me off?" he added, shattering her lustful thoughts, bringing her back to the present. The one where they hated each other.

"You're a dick, you know that."

"I resemble that remark. A very big one!" he called back as he casually walked from the bathroom, still completely naked.

Brin closed the bathroom door behind her and leaned against it to catch her breath, her heart pounding like she'd just sprinted a marathon.

"Get it together," she hissed at herself, splashing cold water on her face. Her reflection in the mirror stared back, wide-eyed, cheeks flushed. "He's an arrogant ass, not…whatever your overactive hormonal brain's turning him into."

But the image of Marcus in the doorway refused to fade. That smirk. His smug confidence. Not to mention his huge meat popsicle.

It also ticked her off that he hadn't seemed remotely self-conscious while she'd forgotten how to breathe.

It wasn't fair. He was infuriating, yes. But he was also delectably hot, and she hadn't had sex in, oh…how long? She'd lost track, it was definitely longer than a year, maybe two. In this frozen wilderness, that combination suddenly made him seem *very* appealing.

Her and Marcus? Nope, that was never going to happen.

Bad hormones.

She took another deep breath, willing her pulse to calm and tried to focus on something else. Anything else. The cabin's warmth wrapped around her like a blanket, the faint scent of coffee still lingered from breakfast. Outside the frosted window, daylight gleamed off endless snow, so bright it almost hurt to look at.

When she finally left the bathroom, Marcus was nowhere in sight. Yet, the air carried the faint trace of his woodsy, masculine scent, and again her pulse kicked up its beat.

Peering out of a window a few minutes later, Brin caught sight of him out along the tree line, moving like someone trying to outrun his own shadow.

Outside, the cold bit hard. Marcus inhaled deeply, letting it burn through his lungs. He needed the sting, something to shock some sense back into him.

The world around him was silent except for the creak of pines shifting under snow and the occasional snap of ice on the frozen river nearby. The blizzard had passed, leaving behind a pristine expanse of white that stretched to the horizon, like the world around him had been reset. If only he could do the same so easily.

He should've felt relief, having some distance from Brin. Instead, unease prickled under his skin.

The burn on his wrist pulsed faintly beneath his sleeve, not painful, exactly, but alive. He flexed his hand, the mark glowing briefly before fading again. The serpent's bite had left a lingering effect on him, although as yet he was unsure of what that was, and until he knew more, he had no intention of letting Brin see it.

Walking along the perimeter of the lodge, Marcus studied the terrain. Animal tracks crisscrossed near the tree line, mostly rabbits, maybe a fox or two. Nothing large. Yet the hair at the nape of his neck rose all the same. His wolf didn't feel any danger nearby, but it *felt something*, faint but unmistakable, like distant roll of thunder.

"Great," he muttered. "Just what I need, mysterious tingles and an overactive imagination."

Circling back toward the cabin, he could see Brin through the frosted window, moving about, tidying the table and pretending not to glance outside every few minutes. She sure was watching him closely for someone who claimed to hate him.

The thought made him smile, then scowled at himself for doing it.

After making two sweeps around the parameter, he headed back toward the cabin, he considered procrastinating and stay out longer. He was tempted to shed his clothes again and shift into his wolf, run free and wild for a while, burn off some of his frustration. But something still didn't feel right with his wolf, and so decided against it.

The simple fact was, he couldn't stay outside forever. Whether either of them liked it or not, they were stuck together. At least for now.

Brin jumped slightly when the door opened and Marcus stepped back inside, boots leaving small wet prints on the floorboards.

"Everything alright?" she asked hesitantly, trying for casual, though her voice came out tighter than intended.

"No tracks out there except mine and a few small animals. I doubt there's anyone out here for a hundred miles."

"Comforting," she said dryly.

He shrugged out of his coat and hung it near the fire. "Sky's clearing. If it stays that way, maybe a rescue team will have a shot at spotting the wreckage by this afternoon." If they know where to start looking, he thought, but didn't voice his concern.

"That's good news," she said, though she didn't quite sound convinced. "And if they don't?"

"Then we adapt." His gaze softened a fraction. "We'll be fine, Brin. We've got everything we need to survive out here for as long as it takes."

She studied him, the set of his shoulders, the steadiness in his tone. There was a quiet authority about him when he wasn't being infuriating, and it drew her more than she wanted to admit. "If you say so," she said quietly.

He met her eyes, something unspoken sparking between them before he looked away, rubbing the back of his neck. "You should rest for a bit. I'll check the supplies again, see if there's anything we can use to make a signal."

Brin hesitated, then nodded. "Only if you promise not to lock yourself in the bathroom for another hour."

That earned a genuine laugh, low and rough. "Deal."

"And I still think you're a dick," she added quietly as she left the room.

Marcus chuckled.

The rest of the morning passed in uneasy silence. Marcus inventoried the pantry and the gear closet, while Brin swept near the hearth, humming under her breath to fill the silence. Outside, the sun broke through in hazy streaks, turning the snow into a glittering sea of diamonds.

Every so often, one of them would glance at the other, quick, unguarded looks that lingered a beat too long when the other wasn't looking. The memory of their earlier exchange hung between them like static, both of them pretending not to feel it, both very aware that they did.

And beneath it all, Marcus' wolf still stirred, quiet but restless, like a heartbeat syncing with hers.

Neither of them said it aloud, but they both felt the same uneasy truth settling into their bones.

The real danger wasn't the cold, or the wilderness.

It was *each other.*

14

The manor was wrapped in the early morning silence. Only the occasional faint crackle from dying embers in the hearth of Alaric's study, and the constant tap of his keyboard, stirred the air. Outside, a mist hung heavily over the grounds, blurring the edges of the world into soft shades of grey.

It was just past five in the morning, too early for the mortal residents to stir, asleep soundly in their beds upstairs, curled snuggled beneath heavy quilts. So too, Doran rested in fitful slumber, his large frame sprawled across the couch in the home's oversized lounge room, one arm draped over his eyes as if shielding himself from the coming sunrise.

The resident vampires however, were all awake and trying to keep busy, quietly. None of them had slept since the lycan team left two days earlier with Brin, to retrieve the serpent armband, waiting diligently for any updates. The lack of sleep didn't pose any imposition, since none of them required more than a few hours every four to five days anyway.

Alaric sat alone in his study, the desk light pooling across maps and reports scattered over his desk. The constant clicking of keyboard keys paused when his phone began to ring. The shrill tone slicing through the stillness like a blade.

He pressed the receiver to his ear. "Sanders?"

"Alaric." The voice on the other end sounded strained, roughened by fatigue and what sounded suspiciously like restrained fear.

Alaric's spine straightened, an icy chill suddenly permeating the tepid air around him. "What's happened?"

There was a short pause, broken only by static and a muffled exhale. "We reached the cave, and Brin retrieved the armband. But unfortunately, we had an encounter with the Guild. We dealt with them and headed back to camp, where we were ambushed. Except, the Guild's men didn't come alone, they brought some very nasty friends. Some type of demon we haven't come up against before. They were fast and aggressive. We dealt with them too with minimal casualties, but…" Sanders hesitated.

"But, what?" Alaric asked, both eager and dreading what followed the unnerving silence.

"The demons targeted Brin specifically, and a couple of them got away. I called for an urgent evac, but was told that the Chinook was on a mission elsewhere to help in a rescue from the overnight blizzard, and were likely going to take at least eight hours to reach us. Since we couldn't guarantee that the demons wouldn't return before then with more of their friends, we decided to get Brin out of there as soon as possible. They sent in a smaller chopper, which was nearby, but it was only big enough for three passengers. We sent Brin and Marcus, and one of the injured men, Farrell, back on that flight. The rest of us waited for the Chinook to swing back around."

Alaric frowned, the pulse ticking in his jaw. "And?"

"That's just it," Sanders said quietly. "The Chinook took longer than expected to reach us because of another storm which blew in. We assumed the other chopper made it back to Fort Mackenzie long before we left base camp. We've only just landed, and there's no sign of them."

The silence stretched, heavy as a stone.

"What do you mean, no sign?" Alaric asked, his voice dangerously calm.

Sanders swallowed audibly. "The other chopper never arrived. We've checked every relay and airstrip within three hundred miles. No signal, no contact. We think…" He hesitated again, as if saying it aloud made it real. "It looks like it may have gone down."

The words hit Alaric like a punch to the ribs. He rose abruptly from his chair, pacing the length of the study as the floorboards creaked beneath his boots. "When exactly, how long ago?"

"Rough estimate, maybe twelve hours ago, assuming it went down during the storm that blew in. We've already launched a search. The storm's cleared but visibility is still poor. It'll take time to pinpoint the likely crash zone."

"Time is not a luxury they have," Alaric snapped. His hand curled around the edge of the desk, knuckles white.

"I know. I'm well aware of that. We'll find them." Sanders' tone was steady, but beneath it lay a note of dread. They'd just flown back over the terrain the smaller chopper had, and there was nothing out there but snow and ice. "We're mobilising a couple of extra choppers and planes now."

"I'll get Doran to meet you at the drop off point, send back any men you don't need, and I'll organise for some replacements to help with the search."

"That would be great. We have to assume they might've been blown off course in the storm, and we'll have to extend the search. Alaric, I have to warn you, there's over a thousand miles of nothing out here, and after two major storms in two days, everything is under metres of snow. Finding them may be easier said than done." Sanders warned him.

Alaric inhaled through his nose, forcing himself to focus. "Yeah. Keep me updated every hour. If there's any change, any sign, any news at all, call me directly. Doran should be there in about fifteen minutes."

"You got it."

The line went dead.

For several long seconds, Alaric simply sat there, listening to the empty silence. Then he exhaled sharply, the sound more a growl than breath. "Fuck!" He drove a fist down onto the desk hard enough to make the lamp flicker.

The study door to the hall creaked open. Narayan appeared, silent as a shadow. His expression was calm, but his eyes reflected quiet concern.

"You heard from Sanders?" he asked softly.

Alaric turned toward him, jaw tight. "Brin, Marcus, and another lycan, Farrell, were sent back in a chopper yesterday. They never made it back to Fort MacKenzie. It looks like it might have gone down somewhere between there and Mount Odin."

"Any idea what would've caused them to go down?"

"Sanders feels they were most likely hit by a storm that went through not long after they took off."

Narayan's eyes closed briefly, his hand forming a half-mudra at his chest. "Have they begun the search?"

"They have," Alaric replied. He pinched the bridge of his nose, frustration and fury warring beneath his composed exterior. "But if they were in that storm, God knows how much ground we need to cover."

Alaric straightened suddenly. "Yeah. Wake Doran, we need him out there now."

Narayan nodded and vanished through the doorway silently.

Alaric stood in his study, staring out through the tall windows toward the frost-glazed garden beyond.

"Seb, Philippe." He called, his voice barely louder than his normal volume, although still loud enough for their sensitive hearing to catch their attention. Clenching his jaw, the faint pulse of his power flickered through the room, freezing the moisture in the air into miniscule ice crystals, falling to lightly coat everything with a crystalline shimmer.

Doran woke with a start when Narayan gripped his shoulder, giving it a light shake. He was on his feet before his brain kicked into gear. "What the…?"

"Sorry Doran, but we need you to head back to Fort Mackenzie."

Doran blinked, checking his watch. "Now? It's barely…"

"Yeah, I know. But we have a major problem. It looks like the chopper Brin and Marcus were in, might have gone down. We need to get the lycan team back and get a fresh team out there to start a search."

"Are you serious?" Doran's foggy mind cleared in an instant with a jolt of adrenaline into his bloodstream. "Oh, fuck. Um, yeah…Right. Just give me two minutes. I just need to make a pitstop in the bathroom."

Doran cursed and swore along the length of the corridor, moving at a clipped pace, and was standing barefoot in the study's doorway in just over two minutes, hair mussed from sleep, eyes sharp and focussed. Looking at Alaric's grim posture and Narayan's folded arms, Doran's heart sank into the pit of his stomach.

"What exactly happened?" he asked, his voice low, already bracing for the worst.

Alaric didn't soften the blow. "Brin and Marcus' helicopter never arrived back at Fort MacKenzie."

For a heartbeat Doran stood very still. "When were they due back?" His voice was eerily calm. Too calm.

"They should've landed hours ago. There's a chance a storm forced them off course."

Seb and Philippe arrived together, their faces grim with concern.

Alaric began to tell them the news, but Seb cut him off. "Yeah, we heard." The conversation having carried to them at the other end of the house.

Doran's gaze flicked between them all, fast, assessing, calculating.

"How long have they been missing?" Doran asked.

"Possibly up to twelve hours," Alaric said.

A muscle feathered in Doran's jaw. "That's not good."

"No. Sanders is launching search and rescue from Fort Mackenzie, but we need to bring his team back and get some fresh eyes out there ASAP."

"I can have a portal open in five minutes. But what about Brin's brothers? They need to be informed. If you want, I can head over there once I've got everyone sorted from the fort."

Alaric nodded. "Thanks, that would be great," he replied, rubbing the back of his neck, the muscles there bunching into tight knots.

"I'll call Oliver. He needs to know too."

Sebastian cleared his throat. "What about the women? Holly, Mrs P and Jocelyn. They're Marcus' family. Shouldn't we…"

"No," Alaric snapped sharper than intended. He softened, but only barely. "Yes. But, let them sleep, for now. They'll know soon enough. At the moment there's nothing they can do to help, no point causing them more stress than necessary."

Narayan inclined his head. "True."

"Thank you." Alaric ran a hand through his hair. "God help us, I hope we're panicking over nothing."

But none of them believed that.

Everyone scattered in different directions, Seb and Philippe headed out to the forest with Doran, Narayan accompanying them as far as the forest path to Cadley, and Oliver's home, leaving Alaric alone in his study once more.

Picking up his phone, he dialled Oliver, although he suspected Narayan would be at his door before the phone finished dialling. Next, he called Saladin and Dray. If nothing else, he suspected he may need them here to help control the wyvern brothers when they arrived.

Doran strode out toward the forest without another word, his long stride making short work of the distance. His footsteps leaving barely discernible impressions on the dew coated grass. He didn't feel the cold. He hardly felt anything at all except the thundering pulse of dread beneath his ribs. The three vampires flanked him like dangerous wraiths, their own inner tension lending a menacing edge to their silent presence.

Reaching a clearing about a hundred meters inside the forest, Doran raised his hand and summoned his power. The air cracked like splitting stone, spiralling and twisting into a vertical sheet of shimmering light.

He stepped through.

The Canadian Arctic hit him like a physical wall, air so cold it flayed exposed skin raw. Wind howled, flattening the snow into shifting dunes beneath the dim pre-dawn sky.

Behind him stepped Seb and Philippe.

Sanders and the remaining lycan team turned toward the new arrivals instantly, weapons ready. Sanders' shoulders sagged with relief.

"Thank Fuck," Callum muttered, his breath fogging the air. "We've got nothing on radar, and the storm has buried most of the search zone."

"Are there any planes or choppers out looking for them?" Seb asked.

"No. Not yet. There's no point until after the sun's up. And to make matters worse, up here, there's only about six hours of decent daylight to search."

"Okay then. So how long before sunrise?" Philippe queried.

"Three hours. Then we'll have to hope the weather holds out."

"In that case, why don't we get you all back to the manor, you can warm up, clean up and grab a hot breakfast while you fill everyone in on what's happened." Seb suggested.

"My men will go back, I'm staying here." Sanders told him, his military stance as stoic as ever.

"With all due respect. Fuck no! Alaric, Oliver and the wyvern brothers are going to want to talk to you, not your men. Philippe and I will stay behind to co-ordinate things."

Seb had a point, Sanders conceded. Brin was his responsibility on this mission, it was also his responsibility to deal with her brothers. Heaven help him, they were either going to be understanding or use him as a dragon chew toy.

Sanders looked away toward the darkened airfield, aware that everyone was looking at him.

"Fine. Then let's move. The sooner we get home, the faster we can get back and into the air."

One by one they stepped through the portal.

The shift in temperature was immediate, a gut-punch of sensation as they left Canada's lethal chill behind and emerged beneath the early morning English sky. Moist, cold air replaced the razor-bite freeze, and the men visibly relaxed, but looked no less uneasy. They had never left a man behind, ever. This time however, they'd had no choice, and it didn't sit well with any of them.

"Never thought I'd be grateful for a British winter," Owen grumbled, rolling his wide shoulders. "Feels downright tropical." That was saying something since his regular environment was the tropics of Far North Queensland, Australia.

"This is where I'll leave you for now. I'm heading over to Avengard." Doran told them. "I should be back within the hour, depending on what happens with Raif and his brothers."

"Good luck," Callum told him, slapping him on the shoulder with sympathy. No one ever wants to be the bearer of bad news with a dragon.

Watching the weary troop of bloody and battered soldiers head back along the forest path, Doran turned away to open a new portal to Avengard and stepped through.

The citadel's great dining hall was warm and alive with morning chatter. The wyvern brothers, Raif, Wade, Seth, and Ky, each sat at the enormous table with their wives and Finn, Raif's eleven year-old son, whose curly hair stood up in wild tufts from sleep. While servants brought in platters of fruit, warm breads and pots of coffee.

"Sir, you have a visitor from the nephilim council." The servant told Raif quietly at his ear.

"Oh? At this time of the morning. Send him in." Raif swivelled in his chair to see who was paying them a visit.

The room fell silent when Doran appeared, his expression grim.

Raif rose first. "Doran? What's wrong? Is it Brin?"

The others looked up. Ky's fork froze halfway to his mouth. Seth stood immediately, and almost as one, all four brothers were standing in front of him.

Doran didn't mince words. "There's been a crash. We think. Brin's helicopter never returned to base."

Chairs scraped. Wives gasped softly. Finn's small brow pinched in concern before his mother pulled him close.

"What do you mean, *never returned*?" Seth demanded, his voice like rolling thunder.

"They found the armband, but were attacked by the Guild, along with some demons," Doran said. The accompanying growls had him taking a minor step backwards, just in case. He wasn't intimidated by them in the least, but he still wanted to keep all his body parts intact if one of them, probably Raif, lost his shit. "There was going to be a long wait for a chopper big enough to bring them all back together, and rather than risking having Brin there if the Guild or the demons came back, they opted to send her and Marcus, and an injured lycan back on an earlier flight, in a smaller chopper. Not long after they took off, a bad storm hit. Sanders' team made it back several hours later, but Brin's chopper didn't."

Raif's face drained of all colour before hardening into lethal resolve. "How long ago did this happen?"

"Maybe up to twelve hours, they don't know for certain."

Seth cursed viciously. Ky's hands balled into fists.

"We'll grab whatever gear we need and leave immediately." Wade suggested.

Their wives Kaitlyn, Yasmin and Branwen were already moving, their half-eaten breakfast discarded. "We're coming too." Kaitlyn told them, her tone rebuking any rebuttal.

"Me too." Finn told them in a defiant manner.

Doran bowed his head. "I'm sure that by now they'll be expecting you all. I have to return to Dunn Turidd to inform my uncle. I'll meet you back at Havenswood."

Raif clapped a hand briefly on his arm. "Thanks for letting us know."

As Doran left the dining room and headed for the citadel's main entrance and the forest beyond, the whole place seemed to come alive with activity and curses. Just two words, "Brin's missing," would have a ripple effect of upheaval and chaos throughout the whole city until such time she was found. Hopefully alive.

It was only about thirty minutes from the time that Alaric received the call from Sanders, that the once-silent house thrummed with activity. Oliver arrived first, along with several soldiers who'd remained behind from the mission, his imposing presence radiating his quiet strength. Soon after Sanders and his remaining team marched across the gardens from Savernake Forest, their boots cutting crisp lines through the grass. They were battle-worn, cold, and carrying the weight of regret, disappointment and failure.

Normally their arrival en masse, could be a little intimidating. However, here among the most powerful beings in this world, they were simply a group of grim-faced warriors.

Every man in the room carried his own version of distress, fear, guilt, anger and helplessness. It swirled about them like a building storm.

The clatter of heavy boots, clipped orders and tense voices echoed through the manor corridors, vibrating through the old stone and polished timber like a war drum. The noise was enough to wake the dead, and certainly enough to wake everyone else in the house.

Grace was the first to appear on the landing, hair sticking up like a disgruntled hedgehog, wrapped in an oversized dressing gown that nearly swallowed her whole.

She blinked blearily at the bustling foyer below. "Uh…why does it sound like World War Three just broke out?"

Holly appeared next, robe cinched tight, immediately stiffening at the sight of Oliver, Callum, and half the manor's male population pacing with grim purpose. Her gaze finding her husband, Sanders, her heart missing a beat at his grave expression.

Paige descended with Riley in tow, the boy rubbing his eyes and mumbling, "Did Aunt Cassie blow up the kitchen again?"

Cassie hurried to Alaric's side, bracing herself for the worst.

"What's going on?" she asked, her voice tight with dread.

Alaric stopped his pacing mid-stride, guilt flickering across his features for a fraction of a second before he masked it. "I didn't want to wake you. There was no point until we knew more."

Grace's stomach dropped. "Has something happened to Brin?" she asked, noting that she and Marcus seemed to be the only ones *not* in her dad's study.

Cassie's breath caught. "Alaric, what's happened?"

"Brin and Marcus are missing," he said quietly. "Their helicopter never made it back."

Paige moved to stand by Narayan, clutching his hand. Riley too moved to stand by his father. Behind her the women collectively inhaled, sharp, staggered breaths like they'd taken a blow to the ribs. Megan and Mrs P arrived moments later, both going pale at the news.

Lastly, Jocelyn, Marcus' mother joined the group. "What's all the noise about. A woman needs her beauty sleep."

"Marcus is missing," Alaric told her sympathetically.

"What? Oh, I'm sure he'll turn up somewhere." She replied, barely any concern in her tone.

Whether she noticed every eye in the room turn toward her, their stunned surprise at her attitude never registered in her demeanour, as she simply turned around and headed down the hallway toward the kitchen.

"Do you believe that?" Paige muttered, shaking her head.

Holly's brow furrowed deeply, her cheeks flushed with anger. "Yep. That's my mum. The most selfish, self-centred…" She huffed, leaving the rest unspoken, everyone was no doubt filling in the gaps with their own sentiments.

"Missing? What happened?" Paige whispered.

Once again, the story was relayed to the women.

Holly pressed a hand to her mouth. "Oh God…"

Riley looked up at his mum, eyes wide. "We'll find them, won't we?"

Paige swallowed hard. "Yes sweetheart, of course we will."

Outside, the sky cracked with the sound of four successive sonic booms, followed a minute later by several more.

Brin's brothers had arrived. And by the sounds of it, they didn't come alone.

The space in the large study was disappearing fast with the addition of the wyvern brothers, Doran who'd returned with his own wife, Zoe, and his uncle, Gwynn Ap Nudd, the nephilim High Lord.

Oliver stepped forward, tone firm and controlled but tinged with restrained emotion. "We've already begun organising a search. Sanders will return to the fort with fresh troops to co-ordinate the search with the locals, utilising their planes and helicopters. Raif, you could go along too if you want, but there's not much anyone can do for now, there's a very large search area to cover. You might all be more comfortable back at home. We can send word to you as we get news."

A low rumble echoed from the study doorway where the brothers stood, already dressed for battle in heavy dark leathers. Their expressions were carved from stone, hard and merciless.

"We'll be going to Canada, but not to sit around and do nothing. A few flimsy planes and choppers can't cover nearly enough ground. But, we can." Raif said, his voice colder than any Arctic wind. "We've brought a dozen of our soldiers. Between us we can cover a hundred miles in an hour and our eyes are far sharper than any of yours or the humans in those planes."

Mrs Philpot piped up, “Is that wise? Humans might see you?”

Seth’s lip curled into a humourless grin. “Let them.”

Narayan stepped forward. “Risking exposure will have consequences.”

Ky cracked his knuckles. “If the Elders have a problem with it, they can talk to my arse.”

Raif’s jaw flexed. “Our sister is out there.” His voice thickened with fury and worry. “I don’t give a flying fuck about consequences right now.”

Cassie stepped beside him, touching his arm. “We’ll find her. We will.”

“You’re damn right, we will,” Wade muttered darkly. “Preferably alive so she won’t haunt us for the rest of our lives. She likes to hold a grudge.” He said, trying to lighten the mood in the room.

Grace made a small sound, a snort of amusement.

Alaric forced himself to stay composed. “We’ll coordinate from here. I’ll keep all communications open with both realms.”

“And I’ll maintain a clear link from Fort MacKenzie,” Sanders added.

Grace wrapped her arms around herself. “What if they’re lying out there, hurt?”

Alaric looked at his daughter, his voice gentle but firm. “Grace, you know Marcus, he’s well trained in survival techniques. He’ll keep her safe, I’m certain of it.”

“And Brin’s stronger than she looks,” Seth said, rubbing absently at the back of his neck. “And stubborn enough to outlive all of us.”

“Let’s hope so,” Paige whispered.

Cassie squeezed her daughter’s shoulders, then looked toward the men again. “What exactly is the plan?”

Sanders outlined it concisely.

The air hung thickly, a short silence filling the study, too full of emotion for the early hour.

Then Alaric exhaled deeply. “Everyone who isn’t part of the planning or the search, stay here, eat something. Use the gym or pool. Do whatever you need to, to stay busy.”

Holly nodded numbly. “I’ll put a pot of coffee on.”

Mrs P wiped her eyes. "I'll make some breakfast. I assume no one's eaten yet?"

Paige hugged Riley close. "Come on, sweetheart, how about you go and get dressed."

"Mum, if Uncle Raif and all the other wyverns are going flying to find them, maybe Finn and I can too?" he asked, hope and excitement on his face. While Riley did have a pair of angel's wings, which he could use very well, and Finn was also a wyvern with his own pair of dragon wings. The two boys were just that, only eleven year-old boys.

"Not this time." Narayan told him, sympathising with his son's disgruntled response.

As Havenswood Manor surged into coordinated chaos, one truth weighed heavy in every heart; Every hour they remained out there, freezing, possibly wounded and alone, was another hour stolen from Brin and Marcus' chance of survival.

"Owen." Alaric called as the room began to clear of people.

"Yeah?"

"I have a proposition for you. I'm told you were stuck by one of the paralysing darts that may be carrying a virus."

"I was," he replied cautiously. "But I wasn't affected, I'm immune to all toxins."

"I know. That's why I want you to go to the Ukraine, to Gustav's headquarters where they're holding the lycan who was infected a few days ago. I'm hoping you can work with Alex to find a cure for the virus."

"I don't know how I can help. Like I said, I'm immune. Farrell would be a better candidate than me, he was hit too."

"And he was on the chopper with Brin and Marcus. If…when they're found, I'm sure he could help too, but in the meantime you're our best option. I've spoken to Alex already, he's still in the process of setting up a lab over there, but he thinks that your immunity is exactly what he needs to make the cure."

"He wants to use the live virus from the current victim over there, and needs any antibodies that I might be carrying, you mean?"

"I guess so, something like that. However it works, Alex has asked for you to head to the Ukraine to work with him."

"Alright," Owen replied, his voice grave but steady. "If you think I'll be of use, sure. I'm damn well of no use here at the moment."

"Good lad. Pack whatever you need, I'll get Doran or Gwynn to take you there later this morning."

Great, another cold climate. At least this time he'll be inside....even if he will be used as a human pin cushion. Regardless, he conceded, he was still doing better than Marcus, Brin, Farrell and their pilot.

15

Brin had never been great at sitting still at the best of times, and now, the storm-battered wilderness on the other side of the walls, and a six-foot-three lycan with the morals of a pirate and the body of a Greek God prowling the lodge like a caged tiger, her nerves needed somewhere to go.

So, she gave them jobs to do.

First, the dishes. She stacked the empty dishes from breakfast, rinsed out the mugs, and scrubbed the pan until the smell of bacon grease was replaced by dish soap and hot water. The lingering aroma of coffee still clung to the air, cozy and domestic, mixing with the faint smoky aroma of last night's fire. It should've been comforting. Instead, it only highlighted how surreal it all was, like they'd escaped a war, and crash landed into somebody else's off-grid holiday.

The fire they'd built the previous night had collapsed into a bed of glowing ash and blackened wood, but the stone hearth still radiated residual warmth. The thick log walls held it in, cocooning the main room in a steady, pleasant heat. Brin padded from window to window every few minutes, pretending to straighten curtains that didn't need straightening, her breath fogging faintly on the glass as she peered out.

Nothing but white. White sky, white drifts, white glare off the frozen river. No moving specks in the distance. No chop of rotor blades. No whine of engines.

No rescue.

"Stop it," she muttered at herself, tugging the curtain open fully and tying it back against its frame. "If someone was coming, you'd hear them."

And if they couldn't find them... That was a thought she refused to finish.

The uneaten remains of breakfast sat in a bowl on the counter, half a stack of pancakes and a few strips of bacon she'd been too full to finish. They'd gone cold and rubbery. She stared at them, chewing her lip.

Tossing the food in a bin outside probably wasn't wise, the smell might draw in wolves…or bears. The idea of a curious bear nosing around the windows made her stomach clench. "Come and get your free buffet here! When you're done with the scraps, feast on the juicy people inside."

In the end, she scraped the leftovers into a sealable container she'd found in a cupboard and shoved it into the fridge. Totally a problem for the future. Maybe if they were there long enough, she could befriend a few of the four legged locals and hand feed them their leftovers.

Sure.

That was like suggesting hellhounds might take up knitting.

When the kitchen had no more excuses to offer, she headed downstairs.

The basement greeted her with a selection of new smells. Old timber, the sharp tang of diesel seeping from the generators, undercutting the musty dampness, suggesting the place had been sealed up for months between visits. Her breath puffed out in white wisps as she descended the last few steps. Down here the cold concrete beneath her feet, gave off as much chill from the buried earth beneath, as the fire upstairs gave off warmth through its stone hearth.

The big generator thudded steadily, vibrating the floor faintly under her boots. Behind her, the smaller one chugged more quietly, still hooked to the chest freezer humming faithfully in the corner. She couldn't help thinking of all the movies that started with a freezer in the basement of a home in the middle of nowhere, and ended in blood and bad decisions.

"Relax. There's only meat here, not murder," she told herself, lifting the lid just long enough to check inside. Moose, caribou, bags of vegetables, a small mountain of bacon. No severed fingers. Always a plus.

Brin pulled out a notebook she'd found in a kitchen drawer, clicked a pen and began taking inventory.

"Freezer," she murmured. "Moose steaks - lots. Caribou - assorted bits. Veg - peas, beans, carrots, potatoes. Enough bacon to feed an army…or feed one lycan for a month."

She moved to the shelves hidden behind the curtain of heavy fabric. The pantry was a prepper's dream, rows of canned tomatoes, beans, soups, stew, dried fruit and tinned fruit, bags of rice and pasta, jars of pickled…something green. She wrinkled her nose as she passed one cloudy jar. And alcohol. Several cases of wine and two cases of whisky.

Tallying up the horde, she concluded they had a ridiculous amount of everything. "There're enough rations here to last weeks, maybe months, if we're careful. That's good." She muttered to herself.

Her voice sounded small against the low ceiling, but the act of listing things grounded her. Numbers were something she could control. Two people. One lodge. And enough food to outlast a very stubborn winter.

Assuming they didn't die of frostbite, demon or animal attacks, or strangle each other first.

Taking a seat on one of the lower steps on the staircase, Brin scribbled down rough portion estimates, doing quick mental maths on how long the supplies would last if no one found them before spring. Every line of ink seemed to add a little weight to the reality. They might be here a while. Certainly long enough to share some decent meals. Long enough for more arguments. And long enough for…other things that might happen between them that she absolutely was not going to think about.

As soon as Brin tried not to think about Marcus in the bathroom that morning, naked, palming his heavy erection as it jutted proudly from his body, its broad head flushed with a bead of moisture dampening its tip, she couldn't help but groan in frustration at the flush of heat that pulsed at her clit, making her squirm on the step uncomfortably.

Seriously though, how could she not think of him, he had the most magnificent physique she'd ever seen, and he knew it too. It was in his cocky grin, in the smug glint in his eyes and the over confidence in his stance. He knew he got under her skin, and he prided himself in making her feel uncomfortable.

The diesel smell thickened the longer she stayed in the basement. Her head began to develop a faint throb, and she rubbed at her temple. Upstairs was warmth and light. Down here, was necessity and fumes. Opting for the former, she finished tallying the last column and snapped the notebook shut. "Right, inventory done. Survivability - cautiously optimistic. Sanity - questionable," she muttered to herself. Using the sturdy railing to pull herself up, she began the climb to the top of the stairs. At the halfway point she paused, listening.

Silence, except for the muted thump of the generator and the occasional creak from the lodge's timbers settling. Climbing the last few steps, she stopped again on the landing.

"Marcus?" she called.

No answer.

Her pulse kicked up a notch as she reached the main room, scanning automatically for his large, irritating shape. The couch was empty, the blanket folded in a lumpy heap. His boots were gone, along with his rifle, but his jacket still hung on a hook beside the front door.

She hurried to the front window and searched the white expanse. Following a line of boot prints, she found him.

He was a dark figure against the never-ending white, pacing along the edge of the forest like an animal patrolling a fence line. He wore no heavy jacket, no hat, no gloves. Just his trousers and a t-shirt stretched over those broad shoulders of his, like it was a mild winter's day instead of the middle of the Arctic.

"Idiot," she breathed, shaking her head, her hand flattening against the glass.

The cold outside was the kind that stripped you of your breath and your skin, if you gave it half a chance. Even from where she stood close to the window, despite the heat of a fire warming the air, she could feel the icy bite radiating a chill that made her shiver.

Outside, the wind caught stray snowflakes and flung them sideways, yet Marcus moved about as though the sub zero temperature was nothing more than an inconvenience. He trudged a hundred metres one way along the tree line, turned on his heel, and trudged back. Over and over. Sometimes he veered farther into the trees, sometimes he widened his loop out around the cabin, never staying too far from the lodge.

Or was it that he chose not to stray too far from her?

If that was the case, no doubt it was only out of duty since she was still wearing that damned armband. Any feelings he had toward her personally, were those of loathing. Offering her a kind word wasn't in his vocabulary. Not when tormenting and annoying her seemed to bring him so much enjoyment.

So why should she worry about him out there, exposed to the elements like he was. He wasn't a child, if he didn't want to wear a jacket, that was his choice.

He's your…Bodyguard. Babysitter. Thorn in your side. Take your pick, she told herself, letting out a huff of exasperation.

Her concern definitely had nothing to do with the way his muscles rippled beneath his shirt as it clung to his torso, or the memory of his ridiculously gorgeous naked body in the bathroom...

Heat prickled under her skin at the memory. She scowled and spun away from the window, as if putting her back to him would somehow shut off the treacherous thoughts her brain kept replaying.

"Don't do this to yourself. He has a girlfriend," she muttered to herself, yanking a pan from the sink's drying rack with a little more force than necessary. "He's off-limits. Emotionally, physically and morally. Completely off-limits. So, stop it."

Her traitorous imagination ignored the order.

Fine. Then she'd drown her thoughts in domesticity.

She laid out the smorgasbord of ingredients on the counter, more bacon, potatoes to slice and fry, a couple of cans of tomatoes, beans and a large portion of the casserole meat, along with some flour to maybe bake something later if she had the energy. The thought of a warm, hearty meal that didn't come straight from a tin, made her chest ache, in a good way.

She lit the stove, waited for the pan to heat, and listened to the sizzle as she laid the bacon down. The fat crackled and spat, sending up a divine smell that threaded through the lodge. Soon, the kitchen filled with the sound of frying and the scent of comfort food, thick and rich.

It helped. A little.

Every few minutes she drifted back toward the window under the guise of washing something or checking something. Every time, Marcus was still there, a dark figure carving the landscape into manageable pieces, his movements growing sharper, more frustrated as the hours wore on.

"What are you doing out there?" she whispered to his distant figure. "Walking off your bad mood or thinking up something new to annoy me with later?"

Her chest squeezed. He'd been…off, all morning. Moody wasn't a strong enough word. Agitated, restless, like he'd been wound too tight and couldn't find the pressure release valve.

Brin clenched the wooden spoon, stirring viciously at the food in the pot. If he would just talk to her, tell her what was wrong, she might be able to help. But this was Marcus. Talking was not his default setting.

He's fine, she told herself. He's a lycan. A soldier.

He also saved your life. Twice.

Her throat tightened.

Brin inhaled deeply, filling her lungs with the smell of food cooking and a fresh pot of coffee. "He'll be fine," she said aloud. "He's too stubborn to freeze to death out there."

Outside, Marcus welcomed the cold like a punishment.

Or, he tried to.

He strode out of the lodge just before midday, fury and something more dangerous gnawing at his insides. The first blast of frigid air had hit him head-on, stinging his cheeks, biting at his ears, turning the moisture in his nose to ice. For all of thirty seconds it felt glorious, shocking his overheated skin and rattling his sensitised nerves into submission.

Then the relief faded, leaving the same itch under his skin. The same heat in his blood.

And the cold? He barely felt it.

He pulled in a breath until his lungs burned, fogging the air in front of him. "Come on," he muttered to himself. "Snap out of it."

The wolf inside him prowled, restless and…wrong.

That was the part that scared him.

It wasn't like any other agitation he'd felt before. Normally, his wolf stirred with clean, sharp purpose; attack, defend, hunt and protect. This…this felt muddied. Like someone had rewired the connection between man and wolf, and forgotten to label the switches.

The bite on his wrist throbbed, a dull ache edged with heat. Under his sleeve, the rash had darkened, swirling lines threading the skin like faint, smoke-coloured veins. They stayed contained in a rough circle around the puncture marks, not creeping up his arm. He checked every so often to inspect the rash with clinical detachment.

It's not spreading. Thank goodness for small mercies, he thought.

He counted it as a victory while ignoring the rest, the way the patch of skin seemed to pulse faintly when he thought about Brin. The way his wolf reacted every time he stepped farther from the cabin, as though there was an invisible leash threaded through his bones tugging him back.

By early afternoon, annoyance had curdled into alarm.

Entering the shelter of the forest, the thick pines creaked under their heavy snow loads. Here, the wind was broken into gusts and whispers, the air full of the soft hiss of falling flakes shaken from branches.

Marcus closed his eyes, drawing in several deep breaths, he rolled his shoulders to relieve some of the built-up tension that had accumulated there. He needed more relief than that simple manoeuvre could offer. He needed to run, free and wild. Blow off some of the steam pumping in his veins.

Marcus reached for his wolf.

The transformation came on like it always did, bones loosening, muscles tensing, something vast and ancient rising in his blood, stepping forward with a snarl of eager relief. His skin prickled, the first twinge of change flaring along his fingers and spine.

Then he hit a wall.

Pain lanced through his body, not sharp but heavy, like trying to push a door that had been welded shut. His wolf surged, confused and frustrated, claws scraping against whatever barrier had formed between them. Marcus staggered, bracing a hand against a tree, and gritted his teeth.

"Again," he growled.

He tried. Again and again. Calling forth the shift, coaxing, ordering, swearing.

All he managed was a partial change rippling beneath his skin.

So close, but the shift never fully took. His nails thickened, then smoothed back. His teeth ached, his vision tried to sharpen and failed.

The block held.

Sweat broke out down his spine despite the cold. Panic nipped at the edges of his mind, claws sharp and mean.

"No," he snarled, breath coming fast. "No, no, no. What the fuck is going on?"

Lycans didn't just…lose their wolf. It wasn't an illness you caught, something you shook off with rest and chicken soup. The beast was built in, born into his blood and bones.

His hand clenched around his wrist. The skin there burned hotter, itching with maddening insistence. He scratched at it. Rubbed at it. All he achieved was a bleeding rash and even more frustration and anger than before.

"This is your fault," he told the unseen serpent, as if the armband could hear him from where it sat coiled on Brin's arm. "You and your fucking bite and your fucking prophecy."

The last word hung in the air like frost.

Prophecy.

He hated that word. Hated what it implied. That his life wasn't his own, that his choices were pre-written into some ancient rhyme about dragons and wolves being bonded together.

"Not happening," he muttered, pushing away from the tree. "I'll destroy the fucking armband before I let it…"

His stomach twisted. The thought of the armband destroyed made his wolf rear with furious denial.

"Oh, that's new," he snapped at himself, stalking out of the trees again. "Fantastic. Now you like the magic snake jewellery?"

Marcus strode along the tree line, a violent shiver climbing his spine. However, it wasn't relief of his overheated skin in the frigid air.

Instead, a feverish heat crawling under his flesh, adding a faint lightness to his head.

Was he sick? That made no sense. His wolf burned off infections like tissue paper. At least it did when their connection worked without his current limitations.

From the corner of his eye, he caught movement in the cabin, a flicker behind the pane of glass in the window. Brin, watching. Checking on him. Again.

His wolf instantly calmed, and the heat in his blood eased a fraction.

Marcus swore under his breath and tore his gaze away. The last thing he needed was more proof that being near her made things better. He'd already had an awkward kiss, and an even more awkward bathroom encounter to complicate that truth.

And then there was his other problem.

He glanced down with a grimace. The cold should have taken care of that. Any normal bloke would've lost interest the second the wind hit his balls. But he wasn't normal, and his body hadn't gotten the memo. His turgid arousal continued unabated, adding yet another layer of misery and uncertainty to his already infuriating situation.

He'd tried dealing with it in the bathroom earlier. His hand, his usual no-nonsense solution, had done nothing but wind him up tighter. It wasn't just physical need, he realised with reluctant dread. Nor was it just a case of blood flow to his heavy length. Something deeper was entwined, driving his need, something he didn't have a label for beyond the one he refused to say.

Bond.

"Fuck that," he muttered, kicking at a snowdrift hard enough to spray powder in a wide arc. "You're horny, not cursed."

But even the self-mockery rang hollow.

He paced back and forth, along a hundred-metre stretch of the trees until the snow was churned and packed by his boots. Every so often he'd widen his route, circling the lodge, scanning the sky for any sign of aircraft. None came. The only sounds were wind, the distant creak of ice, the occasional caw of a crow flying overhead like a smudge on the clouds.

Each time he drifted too far from the cabin, far enough that he couldn't see the windows, his wolf snapped awake, agitation spiking so sharply he could taste it in the back of his throat. His chest tightened, his breathing became shallow and his skin prickled with the urge to turn back.

It was a stalemate. He needed distance, while his wolf needed proximity. Neither got what they wanted. Compromise was pacing within sight of the lodge like a very angry, very confused metronome.

By the time the low winter sun began its lazy slide toward the horizon, the muscles in his legs burned agreeably from fatigue. The nerves under his skin did not. The heat remained, pulsing in time with the mark on his wrist.

He stopped at the edge of the trees and leaned one shoulder against a trunk, dragging in a slow breath.

Through the nearest window, he could see Brin moving around the kitchen, haloed in warm light. She was at the stove, stirring something, hair tied up and jaw set in that determined line he was getting used to. The room behind her glowed, orange and gold, radiating comfort.

It hit him, abruptly, how stark the divide was.

Out here, cold, isolation, the endless monotony of snow and sky.

In there, warmth, food, the soft clink of dishes and the crackle of fire.

And Brin.

His fingers flexed against the bark.

"I'm going to have to go back in there eventually," he told himself. "Play nice. Eat dinner. Pretend everything's fine."

His wolf answered with a low, satisfied purr.

His erection twitched unhelpfully.

Marcus scrubbed a hand over his face. "Yeah, that's going to be a fucking breeze."

He pushed off the tree and started back toward the lodge as the last light bled out of the sky, a dark silhouette moving toward the only pool of warmth for miles, and toward the woman he desperately didn't want to need.

The Arctic sky faded from pale grey, bleeding with the shadowed landscape stretching out toward the horizon as the last sliver of daylight began to fade.

Sanders stood on the windy tarmac of Fort Mackenzie, collar up, hands numb despite his gloves, his comms crackling with static and strained voices. Behind him, the snow-swept runway glinted under flickering floodlights, endless white stretching out into nothingness.

"Chopper One, report current status," Sanders said, tightening the earpiece against the rising wind.

A burst of static crackled, followed by a weary voice. "Fuel's at fifteen percent. Visibility's dropping fast. We can make one more pass, but that's it."

Sanders shut his eyes briefly. "Negative. Return to base. You wouldn't spot a bloody rainbow in this weather. We'll resume at first light."

Another voice cut in, the second aircraft offering a similar report.

They had started the search only fifty miles from their take-off point at Mount Odin, sweeping back and forth in grid fashion. No heat signatures, no radio noise, no movement. "We're heading back now."

"Copy that," Sanders replied, the words leaving a bitter taste in his mouth. "Good work today. We'll have better luck tomorrow."

He lowered the radio, exhaling through his teeth. Beside him, Callum scrubbed a hand over his face, exhaustion etched into every line.

"No sign of them yet," he murmured. "I thought…hell, I thought we'd see something."

"We will," Sanders said automatically, even though his stomach churned.

The sky tore open again as another wyvern broke through the atmosphere, wings beating hard, scales shimmering like forged metal in the fading light.

Raif was the last of the brothers to call off his search.

Another sweep? One more? his instincts snarled.

But even wyvern eyes, supernaturally sharp, were no match for the approaching darkness. The whitewashed landscape swallowed everything, no tracks, no movement, no clues. Just frozen silence stretching into infinity.

Ky's voice carried over the wind. "Raif. Enough. We'll find her tomorrow."

Seth circled down, voice ragged. "He's right. We're flying blind."

Wade punched through the cloud layer, swearing under his breath. "I hate this bloody frozen hellhole."

One by one, the wyvern soldiers vanished, punching through the atmosphere back to Fey, their enormous bodies disappearing with a sonic boom of the cracking dimensional barrier. The brothers shifted mid-air, only feet from the ground back at Havenswood Manor, landing lithely on the lawn in the early evening.

Their expressions were grim, eyes burning with frustration and fear.

"Nothing," Raif said simply as they approached the manor, marching past Narayan who'd waited for them on the path.

That single word felt like a knife to his heart.

The manor was dimly lit, its tall windows glowing warm against the cool night outside. But the mood inside was anything but warm.

The moment the wyvern brothers stepped into the foyer, all conversation ceased.

Alaric moved toward them first. "Anything?"

Raif shook his head once. "We've covered everything we could before dark. Nothing yet though."

Grace wrung her hands anxiously. "You're going back out again tomorrow though, aren't you?"

"Absolutely." Ky told her, patting her shoulder gently, before dropping heavily onto a chair. "Just after sunrise." Northern Canadian sunrise, not their English sunrise, which was more than five hours later than England.

Wade paced back and forth through the room. "We're not giving up."

Seth's jaw worked. "We'll keep looking until we find them. Even if I have to rip that entire frozen continent apart."

Cassie placed a gentle hand on his arm, but it did nothing to soften the tension radiating off him.

Alaric cleared his throat. "We're not giving up hope." He said, continuing in a reserved tone, "I spoke with Emil Wagstaff while you were out."

Several heads lifted.

"He's been doing some digging and learned something that will hopefully prove…useful." Alaric hesitated. "Apparently the Guild is still searching for Brin too."

"What?" Wade snarled. "Why in the seven hells would *they* still be looking for her?"

"Because they're convinced she's alive," Alaric said grimly. "And they want the armband. According to Emil, their certainty is absolute. How they know, he doesn't know."

Ky crossed his arms. "If they're confident she's alive and they're still looking, that means they haven't found any bodies."

A breath of hope fluttered through the room.

"Emil's also identified the demons you encountered," Alaric went on. "They're called *Scree*. They're trackers."

Seth let out a humourless huff. "Great. So, we've got frostbite, storms, a crashed helicopter, and demon bloodhounds on the loose."

"Emil is trying to get more information about them," Alaric finished. "He'll report back the moment he learns anything."

No one spoke for a long moment.

Outside, the gentle wind scraped across the windows with the rustle of dried leaves scraping the paved path outside.

Inside, the air seemed to thicken, anxiety, determination, and a tiny spark of stubborn hope all mixing in equal measure.

Narayan poured tea into a mug and set it beside Paige, who hadn't moved since the brothers walked in. "We'll find them," he said gently.

Paige nodded, though her eyes were glassy. "I know. They're strong," she whispered. "Both of them. They'll hold on until we get there, I'm sure of it."

Grace wrapped her arms around herself, her voice brittle. "Just, tell me again. Someone out there is *sure* they're alive?"

"Yes," Alaric confirmed. "Even if it's the wrong someone."

Ky cracked his knuckles. "Then that's enough for me."

The brothers drifted together like shadows, four mountains of muscle, filled with fury and determination.

"We'll head out there again at dawn," Raif said, his voice an order and a promise.

Sanders nodded. "My team's ready."

Doran leaned against the doorframe. "I'll be ready too."

Paige squeezed his hand. "Anything you need, we're all here to help, any way we can."

Across the room, even Jocelyn paused her dramatic sighing long enough to look concerned, for half a second, before huffing her way into the kitchen muttering about needing her evening tea. Holly shook her head sadly. She had held higher hopes her mother would feel more concern for her son. Regrettably, she was wrong.

But no one bothered wasting their ire on her. Not tonight.

Tonight, all attention was fixed on maps, strategy, and the burning hope that tomorrow might bring better news.

The kind that ended with warm arms around missing loved ones…not cold bodies in the snow.

Havenswood Manor settled into a tense quiet as midnight approached. Fires crackled in several rooms. Boots were lined near radiators. Coffee brewed in regular cycles. Maps were rolled and unrolled. Equipment checked and re-checked.

Everyone moved with purpose, but voices were hushed, subdued. Movements slow and lethargic.

They would not give up. Not now. Not ever.

And though fear stalked every corner, something else lingered too…Hope.

Hope that Brin and Marcus were alive.

Hope that they were together.

Hope that tomorrow, finally, someone would spot something, a plume of smoke, a flicker of movement, a shape or splash of colour against the snow.

Hope that they could bring them home.

Alive.

16

Grey light seeped through the frost-fogged windows of the lodge, dull and cold. The air smelled faintly of woodsmoke, reminding her that this home wasn't hers, and the safety it was providing, felt increasingly temporary.

Brin rubbed her eyes and yawned as she descended the stairs slowly, muscles stiff and sore from another night of restless sleep, plagued by memories of the previous few days, replaying over and over in her mind whenever she closed her eyes. And when she did manage to doze off, she was tormented by dreams of Marcus' hard, naked, and impossibly tempting body, waking only to roll over and pretend none of it mattered, that *he* didn't matter to her.

She hoped if she told herself that often enough, she might actually begin to believe it.

Pigs might fly too, she sighed miserably.

The one thing she was certain about, she was stuck, alone, with Marcus. The one man who had the power to turn her world upside down just by breathing the same air as her. Why was it that he hated her so much? She'd never understood. What had she ever done to offend him to the extent that he'd gone out of his way to either completely ignore her, or when he couldn't do that, he went out of his way to piss her off. It just didn't make sense.

Not that she was going to waste any time on that thought this morning, her sleep deprived mind felt as fogged over as the cabin's windows.

The main room was warm, the fire steady now, but the man standing near it…wasn't.

Marcus looked carved from misery and irritation. Dark circles bruised under his eyes. His jaw was clenched so tightly she wondered how it hadn't cracked. His posture was a coil of tension, shoulders hunched like he couldn't find a position to stand that didn't make something hurt.

"Good morning." She told him tentatively, her eyes watching him, assessing his mood warily.

"Morning." He grunted back.

"I'm putting the pot on for some coffee, would you like some?"

"Umm, yeah. Thanks." He replied absently.

"Are you okay, you look like you haven't slept a wink all night." She took a step closer toward where he stood by the fireplace, but he took a step further away.

Okay, she thought. They were off to a great start this morning.

"Do you think they'll be looking for us today?"

"I fucking hope so."

"Our helicopter crashed two days ago, surely they'll find us today, won't they?"

Marcus wanted to reassure her, calmly and politely, but what came out of his mouth was the complete opposite. "How the fuck would I know. Do I look like a mind reader to you?"

"A simple yes or no, would've been sufficient," she snapped back. "I know how much you hate it that I'm the one here with you, no doubt you wish it was your girlfriend, Cindy…Candy…or whatever her name is," she waved a hand to discard her as insignificant. "But, suck it up, buster. Whether you like it or not, you're stuck with me."

Yeah, that was exactly what he was afraid of.

Marcus looked down at his wrist discretely, the rash looked as red and raw as it had yesterday, and the same as it had an hour ago when he last checked it. Only, now the swirling black lines beneath his skin had begun to thicken.

This was not good. Not good at all.

Even so, he covered it up with his long sleeved shirt and turned toward Brin. "I need coffee, not a lecture." He snapped before he could rein in his temper, forcing a half-hearted, lopsided smile in an attempt to backtrack on his statement, which in hindsight, probably looked more like a spiteful sneer. He wanted to kick himself. There wasn't a single thing that he did or said that didn't come out wrong.

"Is that so. Well, you can get your own coffee. I'm going to have a shower." She told him in a cold, hard tone.

His head jerked to give her a sideways glance. "Fine. Whatever."

Turning on her heel, she stomped toward the bathroom, slamming the door behind her and locking it.

Marcus didn't move, he just watched her walk away. More specifically, he watched the way her hips swayed provocatively as she walked away, watched the way the silken strands of her long red hair bounced and brushed against her skin, drawing his eyes down lower toward the small of her waist enticingly.

It took more effort than he would have liked to tear his eyes away, turning to face the fireplace to stare down into the crackling fire in self-loathing.

He really was an arsehole. He couldn't deny it, nor could he change it. Especially it seemed, now. With every passing hour, he was feeling less and less like himself. He was doing his best to appear stable, in control, but he was barely holding it together.

He needed to be doing something, anything to keep his mind distracted. Coffee, he thought. That was a good start.

Opting to leave the warmth of the open fire, he headed into the kitchen and lit the stove.

The moment Brin stepped under the hot spray, her breath trembled out of her.

The water was blissfully hot, almost scalding, turning her skin pink and loosening muscles that had been knotted since the crash. She let it run over her face, her hair, her shoulders, until the heat finally cracked something inside her chest.

A whimper escaped, then a full sob.

The sound echoed off the tiled walls, swallowed by steam.

She pressed her forehead against the wall, hot water pounding over her neck as tears streamed freely, safely. Away from Marcus. Away from his anger. Away from the interminable fear that lurked in her gut like a dark shadow.

They were lost, stranded and alone. Marcus was acting strangely, stranger than usual, and she didn't know how to help him. Or if he'd even let her.

And beneath all of that was the traitorous truth.

She cared what he thought about her. She enjoyed his company despite his attitude toward her, and how sick was that. She was a total masochist. She had to be, right? To want to spend time with a man who despised her. Even when he was being a complete dick, he turned her insides into a syrupy mess, and heated parts of her that hadn't been touched by a man in a very long time.

Maybe that was her problem. Not having had sex in so long, her sex drive was in overdrive, making even Marcus seem attractive.

Regardless, Brin had no intention of leaving the bathroom in a hurry. Definitely not until she had her fickle emotions under control.

Standing beneath the warmth and solitude of the shower, she let the tears continue to fall. Alone. She was always alone.

Marcus waited in the main room by the fire, pacing back and forth as he polished off his third cup of coffee. Not the best move he decided, having now added caffeine jitters to his already lengthy repertoire of emotional and neurological defects…and a very full bladder.

He waited another fifteen minutes, and then waited a few more. By this time his urgency had increased to a point where he was either going to have to find relief outside, or he needed to get in that bathroom.

He considered his first option, quickly discarding it. While he had no problem being outside in the cold, he preferred to keep his pants on in sub zero temperatures. The way that wind had whipped up over the past hour, he wasn't all that keen to find out if it was true that arctic winds such as these, could freeze his pee mid-stream…and his dick.

He continued to pace back and forth, only now he was walking the length of the corridor outside the bathroom.

Just the thought of her under that hot spray of the shower with her hands between her thighs, her nipples beading, her hips swaying. It made him insane with lust. Or was it his wolf's libido that was going crazy? He honestly couldn't tell.

The end result was the same. His pissy mood continued, kicking up a notch to become irrationally outraged.

"Brin. Enough. You've been in there over an hour."

"Really? You didn't seem to care about hogging the bathroom when it was you in here for an hour yesterday." She called back, her own mood improving at the sound of his surly growl on the other side of the door.

"Brin!"

"Oh, for God's sake. I'll be out in two minutes."

Almost immediately, pounding rattled the door.

"Brin! Open the damn door!"

She smiled to herself, wickedly satisfied. "Just a moment!"

"You've been in there forever…"

"Let's just call this payback, shall we?" Taking another couple of minutes to fix her hair and add another coat of lipstick.

"Brin…"

She took her sweet time before finally unlocking the door.

Brin opened the bathroom door and stepped into the hallway, followed by a stream of vaporous steam, lightly scented with the soap, shampoo, facial creams, body lotions, and just the faintest hint of her own natural body scent. The last of which tormented Marcus' senses far more than he wanted to admit.

It was tantalising, tempting and tormenting.

His skin began to itch as his wolf stirred, his mouth felt dry, and his blood pulsed ferociously toward the organ beneath his belt line. The combination was sheer torture, but did Brin care? No! She didn't even seem to notice the effect she was having on him.

Pushing past her to get into the bathroom, Marcus growled, a fierce sound that came from deep within his chest.

"I don't care if you don't like me," she muttered at Marcus without looking away from him. "The last time I checked, the path to heaven wasn't through your yard."

Marcus' smile was closer to a snarl, tainted by bitterness and the frustration of his inner struggle. "No, it's through yours. If I tended your garden, I'd have you calling me God. Not that I would…" his gaze dipped, wicked and defensive, "…that bush of yours probably has thorns."

"Wait. What? That had come out completely wrong, you've twisted what I meant," Brin said under her breath, furious with herself for caring how he'd misinterpreted her.

"Unless you want to do the honours and hold this for me," he said.

Brin's eyes glued to his hands as they unfastened the top button on his pants and slid down the zipper. It wasn't until he placed his hand between the flaps to pull it out, that she seemed to snap out of her trance-like state. Without even realising it, she'd followed him back into the bathroom. Her cheeks burned with heat, she opened her mouth, then closed it again, turning about, she almost ran from the bathroom.

Having relieved the pressure off his brain with that simple deed of emptying his bladder, Marcus stripped off and turned on the shower.

Brin listened to the water begin to flow, listened too as the shower curtain slid across the railing, open and then closed.

"Fucking hell!" he howled as the cold water hit him. "Brin!"

She'd used up all the hot water, and was she proud of herself? Abso-freaking-lutely. She chuckled all the way down the hall.

Disappointingly, it didn't stop him from having an equally long shower. She thought she'd finally got the better of him. Damn it!

Brin's stomach grumbled, it seemed that all her clashing emotions had built up an appetite, so she set to making something to eat. And it kept her busy. Anything was better than being stuck with nothing but her conflicting thoughts for company.

Logic shouted… *He's dangerous…A big mistake!*

But desire whispered…*You need him.*

Marcus was straight jacket material. So how did she find him so…sexy? Why was she so attuned to him? Her body ached for him. He actually made her dizzy when he was near, as if she was intoxicated.

Focus! She berated herself.

She had to get away from him.

She should want nothing to do with the infuriating bastard. Frustratingly, even as her mind rejected him, her body ached for him. Her skin felt tight and itched for his touch, her flesh prickled with goosebumps and her insides heated to fever pitch.

Oh, and the man smelled good. Why couldn't he smell like fertiliser and old socks, or something else equally as vile. But no. He smelled earthy and natural, like the forest after rain. He'd make a fantastic air freshener, she thought.

Shutting down her thoughts, she poured her energy into cooking. It wasn't something she thought she'd enjoy doing, she'd probably only cooked a meal half a dozen times without supervision before. But, to her surprise, she really was finding it both cathartic and relaxing. She could stab a piece of meat, over and over, pound out her frustration on a lump of dough, and in the end, she could eat it. What more could she ask for, it would make perfect therapy, she thought.

She heard the squeak of the bathroom door open and waited for him to appear in the kitchen to give her a lecture. Nothing. He didn't appear.

A few minutes later, metal clanged somewhere in the cabin.

Brin frowned, assuming he'd found something to fix, in an effort to keep himself busy.

"Marcus…?"

No answer.

More clanging. More muttering. And then…nothing. Silence.

Curiously, Brin headed toward the sound of the noise, the bathroom.

She walked along the corridor, rubbing her hands dry on a towel, and froze.

The bathroom door was gone.

As in…completely gone. Removed.

"Marcus!" she shrieked. "What the hell happened to the door!?"

From behind her, he strolled in with the self-satisfied swagger of a man who had done something deeply petty and immensely satisfying, and leaned against the empty door frame.

"Consider this a lesson," he said smugly. "Bathroom hogs lose bathroom rights."

"You…you…barbaric caveman!"

He crossed his arms proudly. "Thank you."

"You are horrible!"

"And you used all the hot water."

"So, you removed the door?"

"Yes."

"I hate you. Put it back!"

"No." He replied, absolutely unbothered by her anger.

She stormed past him, cheeks burning. "You're unbelievable."

He followed her into the kitchen, no shame, no remorse, only to freeze when he saw what she'd made.

The table was covered with food. A hearty stew, freshly fried potatoes, and a loaf of bread she'd baked from scratch, which looked every bit as good as it smelled.

Marcus went very still.

His jaw flexed.

And, for the tiniest moment, guilt touched his eyes.

Then his stomach growled loud enough to echo.

Brin folded her arms contritely. "Hungry?"

He glared at her. But the edge of his snarl softened.

He wouldn't thank her, she knew. He'd rather gnaw off his own leg.

But as he stepped close enough to dish himself a bowl, she caught the faintest, smallest mutter under his breath, so low she couldn't be sure she wasn't imagining it.

"…smells good."

It was the nicest thing he'd said to her in days.

Not that she was going to point it out. But her cheeks warmed anyway. She was happy to take a win wherever she could get it, no matter how small.

Brin needed air untainted by Marcus' scent and mood swings. She waited until he filled his plate and took a seat, before Brin slipped out onto the verandah.

Unless he inhaled his food, and she wouldn't put it past him, he was a Neanderthal after all, she had at least five minutes of privacy.

The cold slapped her instantly.

The sky had darkened through the morning, turning ominous. Heavy, churning clouds rushed toward them from the northwest, moving fast in the blustering wind.

"Oh no…" she whispered.

Another storm.

A big one.

Which meant no rescue today.

Her chest tightened.

She lasted another ten seconds before retreating back inside.

Marcus stomped outside only minutes later, cursing under his breath, although today he was at least wearing his jacket.

But he didn't stay out long.

Not even five minutes passed before he barrelled back inside, jaw tight, icicles already forming in the stubble of his beard and lashes.

"The weather's gone to shit," he grunted.

"You just work that out, did you?" she replied lightly.

"Don't get smart."

"Then stop giving me ammunition."

He glared. She smiled sweetly.

Thunder rumbled through the valley, and snow began to fall in thick, swirling sheets, adding more depth covering the landscape, and also the cabin. The back of the building, sitting on the higher side of the land, had been swallowed up entirely by the snow, having built up exponentially with the past few storms, leaving nothing visible at all at the rear. The stone chimney on the roof poked through the thick snow deposit, emitting a wispy smoke plume which blended in with the dark clouds. Only the front of the building remained relatively free of the mountainous snowy deposits. Every new snowstorm made any search for them that much more difficult, with the cabin becoming almost indistinguishable from their surroundings.

Outside, snow fell intermittently and the wind continued in fitful gusts.

Inside, the two of them stood facing each other in simmering silence, trapped together with the weather closing in and tensions rising.

There was a storm brewing outside…and an even bigger one building between them.

"I'd like to make a proposal," Brin said.

"What kind of proposal?" Marcus eyed her suspiciously.

"I propose a truce, at least for today. We're stuck inside together until this storm passes, and I'd rather try and get along, if possible."

Marcus looked at her doubtfully but nodded his agreement.

"Great. In that case, pick your poison," she told him, pulling from behind her back two bottles, one being whisky, the other red wine.

"Hey, I like your way of thinking. Give me the whisky," he smiled, a broad, uncensored grin.

Brin's smile was just as relaxed. "I'll get some glasses." She told him.

"Fuck that. Just give me the bottle," he said, reaching out his hand to take the bottle from her, walking around to an armchair beside the fire and cracked the lid.

"Okay then."

Brin followed his lead, taking a seat in the opposite armchair and unscrewed the top on the bottle of wine.

She stared in stunned awe at the smile upon his face. If she thought he was gorgeous with a frown, he was breathtaking with a smile, and those infuriatingly kissable lips were enough to torment any woman with wet dreams.

"Do I have something on my face?" he asked.

"No. I was just thinking it was nice to just sit and relax, not stress about everything out there," she pointed toward the door.

Something in his expression shuttered instantly. Something unreadable, and disturbing.

Did he know something about their situation that she didn't? She wanted to ask him, but this really did feel like they'd achieved a reprieve from the tension between them, and she was loathe to destroy that.

Instead, she took a long draw from the bottle of wine, coughing when it went down the wrong way.

Marcus' brow furrowed in concern, poised on the edge of his seat to go to her.

Brin wiped at her eyes when her coughing fit was over, taking another swig from her bottle of wine, watching him, watching her. She hoped, more than believed, that in his own way, he did actually care about her.

A warm fire and alcohol made for a peaceful atmosphere. So much so, that by the time they had each consumed half a bottle, they had migrated from their opposite armchairs to sitting side by side on the couch as their conversation flowed freely. They laughed and joked like old friends, and then…

Brin sat on the couch, her knees bent and her bare feet resting on one of the soft cushions.

Marcus took a seat at the opposite end. "Are you comfortable?" he asked.

"I am now," she replied. Equally as casually she laid one of her feet across his thigh. Without thought, Marcus began gently massaging the arch of her foot, her ankle, and right down to her toes.

"You've gone quiet. What are you thinking about?" he asked suspiciously. Her eyes watched him intently and it made him nervous.

About what it might be like to touch your hard erection, or have my lips wrapped around it...or maybe both at the same time. "Not much. Just enjoying the foot rub."

She could feel his eyes on her. Like a physical touch, they stroked over her thighs, higher to her full breasts.

Sexual tension had existed between them since the day they met, and now locked in together, it seemed to have increased with each successive day they stayed in such close proximity. At least, that's what it felt like to Brin. Yet, despite their mutual covetous glances she doubted Marcus would make the first move.

Without thinking, Brin pushed Marcus back against the sofa. Leaning forward she kissed him softly. Her lips brushed his so tenderly it stole his breath. Deepening the kiss, she leaned into him further, their bodies melding against one another as the passion between them intensified. Brin controlled his hands, letting him caress her back and along her waist with soft, even strokes, keeping his pace slow and in time with their passionate kiss.

Marcus had never kissed anyone this way before. Kissing a woman had always been intense, a means to an end, that end being sex. This tender, slow kiss took him by surprise. The emotions it instilled in him, adoration, longing. He felt closer to Brin in this moment than he had during the most intense moments of sex with any other woman, and this was just a kiss. If he'd known how wonderful it could be, he would have done it much sooner.

Brin pulled back from the kiss, his eyes glowing fiercely with his wolf's presence, hot, intense and incredibly sexy.

"Marcus, I'm sorry. I shouldn't have done that." She'd shocked herself with the bold move, and now felt even more confused than ever, blaming the moment of lust on the wine. "I'm going to bed," she said, rising from the couch and running for the stairs and the safe seclusion of her room.

Marcus held back a groan. It was amazing how, when Brin spoke that particular combination of words, he was guaranteed to suffer a raging hard-on.

Subtly he rearranged himself before the circulation into his femoral artery was cut-off completely by his erection. The one that had plagued him unrelentingly for the past few days. Now, it was twice as hard, and he felt twice as conflicted. He could still feel the phantom weight of her hot little body on his lap, and every curve and peak his hands had caressed.

Holy hell, he was in serious trouble.

How had his life become so complicated, so quickly? That question seemed to have become a repeating mantra in his head recently. Seriously though, what was he going to do? He just wanted a normal life. A quiet life. A simple life. Looking at his wrist, that hope seemed like an impossible dream.

Sucking in a couple of deep breaths, Marcus took another long swig of his whisky. If he couldn't have the life he wanted, he was going to have the illusion of it, at least for today.

17

They seemed to be falling into a daily routine that began with the smell of coffee drifting through the main room. Marcus breathed in deeply as he trudged down the stairs. Stopping halfway, his pulse tripped with a pang of anxiety.

Entering the kitchen, Brin looked up at the exact same moment he entered.

Marcus held his breath. For one suspended second, neither moved, neither blinked. Even the fire in the main room seemed to crackle more quietly, as if it too sensed the emotional minefield under their feet.

Brin was the first to look away, fussing pointlessly with a spoon on the counter.

Her cheeks were pink, not from the heat of the stove.

Marcus cleared his throat. "Morning." His voice came out lower, rougher than he intended.

"Morning," she replied softly, nervously.

And Marcus hated the sound of her uneasy apprehension, hated that he was the reason her shoulders were tight and her eyes watched him too warily.

He also hated that the only thing he could think about, the only damn thing, was the memory of her lips brushing his…slowly…sweetly…like she had meant it.

No, nope, not going there.

Brin turned to pour coffee, hands steady enough to pass as calm, yet her eyes gave her away.

"I, um…" She swallowed. "About last night…"

Marcus froze. "Yeah," he said quickly, words tumbling out before she could continue. "About that."

Brin winced as if she expected him to mock her.

He hated that too.

So, he forced himself to soften. "We were drinking. A lot. It was…just one of those things."

Her chin lifted, but her voice was hesitant. "I'm still really sorry. I shouldn't have kissed you like that."

Was there another way she would've preferred to kiss him? He wondered.

For a moment his pulse kicked up a notch, the blood flow focussing on the appendage inside his pants. The kiss had been the softest, slowest, most devastating thing he'd ever experienced.

And yet…

"It's fine," he managed. "Really. And you don't need to apologise again. I'm at fault every bit as much as you. Probably more," he told her regretfully.

"Good," she breathed out, visibly relieved. "Um, I don't mean it's good that you feel it was your fault, really it wasn't. I mean, good, we don't ever need to speak of it again."

Marcus paused, not because he disagreed, but because the irrational, wolfen part of him snarled at the idea of pretending the kiss never happened, that it didn't matter.

"That's…probably for the best," he said tightly.

"Good."

Awkward silence followed.

Brin fidgeted with her sleeve. "So, um…what do you think the chances are that they'll find us today?"

He exhaled slowly. "Depends."

"On?"

"The weather. It might be clear now, but yesterday buried us. They can't fly any planes or helicopters if it looks like it will turn dangerous again, and right now…" Marcus looked outside the kitchen window, the small portion that was free of snow. "I'm not hopeful that this reprieve in the weather will last. That sky is still pretty dark."

Brin's eyes dropped to the floor. "It's our third day here."

He heard the anxiety and disappointment she tried, and failed to hide.

"Don't worry. They will find us," he said firmly. "In the meantime…"

Her gaze lifted, her green eyes looking directly into his. "We have to stay positive." He told her, holding her gaze just long enough for her smile to falter, before forcing conviction into his tone. "It's not so bad here. We're perfectly safe until they find us."

Brin nodded. "Yeah. We just need the weather to hold." It wouldn't. This was just another lull, the calm before the sky tore itself open again.

"And until then, we need more firewood, and I think I'd better dig some of that snow out from around the cabin, and probably off the roof as well, before it caves in from the weight."

"Is that actually a thing? I mean, I've heard people talk about stuff like that, but I always thought they were joking."

"Oh, it really happens."

"Right. Good to know. Would you like some help?"

Marcus gave her a hooded sideways glance. "We've already discussed this. You're not going outside. We might be in the middle of nowhere, and the weather may be so shitty that not even the wildlife is game to come out of their hiding places, but I'm not taking any chance that the Guild and their pet demons aren't still looking for us."

Brin rolled her eyes with a huff but didn't argue. Nor was she going to point out that she'd slipped out yesterday when he wasn't looking, even if it was only for a couple of minutes.

Maybe he was being over cautious, but his gut told him otherwise. If there was any creature crazy enough to tempt their luck in blizzard conditions, it was them.

As soon as Brin turned away to rinse a mug, Marcus grabbed his jacket and made for the door.

Outside, the world felt deceptively still.

The pale sun pressed weakly through the broken clouds, hitting the mountain ridge with a muted glow. The cabin, however, had been buried by yesterday's storm, making the only part visible being the middle third of the veranda and the front door, which now resembled a hobbit's doorway between white mounds of snow.

"Perfect," he muttered. Despite their easy manner this morning, he still needed distance from her. Now more than ever.

Work was the perfect distraction. And looking at the size of the snowbank pressing against the lower wall of the cabin, there was plenty to do, certainly enough to keep him busy for the majority of the day.

Grabbing a shovel from the basement, he began clearing it away.

Every muscle in his back and arms burned with effort, but the physical strain calmed him more than the whisky had the night before.

Shovel. Lift. Throw.

Shovel. Lift. Throw.

His movements grew harsher, faster, venting tension he had no other outlet for.

He shouldn't have kissed her.

He shouldn't be thinking about the way their mouths met, their tongues danced together or how she tasted like the finest wine.

Nor should he be thinking about how her soft form felt beneath his hands…

"Fuck," he growled, jamming the shovel into the snow with enough force that it clanged against buried ice.

He turned his attention to the roof next, scaling the remaining half-buried side of the cabin to reach the massive drift smothering the shingles.

Chop. Drag. Toss.

The wind kicked stray flakes into his hair and face, but he barely felt the cold. By the time he climbed back down, sweat slicked his neck, his T-shirt clinging to his chest and back beneath his jacket.

He stacked firewood next, splitting logs rhythmically with the axe, letting the repetitive thud of blade to wood drown out the memory of Brin's tempting mouth.

He needed a shower.

A long one.

Preferably hot, but he had no problems with a cold one again.

While Marcus worked, Brin had retreated downstairs, telling herself she was being productive rather than avoiding him like he was emotionally radioactive, which in a way he was. He was definitely her personal brand of Kryptonite. Never in her life had she behaved so brazenly, so appallingly, kissing another woman's boyfriend.

Yet, in truth, every other time she'd put on some sort of embarrassing performance, it was only ever when she was around Marcus, or was thinking about him. What did that say about her, she wondered, shutting down that particular inner dialogue before her mind came to a conclusion she didn't want to acknowledge.

Instead, keeping busy was the best option.

Entering the basement the familiar mix of diesel fumes, cold concrete, and musty air greeted her. She grabbed a small crate and started loading it with supplies, rice, beans, a jar of pickled…something green that looked vaguely suspicious, even if it wasn't edible, she was curious to see what it was.

Finally, she reached for the bag of flour on the top shelf. Or tried to. Her fingers brushed the edge of the sack, nudged it. And gravity took care of the rest.

FSSSHHHH.

A white cloud exploded over her like a baking-themed avalanche.

"No, no, no, no, no!" She screeched.

Flour rained down over her hair, face, shoulders, coating her sweater, sticking to the faint dampness on her skin, turning her into a ghost-shaped disaster.

She spluttered, coughing out a small puff of flour like a wheezy dragon.

"Crap!"

Brin shook her hair and watched the white cloud drift to the floor to join the rest of the flour, and attempted to wipe it from her eyes and face, yet only smeared it further across her cheeks.

"Perfect. Absolutely perfect. This is exactly the level of dignity I hoped to maintain today. Not!"

She sighed, grabbed the crate of food, and trudged upstairs.

Marcus pushed through the front door just as Brin emerged from the basement.

He stopped dead.

Brin froze too, her shoulder's slumping on a huff.

The silence lasted half a heartbeat.

Then…

Marcus burst out laughing. Not a smirk. Not a mocking huff. A full, belly-deep, uncontrollable laugh.

Brin stood rigid, coated in flour like a disgruntled pastry.

"Don't," she warned.

He bent slightly, wheezing. "Too late."

"It's not funny!"

"You look like…" he snorted, wiping his eyes.

She scrunched her nose, sending another puff of flour drifting off her face. "Shut up. Don't say it. I know I look a mess."

"You need a shower," he said, still grinning.

She glared. "So do you." She told him, scrunching up her nose at the odorous evidence of his labour.

He glanced down at his sweaty shirt. "Fair."

Her shoulders sagged, the corner of her lips twitching despite her best effort to stay annoyed.

But the awkwardness from earlier crept back between them, softening the moment.

Marcus cleared his throat. "I'll, uh…wait till you've had your shower."

"No, it's okay. You'd better go first, I think I'll probably use whatever hot water's left," she told him, pulling a face as she plucked at a piece of hair, with another flutter of flour to the floor.

Marcus watched with amusement, although he did his best to restrain his laughter to a smirk.

"If you're sure" He nodded once.

"I am." She nodded back.

Brin waited a few minutes after she heard the shower turn on, before casually entering the bathroom, since there was no longer a door there.

"Don't mind me, just using the loo." She told him, flushing the toilet and leaving again, laughing at his girlie squeal when the cold water was diverted to the toilet's cistern.

She tried not to take a peek at him behind the shower curtain, but couldn't help herself. Not that it mattered, the opaque plastic barely showed more than his body's outline. His very manly, muscular, likable outline.

Why did she torture herself like that. Now she'd spend the rest of the afternoon filling in all the unviewable body parts with her imagination.

A few minutes later Marcus stomped from the bathroom with only a towel about his waist, and her eyes were immediately drawn toward a single droplet of water as it dripped from his hair and down his chest, catching and hanging on his pert male nipple, sending a ripple of heat straight to her core.

"Was that really necessary?" he demanded heatedly.

"Yes. I'm afraid so. You can't take the door off and expect me to not get payback somehow, do you?"

Her grin was wicked and playful, and Marcus' temper cooled instantly.

"Touche. I'll give you that one. Now, I believe it's your turn for a shower," he told her, the glint in his eye equally as devious as hers had been.

Brin glared at him in warning, pointing a finger in his chest. The feel of his hot skin, still moist from his shower, had her fingers curl up reflexively, desperate to scrape the tips of her nails lightly over those taught muscles that rippled so delectably across his broad chest.

"I believe we're even now," she told him, more a warning than a statement.

Quickly, she pulled her hand away and entered the bathroom. At least she knew the shower curtain wasn't see through, thankfully.

Brin wasn't wrong about using up the rest of the hot water. It took two lots of shampooing to remove the claggy mess from her hair, meaning that her shower was finished in a hurry as the last of the tepid water ran out to become almost as cold as the snow outside.

Pulling the curtain aside just a little, she reached for her towel. She stretched her arm a little further, but found nothing.

Opening the curtain a little more she looked to where she'd left the towel. It was gone.

It seemed that at some point during her shower, Marcus had decided to extend their tit-for-tat pranks and removed her towel, leaving her with two options, using either the bathmat or hand towel to dry herself.

Right. Well, if he thought she was going to have a meltdown over it, he was going to be sorely disappointed.

"Ha ha. Nice one. I'm sure you're very proud of yourself," she called out from inside the shower, towelling herself off with her bath towel's shrunken cousin.

She could hear him chuckling from the hallway outside the bathroom and the sound tripped a switch in the naughty part of her brain, the part that did stupid things like drunk kiss him.

Marcus fully expected Brin to have a hissy fit and demand he give her back her towel, and he fully intended to do just that. He only wanted to make her squirm a little. Instead, she did something that surprised the hell out of him, and made him regret ever considering the prank.

Brin placed the hand towel over her abdomen, covering the curls at the apex of her thighs. But that was all it covered. Every other inch of flesh remained open to the air.

"Listen, you annoying asswaffle, if you don't change your attitude I'm going to remove your family jewels." She told him headedly as she stepped from the bathroom, her eyes instantly dropping toward the region under threat.

Her cheeks burned, although she couldn't tell if it was because she was so angry or because she couldn't drag her eyes away from his abundant man jewels which had suddenly begun tenting his pants with a huge bulge. On second thoughts, her anger had nothing to do with the heat in her cheeks, the same heat seemed to have also set her lady parts on fire too.

"Hey, my eyes are up here," she growled dryly.

Yep, he knew that, but she had the most magnificent breasts he'd ever seen, and he couldn't seem to pry his eyes off them. He licked his lips and groaned inwardly. He also couldn't help noticing the gold armband that still adorned her upper arm, and he swallowed, hard.

"Did you just call me an *asswaffle*?"

"If the shoe fits." She told him, one hand holding her miniscule towel in place, the other planted haughtily on her hip, making her breasts bounce a little at the movement. Oh, and didn't that heat his blood.

"Come here," he said softly.

"In your dreams." Despite her determined voice she had to fight her body's response to put one foot in front of the other.

"Brin, come here," he repeated, his golden eyes boring into hers with a mixture of amusement and lust.

Dammit, he was sexy, his voice was like honey and she hadn't had sex in....forever. Not a good combination. Like a moth to a flame, she felt helpless to fight his command.

"Here's your towel," he told her, holding it out for her to take.

She blinked, and blinked again, dragging herself out of whatever hormonal pool her brain cells had decided to drown themselves in. For the barest of moments, she actually thought he was going to fulfill her every lusty desire. But no. Of course not. So, it seemed she was headed back to the Bad Decision Department in her brain store.

Dropping the small hand towel to the floor, she stood stark naked in front of him and took the towel from his hand, smiling at the way his jaw dropped and his whole body went rigid in response.

Serves himself right she thought, wrapping the towel around herself, she returned to the bathroom.

Marcus turned to walk away, then stopped, turned back and then moved to walk away again, but he couldn't get his feet to move.

"Fuck me dead. I need to put that bathroom door back on."

"Did you say something?" Brin called out smugly.

Despite their continued bathroom pranks, the animosity and anger seemed to have petered out, much to both their relief. As much as she really did enjoy tormenting him, she was tired of the constant tension between them.

Even so, he still made a point of keeping some distance between them which confused her. Ignoring the couple of poor judgment lapses, like drunk kissing him and flashing him her birthday suit, they were getting along much better, even having whole conversations without arguing. So why was he still so standoffish?

She hovered near the bottom step of the staircase, watching him leaning against the mantel over the fireplace, examining him more closely.

He didn't look like himself, not the snarling, cocky, aggravating bastard she'd grown used to. He looked…unwell.

"Marcus?" she said softly, coming to stand beside him. "Are you okay? You don't look like yourself."

He lifted his head sharply, eyes bright with warning. "Of course I'm me. Who the fuck else would I be?"

Brin blinked at the venom in his tone, clearly she'd hit a sensitive nerve. She tried again. "Calm down. I just mean…you don't look well. Are you sure you don't have any wounds I can heal? Maybe something you missed? Internal bleeding? Something hidden?"

His nostrils flared. "You've seen me naked. Did I look like I had any wounds to you?"

Not physically, no. What she had seen was, well…glorious, indecently well-crafted man candy, sculpted to perfection in all the right places. His broad shoulders, chiselled abdomen, the perfect curve of his ass that really should have been illegal, and…Nope. Not going there again, she thought, shutting off the image of him palming his hardened erection in slow strokes, up and down, over the flushed head and the glistening bead at the tip.

Crap! She went there.

Brin cleared her throat and looked away quickly, her cheeks warming with frustration.

Marcus watched her, gaze narrowing, and for a moment she feared he somehow knew exactly what she was thinking.

The tension between them once again thickened like fog.

Marcus raised his hands, running his fingers through his short hair, the sleeve of his shirt pulling back just enough to expose his wrist and her eyes widened.

"Are you sure there's nothing wrong? Would you care to explain this?" Stepping forward she grabbed his hand and pulled his sleeve back further to expose the rash.

Oh, the flying faecal matter….Shit!

"Not really."

"Marcus. I know you don't like me, but I thought you at least trusted me. If there's something wrong that I can fix, then why don't you let me?"

"No. This is none of your concern," he snapped back, snatching his hand free of hers and dragging the sleeve back into place angrily.

She was getting whiplash trying to deal with his hot and cold mood swings.

"Marcus, just let me see it, I can help you." She tried again.

"Brin, just fuck off, and leave it, okay. I don't want your help. This is your fault."

"What?" she looked toward his wrist, although didn't dare try to touch him again. If she wasn't mistaken, that was the wrist the serpent armband had bitten, but she thought that had healed without any effects. Clearly, she was wrong.

"Marcus. You're scaring me. What's going on. Talk to me, please."

His growl was his only response as he stormed toward the door with Brin hot on his heels, trying to head him off at the door. He simply pushed her aside and opened the door, disappearing out into yet another snowstorm.

Closing her eyes, disappointment and frustration bubbled to the surface once more. Biting her bottom lip to stop it from quivering she took a step away from the doorway. Had she really been the cause of some injury or illness he's suffering? It had been obvious for the past couple of days that something was off with him, but she had naturally assumed it was only his resentment of her, blaming her for the fact that he'd been the one ordered to escort her back.

Brin pulled her arm from the sleeve of her top, examining the armband more closely, tugging at it, it refused to move. It was a magical artefact, that much was obvious, but was it truly capable of causing permanent harm to someone? To Marcus?

She honestly hoped not. As much as he infuriated her, she really cared about him, far more than she probably should.

Marcus stood on the other side of the door, grateful for the biting cold, its numbing effect was only skin deep, but it offered a reprieve from his close confines with Brin.

The woman could give lessons to a mule on sheer determined pride and stubbornness.

He had no intentions of sharing his secret with her. To do so, felt like admitting the inevitable, and he wasn't ready to do that. He was happy living his lie.

That's what it was though. A lie. A very big, fat lie he'd been telling himself.

Pulling back his sleeve, he stared down at the evidence of that lie. The red rash still remained, but the black lines beneath his skin had begun to settle into a fixed image.

An image of a dragon.

Fuck! He was so screwed.

18

Owen stepped through the portal that Doran had opened for him, emerging on the other side in yet another forest. This one much colder than Savernake. How was it, he wondered, for someone like himself born and raised in the tropics of Far North Queensland, Australia, he seemed to be spending so much time lately in freezing cold countries. In the past week he'd been in Canada, England and now Ukraine.

Cold. Cold. Cold.

He hated the cold.

Nevertheless, this is where the Alliance needed him to be. This is where Alex was, and the lycan who had been injected with the new, as yet still unknown virus.

So, here he was, arriving for duty as a pin cushion to hopefully find a cure.

Following the path, he reached a small car park at the edge of a clearing where a dark SUV waited for him.

"You Owen?" a gruff voice asked.

"At your service." Owen held out his hand, but the man just stood and stared at him, his face looked like it had been set in stone.

Okay, so the locals aren't so friendly around here, he thought.

Pulling back his hand awkwardly, Owen threw his gear in the back of the SUV which his escort had opened, and then climbed into the front passenger seat.

"You're one of Gustav's men?" It was both a statement and a question.

"I am. Dieter." He answered, starting the engine and driving out onto the road without so much as a sideways glance in Owen's direction.

"How far is it to Gustav's base?" he asked.

"One hour, if we get good traffic."

It might have been cold outside, but it felt just as chilly inside the car, and an hour long trip with Dieter felt like an uncomfortable lifetime. Either the man had a problem with him in particular, being the only human druid working in the lycan military, or he was just a surly bastard. By the time they reached L'viv, he'd decided it was probably the latter. Throughout the trip he'd grumbled about everything from the other drivers, having to stop at stop signs and a billboard about a haemorrhoid cream. Not that he was going to point out to him that his attitude could use some improvement, he was almost twice Owen's size, and he himself, was no light weight.

So, he stayed silent and took in the scenery.

Owen had expected that the Northern European and Baltic Region Alliance Headquarters would be situated along some off-the-beaten trail somewhere, out of the way and hidden from the rest of the world, like it was in England and Australia. However, Dieter pulled up outside the Bunker Restaurant, downtown L'viv. He didn't say anything, just glared at Owen as if to say: *Well, what the fuck are you still doing here?*

Getting out of the SUV, he grabbed his bag from the back.

"In there." Dieter told him through the open window, pointing at the front entrance of the restaurant.

"Great. Thanks. Nice chatting with you," he replied in a slightly sarcastic tone, and saluted him as Dieter drove away.

Okay, now what? Was this another rendezvous point? Whether it was or not, he wasn't going to find out standing on the footpath staring at the front door.

As the name suggested, the restaurant was actually an old WWII bunker, which also surprisingly was quite pleasant inside. Although not much about the place had changed since it was first built early last century. The domed stone ceiling and walls had certainly retained their original, rustic condition, although the walls were now adorned with WWII memorabilia, making the restaurant popular with tourists. The only thing that had been drastically altered was the uneven blue stone floor, replaced by flat, grey slate tiles to meet public liability requirements. While the premise's primary use was as the Alliance's Headquarters, it was also a legitimate business and had to conform to strict health regulations.

"Hey, Owen. Over here."

Looking about the mostly empty booths, he spotted Alex scribbling away on a napkin at one of the tables.

"Alex. Nice place, but where's the Alliance compound?"

"You're standing on top of it," he replied, pointing toward the floor. "How about I show you around. Gustav would've, but he's occupied at the moment."

"Sure. That would be great."

Alex took him through the kitchen to a service door which led to a lift. "This is not the entrance to the compound that most of them use, but since you'll be staying in Gustav's home, not the barrack quarters, you'll use this entrance."

Owen gave him a questioning look. "I just assumed I'd be bunked in with all the other soldiers."

"Not this time. You've already been exposed to the virus, and even if you're immune, that doesn't necessarily mean that the lycans you might come into contact with, will be. Not that you're likely to, virtually everyone has been sent away to minimise the risk. Either way, you'll be staying in the family's private quarters."

Ah, that made sense. "That explains Dieter's cold shoulder towards me."

"Nah. That's just Dieter."

Right. Good to know.

Pressing the button, L1 on the keypad, the lift doors closed. Interestingly, there appeared to be three lower ground levels. Clearly the compound was deceptively larger than he thought, especially considering the restaurant, was also below the street level, marginally.

Gustav's private quarters were also larger than expected with two large main rooms, a kitchen and six bedrooms, of which it appeared five of those were currently being occupied by family and visitors, including him.

"This is your room, next to mine." Alex told him.

Dumping his gear on the bed, Owen followed Alex to a staircase that took them down to the lower levels.

"Here's your code to access these internal doors to the private quarters, and you'll also need it in the lift."

"Got it. Thanks."

Opening the door to level 2, they stepped into a large gym area, well lit with fluorescent lights and filled with all manner of equipment. It was a gym junkies dream, much like the gym at Havenswood Manor. At the far end of the room, a large sparring mat was currently occupied by an unlikely pair, a dark headed, lean but well muscled man who was just shy of seven feet tall, and a much shorter woman.

The woman was stunningly beautiful, the kind of woman who made a man do stupid things just get a smile from her. Her long dark hair was pulled back in a ponytail that swung behind her as she moved, and her figure hugging lycra pants and tank top showed every curve to mouth watering perfection. And the way she could throw that roundhouse kick, it almost made him come in his pants.

"Don't even think about it. She doesn't date."

"What do you mean, *doesn't date*? Anyone? Ever?"

"You got it."

"Okay, so how about just straight sex, no strings attached?"

Alex laughed, he liked Owen's style. "You could ask, but she'd probably just break your legs, or Gustav would."

"Gustav?"

"Yeah, her dad."

"Oh fuck. *That's* Elise? The youngest druid sister?"

"Sure is."

Elise didn't pay them any attention as they walked by, but the man she was with did, his eyes glued to Owen curiously. That momentary lack of concentration cost him dearly, landing him flat on his back with Elise straddling his chest.

Lucky bastard, Owen thought silently.

"How do you know she doesn't date?"

"She spends almost as much time at the manor as she does here. If she so much as looked at a guy, all the women in the house would know about it. Trust me, don't waste your time asking her out, at least, not unless you've got an undentable ego."

"What about the guy she's sparring with, who's he?"

"That, is Eytan. He's the other person staying in the private quarters. He's the nephew of the High Lord of the nephilim, Gwynn ap Nudd, and he's one of the only nephilim who was born inside the Valley of Vardin, when the rephaim, the rogue nephilim were imprisoned fifteen hundred years ago. No doubt you know the story about how Morganna stole the Thunderstone from the Valley, and broke the barrier containing them there."

"I recall something about it."

"Yeah, well, fortunately he's one of the good guys. Some of the rephaim reformed their ways during their imprisonment, but some of them are still loyal to Morganna. Nevertheless, all of them had a hard time transitioning back into society. Eytan has been working with us quite a bit lately. Right now, he's here to help with the two lycans we have downstairs who've been infected by the virus." Alex told him as they reached another doorway leading down another set of stairs.

"What do you mean, I thought there was only one man who was infected." Owen asked.

"Oh, right. You wouldn't have heard yet. Klaus, Dieter's brother was the one who picked up the infected soldier from the forest after a nephilim opened a portal for him, and brought him here. That was four days ago. Yesterday, Klaus started coming down with symptoms too."

"Crap. That's not good. Don't suppose Klaus was bitten or scratched, was he?"

"They had no direct personal contact, which leads me to believe that once the virus has taken hold and shifts to the contagious phase, it becomes an airborne pathogen."

Reaching the bottom of the stairs, Alex put another code into the keypad and the door unlocked. Inside were rows of barred cells, of which only three were occupied.

"I've set up my lab down here so that we can work completely autonomously. No lycans are allowed down here, not anymore. Which is why Eytan is here, he'll be helping with the experiments. Being a nephilim, he shouldn't be affected by the virus, like you."

"When you say, *experiments*, I'm assuming you mean me. That you're going to experiment on me?"

"Well, duh. What else did you think I was going to do, you're the only one who might have some antibodies that we can use to make a vaccine."

Yeah, he knew that, it just sucked hearing it out loud.

Reaching the first of the occupied cells, Klaus sat on a cot, his head resting against the wall.

"Hey buddy, how you doin' today?" Alex asked him.

"Fuck off cockroach," he growled back.

"I see the virus hasn't affected you much yet, that's great." Alex smiled.

Owen took another look at Klaus, there was definitely a family resemblance between him and Dieter, except for a long scar down Klaus' cheek. They definitely had the same congenial personality…Not.

"This is Owen, he's going to be helping me find the cure. So, just stay tight and don't go losing your marbles just yet, okey dokey?" Alex told him.

Stepping up to the next cell, the lycan who'd originally been infected paced the floor back and forth incessantly, eyes angry and red, fixed on something that only he could see, and a line of white foam trickled from the corner of his mouth.

"This is the guy who was infected a few days ago?" Owen asked. To say he was surprised at the man's appearance was an understatement.

"And deteriorating quickly. From what I've been able to determine, the virus is a derivative of the rabies virus. Only, it's effect is much faster. Within two days of the symptoms showing, this is the result." Alex told him.

"Any idea what the next stage of the symptoms might be?"

"Complete mental breakdown, loss of speech and general reasoning. Then, probably death."

Owen nodded in acknowledgement. "Any idea how long that might take?"

"I'm assuming only a matter of days."

"So, now you've had the tour, how about we get started. I've set up my lab down here at the end of the hallway. What would you like to donate first, your blood or your skin?" Alex asked him excitedly, slapping him on the shoulder.

Owen gulped.

The mood within Havenswood Manor had changed. Usually, the estate breathed with a kind of calmness, even in chaos. But tonight, frustration pulsed through every stone, every shadowed corridor and every living and un-living soul within its walls.

Restlessness, tension and simmering dread thickened the air like the static humidity before a storm.

The wyvern brothers paced the manor like caged predators. Even Wade, normally the calmest of them, was snapping at shadows. Raif snarled every time someone brushed past him. Seth and Ky had retreated to the back terrace earlier, but came storming in minutes later arguing over nothing at all.

They were becoming almost as intolerable as Cujo, who was himself a snarling, anxious, pacing menace as Tilly waddled around, heavily pregnant and cranky. Every creak of the floorboards had the hellhound baring his teeth.

"I swear," Sebastian muttered to Alaric, "if Tilly goes into labour tonight and the brothers keep pacing like that, the manor will implode."

Alaric didn't disagree.

Even the usually unflappable vampires were on edge.

Narayan stood at the window overlooking the gardens, arms folded and jaw tight. Doran hovered near the fireplace, his pensive mood not much better than the wyvern brothers.

Every minute that ticked past was another minute Brin and Marcus were out there.

Alive? Frozen? Hunted?

No one knew.

And the not knowing was destroying them.

The manor fell into a kind of brittle quiet just as Alaric's phone buzzed and every wyvern head snapped toward him.

"Emil," Alaric announced, lifting the phone, putting the call on speaker.

The brothers moved closer.

"Please tell me you have something," he queried without preamble.

On the other end, Emil Wagstaff sounded exhausted.

"I have news," he began. "Not much of it good I'm afraid, but not all of it is bad either."

"What do you have?" Raif barked, sounding unintentionally harsh.

Emil didn't even flinch. "The Guild hasn't found them."

A wave of relief filtered through the room.

"Neither have we," Ky snapped. "The weather's been a bloody nightmare."

"That's exactly it," Emil replied. "The storms have been so brutal, visibility has been next to zero. Not even the demons can track through whiteout conditions. Like us, the Guild air search has been grounded."

A beat of silence.

"So, no one's searching," Doran said quietly.

"In this weather? Nobody would survive being out in the open for longer than a couple of hours," Wade growled, pacing again. "Not even Marcus."

"You're right, they wouldn't," Seb said firmly. "They must have found shelter."

Everyone froze.

Seb sighed. "Think about it, if the Guild is still adamant that Brin's alive. They're not guessing. They're not speculating. Somehow, they know."

Ky's eyes sharpened. "How can they possibly know though?"

Emil hesitated in thought. "They're not saying," he answered. "But they certainly haven't wavered in their conviction. Which leads me to think that the Scree demons have some way of sensing Brin, whether it's because she's a healer or they can sense something else about her, I don't know."

"That makes perfect sense." Alaric agreed.

A flicker of hope, tiny but bright, fanned through the room.

"If they have shelter," Narayan said, "that's great news."

"Exactly," Emil agreed. "But that's all I have, I'm sorry."

"Thanks," Alaric said. The relief in his tone was fragile, yet real. "Call again if you learn anything more."

He hung up.

Silence.

A breath, long, deep, shaky, seemed to sigh through the room collectively.

"They're alive, we can hold onto that." Narayan told them.

The wyvern brothers weren't relieved, not fully, but something in their posture loosened. A fraction.

Sebastian pushed off the wall. "If they have shelter, then we need to figure out where. How many structures are in that region? Hunting cabins? Rangers sheds? Weather stations?"

Alaric nodded briskly, stepping toward the mantle where maps had been spread since day one.

"I'll call Dray. He can access records across multiple jurisdictions. Property registries. Old ranger maps. Historical documents." He exhaled sharply. "Even old ruins and mines."

"It's over a thousand square miles out there, there are probably hundreds of properties to search, if not more." Raif reminded him.

"Then we start narrowing it down," Alaric replied. "Anything with a roof goes on the list."

"We'll take whatever Dray finds and cross-reference it with the helicopter's likely flight trajectories."

Sanders, silent until now, added, "And with fuel burn estimates and flight records, we can reconstruct probable flight paths within a few degrees, give or take the storm's drift."

Ky stepped forward. "Please tell me tomorrow's weather is clearing?" he asked.

Alaric checked the Canadian meteorologist website, the radar view filling the screen.

"The storm system seems to be weakening. The whiteout conditions look like they'll ease to be mild to moderate. Visibility looks like it'll improve a bit tomorrow too."

The room held its breath.

"There's likely to be a window of clearer weather by the afternoon."

"It'll do," Raif said. "We'll fly out at first light."

"It might close in again by the later part of the afternoon," Seth argued.

"Then we search ten times faster," Raif snapped.

“Take a breath, we’re all working together here,” Wade murmured, steadying them.

Alaric nodded once, authoritative and final. “We’ll resume the search at dawn.”

Brin’s brothers exhaled sharply, tension coiling into purpose.

“We’ll find them,” Ky promised, more to himself than anyone else.

Holly stepped into the circle of men, her expression chiselled with determination. “Just bring them home.”

The manor’s inhabitants moved about with renewed energy. Hope was a tenuous thing, but they all clung to it like a lifeline.

Outside, the mild English evening drifted carelessly into peaceful silence.

Inside, they kept themselves busy with new investigations and enquiries, and preparations for another day of searching.

19

Brin rummaged through the pockets of her jacket hanging on a hook by the door and pulled something free, following Marcus outside, although she was too distracted to think to just put the jacket on.

"Look here, I don't care if you don't like me, you're going to talk to me." She called out.

Marcus stopped to look over his shoulder at her, his smile tilted into a snarl, bitter with the frustration of a fight he couldn't name. "I'm not one of your subjects you can order about, princess. Fuck off and leave me alone." His inner conflict at that statement flashed in his eyes, his hands curling into fists.

Her eyebrows rose but she bit her tongue, worried she'd say something stupid to make him even more irritable, after all, she had a bad track record of foot in mouth disease around him. Instead, she continued on towards him, keeping pace with his long stride when he started walking away from her again.

Something wasn't right with him, it was plain to see. Not only did he look to have a fever and a rash on his arm, there was something wrong with his eyes. They glowed with the familiar golden colour they always did when he was angry with her, but now, his pupils weren't round, they were vertical slits. Was this a side effect of that damned serpent armband bite, she wondered.

They pushed on. Snow squeaked. Breath fogged. Somewhere in the white wilderness, Brin's courage did a small, unsteady two-step.

"Marcus. You're going to talk to me whether you like it or not. I'm not going to leave you alone for a second until you do."

"I would despair if you did," he sniped angrily.

Brin was more disappointed than upset by his attitude toward her. They may not be friends, but she thought they'd at least reached a level of understanding where he trusted her.

"Marcus. Stop!" she yelled at him, puffed from walking and talking at the same time. "Just stop. Please," she begged.

Marcus did stop, turning around slowly, although his shuttered expression and hard glare gave nothing away of what was going on beneath that hard exterior.

"You're a nosey bitch, you know that? My issues are just that, mine. They have nothing to do with you. What do I have to do to make you leave me alone?"

"I-I only want to help you." She stuttered, the cold making it hard to get her words out.

"Give me a sec. I'm trying to decide whether I don't give a shit, or I don't give a fuck. I don't care what you want, it's none of your business."

"Y-You know what Marcus, I'm d-done with your snide remarks and condescending glares, and the way y-you push your weight around, like y-you think you *are* G-God."

"Excuse me?" his eyes narrowed on her.

"You h-heard me. And, the next t-time you speak to me like that, ask yourself one question. How h-hard would it be to remove my size ten shoe from y-your arse. The answer? Very hard." Brin drew up to her full height, tilting her chin up defiantly to stand nose to nose with him. "I will not stand h-here and be insulted by the likes of *y-you!*"

Marcus sneered, his eyes glowing more brightly than she'd ever seen them before.

"The truth hurts, d-doesn't it? You can dish it out, b-but you can't take it."

"Fuck off and just leave me alone."

Arsehole! Brin straightened her spine. Right.

"Fine. If y-you want to behave like an obnoxious beast, I'm going to treat you like one."

From behind her back, she pulled out the can of bear mace she'd taken from her jacket, and held it up ready to spray him with it.

A deep growl rumbled through his chest. Something primal coiling inside him, threatening to burn him to the core. The way she stood her ground so tenaciously, it stirred his wolf into a frenzy of demanding need, and it was taking every ounce of his willpower to control it.

She stepped back a pace.

Oops! That might have been a mistake, she realised.

"Brin, listen carefully. You have till the count of three to leave. Go back to the cabin. Run, don't walk, and don't look back," he told her, his voice unexpectedly gravely from the accompanying growl. "Do you understand me?"

"I s-see your lips moving and there's sound c-coming out, but I've got n-nothing," Brin told him defiantly, although on the inside she was severely reprimanding herself for taunting him further. She was playing with fire and she knew it, but she just couldn't stop herself.

Marcus' body shook, every muscle pulled taught from his internal struggle. His hold was slipping, his wolf, normally so compliant to his will, clawed at him until…his restraint snapped.

Marcus suffered an emotional response without any input from his brain.

Blinded by his own fury and his wolf's domination, Marcus gripped her by the arms, hauled her up against him and took her mouth. There was nothing gentle about the kiss. It was raw and demanding. It was about dominance and all that male tough-guy crap she'd accused him of. It was about making sure that all his intimacies with her were about anger or pure lust, because he couldn't accept that he was beginning to need physical contact with her, even if *her* touch, was the only one his wolf *did* want.

Obviously, she couldn't accept that notion either. She squealed in outrage and stomped on his foot, punching him in chest with fury.

"You can't stay here any longer, it's not safe." Marcus' voice rumbled, he couldn't hide his need for her, nor his anger.

"W-watch me." Her voice rose right back.

He smiled tightly, tamping down the need to spank her stubborn, pretty arse. Brin's eyes narrowed dangerously with her own rising anger.

"No. You can't." He growled again. Marcus started to offer a condescending smile at Brin's sharp words, freezing as his heated gaze noticed how she was shaking uncontrollably. Her yoga pants and cotton top provided not even the slightest barrier against the frigid wind, the temperature being somewhere between holy-hell and nutcracker-cold degrees below zero. Five more minutes out here and she'd die from hypothermia.

Brin's body trembled violently, her breath a thin, ragged gasp in the frigid air.

Marcus saw it all at once, her skin blanched nearly the same shade as the snow drifting around them, her lips a frightening, brittle blue, her jaw clattering so hard he half-expected her teeth to crack. Her clothes were soaked through, clinging to every trembling contour of her body, the thin cotton and lycra no match for the Arctic's vicious bite.

A bolt of fear cut through him so sharply it bordered on panic.

Not anger.

Not frustration.

Not even lust.

Just raw, instinctive terror.

"Brin," he rasped, voice barely human. "You're freezing."

"I…I'm f-fine," she lied, her voice barely audible, her chattering teeth breaking the words apart.

"Bullshit."

Brin wanted to give him a piece of her mind, but the colder she got, the less energy she seemed to have to continue the argument.

Before she could protest, Marcus scooped her up, one arm under her knees, the other locking firmly about her waist and pulled her into his arms, drawing her cheek against his chest. When she wrapped her own arms about his neck, he practically ran with her back to the cabin.

Her frozen fingers clutched at him reflexively, the contact so weak it made something inside him break.

He didn't think. He just moved.

His long, powerful strides ate up the snow, boots crunching as the wind whipped at their faces, but Marcus didn't seem to feel it anymore. His wolf surged so fiercely that his body heat spiked, sweat beading along his spine despite the cold.

Brin shuddered once. Twice. Then violently, her whole frame shuddered against his chest from the chill that had reached her bones.

"Stay awake," he ordered, voice shaking despite his effort to control it.

"I-I'm…awake," she tried to say, but the words came out slurred.

"Stubborn woman, don't you fucking do this to me," he muttered, tightening his grip as he reached the porch.

The moment they got inside, Brin went limp in his arms.

"Brin!" His heart seized.

Her eyes fluttered weakly. "C-cold…"

That single word obliterated every wall he'd built.

He kicked the door shut with enough force to rattle the frame.

For a heartbeat, he considered the bathroom, throwing her under the hot shower, holding her up under the spray until she thawed. But the second he imagined letting her out of his sight, letting her *go,* releasing her from his arms, his vision blurred with blind refusal.

No. He couldn't do it. He *wouldn't* do it.

Every instinct screamed in one unified demand:

Keep her close.

Keep her warm.

Keep her safe.

Marcus carried her upstairs, her head lolling against his shoulder, her breath shallow and trembling. His wolf prowled just under his skin, pushing harder, demanding he hurry, urging him to protect what was his.

No. *Not his.*

But God, he wanted her to be.

That revelation nearly had him halting in his tracks, but the urgency of her plight had his feet taking two stairs at a time.

He nudged open her bedroom door and laid her gently on the bed. The mattress dipped under her weight, and she shivered so violently the bedframe shook.

"Brin," he whispered harshly, fingers trembling as he brushed damp hair from her forehead. "Stay with me."

"H-h-hot shower," she whispered. "D-don't…n-need…help."

"You need heat, *now*."

"I c-can warm myself."

"You can barely breathe." His tone cracked, rough and furious. "For once woman, don't argue with me. Just…let me do this."

She tried to bat his hands away, weakly, pathetically.

That broke him too.

He stripped off her outer layers, her soaked top, her icy yoga pants, his movements swift but careful, precise. He worked by necessity, not desire, the sight of goosebumps pebbling her skin sending a tremor through him.

He left her in her silken bra and panties, and quickly shrugged off his own clothes, shirt, jeans, everything…until he stood beside the bed in nothing but his boxers, his skin scorching with unnaturally high heat, for once he was grateful for whatever changes were taking place inside him.

Brin blinked up at him, barely conscious.

"M-Marcus…?"

"Shut up," he said gently, voice unexpectedly soft. "I've got you."

He slid into the bed and pulled her against him, wrapping his entire body around hers, his chest at her back, arms encircling her waist, legs tangling with hers. His heat engulfing her instantly, a blazing cocoon surrounding her chilled frame.

She gasped at the temperature, then sighed, a faint, broken sound, and leaned helplessly into him.

Marcus groaned under his breath.

This felt…right.

Too right.

"Don't fight me," he murmured against the back of her neck, his breath warm on her icy skin. If only he could take his own advice, he thought. He'd fought his attraction to her every damned day since they met, and it was killing him.

"I'm n-not," she whispered, voice faint. "J-just don't…don't let go."

His throat tightened. He tightened his hold. "Never."

They lay like that, his large frame curled protectively around her smaller, shaking body. His arms completing the cradle of heat around her, one across her waist, the other beneath her head. His nose brushed her hairline, his breath warm against her nape.

Slowly, her tremors eased.

Slowly, her breathing deepened.

Slowly, colour crept back into her cheeks.

Marcus shut his eyes and exhaled shakily.

She was warm again.

Safe.

Alive.

And then the real danger began.

Because she didn't pull away.

Nor did he let go of her.

Neither of them wanted to.

Brin's fingers curled around his forearm, gentle, trusting.

His wolf purred, a sound he didn't know it could make.

Marcus pressed his forehead to her shoulder. His voice was raw, unguarded, unfiltered.

"Brin," he whispered, "You have to stop scaring the shit out of me."

She didn't answer.

Her body had softened into his, melting into his heat, and Marcus tightened his embrace, burying his face against her neck as if he could fuse her to him. Her body relaxed further, as did his.

Without realising it, they both dozed off into a peaceful slumber.

When Brin woke, the sun had begun to set. She'd slept for hours.

She moved to turn over, but Marcus' sleeping form was still wrapped firmly around her.

She lifted up his arm holding her about the waist and attempted to remove it, but he only tightened his grip, a low growl rumbling from his chest, followed by a soft snore. Brin chuckled, she couldn't help herself, the sound was just…adorable.

Then she noticed something else she didn't expect.

Behind her, where his hips curved and his legs intertwined with hers, a very large, thick bulge pressed firmly between her butt cheeks.

As she moved, it flexed. It was so engorged, she could feel the pulse in the veins along its surface.

Brin flexed her hips, Marcus' hips moved with hers, providing a little more friction and slide of his thick shaft between her legs.

Brin's pulse quickened, the moment felt like the best dream ever and a dangerous game of Russian roulette. She had always wondered what it would feel like to touch him so intimately, stroke him, grip him in her palm. But, doing that now, while he was asleep felt like a violation. Regardless, she couldn't help herself. She had to know what he felt like beneath her fingers.

Reaching behind her, she slipped her hand between them, her fingers touching the soft cotton fabric of his boxers which hugged his form like a glove. Tentatively, she slid her hand down further until they came into contact with that heavy shaft, the minor contact made it jerk and flex again between her legs and she pressed herself harder against it. She knew she should stop, that it was wrong, but she couldn't. Her body seemed to have developed a mind of its own.

Marcus' breathing changed, quickened and another soft growl rumbled from his chest.

Carefully she turned in his arms, his heavy body barely moved.

Brin looked at his sleeping form, his relaxed face was absolutely gorgeous. He had the most incredible bone structure, long dark eyelashes that would make any girl envious, and full kissable lips that were only inches from her own. Did she dare risk a soft kiss, risk waking him? Or did she simply lie there and enjoy the feel of him wrapped around her until whenever he woke? There was a third option, she could do both.

She touched a few strands of his chocolate brown hair, imprinting the feel of it into her memory. Maybe she was just torturing herself, wishing for something that would never happen, but she was ready to acknowledge the truth, at least to herself, that she was in love with him, and probably had been since the day they met. It was no doubt very one sided, but she felt contented to have just this one moment of intimacy with him.

Lightly, she stroked a finger over his chest, relishing the heat that radiated from the perfectly muscled physique.

Marcus stirred.

Brin stilled, her fingers still pressed against his chest, her eyes flicking up toward his face as she held her breath, and nearly forgot how to breathe altogether when her eyes met his. Eyes that weren't quite his. The same eyes she'd seen outside in the snow, glowing golden eyes with slitted pupils.

Oh crap! She'd been caught red handed. There was no talking her way out of this one.

The growl that rumbled from his chest vibrated through her, going directly to her core with a sensation of need that set her clit on fire and her pulse quickened, yet she dared not move a muscle.

Marcus' mind felt foggy, his thoughts detached, like he was in a dream. A very sexy and horny dream. He definitely wasn't in control of his body, so it must be a dream, he surmised, allowing himself to just go with it.

It never occurred to him that he was in fact awake and taking a backseat to the beast inside him.

Before she could say a word, Brin found herself flat on her back. Marcus hovering over her, poised between her legs looking ready to pounce, his iridescent eyes glowing like lampposts as he licked his lips hungrily.

He stared at her so intently, she could swear he was looking directly into her soul. His brow furrowed, as though understanding, but not accepting her inner turmoil. Then his head descended, and his mouth covered hers, and she lost all sense of reason.

The kiss started soft, his tongue drifting across hers, tasting and teasing with infinite care. He tasted like rain and sunshine and flammable substances. It grew quickly like a wildfire, intensified, became savagely fierce and demanding as he plundered her mouth, explored and invaded it with a driving primal need. The kiss siphoned away every last bit of uncertainty she'd tucked away in the recesses of her mind, and kissed him back every bit as fiercely.

He fitted into the heated cradle of her hips, made perfectly to take his weight. Brin moaned at the feel of him, his hard shaft wedged between their bodies, pressing against her inner thigh. She gripped his backside and rocked her hips against him, desperate to feel that steel rod wedged where she most needed him. Filling her. The hollow ache inside her was so intense she didn't think she would survive it a minute longer.

Breaking the steamy kiss, Brin lay stretched beneath him, her face flushed with need. With purposeful movement Marcus removed her bra and then her panties, leaving his own boxers until last, sliding them below his knees to kick them off.

As his rigid cock sprang free, his eyes fixed firmly on her face. Brin's eyes filled with covetous delight. She licked her lips at the sight of his turgid length jutting invitingly from his hips. Her slender fingers wrapped around it with tentative fascination and revelled in the desperate male sound that broke from his throat.

Brin held the heavy shaft in her hand, marvelling at its feel. It felt like silky soft skin covering solid steel. So much better than her tentative strokes through the barrier of his boxers, she thought with delight. Her fingertips traced the length of the pulsing thick veins along its length and was amazed at its heat. So much hotter than the rest of his body. She couldn't quite close her fingers around its girth. Slowly, Brin pumped her fist along his shaft, building momentum as his hips flexed into her touch, then lightening her strokes to only use the tips of her nails, teasing him and driving him into a frenzy of need.

Marcus watched her intently, thoroughly engrossed in his vivid fantasy. It felt so real, he could feel the pressure building inside him as she stroked him, could feel the softness of her body beneath his. He wanted her so badly it hurt. He'd been suffering a major case of blue balls for nearly a week, and now, finally he could feel that inner tension loosening, the one that had kept his release locked inside his balls without relief. But for that, he needed to be inside her. He would only claim her at the height of her pleasure.

That was an odd thought, but as this was just a dream he ignored it in favour of enjoying more of it.

Removing her hand from his cock, Brin fought against him to regain her grip. That was until Marcus slipped a hand between her thighs, finding a delicious spot to play with. Brin lay back to give him control, quaking visibly when his fingers brushed over the silken folds. When he sank them deeper, she shuddered, the sensation so exquisitely intense. Those magically dextrous fingers began a steady stroke which had her groaning in increasing anticipation.

Pleas rolled off her tongue, overwhelmed by the onslaught of ecstasy, even as she forced herself to bite down on the words of love saturating her every molecule.

As Brin stretched against him, reaching for him, another moan whispered past her lips, so too her hips tilted up further into his touch. His fingers continued their dextrous tease, his arm bracing his body above hers and watched in fascination as she cried out and convulsed as her orgasm overtook her.

But he wasn't done, far from it. Now that she was primed for him, her tight channel relaxed and ready to take his size and length, he moved his body over hers, he slid the length of his lethal arousal intimately through her cleft. With every glide, the tip of his shaft rubbed against her sensitised clit, sending shockwaves through her of the orgasm she hadn't yet recovered from.

Marcus flexed his pelvis, his hard shaft delving lower, over her moist welcoming entrance, the beading tip gliding easily, joining with the slick juices seeping from her core.

Her gaze lifted to his, locking the breath in his chest.

Sweet Jesus! She was so incredibly beautiful and sexy as hell.

How was it that he'd never had a dream like this before? It was so damned hot, he never wanted to wake up.

Their gazes locked as he slid into her welcoming heat with one smooth stroke.

Marcus froze as a stunning ecstasy combined with a sense of…rightness, blazed through him.

Mine!

That thought jolted through him like a lightning strike.

Brin cried out at the sudden intrusion, pleasure washing over her. She opened her mouth to scream, and Marcus covered it with his aggressive kiss, driving her higher and higher with his hungry demands. Her body eagerly devoured every inch of his hard length, squeezing it tightly between her inner walls as he pushed inside her, craving more.

The sweet, hot flesh that surrounded him, clasped at him in an incessant embrace, so eager and wild, doubling the sensation of every movement he made into her. Flexing around him, tiny flutters of sensation, tight, rippling caresses washed over his erection as he worked it into her. First short, desperate thrusts, and then hard lunges as he began to fuck her with all the strength and desperation of the hunger that surged through him.

Brin bucked under the onslaught, meeting him thrust for thrust.

A growl tore from his lips, he tried to hold it back. He wanted to hold back the orgasm he was rocketing toward.

He wanted to draw out the dream, make it last infinitely longer, explore her body thoroughly and let her explore his, but Marcus wasn't in control.

Marcus' body tensed further, the rhythm of his pumping hips changing, seeking and yet trying desperately to delay his own release as he deliberately drove her back up and over the edge of insanity once more.

Marcus felt her orgasm then in a way he had never imagined possible, it roared through his senses as if it was his own. Her muscles clamped down, flexed, drawing his release from his pulsing shaft as he buried himself to the hilt, deep within her. His powerful release began to surge inside the milking depths of her womb as her inner muscles rippled around him. Lava-hot spurts, it sent her spiralling into the realms of sensation so exquisite she could only sink into it, allow it to explode around her, through her, until she dissolved into the sweet effervescent mists of peace. His hoarse male shout, mated with her feminine scream as she began to buck in his grip, orgasming with a violence that filled him with such a rush of male pride that his chest clenched with emotion. Hard blasts of his seed jetted into the tight confines of her clutching grip.

Mine!

Marcus felt his body vibrate as though he was about to shift, his facial features elongating into his wolf, his jaw primed ready to bite Brin between her neck and shoulder, to mark her as his.

Claim her as his.

Fuck!

This wasn't a dream. This was really happening, and the beast within him was about to claim Brin as his *mate*.

Shock hit him as effectively as though a bucket of iced water had been dumped on him, and he roared at the beast within him, demanding its submission, taking back control of his body with a jolt.

Brin was oblivious of his struggle as she cried out from the powerful implosion taking her apart from the inside, expanding outward with earth-shattering aftershocks. The cataclysmic explosion rendered her breathless and boneless. Her inner walls convulsed and shuddered around him, adding a new layer of desperation to his predicament.

While he narrowly avoided claiming her, he felt no less bonded to her as his own orgasm continued to surge through him.

If he'd had any doubts before about being the cursed lycan in that damned prophecy, he had none now. Except now, he didn't see it so much of a curse as a complication. A huge complication.

For one thing, Brin despised him.

For another, he still had a girlfriend…technically.

They collapsed against one another, shaking and shuddering. Neither of them spoke, just lay there in silence, enjoying the warmth of each other's embrace, knowing it wasn't likely to be repeated.

Marcus held her close, until she drifted off to sleep again, his hand gliding up and down along her upper arm, his fingers tracing the outline of the serpent armband, and his eyes locked onto the mark on his wrist.

The rash was completely gone, and the image of a dragon was now fully formed beneath his skin.

That wasn't the only thing he noticed. He no longer felt as though he had the fires of Hell burning his body from the inside out, and he felt like himself again…only stronger.

What did that mean, he wondered.

20

"What happened to your face?"

"It's nothing, really. It was one of those rock meets a hard place, type situations," Owen said, touching the dark swelling around his eye.

It was getting harder to contain the lycan who'd been infected only five days before. He was becoming much more violent and seemed to have lost the ability of any reasoning at all. His cell was now a battle ground of strength and brutality just to get a blood sample from him.

And to make things worse, Klaus was also beginning to go down the same path.

"Is the bastard alright?" Alex asked.

"Him? What about me? I was the one who got hit. The man is completely feral."

"Did you kill him?"

Owen smirked. "No, of course not. He'll be fine....once the bruises on his face...and bones mend."

"You broke his bones?" Alex asked.

"Only his collar bone. It was either that or his neck, and since the objective here is to cure him, *not* kill him…"

"I'm sure he'll forgive you one day. If not, well, I guess he'll repay the favour." Alex told him.

"That's assuming he'll remember anything that's happened to him recently. I don't think there's much going on inside that mind right now."

"That's assuming we can save him, or Klaus…or Gustav," Eytan told them as he entered the lab.

"What do you mean, Gustav?" Alex asked.

"Gustav is starting to show symptoms as well. He's waiting in one of the cells to speak with you."

"Hell's hairy balls. This isn't good." Owen muttered to no one in particular.

"It's all the more reason why we need to take drastic measures to find a cure," Alex said. He left off the end of that statement...*Before it's too late.* They were all thinking it, there was no need to say it out loud.

Grabbing something off a medical trolley in the corner of the lab, Alex walked over to Owen.

"Ouch. What was that?" Owen asked rubbing at the back of his neck where Alex had jabbed him with a needle.

"Nothing."

While Owen was busy rubbing his neck, Alex grabbed his other arm, and with lightning speed, sliced a piece of flesh from his forearm.

"Fuck! Why'd you do that?" Owen cursed, forgetting about his neck to stare at the bleeding patch on his arm.

"Do I need a reason?"

"Fuck you, arsehole. That hurts."

"Yeah, I feel real bad," Alex said without any sincerity. "Actually, I did have a reason. I needed a bigger skin sample, and I figured a poisoned needle was a good distraction."

"Seriously? Poison? You could've just used a local anaesthetic."

Alex thought on that for a moment. "Hmm, I didn't think of that. Oh well, next time."

"Next time? Hell no!"

"Plus, I wanted to know what effect the poison would have on you. How do you feel?"

"From the poison, I don't feel anything. My arm however, has a huge fucking hole in it and hurts like a bitch." Oh, he spoke too soon.

"You okay buddy?" Alex asked, his tone heavily laced with excited curiosity.

"Give me a sec. I'm not sure whether I want to vomit up my liver or shred yours. What poison did you use." Owen growled as his balance tipped to one side and he fell, collapsing on the ground, landing flat on his back.

"Only cyanide." Alex replied matter-of-factly.

Only! Only?!

Fortunately, Owen recovered quickly, sitting up within a minute, shaking his head as though his ears were ringing. The only side effect being a mild headache.

He had come to the Ukraine base, knowing he was going to be used as a pin cushion and virus incubator, but Alex had just taken it one step too far.

Getting to his feet, he walked to the trolley where Alex had placed the knife, picked it up and marched over to Alex, who had already lost interest in Owen, since he'd recovered so quickly from the poison, and had moved onto placing his skin under a microscope.

Owen raised the knife and drove it down. Hard.

Alex reflexively stood up.

"You stabbed me, fuck nut. Why'd you do that?" Alex inspected the sharp metal tip poking through the front of his right shoulder from the blade buried to the hilt in his back.

"Why do you think?"

"Well, are you going to just stand there, or pull this knife from my back?" Alex growled indignantly.

An evil grin crossed Owen's face.

"If you insist."

Owen put one hand on Alex's shoulder, then gripped the knife handle with the other. "I'm going to count to three. One, two…"

"Son of a bitch. FUCK YOU! That hurt." Alex cursed.

"I don't know why you're complaining, I thought you were into pain?"

"FYI, for future reference, I only like pain when my *mate* inflicts it."

In a matter of seconds, the wound had healed and all traces of it had vanished. "Damn, that's another shirt ruined," Alex muttered disappointedly.

"Okay, now tell me what that felt like?" Owen asked in a biting tone.

Alex curled his fist into a ball and punched Owen in the gut. "Something like that."

"Unbelievable. Would you two morons get your shit together, please. We don't have time for this bullshit." Eytan told them, although he wondered why he bothered wasting his breath, neither of the two men seemed to pay him any attention.

Owen looked at his bleeding arm where his skin used to be.

"Look what you did to my arm, this is going to take months to heal, and it'll probably need a skin graft. Arsehole."

"It's a small sacrifice to make for science." Alex shrugged, then turned to look at the wound, a sly grin turning up the corner of his mouth with a devious look. "I could speed up the process if you like."

"How?"

"Give me your arm." Alex told him.

Reluctantly, Owen lifted his arm, holding it out in front of him.

"Do you trust me?"

"Not as far as I can throw you," Owen growled, but left his arm stretched out in front of him, more curious than worried about what Alex might do next.

Alex placed a hand beneath Owen's forearm to support it, lifting it higher as he bent his head down, his tongue giving the flesh wound a few long, slow licks.

Owen's eyes widened as he watched the effects of Alex's healing hormone in his saliva go to work. First the blood stopped oozing, then the edges of the wound began to repair themselves, the five-centimetre sized hole in his arm shrinking by the second until there was no trace of the injury.

"Wow! That was cool."

"Great. Now, if you're both finished, can we get back to work?" Eytan growled.

Alex rolled his eyes and turned toward the corridor. "Come on. Gustav's waiting."

Owen shot Eytan a look. "How bad is he?"

"Only a fever so far, but…" Eytan replied with a worried shrug.

They moved down the dim corridor, the lights humming faintly overhead. The nearer they got to the occupied cells, the stronger the stench of sweat, fear, and rabid aggression became.

At the first cell, the originally infected lycan continued pacing in erratic, jerking motions, foam streaking down the corner of his mouth. His fingernails, now blackened, thickened talons, scraped against the walls, and one arm hung a little lower from his broken collar bone near his shoulder. The crude sling used to try to support the arm was shredded into pieces on the floor. He barely registered their approach except to snarl at them, red eyes bulging with animalistic fury.

The next cell held Klaus. He was still lucid enough to glower at Owen with venom, though the fog in his eyes told them his lucidity was fading by the hour.

Then they reached the far cell.

Gustav sat on the edge of the cot, elbows braced on his knees, breathing hard. Sweat plastered his dark hair to his forehead, and his normally sharp brown eyes were now rimmed with feverish yellow. He lifted his head as the trio approached.

"You're late," Gustav rasped, though the words lacked bite, more resigned than accusatory.

Alex stepped closer. "You look like shit."

Gustav ignored him and gestured toward the other two prisoners. "You see what's happening. Five days for him," he nodded toward the feral lycan. "Two days for Klaus. And now me." He swallowed hard. "We don't have much time, and if I'm right, I'm not going to be the last one in one of these cells. And I don't want my daughter to end up in here too. If I have it, then there's a good chance that she does too. I've confined her to our private quarters, just in case, but I need you to keep an eye on her."

Eytan's expression softened. "Of course. And we're working as fast as we can."

"I know you are." Gustav leaned back against the wall, every movement stiff, deliberate. "But it won't be fast enough unless you use every option available."

Alex frowned. "What do you have in mind?"

"Teagan. When Oliver was bitten by the hellhound a few years ago and was dying, we needed to buy some time to save him." He looked at Eytan. "She created a stasis spell. Put him in suspended animation just long enough for her to make a cure."

Understanding dawned on all three faces.

"Bloody hell," Owen breathed. "Would a stasis spell freeze the progression of the virus?"

"Yeah. And make collecting samples easier and safer for everyone" Eytan finished. His gaze flicked again toward the feral lycan a couple of cells down the hall. "He's not going to last another twelve hours at this rate. And Klaus…"

Klaus groaned from his cell, barely conscious.

Gustav exhaled shakily. "I'm sure Teagan still has the spell, but she'll need to make the potion again, and that's going to take time." Time that they didn't have.

Eytan straightened. "I'll call her now."

He strode down the corridor, already lifting his phone.

Gustav sagged back against the wall, relief softening his grim expression. "Good."

Alex gripped the bars. "We're not letting you die."

A faint smile crossed Gustav's lips. "I know. I trust you." His gaze flicked to Owen. "All of you."

Eytan returned moments later. "She's at the manor and she says she has all the ingredients there that she needs for the potion. She'll have it done in a couple of hours and they'll arrange for one of the nephilim to bring it to the forest. I'll organise one of the men to collect it from there. We should have you all in stasis within a few hours."

Alex nodded sharply. "Just hang in there."

Gustav nodded.

As they turned to leave, Gustav's voice followed them, low and strained. "Whatever happens…thank you."

None of them spoke until they reached the laboratory again. The silence wasn't uncomfortable, just heavy, weighted with urgency.

Inside the lab, Owen glanced around as Alex arranged blood vials and labelled petri dishes. "Alright," he said, exhaling. "Before we start, do you need more skin? Blood? Bone? Hair? Whatever. Just tell me now so I can mentally prepare myself."

Alex tapped a pen against his chin thoughtfully. "Actually, since you're offering…" His eyes gleamed with unholy scientist glee. "…probably."

Owen muttered a curse and rubbed his healed forearm. "Of course you do."

Eytan sighed. "Try not to carve him up like a Christmas ham."

"No promises," Alex said cheerfully, reaching for his scalpel.

Owen stared at him flatly. "…I hate you."

Alex grinned. "Good. Hold out your arm."

"You'll heal whatever you cut off, right?" Owen asked, his voice tight with nervous anticipation.

"Sure…eventually."

"You might want to hold off of that. Teagan also told me something else about putting them all in stasis." Eytan began, waiting until he had their full attention before continuing. "They need to drink the potion, but there is a spell that has to be performed at the same time. I'm not a druid, so I can't do it," he said, looking directly at Owen.

Owen's mouth opened and then closed again on its hinges. "I can't do it, my magic isn't powerful enough."

"What if there were two of you?" Alex asked.

"Sure, two druids together could probably do it? But who do you have in mind?"

"Elise. She's not as powerful as her oldest sister, but she's already here and she's done similar spells in the past."

"What? No way. Are you forgetting Elise is Gustav's daughter, a lycan. She's just as susceptible to this virus as any other lycan. Gustav has confined her to her quarters and that's exactly where she should stay." Eytan countered angrily.

"I have an idea that would keep her perfectly safe."

They both looked at Alex as though he'd lost his mind. That was, until he walked to a cupboard in the lab and showed them what was inside.

A hazmat suit?

"This isn't just any hazmat suit, I brought this with me from my lab at Oxford. It's been especially made to be safe from nuclear radiation contamination, not for me of course, but my lab assistants get nervous working with me. Anyway, if Elise was wearing this suit, she could enter the cells and perform the spell with you, and she'd be completely safe."

"Huh. I guess we have a plan." Owen agreed.

Next to him, Eytan just shook his head. He could see this plan going sideways very easily, but made no comment. What was the point, he was outnumbered.

The air inside Havenswood Manor thrummed with tension, activity, and the low-grade hum of magic.

Teagan stood at the enormous bench in the kitchen, sleeves rolled up, hair twisted into a messy knot, grinding something that looked suspiciously like a pink shimmering moss with a mortar and pestle. Mrs P, bustled beside her, sorting jars and herbs with the brisk efficiency of a woman used to general kitchen chaos, and determined to keep it from spilling onto her tiled floor.

"Right," Mrs P muttered, squinting at a shelf. "Heavens above, who moved the powdered mitragyna speciosa? I placed it next to the mint. It's an easy system, logical. They both start with M!"

"That depends entirely on your definition of 'logical'," Teagan said, not looking up.

"And your point is?"

Teagan sighed and pointed to the clearly labelled shelf above the counter. The sign read in Mrs P's neat cursive:

Ingredients to Turn You Into a Chicken — Not Ingredients to Use On Chicken.

Beneath it were neatly arranged jars, glittering powders, dried herbs, pickled roots, odd vials of condensed substances, and other things better left unlabelled for the sake of visitors' mental health.

Mrs P grunted. "See? Easy."

Teagan snorted. "I never should've asked."

"Find what you need love?"

"Yes. But keep everyone out of the kitchen for the next half hour. This stasis potion needs to be exact. I have to make more of it, and make it stronger than the one I made for Oliver. We don't know how long we'll need to keep them under."

Mrs P sighed, nodding. "Yes love. Let's get to it then."

Before Teagan could answer, the back door swung open, letting in a blast of cold air, and four large wyverns, covered in frost and looking like the world's most furious selection of hot, pissed-off male models.

Raif, Seth, Wade and Ky strode in, shedding snow and irritation in equal measure. They moved through the kitchen like a storm front, boots thudding, tension radiating off them in palpable waves.

"We're back," Raif announced unnecessarily.

"The weather turn bad again?" Teagan answered without looking up.

"What gave that away?" Wade asked.

Seth leaned on the counter. "And we're freezing our bollocks off."

"You have my sympathies," Teagan lied flatly. "Now don't breathe on the cauldron. Contamination risk."

They wisely retreated.

The brothers found Alaric, Narayan, Sebastian and several of the manor's inhabitants gathered in the lounge room. Grace and her cousins, Riley and Finn, were curled along one of the couches watching TV, while Nadia, Kaitlyn and Paige, talked quietly amongst themselves with anxious expressions.

Alaric was pouring himself a drink, looking like a man who had exceeded his daily limit of stress by approximately one millennium, and while he lifted glass number whatever, to his lips, he silently wished he could actually get drunk.

Seb lifted his head. "How'd you go?"

Raif exhaled through his nose. "We covered more ground today. Dray's list helped. We eliminated at least two dozen structures, cabins, an old ranger huts, a few long-abandoned research shacks."

"That's good," Grace piped up from the couch. "Isn't it?"

"It's progress," Ky agreed. "But…"

The unfinished sentence weighed heavily.

"But?" Narayan pressed.

Raif rubbed the back of his neck. "We're guessing. We're going from one cabin to another, and for all we know, we're going in the opposite direction to where we should be."

Wade frowned. "And the weather cut us off again."

"If we're lucky, we only seem to get a small window each day," Seth growled. "Barely enough to cover proper ground."

Raif's jaw clenched. "And if Emil's right and the Guild's demons have a way to track Brin directly…then while we're flying blind, those bastards are closing in on her."

A horrified silence fell over the room.

Paige looked up sharply. "Hold on. What about the charm?"

Kaitlyn blinked. "What charm?"

"The watch," Nadia said. "The one we gave Brin with the forgettable charm on it. The one to keep people from noticing her."

"Oh, right!" Paige sat up straighter.

Nadia nodded slowly. "Could we track it, do you think?"

Kaitlyn's eyes lit with hope. "Use it like a GPS?"

"We'd have to write a whole new spell to do that. A big one. It would be more than simple scrying. We'd need an anchor object on this side as an indicator, something the spell could essentially tether the watch's signature to."

Grace gasped suddenly. "What about Riley's snow globe!"

All eyes turned to her.

"It lights up already," she said quickly. "Dad bought it from that knick-knack store in Oxford. You shake it and it changes colours based on your mood."

Paige blinked. "That's brilliant. If we imbue that with a directional charm…and craft a link so it lights up and glows stronger the closer it gets to Brin…"

"That could definitely work," Nadia whispered.

"It would be primitive, but hey," Kaitlyn added dryly, "We don't have time to get too fancy."

Nadia's eyes sharpened. "But someone will need to hold it. It's not going to work remotely. Someone will have to be riding a dragon and navigate."

All eyes then turned toward Kaitlyn.

Kaitlyn blinked. "What? Why are you…what?"

Paige smirked. "You're the only one who's ridden a dragon enough times to stay on without falling off."

Kaitlyn swallowed, looking toward Raif. "Well…yes. I suppose flying is kind of second nature now," she agreed.

Raif's entire body softened, pride and worry flickering in equal measure. "Are you sure about this?"

Kaitlyn straightened. "Yes. Absolutely."

"I'll get my snow globe," Riley told them excitedly, jumping up from the couch in an instant, running out the door and up the stairs to his bedroom.

Seth let out a long breath. "How long will it take to create the spell?"

"We'll have it ready by the morning. Promise." Paige replied. They were probably going to have to work on it all night, but it was worth it, if it works.

Ky nodded.

Nadia grabbed their family's Book of Shadows, hoping to find a similar spell they could use as a base for the new one they had to create. "Let's charm a snow globe. I never thought I'd say that." She said with a shrug.

The entire manor became a buzzing hive of frantic, hopeful activity, magic scribbled on parchment, potion fumes drifting under the doors, wyvern pacing echoing through the corridors, and one snow globe on the dining table beginning to glow faintly, as if sensing its purpose.

21

Brin woke alone.

For a long, disoriented moment, she lay still beneath the quilt, breathing in the scent that clung to the pillows, warm cedar, smoke from last night's fire, and beneath that…Marcus.

Her heart squeezed, the memory of his hands on her skin, his mouth, his body moving with hers, too vivid, too consuming. Heat flushed up her neck. What had she done?

What had they done?

She rolled onto her back, covering her face with both hands. It had been incredible, yes, earth-shatteringly incredible, but it was also an enormous mistake. A mistake with consequences she wasn't ready to face.

Sliding her hand across to the other side of the bed, it felt cool. Marcus must have been gone for a while.

Good, she told herself. Distance is good. Space is good.

Mortification needs room to breathe.

Brin pushed herself upright, aware of the moist tenderness between her thighs, a reminder that the incredibly hot sex they'd had during the night hadn't been a dream.

"Pull yourself together, Brin," she muttered to herself.

She showered quickly, letting the warm water wash away the lingering tension in her muscles, buying herself a precious few minutes to gather her thoughts and courage to face him.

Switching off the water, she pulled back the curtain to grab a towel and was met with the smell of something utterly divine drifting up the hallway and into the door-less bathroom.

Food.

Her stomach growled loudly, louder than her pride, and she followed the scent like a starving bloodhound.

Marcus stood at the gas stove, shirtless except for a pair of worn, grey sweatpants slung indecently low on his hips, flipping French toast in a cast-iron pan. Sun poured through the large kitchen window behind him, warming the room with honeyed light. The entire space glowed around him like he'd stepped out of a painting titled *Domesticated Greek God.*

Brin's heart did an impulsive somersault at the sight of him, ending with another flush of moisture between the already sensitive folds between her legs.

Marcus glanced over his shoulder and smiled. A small, uncertain, but devastating smile.

"Morning," he said quietly.

"Morning," she echoed, voice embarrassingly breathy.

He nodded toward the table. "Sit. Breakfast's almost done."

She did, trying not to stare at the play of muscles across his back as he plated everything, bacon crisped just the way she liked it, golden French toast dusted with sugar, eggs cooked perfectly over-easy. A pot of rich-smelling coffee steamed beside two mugs.

"You cooked all this?" she asked, genuinely surprised.

Marcus shrugged as he brought the plates over. "You've met my mother, haven't you?"

Brin snorted. "Yeah." Jocelyn was definitely memorable, but not for any good reasons.

"Well," he continued, sitting opposite her, "It probably won't shock you that it wasn't her who taught me anything useful." His expression softened. "Gran raised me, mostly. Growing up, I spent more time at the manor with her than at home, from the age of about 5, she let me help cook. Or…annoy her, depending on the day."

Brin's chest warmed with a chuckle. "She taught you very well. This looks incredible."

"Looks?" he lifted a brow. "Taste first. Praise after."

She cut into the French toast and her eyes fluttered closed on the first bite.

"Oh my God," she moaned. "I didn't realise how hungry I was. Marcus, this is delicious."

A faint flush of pride coloured his cheeks. "It's just breakfast."

"It's culinary artistry."

That earned her a small laugh, a genuine heartfelt laugh that pulled at something inside her chest.

They ate in relative silence, both trying to ignore the enormous invisible elephant in the room, wearing a neon sign that said: *WE TOTALLY HAD SEX LAST NIGHT.*

Brin kept her gaze on her plate. Marcus kept his on his coffee mug. And both of them were two seconds from spontaneously combusting from the awkwardness of the situation.

As a cloud drifted by, the sun beamed through the kitchen window, warming the wooden floorboards and lighting dust motes in the air. Outside, the world looked brand new, blue skies and powdery soft snow. After the last few days, the bright sunlight seemed to bounce about the room, giving their moods an injection of hope.

"Looks like the storm's gone," Marcus said.

Brin nodded. "Yeah. Finally. Maybe, today's the day," she said, but her voice lacked enthusiasm.

"Hopefully," he said, but there was a hesitation, barely noticeable, yet it was there.

Because being rescued meant…losing this.

Losing the strange fragile peace between them. Losing the soft glow of something growing in the quiet hours between crisis and survival.

The silence stretched, heavy now. Too heavy.

Brin swallowed hard, then blurted out, "I'm sorry."

Marcus blinked. "For what?"

"For last night," she said quickly, words tumbling out. "It was…it shouldn't have happened. I rushed outside without thinking, without putting on my jacket. If I had, what happened last night, wouldn't have happened. It was my fault."

He set down his fork. Slowly.

"No," he said firmly. "Brin, you didn't force me. I knew what I was doing."

"Marcus…"

"I couldn't stop myself," he admitted, jaw tightening as he looked down, unable to meet her gaze. "That's on me. I crossed the line."

"My behaviour wasn't…"

"I've been a bastard to you for years," he cut in again. "You didn't deserve any of it."

Her throat tightened. She stared down at the last bite of French toast, her stomach clenching too tightly to eat it. "But you have a girlfriend, Marcus. I knew that, and I still…"

He flinched, even that tiny reminder hit deep.

"I know." His voice was gravel. "And that's why I'm saying this. I don't want to hurt you, not anymore."

A sharp pulse of pain stabbed beneath Brin's ribs.

Of course he still cared about his girlfriend.

She forced a nod. "Right. Yes. Exactly. It was…just a mistake."

She said it lightly. Casually. A lie that tasted like ash on her tongue from her burning heart.

Marcus stared at her for a long, quiet moment.

He wanted to tell her. God, he wanted to tell her everything.

Tell her that sex with her wasn't a mistake. That she was the only right thing in his life.

That she was his *mate*.

Last night he'd almost bound them together forever, and a selfish part of him wished he had.

He wanted to tell her how much he truly cared about her. He wanted to tell her he didn't want this fragile intimacy to vanish when they were rescued, he wanted it to grow into so much more.

But he couldn't, not while he was still technically with someone else. Not until he put things right.

So, he said nothing.

And the silence that settled between them, hurt them both.

When breakfast was finished, Marcus stood. "We're getting low on firewood, I'll be outside if you need anything," he said, unable to look directly at her.

"Okay," she said softly. "I'll, um…clean up a bit."

She watched him pull on his boots, his broad back tense beneath his shirt, and felt something inside her deflate.

The moment the door shut behind him, she pressed both hands to the edge of the counter and exhaled shakily.

He doesn't want you the way you want him, she told herself. *Last night was just a moment of weakness. Nothing more.*

But even as she tried to convince herself, she wasn't sure she believed it.

Outside, Marcus swung the axe hard, splitting a log cleanly through the centre. The wood cracked sharply, echoing back from the trees like a warning shot.

He didn't feel cold. He didn't feel tired. Nor did he feel feverish like he had for the past few days. In fact, he felt…incredible. As though he'd suddenly been injected with a shot of energy and vitality.

The serpent's bite had done *something* to him. And whatever it was, seemed to have settled overnight, fixed itself.

The wolf within him felt calm, the unsettling agitation now gone. For the first time since they were in the cave, he felt steady and whole.

Marcus exhaled, his breath steaming in the crisp air.

I have to tell Brin the truth.

He needed to tell her everything…about the prophecy, and how he felt about her and what he wanted for their future.

He owed her that, she deserved better than silence and regret.

At lunch, he decided.

He'd talk to her then. He'd lay everything out, and he'd deal with whatever consequences came of his confessions.

Today felt like the beginning of something new, something right.

Nothing could possibly ruin that.

Or so he believed.

The sky was an endless, crystalline blue, an almost mocking contrast to the fear and desperation thrumming through Raif and his brothers.

Four enormous green dragons soared in tight formation above the vast Canadian wilderness, their massive wings slicing through the cold air with effortless ease. Sunlight shimmered over their scales, making them blaze like living emerald coloured jewels against the white expanse below.

Kaitlyn sat against the ridge of Raif's neck, nestled between two protective spines, bundled in so many layers of winter gear she resembled a colourful, marshmallow. Her gloved hands clutched the snow globe, like her life depended on it. The charm they placed on it, lighting it up like a beacon,

The wind stung her cheeks, the only part of her not covered, reminding her just how high they were, and how cold the world beneath them was. At least the sun was out, providing a little comfort, softening the harshness of the climate.

Far below, stretched an endless sweep of white rolling hills, drowning under metres of snow, ribbons of frozen rivers, and dark patches of forest where skeletal trees clawed at the sky. Every gust of wind sent glittering flurries swirling upward like shaken diamonds. It was beautiful, and yet so brutally unforgiving, Kaitlyn thought.

Leaning forward a little more, she touched the scales on Raif's neck.

"It's still green," she told him through their mating bond. *"Keep heading north-east."*

Raif dipped a wing and banked smoothly, his brothers adjusting in perfect unison.

As they crossed over another mountain, the swirling colours abruptly flashed. *Red!*

"Stop! Wrong direction!" she shouted aloud, though Raif was already correcting his course.

He growled deep in his chest, wings beating harder. *"It changed again?"*

Kaitlyn clenched her jaw. *"Sorry! This thing's basically a magical mood ring having an identity crisis!"*

"It's working though," Raif soothed. *"Crude doesn't mean useless."*

That was true. Thankfully. Hopefully it wouldn't be too much further.

They carried on, flying lower, faster, more deliberately than they had on any previous day. Hope buoyed them all, for once they weren't searching blindly.

Twice they veered toward isolated cabins tucked between trees or perched on hillsides. Each time they landed in a thunder of snow and pounding wings, shifted back into human form to investigate each of the properties thoroughly.

Empty.

"We're close," Kaitlyn whispered, her heart hammering. "I can feel it."

They covered a few more miles, flying over more of the white landscape when Kaitlyn gasped. The snow globe, once swirling with a pale green, suddenly blazed a bright, vivid green.

"Raif! We're getting close!"

He surged forward in a blast of speed, his brothers flanking him in tight formation, casting long shadows across the treetops below like dark omens.

The land began to shift, forests thickening, slopes growing steeper.

"Smoke! Eleven o'clock!" Seth told his brothers.

Kaitlyn spotted it too. "There! Raif, there! That's definitely from a chimney!"

The dragons banked hard, excitement flaring through each of them.

We've found them! Raif thought with relief.

But the thrill of excitement lasted only seconds when Ky's telescopic sight spotted something amongst the barren trees below them a little way ahead. *"Movement. In the trees."*

Raif whipped his head toward the far edge of the forest.

And saw them.

Six dark shapes moving fast between the snow-laden trees, four men, armed, pushing through the drifts as though driven by purpose alone. And two creatures moving beside them. Long-limbed. Wrongly shaped. Their bodies cutting through the forest like shadows refusing to obey physics.

The Scree.

A cold wave of fury rippled through all four dragons.

Kaitlyn's blood turned to ice. "Raif, they're heading for the cabin!"

"We'll get there first. Hold on!" Raif's voice thundered through every mind in the formation.

The brothers streamlined their bodies and put more power into their wings, cutting through the air, as fast as the wind would carry them. Flying over the forest, they dipped lower, their senses and instincts sharpened like the razor edge of a knife.

The Guild and Scree were moving fast.

But, the dragons moved faster.

Reaching the far side of the forest, the cabin was only a hundred meters from them. Raif hit the ground so hard snow exploded outward in a powdery wave. The others landed beside him, an emerald wall of fury and lethal intent.

Kaitlyn scrambled down his paw, boots slipping, heart galloping. She sprinted for the cabin, nearly falling up the steps in her panic.

She pounded on the door with both fists, hoping and praying they were here. "Brin! Marcus!"

No response.

She struck the door again, harder. "Brin! Marcus! It's me, Kaitlyn. Open the door!"

From the corner of her eye, Kaitlyn saw the dragons form a line facing the forest, their heads lowering and wings half-spread, their tails lashing behind them and their lips curling back to reveal rows of gleaming teeth, shark-like teeth. Their enemy was nearing the edge of the forest, they could sense it.

"Kaitlyn?" a voice called.

She spun.

Marcus rounded the cabin from the far side, axe still in his hand, chest heaving, sweat glistening across his skin despite the cold.

Marcus broke into a broad grin, dropping the axe as he rushed to give her a huge hug. "What took you so long?"

Just as quickly, his smile slipped into a frown when he saw the terror on her face, and the dragons, restless and ready to kill something.

"What's happened?" he asked.

"Where's Brin and the others?" Kaitlin demanded urgently.

"Brin's inside. The others didn't make it, they died in the crash." Marcus told her, his own anxiety rising with her distress.

"Marcus, the Guild's found you. They're coming RIGHT NOW. They're in the forest and moving fast. And they've got demons with them. They'll be here any minute!"

Fuck!

Marcus didn't waste a breath.

He took the porch stairs in three long strides and slammed the door open.

"BRIN!" he roared. "We have to leave. Now!"

Brin appeared from the basement stairs, the concern on her face turning to confusion. "Marcus, what…?"

"Kaitlyn and your brothers are here," he told her, grabbing her hand and pulling her toward the door. "Come on. Get your jacket on. We have to go, right now. The Guild and their pets are here."

Her gaze darted to the doorway, and she froze at the sight of a terrified Kaitlyn waving frantically.

"RUN!" Kaitlyn yelled. "They're here! Come on!"

Brin snatched her jacket, only getting one arm through the sleeve before Marcus seized her hand.

"No time, MOVE!"

He dragged her out onto the porch as the dragons roared, an earth-shaking sound that sent birds exploding from the treetops. From within the forest, answering shrieks cut through the air, a high pitched, unnatural screech of the Scree announcing their approach.

"Marcus?" Brin looked over her shoulder in time to see the group emerge from the trees only a couple of hundred meters from them.

Snow shook loose from the branches above, as they burst from the forest, closing the distance between them at an unnervingly fast rate.

Brin didn't hesitate.

She leapt onto Seth's paw, scrambling expertly up his side before settling onto the ridge of his back like she'd been doing it since birth, which she had.

Marcus wasn't so graceful.

He grabbed onto the dragon's scale ridge, swung one leg over, and almost slid right off the other side as Seth's wings flexed.

"Hang on!" Brin grabbed his arm, steadying him in place.

"Let's go!" Marcus barked, wrapping both arms around her tightly.

Seth crouched, muscles coiling.

The demons shrieked, breaking into a sprint as Seth launched skyward with Brin and Marcus.

All four dragons exploded upward at once, snow blasting in every direction, wings beating hard as their powerful legs kicked them off the ground with seismic force.

Marcus clung to Brin with a death grip.

"Holy…SHIT!"

Brin twisted enough to shout over the wind. "Grip with your knees and hold onto his spine! And don't look down."

She told him not to look down. So naturally, that was the first thing he did. He'd only ever ridden on the back of a dragon a couple of times, and each time he'd been shit-faced terrified. This time seemed so different somehow. Maybe it was the adrenaline of the moment, he thought absently. As he looked down, the distance to the ground was comforting, not terrifying.

Seth banked, wings slicing through the air as they rose, higher and higher. The forest shrank beneath them. The Scree shrieked and the Guild's men pumped off round after round from their semi-automatic rifles, yet they were powerless now to reach them.

The cold wind bit at their faces, but the sunlight was warm and bright.

Brin felt Marcus tighten his arms abruptly, but not in fear. In relief.

They were safe.

Raif's voice boomed across the mental link to his brothers.

"Let's get out of here."

They climbed to where the air felt thinner and the world curved beneath them.

Kaitlyn held tight to Raif's neck spines, heart pounding as the familiar pressure built, static in the air, electricity crawling across the scales beneath her legs.

Almost in unison, the four dragons punched through the dimensional barrier with a sonic boom that rippled across the frozen world.

In the same heartbeat, they burst through again above Savernake Forest, another thunderous boom echoing across the English sky.

The manor came into view below. They were home.

For the first time in days, they were safe.

Descending like floating emerald stars, they each landed lightly, almost delicately, on the grassy lawn of Havenswood Manor.

Brin exhaled a shaky breath against Marcus' arm.

"We made it," she whispered.

Marcus held her tighter.

"Yeah," he said softly. But his heart was pounding with something more than relief.

He wasn't ready to let her go.

22

Brin barely had one leg over the side of Seth's broad neck when the manor doors burst open.

A tidal wave of people poured from the house, across the patio to the lawns at the bottom of the garden. Voices overlapped in a chaotic mix of relief, disbelief and raw, unfiltered emotion.

She slid the rest of the way down Seth's foreleg and hit the ground only to be swallowed by everyone. Grace got to her first, throwing her arms around her neck so hard Brin's breath hitched.

"Brin, I can't believe it, you're really here!"

Then Holly grabbed her.

Then Paige.

Then Teagan, squeezing her so tightly her ribs creaked.

Kaitlyn reached her last as she climbed down from Raif's back, tears streaming freely down her cold-reddened cheeks. "Don't you ever, ever, scare us like that again, do you hear me? Are you okay?"

Brin nodded, overwhelmed, too emotionally drained to do anything but hug her.

Behind her, Marcus climbed down a little less gracefully, only to be engulfed by the family horde too.

And then his mother was there. Jocelyn pushed her way through the crowd to reach Marcus, her overtures of relief loud and a little too forced to be genuine. Even so, she did manage to produce tears. Just one or two, glassing the edges of her eyes as she reached out and cupped her son's cheeks.

"Marcus…" Her voice hitched on a sob. "I was sure you were dead."

He blinked as she pulled him in for a hug. "I'm glad you have so much confidence in me, mum." He told her dryly as he hugged her back, stiffly. Marcus' throat worked around a sound he didn't let escape, but by his expression, Brin felt sure it as probably a growl.

Alaric stepped forward and Marcus straightened automatically, falling into soldier mode.

"Good to have you both home," Alaric said, clapping Marcus on the shoulder, his steely composure fractured by a degree of emotion Marcus had rarely seen from him, despite the fact that Alaric had helped raise him alongside his grandmother, for the majority of his childhood.

"It's great to be home," Marcus replied, giving him a brief hug, stepping back only to find himself surrounded by Brin's brothers.

"We can't thank you enough for keeping our sister safe. We owe you one. Anything you want, just ask." Raif told him sincerely.

Hmmm, hold that thought, Marcus mused, wondering if they'd be quite so accommodating when he told them that he wants their sister as his *mate*.

As the crowd escorted them toward the manor, Brin felt Marcus' eyes slide toward her and she looked over to meet his gaze. There was quiet desperation in his expression, along with frustration, disappointment and also relief, all tangling together and hanging in the space between them.

She offered him a tentative smile before looking away, distracted by the barrage of questions and more hugs coming at her from all directions.

Marcus continued to watch Brin as the women escorted her along the path to the kitchen's backdoor, in the opposite direction to where the men were leading him. He'd missed his chance to talk to her, and he knew that the conversation they desperately needed to have, would not be happening anytime soon.

At least, not today.

Probably not tomorrow either.

Not unless by some miracle, they somehow found time alone. Which, knowing her brothers and the rest of their mutual extended family, was as likely as pigs flying or Jehovah's Witnesses bypassing his house on their door knocking pilgrimage.

The women swept Brin into the kitchen and seated her at the kitchen bench, a cup of coffee appearing on the bench in front of her as they continued to fuss over her.

Questions flew before Brin could breathe.

"What happened?"

"How did you survive the cold?"

"Did you get hurt?"

"Did you see the demons again?"

"What about the pilot and the other guy in the helicopter?"

"What did you eat? How did you stay warm?"

"Was it as bad as we feared?"

Brin's pulse climbed, her breaths shortened.

Only minutes ago, she had been in a quiet cabin, picking supplies from the shelf in the basement to make lunch.

Then she was running for her life again, narrowly escaping the Guild and demons with her brothers very timely rescue.

Now…this.

It was too much, too fast, and too loud.

A pair of warm, steady hands closed around her shoulders. Mrs P.

"Alright, alright, that's enough, you pack of vultures," Mrs P announced in a kind but firm tone. "Give the girl some breathing room. She's just been through a terrible ordeal, give her some space."

The women reluctantly toned down their enthusiasm, but they all remained hovering around her protectively, curiously.

Mrs P cupped Brin's cheek. "Now love, another coffee, or maybe a nice pot of tea?"

Brin gave a weak smile. "Coffee, please."

Mrs P slipped an arm around her shoulders. "You're shaking." She said, patting Brin's clothes lightly, her warm smile turning into a frown. "You're soaked through to the bone, poor pet. Come on, love, we'll get you into something warm. This way."

She guided Brin through the rear kitchen door and down the short corridor to a staircase leading to the first floor, a short cut to Brin's own room in the manor.

"Go on," she encouraged. "Have a hot shower and put on some clean clothes, and come back down when you're ready."

Brin swallowed a lump of emotion. "Thanks, Mrs P."

The old housekeeper's smile broadened. "Welcome home."

Brin climbed the stairs and followed the corridor to her room. Closing the door behind her, she took a set of clean clothes from the dresser and stepped into the little bathroom. Turning on the taps, steam curled around her as she stepped under the shower spray, letting the hot water pound her skin until her pulse slowed and her breathing steadied.

She braced her hands against the tiles and let her forehead rest between them.

She was safe. She was home.

She should be relieved, but all she felt was…lost.

Now that they were back, that closeness between them was over. Marcus would go back to his life, and she to hers. Which was reasonable. Logical. Expected.

So why did it hurt so much?

Why did her chest ache with a hollow, twisting pressure that made her eyes burn? There was no need to debate the answer. Because she knew what last night had meant to her. And she knew what he believed it meant to him.

A mistake. A moment of weakness. A relapse in morality out of his sense of duty as a result of her hyperthermia, or whatever excuse he needed to tell himself.

Brin squeezed her eyes shut as another wave of emotion crested painfully, and for a second time in the last few days, she let herself cry.

He doesn't want you. He has a girlfriend.

Yet Brin couldn't stop replaying in her mind the way he'd held her afterward, like he couldn't bear to let go. And that kiss…that brutal kiss in the snow…and the soft, gentle drunk kiss.

Her hands trembled.

"Get it together," she chastised herself.

But she wasn't sure she could. Not yet.

Her only comfort was a tiny flicker of hope, the look he'd given her on the lawn before they we're whisked away to opposite ends of the house.

A look that said: *This isn't over*.

Could she dare to have hope?

Brin let the water wash over her and finally allowed herself a single, whispered truth.

"I don't want it to be over."

Marcus was led toward Alaric's study before he even had time to shake snow off his boots.

Oliver stood waiting with two other lycans from Cadley, arms folded, expressions grim but relieved. Saladin lingered behind them, hands clasped behind his back like a commander expecting a detailed report.

"What happened?" Alaric asked.

Marcus ran a hand through his hair. "Right. Okay. I'll give you the short version."

Oliver arched a brow. "We want the long version."

"Yes, Sir." Marcus replied.

He told them everything relevant, starting from *near* the beginning when they were at the cave at Mount Odin, where they were ambushed by the Guild, and again back at their camp. He told them about the helicopter being hit by lightning, and the crash, with Farrell and the pilot dying instantly, and how they found the cabin. He told them about the bad weather and blizzard conditions.

He left out the part where he was bitten by the serpent armband at the cave. He also omitted informing them about their constant arguments and the incidents involving the bathroom. And, he definitely didn't inform them about his fever, the mark on his wrist or the fact that for the last few days he had lost his ability to control his wolf. Nor did he mention that he had made love to Brin the night before and had nearly marked her as his *mate*.

Those details remained locked behind his teeth, guarded by a wolf that growled every time someone spoke Brin's name.

Oliver whistled low. "Hell of a week."

"No shit," Marcus muttered.

Narayan stepped closer. "And the Guild? They were closing in fast?"

"Too fast," Marcus said grimly. "We were thirty seconds away from being caught."

Narayan exhaled. "Good thing Brin's brothers found you when they did."

"You can say that again." He cleared his throat. "What's happening with the lycan who was shot with the infected dart on our last mission?" Marcus queried.

Oliver grimaced. "There's a lot to catch you up on. But it's…bad. Worse than we'd expected."

Alaric outlined the situation in the Ukraine base. Despite his own ordeal he'd endured in Canada as a result of the serpent armband bite, Marcus felt he'd been dealt the better of the two hands. If they didn't find a cure for the virus, the lycans currently infected were looking at a guaranteed death sentence. He almost felt guilty that he'd gotten off so lightly.

Marcus nodded, though irritation tugged at him. "I'm just wondering, if you don't need me for anything else right now, can I be excused?"

Oliver smirked faintly. "Eager to get out of here, are you?"

Marcus hesitated. Just one heartbeat, but Narayan caught it. Clearing his throat, he answered. "Yeah. I have to take care of something."

He had to make a phone call that would change his future.

It was a call he dreaded…but needed to make.

He needed to break things off with Candy. He'd missed his chance before they left for Canada, and he had no intention of dragging it out any longer. He owed it to her to be honest, stop living a lie and letting her believe they might have a long-term future together. Then he had to lay his cards on the table with Brin, she deserved the truth from him too.

One thing at a time though.

"I'll make it quick," Marcus said.

Oliver leaned back in his chair. "You'll have to wait a bit longer. Sanders is tying up a few things in Canada and should be here soon. No doubt he's going to want to debrief you too."

Marcus' jaw twitched. Fantastic. More time that Brin would continue to believe he regretted what happened between them, that he didn't care about her.

He needed to talk to her, explain everything and hope she forgave him for being such a huge fucking fool, because the way his wolf paced beneath his skin, told him one very simple truth, he needed her more than he needed air to breathe, and for once he was in complete agreement with the beast inside him.

Marcus was dismissed from the debriefing two hours later, although "dismissed" was probably a bit generous. He felt mentally wrung out, his head pounding so hard he wondered whether a marching band had taken up residence inside his skull, and his emotions felt like he'd been dropped into a tornado, with everything colliding together and spinning out of control, leaving him feeling irritable and short tempered.

The situation in the Ukraine with the virus…Gustav being infected now too. The situation was bad.

And layered on top of that was the Guild. Emil had confirmed to Alaric what Marcus already suspected, they weren't going to stop looking for Brin. Ever. She wore the Serpent Armband which they desperately wanted. More than that though, they also wanted her dead. She was a healer, and they'd systematically been killing off all healers, to what end, he hadn't been informed as yet. For all he knew there probably wasn't any reason, Morganna could have easily woken one morning and on a whim decided to have all healers killed. After all, the evil sorceress was certifiably crazy.

They'd all agreed that Brin's safety was their number one priority, so the decision had been made that she would remain at Havenswood Manor indefinitely, tucked safely behind the impenetrable wards on the property and the protection of Savernake Forest.

No Guild agents or Scree demons could set foot on the land, nor would they be able to detect her presence there. They couldn't say the same for her home in Avengard. Not even the high stone walls of the citadel would keep her safe. If the Scree could detect her, they would find a way to reach her.

Marcus rubbed a hand over his face as he stepped into the quiet hallway. He knew Brin well enough to know exactly how she would take this news. *She'll hate it,* he thought. *She'll feel trapped. Controlled. Caged.*

For once he wouldn't be the cause or the recipient of her anger, which he was very relieved about. But the selfish part of him felt relief for another reason too, one he didn't dare say aloud. If she was to remain at the manor, she would be much closer to him. It felt like the universe had handed him a second chance.

He needed to talk to her. Soon. Before she spiralled into thinking he didn't care about her.

Marcus exhaled, shaking off the tangling emotions long enough to take out his phone.

Time to handle the other mistake in his life.

He walked halfway down the corridor, ensuring he was alone, and pressed *call* on Candy's number.

The phone barely rang once.

"Marcus!" Candy's sparkling voice chimed through the speaker. "Baby, I've been so worried. I wondered if something had happened to you. I haven't heard from you in nearly two months."

Two months? Ah, right. Philippe took her home after her dinner here and wiped her memory, he must have forgotten to replace it with a false one, one where she had seen Marcus somewhere else.

"Candy." He cut her off gently. "Yes, I'm back."

She sighed dramatically. "I feel like I haven't seen you in forever. When can we catch up?"

He closed his eyes.

"Tomorrow night," he said. "Seven o'clock, at Lancasters."

"Perfect! I'll make a booking. You can pick me up and…"

"No," Marcus said. "I'll meet you there."

A tiny pause. Just long enough for irritation to flicker in her tone.

"Right. Okay. Fine." Then her voice brightened again. "Seven it is, babe."

"See you then."

He hung up quickly, jaw clenched. This wasn't going to be pleasant.

The moment the screen went dark, a voice behind him snapped like a whip.

"Well. That's disappointing."

Marcus nearly growled.

He turned.

Jocelyn stood a few metres away, arms crossed in front of her, lips pursed in that perpetual expression of disapproval she'd perfected over decades.

She tilted her head. "*Her* again?"

Marcus stiffened, he really wasn't in the mood for any of his mother's dramas. "Mum, don't start."

"Excuse me? I'm your mother," Jocelyn hissed, stepping closer. "You nearly *died*, Marcus. God knows what horrors you faced, and the moment you're safe you go running back to that…that airheaded social climbing bimbo?"

His nostrils flared. "It's my life, I'll hang out with whomever I choose."

"Have you ever stopped to think that your choices might reflect poorly on me?" she shot back. "You could do better. You could do so much better. Someone like Candy brings nothing to the table except embarrassment and…"

"Mum." Marcus' voice dropped dangerously low. "Enough. I don't want to hear your opinion."

Jocelyn's eyes narrowed. "Why? Because deep down you know I'm right?"

"I'm warning you…"

"I'm your mother," she snapped. "You owe me the respect of hearing my opinion whenever I choose to give it. I nearly lost you this week, Marcus! The thought of it nearly…"

"Oh, spare me," he cut in coldly. "You didn't come here out of a maternal need to see your children. You showed up because your husband is away and you wanted attention from someone. As always. If

I went missing when you weren't here, you wouldn't have given a shit about me, you never have and you probably never will. At least, not unless it suited you for some selfish reason," he bit out, thirty-two years of pent-up anger and resentment bursting the flood gates in an unstoppable rush.

Jocelyn's mouth fell open. "How dare you!"

"No, how dare *you*?" Marcus stepped closer, voice quiet but sharp. "Every time something happens to me, you make it about yourself. Well, I'm done with it. I'm done with the guilt trips you lay at my feet. I'm done with walking on eggshells so your delicate sensibilities don't get ruffled."

"You ungrateful boy."

"Go home mother."

The hallway went still.

Jocelyn blinked slowly. "Excuse me?"

"You heard me." Marcus folded his arms. "You're not welcome here. Go home."

Jocelyn's face contorted, wounded pride mixing with fury. "I will not be spoken to like this."

"Then walk away, leave." Marcus said. "Because that's how I feel."

For one suspended moment she stared at him, trembling with anger.

Then she spun on her heel and stormed off down the corridor, heels clicking sharply against the wooden floor.

Marcus let out a long breath and pinched the bridge of his nose.

"That went well," he muttered sarcastically to himself. "Fuck!"

He had no idea he wasn't alone.

Just around the bend of the hallway, hidden from view by the shadowed archway leading from the staircase, Brin stood frozen, her fingers pressed to her lips, heart racing.

She hadn't meant to eavesdrop. She had been heading back to the kitchen when she'd overheard him on the phone and wanted to give him the courtesy of some privacy. Then she'd overheard his confrontation with his mother, another situation she didn't want to get in the middle of. But it was his phone conversation that had her stomach twisting into knots.

Candy. Seven o'clock, at Lancasters Restaurant.

She knew that place, very upmarket…and perfect for romantic dinners.

Brin swallowed around the lump rising in her throat. He was seeing her tomorrow.

Of course he is, you idiot. And why wouldn't he, she's his girlfriend, she chastised herself.

That didn't mean she had to like the idea.

A bitter sting of jealousy throbbed through her chest, sharp enough to lock her breath in her lungs.

He's not mine. I have no claim on him, she told herself. Knowing that however, didn't stop the ache.

Brin pressed back against the wall, closing her eyes as Marcus' footsteps echoed away.

Her mind began to replay the incredible sex they'd had the night before, the heat in his eyes when he looked at her, and a bond she'd felt developing between them. She wanted to convince herself it was just her overactive imagination, but it wasn't. It was real, she was certain of it. Whether Marcus was prepared to admit it or not, he felt something for her.

Her conviction warred with doubt, culminating in curiosity. Did he look at Candy in the same way he'd looked at her? She had to know.

In that moment, Brin talked herself into going to that restaurant tomorrow night too. Not to interfere or cause trouble. Just to see for herself, to understand his connection to her, and put her mind at rest one way or the other.

Brin exhaled shakily.

And maybe, just maybe, to finally let him go.

23

Brin sat on her bed and looked out the window.

At first the only thing she noticed was the speckled dirt, layered upon the glass from the splattering of muddy rain over time, leaving an opaque film of obscurity when the sunlight caught it. As the sun shifted higher on the horizon, the light left the window's surface, instead catching tiny dew drops on the fronds of the ferns in the pot beneath it, glittering on the fine strands of a spider's web spread between them. There was no sign of the spider which had made it, but Brin doubted it was far away.

Much like those damned demons and the Guild. Always hovering in the shadows, rarely seen but somehow always present. Brin wasn't sure how she felt about that, the spider or demons. They both creeped her out to a degree, albeit for different reasons.

Not that the demons would be bothering her again for a while, not now that she was being confined to Havenswood Manor.

Confined. The word sat in her chest like a stone.

Being informed last night that she wasn't allowed to go back to her home in Fey, had pissed her off, but the news wasn't totally unexpected. She'd seen it in her brothers' eyes, in Alaric's careful tone before he'd even said the words. They'd all looked at her like she was made of glass, precious and breakable.

And while she did enjoy being at the manor, she hated the feeling of having her free will usurped.

It is, what it is, and like it or not, she just had to learn to live with it.

Besides, it wouldn't be forever, only until they could deal with the Guild, Morganna, Scorpion, the demons and Mephistopheles once and for all.

Her mind tried to stack those names into a neat little list of achievable goals, and promptly gave up.

Okay, putting that into perspective, she was likely to be stuck at the manor for a few years.

Years! Holy crap on a cracker.

Brin scrubbed both hands over her face and dragged them back through her hair, exhaling hard.

There was no use complaining about it, she just had to make the most of it, she reminded herself, again.

She pushed herself to her feet. Putting one foot in front of the other, she trudged to the bathroom. Her own personal bathroom…which had a door.

How ironic, only a couple of days ago she'd complained about Marcus having removed the bathroom door at the cabin. Now, she'd give anything to be back there again with no bathroom door…if it meant she could be with Marcus.

Sometimes life just sucked, she thought glumly to herself.

A quick splash of cold water on her face did little to clear the ache behind her eyes, but it was enough to get her moving.

It was still quite early in the morning and while most of the vampires in the house were probably roaming about somewhere, the kitchen was likely empty, which made this the perfect time to grab a cup of coffee and enjoy some peace and silence while she could get it.

Brin slipped on a pair of soft track pants and a loose top, and headed out, walking quickly along the corridor and down the stairs, slowing when she reached the spot where she'd overheard Marcus' conversations last evening, both with his mother and with Candy.

Candy.

Her stomach clenched.

Marcus had his date with Candy tonight, and she was confined to the manor. The timing couldn't be shittier. How could she be a fly on the wall…*or a fly in the ointment …*

Brin quickly shut down that last thought. She had no intention of causing trouble between them, she just wanted to know what he saw in her, that's all.

Yeah, and maybe you'd like to stab yourself in the heart a few more times while you're at it, her inner voice added.

She ignored it. Mostly.

Putting a bit more speed into her steps toward the kitchen, she focussed on getting a large cup of steaming hot coffee. Until she had caffeine onboard, her brain was barely functional, bordering on irrational, as evidenced by her current train of thought.

Right now, all she needed was coffee and a quiet space to process everything.

Obtaining coffee was easy. Finding a quiet place to think however, even in a house this size, was far more difficult.

The kettle had barely finished boiling before she heard footsteps. In hindsight, maybe if she hadn't made the coffee, the women in the house wouldn't have surfaced quite so soon. They all seemed to have a sixth sense for knowing when a fresh pot of the dark caffeinated elixir had been brewed, and flooded toward the kitchen.

"Morning love, how are you feeling this morning?" Mrs P asked, her eyes watching her carefully for signs of emotional turmoil.

"Fine. Thanks," she replied, lifting her cup to her lips in the hopes of avoiding a conversation.

"Hey Brin, how are you?" Abby asked as she grabbed herself a cup, the telepathic vampire giving her a sympathetic look.

"Yep. Good. Thanks." Taking another sip to hide behind her cup.

"Morning Brin, how are things?" Cassie asked cheerily as she breezed in, her gaze lingering on her a fraction longer than necessary, silently assessing her.

"Things are great." Brin forced a smile, lifting her cup to show she had everything she needed.

"Hey Brin, how are ye doing?" Megan asked when she entered the kitchen, her Scottish lilt soft and warm. Her gaze too, remaining fixed on her with concern.

Ohmygod! "I'm fine!" she huffed before she could stop herself.

Silence fell for half a second, Megan raising a questioning eyebrow.

"I'm sorry. It's just…that was the sixth time I've been asked that in the last ten minutes," Brin told her. "I appreciate you all caring, really I do, but I'm okay. I'm not as traumatised as everyone seems to think."

Not by the demons, she finished silently. The exception being Marcus. She was positively tormented by her irrational need to be near him again. Not that she was planning on sharing that snippet of information with anyone. She was quite happy to wallow in her self-pity alone.

Brin took a deep breath to calm her nerves and mood, a feat easier said than done, but she tried.

A little while later, once the coffee pot was empty, the kitchen's occupants scattered to other parts of the house, leaving Brin alone with only one other person.

Megan.

"Ye know, it's not so bad being stuck here in this big house. I'll admit it wasn't easy at first, but I did get used to it. Plus, if I really want to go out somewhere, I have my forgettable charm that the sisters made fur me." Megan told her with a friendly smile.

Brin looked up at her. "Yeah, well. Like you, I'm not being given a choice about it, so I guess I just have to adapt too."

"I kicked up one hell of a fuss when they told me I couldn't leave on my own anymore," Megan admitted with a wry smile. "Thought I'd lost my independence. But…ye learn new ways to live. It's just different from what ye're used to."

Brin huffed softly. "I don't want *'different'*. I want my old way of living back."

Megan's eyes softened. "Aye. I ken that feeling."

The mention of her forgettable charm sparked the first flicker of excitement Brin had felt since she was informed of her new living arrangements.

The sisters had also given her a forgettable charm. Her watch.

What were the chances that she could use it tonight, to slip out and go to the restaurant?

Probably none, she thought darkly. Megan was allowed to use her charm to go out on special occasions, even so, she was never allowed to go alone. She always had an escort. Brin was under no illusion that the same rules would apply to her too. And the last thing she needed was to go and spy on Marcus and his girlfriend, with a babysitter tagging along.

Never mind, she'd think of something else.

The morning seemed to drag on forever, but it eventually ticked over to the afternoon, all the while Brin kept a quiet vigil on the time, counting down the hours until Marcus' date.

Maybe she couldn't leave the house, but that didn't stop her from obsessing over it.

Brin had barely left her stool at the kitchen bench all day, absently swapping between sipping coffee to nibbling on whatever pastry Megan had baked and placed in front of her, fuelling her emotional funk with caffeine and carbs.

"Megan, have you seen mum?" Grace asked as she rushed into the room, worry and urgency in her tone.

"No. Sorry. Is there anything I can help ye with?"

"No. Umm, maybe. Could you talk to Tilly? She's been acting really weird all morning. She won't sit still and she keeps pacing around, and Cujo is driving me crazy with his constant growling." Grace told her.

"Ye don't say? I don't think I need to speak to Tilly to know what's ailing her."

"Oh? Do you think it's being pregnant that's got her so irritable?"

"Aye. Didn't the vet say she was likely to have her pups within a week or so?" Megan prompted.

"Yeah, he did, and that was…nearly a week ago. Do you think she's going to have her pups today?" Grace's eyes widened with a hopeful grin.

"I think it's very likely," Megan told her with a smile that was almost as broad as Grace's.

"Woo Hoo! I have to tell Riley, he's going to want to watch them being born." Grace said as she made a dash for the door.

"Don't forget to find yer mum or dad," Megan yelled after her. "They'll want to know too."

"Okay!" Grace's voice floated back as she disappeared down the corridor.

"Alaric must be thrilled about Tilly and Cujo having pups," Brin commented dryly.

Megan laughed. "Oh, aye. Although his definition of *thrilled* involves a bit more cursing and growling. It's just a good thing this house is so big. Even so, I'm sure that with a few more hellhounds running about, it's still going to feel a bit cramped in here fur a while, at least until they all find new homes."

Brin tried to picture four tiny hellhound pups tearing around the manor and almost smiled. Almost.

"So, if Tilly is going into labour, how long do you think it'll be before she actually starts giving birth?" Brin asked.

Megan thought on that for a moment. Normally she would have answered with something along the lines of: *How long is a piece of string?* This time however, Brin's question seemed to have caught the attention of the angels, who liked to eavesdrop on Megan from time to time, and they were more than happy to answer the question for her.

Her eyes went a little unfocused for a second, then she blinked. "Apparently she'll go into full labour at around 6.30pm and all the pups should be born by 8pm."

"That's a long labour for a dog, isn't it?" Brin asked.

"I suppose it is, although I don't know of any other dog who gives birth to hellhound pups, they're probably a bit bigger than the average pup."

Hmm, true enough. "Poor Tilly," Brin muttered. "Super-sized demon dog puppies. What could possibly go wrong."

Megan snorted.

That had Brin's mind mulling over another thought.

If Tilly was likely to be birthing her pups from around 6.30pm, wouldn't that mean that most of the occupants of the house will be hanging around her to watch…and make sure Cujo doesn't destroy the house in his over protectiveness of her?

And if that was the case…they should all be distracted enough that they wouldn't notice if she slipped out for an hour or so, would they?

Her heartbeat seemed to flutter, setting a faster rhythm.

Don't be ridiculous, she told herself silently. Was she seriously considering sneaking out of the manor to stalk Marcus and his girlfriend?

She took another sip of coffee.

Her pulse didn't slow.

Still, the idea remained. Persistent and tempting.

If everyone's with Tilly…And if she was wearing the watch with the forgettable charm…And, if no one saw her leave, no one would worry about her…a treacherous voice whispered in her mind.

Brin exhaled sharply and lifted her mug again.

She wasn't committing to anything.

Yet.

But for the first time since she'd been told she was stuck at the manor indefinitely, she felt a faint, wicked spark of possibility.

And she couldn't quite bring herself to snuff it out.

The elevator doors hissed open with a metallic sigh.

Teagan stepped out into the underground corridor of the Ukraine base, her arms full, literally, of clinking glass bottles, sealed vials, zip-locked pouches of herbs, and a heavy satchel that looked suspiciously like it could detonate if she sneezed.

She was breathless, flushed, annoyed, and tired enough to kill someone for a cup of coffee.

"Bloody hell," she muttered, kicking the stairwell door open with her boot. Frustrated that she'd had to manage carrying everything on her own. It was perfectly understandable though, Gustav had cleared everyone out of the base except for essential staff. Even the restaurant upstairs was running on minimal staff, since he also employed lycans in the kitchen.

It was unnerving to say the least, the whole place seemed to echo in the emptiness. In all the times she'd come here, she had never seen it deserted, not even when her dad had troops deployed on missions and there had been a skeletal crew remaining. It had never been like this.

The corridor smelled of disinfectant, cold concrete and ozone from Alex's experiments.

Elise entered the family's quarters at the end of the hall, unaware that her sister was there. She looked like someone had sucked the soul out of her. Her shoulders sagging with worry.

"Teagan?" Elise's eyes widened, first with relief, then panic. "What are you doing here?!"

Teagan lifted a heavy bag. "Delivering the potion."

"You shouldn't be here!" Elise scolded. "You're a lycan too, what if you get infected?"

Teagan breezed past her with the well practiced indifference of an older sister. "Calm down. I'm immortal, remember. I can't die."

"That's not the point!" Elise almost stamped her foot. "Have you considered that you might still be able to carry the virus? And if you can carry it, then you could also spread it to every lycan in and around Havenswood and Cadley!"

"Oh, for the love of…" No, actually she hadn't stopped to think of that. Regardless, Teagan sighed and waved a dismissive hand. "Then I'll quarantine myself. Happy?"

"No!" Elise threw her arms up. "But since you're already here, I suppose I don't get a vote!"

Teagan patted her cheek. "Exactly."

Not wasting any more time on family chit chat, Teagan put her bag of clothes down on the couch in the lounge room and picked up the potions and vials, and headed back out the door toward the elevator.

"How's dad?" she asked Elise, who was following close behind.

Elise's brow furrowed and she suddenly looked far older than her twenty-nine years. "Not good. You can see for yourself."

Pushing the button for the elevator, the doors swung open and they stepped inside. A few moments later, they swung open again and Teagan stepped out into the hallway.

"This is as far as I can go without a hazmat suit on, I'm afraid." Elise told her, giving her a brief hug.

"Okay, umm…I'll see you soon."

The moment Teagan stepped into the corridor, the air felt thicker, heavier. In stark contrast to the silence of the three floors above them, down here the sound of feral growls and male cries was deafening and distressing.

Teagan swallowed hard, sharing a worried look with her youngest sister as the elevator doors closed once again.

Putting one foot in front of the other, she walked a steady pace toward the cells, and the lab at the end of the corridor.

Reaching the first cell, Teagan looked inside. The first infected lycan was pacing like a caged tiger, only more feral. His eyes were wild and yellowed, his nails now black talons scraping long grooves into the stone wall. His broken collarbone jutted unnaturally beneath the skin. A sling lay shredded in the corner like tissue paper.

His growls echoed off the walls, vibrating through the soles of Teagan's shoes and setting her teeth on edge.

Reaching the next cell, Klaus sat slumped against the bars, his chest heaving, eyes glassy with the fever. When he saw Teagan, his brows pinched in recognition, and he tried to speak…but only a broken rumble escaped him. Like the first lycan, he was losing his ability to speak.

And then, Gustav.

Teagan's breath caught.

"Dad."

Her father looked up from his cot, sweat darkening the collar of his shirt, his hair plastered to his forehead. Even sick, he managed to look dignified, but the fever trembled through his body in visible waves.

"Teagan," Gustav rasped, shock and reprimand blended in his tone. "What are you doing here?"

"Delivering the stasis potion. You're welcome." She said in a light tone, trying not to show her distress at seeing him in such a state.

His glare could have burned a hole in titanium.

"You're a lycan," he growled. "You could catch it. Or worse, carry it. You shouldn't be anywhere near us."

Teagan rolled her eyes to the ceiling. "Yes, I've already heard that speech from Elise. Don't worry dad, it'll be fine."

"This is NOT fine!" Gustav barked, sitting straighter despite the obvious effort to do so. "If you take this disease back to Havenswood…"

"I won't. I'm staying here until you're better. Even if I could carry it, which I doubt, I won't be passing it onto anyone." Teagan told him calmly, matter-of-factly.

Everyone in the corridor winced.

Eytan cleared his throat. "I, uh…agree with Gustav. You've taken a risk coming here, but also…we're really glad you're here," he told her, walking over to give her a welcoming hug and take the heavy bag from her.

Owen nodded fervently. "God, yes. I'll second that."

Alex waved from inside the lab doorway. "Teagan! You brought snacks!"

Teagan rolled her eyes at him. "The potions are not snacks."

"Oh. Then never mind," he replied, his disappointment evident in his voice.

"But…You will find a few bags of chocolates and lollies in there too." She added, chuckling when he jumped from his stool to take the bag from Eytan, rifling through it and pulling out a bag of rainbow snakes.

Grabbing one from the bag, he put the end in the corner of his mouth and began sucking on it. "You're my favourite sister-in-law."

"If you say so," she said, with a lamented sigh.

Teagan looked about the small lab. There was equipment, vials and machinery covering every inch of the benches, and the glass doored fridge was filled with more vials, mostly blood samples, she noted.

"How did you go writing the spell?" Teagan asked Owen.

Owen pulled it from a pile of papers on the desk and handed it to her. Giving her a few moments to read it. "What do you think?" he asked nervously.

She blinked. "This is…very impressive."

Owen beamed. "Really?" He felt like he'd just received an A+ on an exam from the toughest teacher in school.

"It's almost grammatically correct," Teagan told him.

Owen groaned.

Teagan laughed. "I'm kidding. It's perfect."

"So, when do you want to do this?" Eytan asked her.

Teagan turned toward the cages, her lips pursing with worry. "The sooner the better. The potion's ready to go, and it looks like the spell is too. Why don't we do it now."

"Okay, next question. How are we going to do this?" Owen asked.

"First we need Elise down here." Teagan said, as she sent her sister a message to put on the hazmat suit and come down.

"Then, we'll do each person individually. We'll start with the man who's in the worst shape. I'll freeze him, then you can open the door without getting torn to pieces. Eytan, if you can pour a vial of the potion down his throat, and Owen, if you and Elise can perform the spell."

Eytan nodded.

“That sounds good to me.” Owen agreed.

“And Alex?”

“Yes?”

“You get to play mattress.”

Alex stared at her. “Ahh, what?”

“Catch them when they fall. And lay them on their cots.”

“Oh good,” Alex muttered. “Spinal injury roulette. My favourite.”

Teagan rolled her eyes at him but made no comment.

A few minutes later the lift doors at the of corridor opened and out waddled Elise.

The oversized suit hung on her like a bright yellow, puffed up monstrosity, giving her the appearance of cross between a nuclear handling suit and an inflatable penguin.

Teagan couldn’t help the small snicker that escaped.

“Shut up.” Elise growled.

Clamping her lips tightly closed, Teagan made a gesture to zip it, but her grin remained despite her pursed lips.

“You look adorable,” Owen assured her, holding up his hands in surrender when she turned to glare at him.

“Let’s just do this, please.” Elise told them curtly.

Teagan stepped up to the first cell. The infected lycan lunged for the bars, saliva dripping from the corner of his mouth. Lifting her hand the lycan froze mid-stride, his face contorted in a half-snarl and bared teeth. Suspended in perfect, eerie stillness.

Owen swallowed. “Every time I see you do that, it gives me chills.”

“Yes, well, we all have our talents,” she smiled.

“Eytan, are you ready with the potion?”

Eytan nodded, unlocking the cell door and stepping inside. Tilting the lycan’s head back, he poured the murky green liquid down his throat. It slid down his throat without resistance.

“Owen and Elise, your turn. But first, Alex can you get behind him, please,” Teagan said.

They chanted together, their voices overlapping, harmonising with druidic energy.

The lycan’s frozen body relaxed all at once.

He collapsed like a marionette with its strings cut…straight into Alex's waiting arms.

Alex took a step backwards under his weight. "This guy's no light weight!" he told them, laying him awkwardly on the cot.

Klaus was next.

He didn't pace. He remained slumped against the wall, trembling. When he saw Teagan, his clouded eyes widened.

"Klaus," Owen said gently. "We're going to have you back to normal real soon."

Klaus tried to speak. What came out was a warped croak.

"It's alright," Teagan whispered, in a comforting tone.

Fortunately, Klaus was still coherent enough that she didn't need to freeze him and he took the potion Eytan gave him without any struggle.

Again, Owen and Elise performed the spell and Alex made sure he was laid comfortably on the cot.

That left Gustav.

He stood when they reached him. Barely. Unsteadily.

He looked each of them in the eye. His voice was hoarse. "You have done everything you can. All of you. From here, whatever happens, happens. I don't want any of you to blame yourselves if this doesn't work, do you hear me?" He told them, looking each one in the eye directly.

"Dad…" Elise couldn't get anything else out, her throat closed tight from the emotion she was trying to hold back.

"I love you." He told Elise and Teagan, giving each one a tight hug which only upset both of them all the more. For such a big man, he barely had the strength to put his arms around them.

"Next time you see us dad, you'll be feeling like your normal self again, I promise." Teagan swallowed hard, battling to hold back her own tears.

"Ready?" she whispered.

Gustav nodded.

Eytan gave him the potion which he swallowed in one long gulp.

Owen and Elise performed the accompanying spell.

Alex caught Gustav, lowering him to the cot with surprising tenderness.

The three infected lycans now lay peacefully in their cells, silent, breathing slow and steady, as though merely asleep. But for how long they would remain in this state, none of them knew. It could be days or it could be weeks.

The corridor felt strangely quiet, eerily so.

Elise pressed her gloved hand to the cell's bars. "We'll fix this," she whispered.

"Yes, we will," Teagan replied with determined resolve.

Owen looked at Alex. "Now what?"

Alex grinned, his eyes brimming with a *mad-scientist* gleam, as he lifted a syringe from the lab's bench, filled with a pale yellow liquid.

"Now," he said, "We'll see if this works."

Owen groaned but rolled up his sleeve anyway. "If I grow an extra limb, I'm blaming you."

Alex patted his arm. "Don't worry, you won't. And if it kills you, I'll bring you back," he grinned.

"If that's meant to make me feel better, it doesn't!"

Teagan crossed her arms. "Alex. Stop tormenting him and just inject him."

Alex did just that.

"Okay," Owen said after a moment. "What now?"

"Now, we wait twenty-four hours and I'll take another blood sample and see if we can get any antibodies." Alex told him matter-of-factly.

24

The barracks were quiet.

That in itself was unusual. Normally there was the low thrum of voices drifting from the hallways, footsteps of men coming and going, and the general clatter of movement and laughter in the common room.

Tonight, there was none of that.

The barracks were still, a heavy silence seemed to have settled within its walls. News of the infected lycan in Ukraine, and the loss of their colleague, Farrell, sat uncomfortably with everyone, subduing the normally rowdy bunch of men.

Marcus sat on the edge of his bunk, elbows propped on his knees, head bowed into his hands. The tidy, organized space around him, meticulously made beds, neatly arranged furniture against the wall of the sparsely decorated room, only made the tangled thoughts in his mind feel more disjointed.

He dragged in a slow, deep breath. It didn't help.

The door creaked softly.

Callum stepped inside, his presence filling the room with the familiar steadiness he'd always relied upon. He was the grounding force of reason to Marcus' tempestuous moods. Closing the door behind him, Callum crossed the room and sat on his own bunk opposite him.

For a moment, he said nothing. Callum had always been good at silence, at giving space without making it uncomfortable or heavy.

Quietly he asked, "Do you want to talk about it?"

Marcus let out a rough exhale, dragging both hands through his short hair.

"Nothing to talk about."

Callum snorted. "Bullshit."

Marcus didn't smile.

"Alright. Then let me rephrase that." He leaned forward, elbows on his knees, mirroring Marcus' posture. "It's not hard to figure out what's bothering you. You've just spent the last few days stranded in the Arctic with Brin, and no doubt whatever went down between you is fucking with your mind. You *need* to talk about it."

"Sometimes I hate you." Marcus grumbled under his breath, raising his eyes to meet Callum's.

"You know I'm not going anywhere until you talk to me."

Yeah, he knew.

"You know that prophecy?" he said, sucking in a steadying breath.

"The one you suspected relates to you?"

Marcus nodded and rolled up his sleeve, turning over his hand to expose his wrist.

Callum's eyes widened. "Holy fuck?"

"Yeah," Marcus huffed a humourless laugh. "They were my sentiments too."

Callum reached out, but stopped short of touching it. "Does she know?"

Marcus shook his head. "Not yet."

"Are you…okay?" Callum asked cautiously. "This is your worst nightmare come true."

Marcus let out a breath that was part laugh, part groan. "Yeah, I know. But it's funny how things change," he told him, his fingers lightly tracing the outline of the dragon mark. Lifting his eyes to meet Callum's again, his gaze steady and decisive. "I'm not afraid anymore."

That surprised Callum. "Seriously?"

Marcus' eyes warmed, softening in a way that told the truth even before he spoke it.

"You remember when we left for Canada, you told me it was the perfect opportunity to sort out my differences with her?"

"You actually talked to her? I'm proud of you," Callum told him with a grin.

"Well, not exactly. But we did get to know each other a lot better, and I realised…I need her."

Callum blinked. "Back up a bit. When you say you haven't talked out your feelings, but you've gotten to know her better, are you saying that the two of you shared a bed?"

Marcus nodded once, firmly.

"But there's more."

Callum's brow furrowed curiously, waiting silently for him to continue.

"Do you remember when the serpent armband came alive on Brin's arm and bit the demon?"

Callum nodded.

"Well, that wasn't the only time that happened. When I was helping Brin out of the cave, the same thing happened to me." Marcus rubbed the area on his wrist where the dragon mark was now visible.

"Holy crap! Why didn't you say anything?"

"I didn't see any point. I assumed it wouldn't matter. But…" Marcus' gaze was fixed onto his memory of what happened next. "By the time we got on that chopper, I had started to develop an itch on my wrist and a mild rash. A few hours later I developed a fever."

"Did Brin try to help you?"

Marcus shook his head. "I didn't want her to know anything about it. By the next day the symptoms had increased, the rash got worse and there were dark swirling lines under my skin. I tried to shift so my wolf could heal it, but when I tried, nothing happened. I felt like I'd lost my connection to it, and it felt as agitated as I did. The only time it settled was when I was near Brin. And that was the only time I felt better too. Then, the night before our rescue, there was an…incident, an argument that led to us…you know. But, the freaky thing was, it wasn't me that initiated sex, my wolf did. I had no control over my body, none. I only just managed to stop it from claiming her."

"Claiming her as your *mate*?"

"Yeah. And afterwards, we both fell asleep and when I woke up, the mark on my wrist was fully formed, my fever was gone and my connection to my wolf felt back to normal again. I actually feel stronger now than I can ever remember before. It's really weird."

"And you haven't told Brin about any of this?"

"No. When her brothers and Kaitlyn turned up, I'd just spent the past couple of hours building up the courage, but didn't get the chance, and I haven't seen her since we got back. I'm worried that the longer I leave it, the harder it'll be to have that heart-to-heart chat. Coz, seriously, we've had years of bad blood between us." Marcus said, his voice low. "I was a bastard to her. I've admitted it to her and apologised, but that doesn't mean she's prepared to forgive and forget. She's more likely to tell me to fuck off than accept me as her *mate*."

Callum sat back, studying him. "Marcus, you've forgotten one thing."

Marcus scrubbed his hands over his face. "What?"

"Besides that mark on your arm, the two of you have always had serious chemistry together, the air practically buzzes with the electricity between you. Everyone's noticed."

"I think you're confusing hatred with attraction."

Callum glared at him like he was a moron, which at this point, he'd agree with.

"I've still got two problems."

"Only two? That's progress." Callum jibed.

Marcus glared weakly. "One, I'm having dinner with Candy tonight to break up with her," Marcus said firmly. "I should've done it weeks ago but I'm a coward, I didn't want to hurt her feelings, but now I have no choice."

"Well, yeah," Callum muttered. "But, better late than never though, right?"

Marcus winced. "Not helpful."

Callum smirked. "I'm not here to be helpful. I'm here to be honest, that's what friends do for each other. I'm your voice of reason."

Marcus huffed out a reluctant laugh. "I'll remember that when you're going through shit like this too."

"Yeah, nah. That's never going to happen. I'm a confirmed bachelor." Callum scoffed. "So, what's your second problem?"

Marcus swallowed. "I need to talk with Brin…" He said no more, he'd already outlined his fears on that score. Marcus' breath stilled. "Do you really think I have a chance?"

"Yes," Callum said simply.

Silence stretched between them, not heavy this time but grounding.

Finally, Marcus blew out a long breath. “Who knew that four short lines in a prophecy could have such an impact on my life?”

Callum frowned. “Four lines?”

Marcus nodded. “Yeah. The dragon mark bit. And the…future is sealed part.”

Callum looked at him like he’d grown a second head. “Marcus. There are eight lines to that prophecy.”

Marcus blinked. “Wait, what? No, there’s only four.”

Callum sat up straighter. “Mate…tell me the lines you remember.”

Marcus recited:

“Darkened hordes shall seek the one,
Through whose touch truth is revealed,
The mark of a dragon on a lycan son,
By blood and fate, their future is sealed.”

Callum stared. “Yeah. That’s the first verse.”

Marcus’ stomach dropped. “First verse…?”

Callum nodded grimly. “You’ve forgotten the rest?”

“Apparently.” Marcus’ pulse kicked up. “Alright…enlighten me. What’s the last part?”

Callum did just that, reciting the final verse.

“When hearts collide, the storm shall rise,
Then both dragon and wolf will unify,
Together alive, apart they die,
He must defend her from the sky.”

Marcus went still. Completely still, letting the words sink in. How did he forget lines like: *Together alive, apart they die…*and, *Defend her from the sky.* They seemed like pretty important lines to remember, especially now.

What the hell was it supposed to mean though?

Callum watched him carefully. “You okay there buddy, you’ve gone a bit pale?”

Marcus scratched his head. “No. Yes. I think so.”

His mind raced with images of Brin, the crash, the storm, the way his wolf had nearly claimed her, the heat in her eyes, the feel of her in his arms.

If the first half of the prophecy had already come true…including the first part of the second verse, was the rest of it also inevitable?

He blew out a slow breath. "Seriously bro, what's the point in stressing over it? If it's going to happen, then it's going to happen. I might as well just accept it."

Callum stared at him suspiciously, as though he believed someone had cloned his body but given him a new personality.

"Wow! Look at you, being all mature and grown up about it. Are you sure you didn't suffer a head knock in the chopper crash?"

Marcus snorted out a laugh. "Fuck, maybe I did."

Callum checked the time. "If you're breaking up with Candy tonight, you'd better start getting ready."

Marcus groaned but stood. "Yeah…And, thanks for the talk."

"Anytime bro." Callum headed for the door, pausing with a warm, knowing smile. "It'll all work out, you'll see."

The door clicked shut behind him.

Marcus stood alone, staring at his reflection in the small mirror above the dresser.

The last few lines of the prophecy whispered through his mind again, unsettling and electric: *When hearts collide, the storm shall rise, Then both dragon and wolf will unify,*

Together alive, apart they die, He must defend her from the sky.

"What the hell does *that* mean?" he muttered.

Whatever it meant…Whatever was coming…He would find out soon.

Brin checked the time on her watch for what had to be the seventeenth time in twenty minutes.

6:22 p.m.

Any minute now.

She hovered in the lounge room with the rest of the household, waiting and watching.

Tilly had finally settled herself onto the bed Cassie had arranged by the fire, thick quilts, old towels, and a waterproof sheet underneath, because even in a supernatural household, no one wanted bodily fluids on antique Persian rugs.

Then…

"Oh! I think she just had her first contraction!" Cassie announced excitedly, as Tilly gave a low, guttural groan.

Brin held her breath. Was she really going to do this?

She hovered at the back of the room, debating with herself what to do. In the end, her decision came down to opportunity.

Cujo had paced in neurotic circles for the past hour, but now that Tilly was in full labour, his behaviour stepped up a level to become more problematic, putting himself between Tilly and anyone who dared approach.

He snapped at Cassie as she tried to comfort Tilly.

He snapped at anyone who came within two meters.

"Oh, for Christ's sake, Cujo, stop it!" Grace growled, as if reason had ever once worked on the hellhound.

Cujo responded by puffing up like an enraged bear, bristling, pacing, baring his sharp teeth at anyone with hands near Tilly.

He wasn't attacking. But he was warning. Protecting.

He was also overreacting.

"Brilliant," Paige muttered. "He's gone into full feral father mode."

Then he snapped at Alaric. Big mistake. Alaric didn't like the hound at the best of times, and trying to take a chunk out of him flipped his mood meter to *severely pissed off*.

It was time to put the hound outside.

That was when things began to get a lot more chaotic. Alaric grabbed the huge hound by the scruff of the neck, Cujo's furious growl echoed through the manor…and was answered almost immediately by the rest of his pack in Savernake Forest.

"Someone get the doors." Alaric growled, dragging the snarling, snapping hound out onto the adjoining patio, and down toward the lawns below.

"A little help out here might be helpful, please," he called back toward the house.

Brin heard the thundering of paws outside.

"Oh dear," Mrs P whispered.

A moment later, five full-grown hellhounds charged toward the manor, teeth bared, eyes blazing, their growls harmonising in a terrifying roar.

"Fantastic," Paige muttered dryly. "The whole pack have shown up."

Suddenly, Havenswood Manor's grounds was a war zone as every vampire scrambled to contain the hellhound pack.

It was total chaos.

It was also the perfect time to slip away.

Brin looked about her, the women and kids inside were focussed on Tilly, while every man in the house was currently battling a pack of hellhounds. No one even noticed she was there.

Brin slipped from the room and down the corridor. Her pulse thudded with adrenaline, partly from guilt and partly from exhilaration.

At the front doors, she found the hall table and the ceramic bowl where everyone tossed their car keys. She didn't even bother looking at whose keys she grabbed, she simply snatched the first pair her hand touched.

Slipping silently out the door, she pressed the key fob and one of the garage doors hummed open.

Brin darted inside the sprawling garage containing an obscene number of vehicles. Sports cars, classic restorations, a few military-grade blacked-out beasts that would be a drug lord's delight.

She clicked the "unlock" button. Beep-beep. Headlights flashed.

Brin turned slowly toward the sound…and grinned.

The Maserati.

"Oh, Hell yes," she muttered to herself.

She climbed in, adjusting the seat and mirrors, her heart racing with adrenaline. Turning the key, the engine purred to life with a low rumble.

Pulling out of the garage, she drove slowly, creeping down the long gravel driveway to keep the engine noise to a minimum.

The moment she cleared the laneway entrance at the end of the long driveway, Brin floored it.

The car leapt forward, the engine roaring down the country road as a rush of near-delirious exhilaration washed through her.

She was free.

At least for a short while, she planned on being back in the next hour, before the chaos with the hounds died down and they discovered she was missing.

Her watch read 7:15 p.m. She was right on time.

Spotting the restaurant's glowing windows up ahead, she pulled into a quiet side street nearby. Parking discreetly, she took a few steadying breaths.

"Okay," she whispered to herself. "There's no backing out now."

Stepping from the car, Brin approached the restaurant, peering through the front window.

Marcus and Candy were seated at the back of the restaurant, a candle flickering on the table between them. Candy looked exactly like Brin remembered, gorgeous, glossy, annoyingly perfect. A waterfall of amber coloured wavey hair, sparkly earrings and plump red lips, all presented temptingly in a tiny bright red dress.

Marcus looked…distracted. Stiff. Uncomfortable, as he ran a hand through his hair nervously.

Behind them was a wicker room divider, shielding the entrance to the kitchen.

Perfect.

Brin's heart drummed in her ears, as she edged around the building to the back alley and tried the rear kitchen door.

Unlocked.

Slipping inside, chefs went about their business, too busy plating meals to notice her.

She released a tight breath and relaxed a little. Thankfully, the charm on her watch appeared to be working.

Brin eased through the swinging doors and pressed her back to the wall behind the wicker divider.

From there, she could hear everything.

Candy twirled a strand of hair, her voice dripping with syrupy vanity. "…and honestly, Marcus, the photographer said I was the most photogenic model he'd seen all year. All year. Isn't that amazing?"

Marcus grunted noncommittally.

Candy pouted. "You're not even listening. You used to get jealous when I talked about other men looking at me."

Marcus looked like a man rethinking every life choice he'd ever made. "Right. Yeah. That's…great."

Brin clamped a hand over her mouth to stop a snort.

Candy kept going, her voice rising. "You disappear for near two months, without a single phone call, by the way, and now…this? Our first night together and you're not paying any attention to me at all. It's like you don't even care."

Marcus straightened. "Candy, I…"

Brin's pulse hammered. What was he going to tell her?

Candy reached across the table and placed her hand over his, possessive and petulant.

Marcus took a deep breath, ready to speak.

He lifted her hand gently but firmly, preparing the words in his mind to break off their relationship.

"Candy, we need to ta…"

The kitchen doors swung open, through it a waiter entered the dining room carrying two plates. As he stepped sideways to avoid the spring back of the door…and walked straight into Brin.

Crash!

Porcelain shattered. Food flew everywhere. The waiter stumbled back with a loud yelp.

And like a slow-motion train wreck, every head in the restaurant turned toward the commotion.

Brin froze.

Candy looked up, her expression quickly changing from curiosity to annoyance when she saw Brin, recognition slowing dawning on her that she'd seen her before, although she couldn't quite place where. Regardless, her hackles began to rise.

Marcus swivelled in his seat to see what the commotion was about, his eyes narrowing on the figure standing before him.

Candy's mouth fell open.

The waiter fussed and apologised profusely as he attempted to clean up the mess.

Brin's heart fell through the floor.

Oh, crap!

The forgettable charm made people overlook her. It did *not* make her invisible.

And right now?

She was very, very visible.

"Brin?" Marcus blinked in surprise. "What are you doing here?" he asked, his tone taking on an edge of anger.

Candy stood from her chair. "You know her?" she demanded in quiet outrage.

Brin didn't know what to say and panicked. "That's a lovely dress. It's amazing what a bit of colour can do," she told Candy.

"You'd know, with your complexion," she bit back acerbically.

Brin gasped. Okay, maybe she deserved that, but the woman's catty tone really ticked her off.

"Is there something you want to tell me, Marcus?" Candy demanded, her arms crossed in front of her, almost pushing her full breasts out of her low-cut dress.

Marcus just looked between the two women, caught off guard. He didn't have the first clue what to say that wouldn't land him in more hot water.

"Marcus? Say something. Would you care to explain why *she's* here?" Candy snapped.

Brin looked the other woman over with a much more critical eye. There wasn't anything about her that didn't appear fake. Fake boobs, fake eyelashes, collagen-plumped lips, and by the way virtually no muscle in her face moved, she'd probably had enough Botox to paralyse an elephant.

Candy shifted her attention from Marcus to Brin with a snarl, reading the evidence of a connection between them on their faces as clearly as if they were wearing a neon sign. "You look at me like I'm some cheap whore, but you seem to be the one with all the skills in that department. You'd make a good living on a street corner, slut."

"We all have to work with the gifts we're given. At least I know how to keep a man happy." Brin retaliated in her best tone.

Neatly manicured brows slid fiercely over almond-shaped eyes, Candy's wrath thoroughly tweaked.

"That's enough." Marcus growled at the two of them.

"What can I say, you have to get your giggles where you can." Brin retaliated.

Marcus kept his head low to keep his face hidden, swallowing the bubble of laughter bursting to get free. He shouldn't be enjoying this, but he was. He loved the way Brin held her own against Candy.

A few swallowed snickers and chuckles filled the room, but no one said a word. Candy ignored them all, lowering herself back to her seat with the grace of a queen.

Marcus had barely spoken three words since Brin arrived and made no direct eye contact with her whatsoever.

It was about what she'd expected. And yet considering the amount of energy she needed to put into breathing normally around him, it seemed unfair.

"Marcus, I'm sorry. I can explain."

"We're definitely going to talk about this, later. What were you thinking, you shouldn't have come here." He told her firmly.

"Um…Yeah, um... I'm sorry if I've ruined your meal," she told him, then apologised to the waiter who'd knocked into her, as she backed away toward the front door. "I really am sorry."

What was she thinking? She was such a fool. Marcus had no feelings for her. None. Except contempt. And why wouldn't he after her performance just now.

All because she'd let herself hope, for just one minute.

She'd seen what she thought was a spark of something special in the way he looked at her, and in his manner toward her, and she'd hoped.

Now she was left to marvel at her stupidity. How quickly that hope had been blown apart. How easily it had lashed back to strike her in the heart.

"Brin, wait. I'll take you home."

"No thanks. I drove myself here, I'll drive myself home." It was bad enough that she'd made a fool of herself, she didn't need to endure his pity too.

Brin closed the restaurant door behind her and placed one foot in front of the other toward the car. She didn't pay any attention to anything around her, she was lost in her thoughts and self-pity.

Marcus sat opposite Candy, watching Brin leave.

"I'm sorry Candy, but I have to make sure she gets home safely," he told her.

"Seriously? That bimbo shows up while we're on a date, and you immediately want to chase after her?"

"I don't expect you to understand, but I'm responsible for her safety."

Gone were his nerves about how he was going to break up with her. Seeing Brin there at the restaurant, he almost leapt from his seat with happiness there and then. There was only one reason for her to turn up like that, because she truly cared about him too. It gave him the motivation to say what he needed to with Candy. He was ready to just rip that band-aid off and get it over with.

He opened his mouth to speak but was cut short.

"Marcus. I'm breaking up with you." She told him, her tone almost bored.

Marcus blinked in surprise. "What?" He wasn't unhappy about her declaration, it was just unexpected. "Um…Yeah…I think that's probably for the best." He agreed.

"I've been seeing someone else. I wanted to tell you before you went away, but didn't get the chance," she shrugged.

"Oh. Okay. Well, um…Okay." He couldn't believe his luck. Breaking up with someone had never been so easy. Even so, he had an uneasy feeling in his gut that had his wolf on edge. "I hope you and whoever he is, will be very happy together." He pushed his chair back to stand and leave.

Looking toward the front window of the restaurant, he noticed a black van screech to a stop.

"Brin!" he yelled.

Marcus heard her scream and ran for the door, pulling it open in time to watch her being dragged into the van and speed off with a screech of tyres.

He was too slow to reach her in time.

Fury rose up like a tornado. His heart was in his throat, rage pounding in his head. He wasn't aware of the snarling growls that left his throat or the savagery that glowed in his eyes.

The men who took her, left their scent. Marcus drew in a deep breath, memorising every detail, it was like an identifying fingerprint.

He was going to follow their stench, and when he caught them, they were going to die.

Pulling out his phone, he sent a quick text to Alaric.

With every passing moment Marcus' fury rose, as did the beast inside him. This time, when his wolf demanded release, he would give it full rein to execute its fury.

25

Marcus stood on the footpath outside the restaurant, staring after the black van as its tyres screeched against the bitumen and tore away into the darkness.

For one fractured heartbeat, he stood frozen, terror didn't just grip him, it detonated. It punched through his chest and ripped the air from his lungs.

Brin.

No, no, no!

A sound tore from his throat, raw and primal.

He didn't wait for Alaric's reply to the frantic text he'd fired off seconds earlier. He shoved his phone into his pants pocket, tore off his shirt, ignoring the startled gasps of restaurant patrons behind him, and ran.

The cool night air lashed at his bare skin, but he barely felt it. Rage and fear were fighting for dominance inside him, the kind that made his vision blur at the edges.

His body moved before his mind caught up, sprinting after the van, adrenaline scorching through his blood like napalm. His boots hammered the pavement, muscles burning with a frantic, violent need to catch up, to rip apart the van's metal doors and tear the Guild bastards, limb from limb.

He didn't give a flying fuck who saw. Nor did he care that he was about to shift in the middle of a public street.

He had to find Brin, that was the only thing that mattered.

His wolf surged, wild and furious, answering his call before his breath fully left his lungs.

Marcus didn't slow. He'd shifted mid-run a thousand times before.

He felt bones shift and lengthen, muscles realigned and tendons coiled like steel wires. His body blurred from man to beast...

But something was wrong. Very wrong.

Instead of exploding forward with triple his speed, his legs felt…heavy. Sluggish.

What the hell?

He stumbled, nearly tripping, and caught himself with a growl. His lungs heaved in confusion. Normally the shift amplified everything, speed, power, senses.

This time, he felt like he was moving through thick mud.

And the world…It looked different. Everything was…smaller. His centre of gravity had changed, it felt higher, more weight pulling on his back.

His wolf's body was the size of a small horse, but this time he felt larger. Taller.

Marcus skidded to a halt, turning toward a shop window…and froze.

For a second, he thought his mind had snapped under the panic, because the face in the window's reflection was his wolf's, thick fur, broad muzzle…except the eyes staring back at him were ringed in molten gold with slitted…reptilian pupils glowing faintly even under the dull streetlights. And his fangs were longer, sharper, almost like curved daggers.

And the rest of him…

The rest of him looked like a creature pulled from myth and legend. His body gleamed with reptilian scales, covering his shoulders, chest, and powerful limbs. Dark bronze near the spine, shifting to burnished copper toward the claws.

And on his back…two wings were folded awkwardly against his sides, each membrane a deep russet shade that shimmered as he shifted their weight. He stretched them instinctively, and they expanded wider…wider…stretching to the width of the entire shop frontage.

He had wings!

For a moment, he couldn't breathe. Couldn't think.

What the fuck happened to me?

And his tail…OMG…his tail was long and serpentine, covered in overlapping scales. And heavy, so heavy he could feel the weight of it when he lashed it experimentally, with muscles rippling under impenetrable scale plating.

His breath came in puffs of white steam in the cold air.

That serpent armband bite hadn't just given him a temporary rash and dragon tattoo on his wrist, or a fever. It had rewritten his DNA. Transformed his wolf into something else entirely.

Something deadly.

No longer a wolf but not quite a dragon either. He'd become…something else.

He was a fucking hybrid.

Marcus stared at himself, his heart slamming against his ribs so hard he thought he might be having a heart attack.

"What the hell…?" The words rumbled from his throat in a warped growl. This wasn't right. This was the most bizarre thing he'd ever encountered, and he'd encountered a lot of strange stuff.

Regardless, he didn't have time to give his new form any further contemplation. He had to figure out how to use it. And fast!

He snarled aloud, snapping himself back into focus.

Marcus tore his gaze from his reflection, his thoughts shifting to Brin.

His panic sharpened into razor-edged fury.

He flapped his wings experimentally. They were heavy and he felt unnaturally awkward, his first attempt nearly toppled him sideways.

"Come on…" he growled at himself.

The second attempt was better.

The third, nearly lifted him off the ground.

He remembered then the prophecy: *He must defend her from the sky.*

"Fucking get your shit together," he snapped at his spiralling thoughts.

He spread his wings fully and they caught the cool night air like sails.

The wind rushed beneath him, cool and sharp with the faint scent of approaching rain. The streetlamps cast long pools of light across the empty road, shadows stretching like fingers as he crouched low.

He launched himself into the air.

The wings caught the wind, wobbled a little, dipped…then lifted.

He was airborne. Awkwardly. Unevenly. But he was flying. Initially his wings flapped too wide, his tail dragged beneath him, throwing off his balance, but by the time he reached twenty, thirty, fifty feet from the ground, his body began to find its rhythm.

The town shrank beneath him in a blur of rooftops and glowing windows as he soared higher. The cold air sharpened his focus, feeding the fire roaring through his veins.

He rose a hundred feet above the streetlights, following the Guild's scent trail.

Holy shit! His enhanced nose picked up everything. The Guild. Their sweat. The rubber scorch of their tyres…and a Scree demon.

At the forefront of all those scents, he caught Brin's fear. It struck him like a blade to the chest and seared his soul.

He roared, the sound tearing across the sky like thunder.

He was angry with her for leaving the manor, for risking herself, but mostly he was furious with himself.

I should've walked away from Candy the moment I saw her in that restaurant. This is my fault.

Tucking his wings closer, he swept them back and rocketed forward through the cold night sky as the scent trail sharpened, curving toward the outskirts of the next town, crossing the main highway.

He was going to find her.

And God help the Guild when he did, because this new form of his…whatever the hell it was, was built for hunting.

And he had never been more ready to kill.

Then he saw them. The black van was parked in the middle of a long arched stone bridge. Another vehicle parked beside it, a grey, unmarked SUV.

A transfer.

Brin didn't get more than three metres from the restaurant when the van screeched to a holt beside her. And it took another moment to realise they were there for her, as the side door slid open and a man dressed in all black, jumped out and grabbed her. She screamed just as a hand clamped over her mouth and an arm locked around her ribs like an iron band.

Her scream was swallowed.

Her feet left the ground.

She kicked, twisted, fought, but the man hauling her backward was twice her size and terrifyingly efficient. A second man held open the sliding door of the black van as the first man shoved her inside, as though she weighed nothing at all.

Brin hit the metal flooring hard, pain exploding through her hip.

"Got her," someone said behind her.

A boot connected with her stomach when she tried to scramble away, knocking the wind out of her. Before she could inhale, a fist slammed into the side of her face and white-hot pain exploded behind her eye. Her vision blurred and the metallic taste of blood coated her tongue.

Strong hands wrenched her arms behind her back and cinched plastic restraints around her wrists until they burned. A strip of tape was slapped over her mouth so roughly her head snapped to the side.

She couldn't breathe. She couldn't think, her head was spinning from shock and pain.

She was pulled upright by the restraints and shoved into a narrow bench seat along the van's wall.

And then she felt it. A presence.

She turned her head…and froze.

A Scree demon sat crouched at the far end of the van, no more than a metre from her.

Close. Too close.

Its waxy, greyish skin stretched over sharp bones, its black eyes glowing faintly, with its long fingers curled into its lap like talons waiting to unfold.

It didn't blink. It didn't breathe. It didn't move. It only stared at her as though it was waiting for someone to say, *Go on then. She's all yours.*

Brin's heart slammed against her ribs so hard it hurt, as she pressed herself up against the van's wall, angling herself as far away from the demon as she could possibly get.

The inside of the van was dimly lit by the lights radiating from the dashboard, a faint smell of diesel, sweat and gun oil permeated the air, along with the scent of something sickly sweet which she suspected was the demon itself. Heavy shelving filled the opposite wall, crates of weapons strapped down with chains and zip ties.

Two men sat in the back of the van with her, and two more in the front. Stone-faced. Cold hard killers every one of them. One looked at her and grinned.

"Well, well. The little healer," he said with a sneer. "Didn't expect you to fall into our laps this easy, hey boys."

Another laughed. "Easiest job we've ever had. We'll get a week in the Emerald District brothels for this. All expenses paid."

"Waste of good coin," the man beside him muttered. "I'd rather be the one to toss her into the wood chipper," he sneered, drilling Brin with his evil stare as he said it, enjoying the way her eyes widened and she squirmed in fear.

The first man elbowed him. "Not until after she hands over the armband. If she doesn't give it willingly, maybe they'll let you keep the arm as a souvenir."

They all laughed.

Brin's blood turned to ice.

She tried to speak, to scream through the tape, but all that came out was a muffled, panicked choke.

"Shut her up," someone snapped.

"She's already shut up."

Another laughed. "She won't be once the cutting starts."

Brin stomach flipped and churned, and she prayed she wasn't going to be sick, especially since she had a gag in her mouth.

Her thoughts spiralled, frantic and jagged. *No one at the manor knows I'm gone. And Marcus thinks I've gone home. Oh, why did I leave? I'm so screwed!*

She hadn't believed that the Guild would come for her again so soon. She'd thought she'd have time. She'd thought the forgettable charm on her watch would protect her. Certainly by now, everyone at the restaurant who'd seen her, would have forgotten all about her. Probably even Marcus.

No doubt these douche bag arseholes would also forget about her the moment she was out of their sight…if she could only find a way to get away from them. That raised a very important question. How did they find her so easily?

Her gaze flicked sideways toward the Scree demon.

The Scree could track her anywhere, she realised. That's how they'd tracked her in Canada, and no doubt that's why the creature was here in this van too.

How could she be so stupid.

The van jolted over a bump, metal chains rattling on the opposite wall. Brin's cheek throbbed with every vibration, her eye beginning to swell.

And through the burning pain she felt something deeper, sharper.

Regret.

She swallowed hard behind the tape.

Marcus…

Her chest constricted painfully. She'd ruined everything. Every fragile possibility between them was now gone. She'd been jealous. Yes, she can admit it to herself now. It wasn't curiosity about Candy that had her following him to the restaurant, it was pure green-eyed jealousy.

And now she was going to die without ever telling him the one thing she should have told him a long time ago.

I love you.

If she'd told him, maybe things might have turned out differently. The thought gutted her more brutally than the Guild's threats.

Her eyes stung. She blinked rapidly, fighting tears, fighting terror, fighting the crushing hopelessness clawing up her.

Outside, headlights streaked past in blurred lines. The van left town quickly, moving into the darkness of the open highway, the hum of tyres steady and merciless beneath them, taking her further from any hope of rescue.

All the while the Guild men kept talking, cocky, confident, congratulating themselves on a flawless catch.

"We'll be heroes for this," one said. "Morganna herself might even reward us."

"Wonder what she'll do with the healer," another chuckled. "I heard Morganna wants to interrogate this one herself. Apparently, she's *special.*" The sneer that accompanied his statement inferred that he didn't believe that. To him, Brin was just another Alliance bitch to be put down.

"She's got the armband, dipshit. Of course she's special," the driver told them.

"Nah, I heard she's got some ability besides healing that Morganna's interested in."

"If Morganna's coming for her, I don't care how *special* she is, she won't live long, the ones Morganna plays with never do." The fourth man leaned back smugly.

Brin squeezed her eyes shut. It seemed her situation was going from bad to worse.

She needed a miracle.

No one at the manor knew where she was, and Marcus was still at the restaurant with Candy, finishing his dinner, living a life she had no place in.

The van slowed.

The crunch of tyres on gravel echoed under them as they left the main road and took a lesser used road, following it for another mile or so.

As the van slowed again, Brin leaned forward to look out the windscreen and her heart lurched.

They'd reached a bridge.

The men straightened, confident, relaxed. The Scree demon finally moved, its head turning toward the doors as though sensing something beyond.

"Alright boys, let's go," the driver said.

The van doors slid open.

Cold night air rushed inside and Brin flinched, shaking her head, she screamed behind the gag as she strained against the man who grabbed her, dragging her from the van. She kicked out at him with all her strength. Maybe she couldn't stop them from handing her over, but she damn well wasn't going to make it easy for them.

"You'll regret that, bitch."

He raised a hand to punch her again, stopping at the sound of an unearthly roar echoing across the dark stretch of sky. The sound was unlike anything any of them had ever heard before.

As the man yanked her from the van, Brin heard it again. It was much closer and was travelling fast.

One of the men frowned. "What the hell is that?"

Another stepped out, craning his neck upward, pulling a rifle from the van.

"Oh, fuck…what is that?"

Brin's pulse spiked.

A shadow dropped from the night sky, its wings blotting out the stars behind it.

The men's confidence evaporated in an instant.

The last thing Brin saw before chaos erupted was the pure, stunned terror on the men's faces.

"Is that a dragon?" one muttered in disbelief.

Marcus roared, a sound that shook the air and echoed for miles around.

The Guild soldiers jerked their heads upward in terror, but he barely gave them a thought. It was the creature crouched beside the van, greyish skin, limbs too long, eyes like dark embers that held his attention.

A Scree demon.

Of course. That's how they'd found her.

The Guild soldiers shoved Brin between them like she was a parcel being passed over a counter. Cable ties around her wrists. Tape around her mouth. She stumbled but held her balance, eyes wide with terror.

Marcus' vision tunnelled in white-hot fury.

He folded his wings, dropping from the sky like a meteor as gunfire erupted. Bullets rained up at him and he braced instinctively, expecting the biting pain of impact.

But…the bullets hit his scaled hide and ricocheted off like pebbles hitting a tank.

The Guild men froze as Marcus kept on coming.

"Oh, shit!" one yelled in horror.

Marcus hit the bridge with the impact of a falling tree, cracking stone beneath his taloned feet.

His roar split the night.

The Guild panicked and opened fire again. Pointless and completely ineffectual.

Marcus surged forward. The first soldier didn't even have a chance to start screaming before Marcus crushed him beneath his claws.

A second tried to run. Marcus grabbed him with his jaws, felt bone snap and flung him aside.

Another raised his gun. Marcus' tail-whipped him so hard he flew over the bridge railing and vanished into the black water below. Each of the Guild mercenaries dying in quick succession.

Brin screamed behind the tape, scrambling backward, terrified. Not only of the Guild and Scree demon, but also of this new creature dispatching the men like they were mere dolls, fearing that she was next on the menu.

The SUV driver and passenger tried to make a run for it, but Marcus quickly reduced them to body parts scattered about the bridge, which only left the Scree demon.

It didn't flee nor did it hesitate. Why would it, it felt no fear and it was near indestructible.

It launched itself over the SUV at Marcus, landing with claws scraping on stone. It hissed, its jaw widening in a snarl of razor-sharp teeth.

Marcus roared.

The demon moved quickly, slashing across his flank but couldn't penetrate his tough scaley hide.

Marcus retaliated, biting down on the demon's shoulder.

It shrieked, twisting violently. Then…It stopped.

Black veins began to spread outward from Marcus' bite like cracks in glass. The Scree demon staggered backward, choking, clawing at the wound desperately.

Then it collapsed. Convulsed and went completely still.

Dead.

Marcus stood over the corpse, chest heaving, wings half-spread, dripping venom-black demon blood onto the pavement.

His monstrous form breathed hard, steam curling from his nostrils.

His eyes snapped to Brin.

She was watching him.

Wide-eyed. Terrified and shaking.

Marcus took one step toward her, and she stumbled backward until her spine hit the guardrail.

He froze.

Her name rose in his throat, but his dragon-wolf jaws couldn't form it.

Brin…it's me.

He lowered himself slowly to the ground, trying to look less threatening.

Her heartbeat pounded like a drum in his ears.

She muttered behind the tape…"Marcus?"

And his entire world shifted.

Marcus shifted back to his regular form, his beast happy to take a backseat for the moment. The instant she saw him, her eyes began to tear up with relief. Wasting no time, he rushed over and broke the bindings about her wrists, then removed the tape from her mouth. All the while she just stood there staring at him.

He'd almost lost her.

That thought had every bone and muscle in Marcus' body tightening with fury. And fear.

For years he'd avoided her at all costs, ignored that tiny voice in his mind that drew him toward her. He'd scoffed at the prophecy which surrounded her, and fought tooth and nail against the eventuality of it being a reality, even when it reared up and struck him, literally.

Marcus glanced at Brin's pale face, the quiet determination in the tilt of her chin had him rubbing a hand wearily over the back of his neck.

What would he do if he lost her?

"Marcus?" she asked, a thousand questions all rolled up into the two syllables of his name. But, instead of asking him about his new beastly form, she asked something that completely flawed him. "You came for me?"

"Of course. I'd tear this whole world apart to protect you," he told her quietly, his voice even, his gaze holding hers with unwavering determination. "Are you alright? Did they hurt you?" he asked, the last words accompanied by a growl when he saw a bruise around her eye beginning to shine through.

"I'm fine, it doesn't matter. Just leave it, okay," she rebuked.

"The Hell it doesn't matter," he bit back, lowering his head to capture her lips in a possessive kiss, wracked with guilt, frustration and a need to replace the scent of the men who'd kidnapped her with his own.

Pulling back from the burning kiss, Brin once again just stared at him, unsure what to make of his behaviour. Was it a side effect of his new beastly form, adrenaline from the hunt, or something else? She was too scared to put words to the *'something else'*. Even so, her heart skipped a beat with renewed hope.

"I'm sorry I ruined your dinner with your girlfriend. I…" she began to apologise.

"Candy's not my girlfriend," he quickly cut her off.

"What? But…"

"I went out with her tonight for one reason only. To break up with her. I don't want to be with anyone but my *mate*." He told her, his eyes watching intently for every muscle twitch on her face and the hitch in her breath, assessing her reaction.

"That makes sense. You shouldn't settle for second best. You deserve someone who makes you happy. I hope you find her one day." Brin told him with a gentle smile, even as the light of hope in her eyes dimmed and her shoulders slumped a little.

It was Marcus' turn to stare at her in bewilderment. Was she so clueless that he was talking about her?

Clearly…Yes, she was.

"Brin, didn't that kiss give you a clue as to who I was talking about?"

She stilled for a moment, blinking once, twice, as the cogs in her mind turned, processing his words.

"But…I thought you hated me."

"No. Just the opposite. Although that's not a discussion I want to have out here." He told her, looking about at all the dismembered corpses surrounding them. Pulling his phone from his pocket, he noticed a reply from Alaric.

"Where are you?"

He shot back a quick reply, and another one to Oliver to organise a clean-up crew. They had about five minutes before everyone started arriving.

"Does this mean you're not annoyed with me for going to the restaurant?" she asked sweetly.

He glared down at her. To say he was annoyed with her was an understatement, but relief at seeing her standing there unharmed and safe trumped his anger. That didn't mean he wouldn't punish her for going against instructions not to leave the manor, or for leaving the restaurant without him.

For good measure...and because he really wanted to...he slapped her on the rear.

Her miserable attempt at glowering at him actually had him grinning. She might look timid and shy on the outside, but she had a spine of steel, which he respected and admired. It was only fitting that his *mate*, would be his match in every way.

His grin showed bright white, even teeth. Brin wasn't sure if she wanted to smack that smile off his face or yank him closer so she could kiss it away.

"You're in so much trouble for doing that…" she told him defiantly, stopping dead mid-sentence when she realised how close he was now standing to her.

Each inhale grew shorter, faster, as Marcus once again wrapped an arm about her waist, drawing her flush against his overheated body.

As he watched her, the simmer of arousal that never seemed to completely disappear, began to build within his body. The reaction didn't seem unnatural, she was his *mate* after all. His wolf had sensed it, and the universe had ensured it.

Gripping her tighter, Brin stared up at him, watching as his gaze began to burn with lust.

Swallowing, she licked her dry lips and tried to control the pounding of her heart.

"You know, that new beast of yours is kinda hot." She told him with a sexy lilt in her tone.

"You really think so?" he asked curiously.

"Ahh huh. And being a wyvern myself, there's no better way to travel than with a beast between my legs. That's assuming you'd want me to ride you." She told him cheekily, drawing a deep guttural lusty growl from his chest at the dual meaning.

If Alaric hadn't arrived at that very moment, Marcus probably would have wrapped Brin's legs around his hips and filled her hot body with every throbbing inch of manhood that was straining against the zipper of his pants.

"Brin, are you okay?" Alaric asked, his sharp gaze examining her so closely, she was certain he could see inside her soul.

"I'm fine, thanks." she replied, unable to meet his gaze, feeling more than a little guilty for being the cause of all the drama and carnage. Fortunately for her though, it didn't appear that he was going to hold it against her. At least not for too long. No doubt there was a lecture coming and not just from Alaric, it would be repeated, probably verbatim from her brothers too.

Alaric searched through the body parts for identification on the dismembered men when several others from the manor, along with Oliver and his fellow lycan soldiers, and Marcus' commander/brother-in-law Sanders, arrived.

Picking Brin up carefully, he carried her to the far side of the bridge. People were talking all around him, but he ignored them. The pounding of his own heart beat loud enough to drown everything else out.

"Oliver, Sanders," he called. "Could I have a word with you both for a second?" he added when he had their attention.

Both men came to stand before him, brows furrowed questioningly.

"If you don't mind, I'd like to take Brin, ah…my *mate,* home."

Oliver's eyebrows rose with a knowing smile. "I see you finally came to your senses. Congratulations to the two of you. You can take my car, it's just down the road," Oliver told him, pulling a set of car keys from his pocket.

"Umm, thanks. But…um, I don't need the car." Marcus said, looking from Oliver to Sanders and back again nervously. "There might be a couple of things I left out of my debriefing report from Canada, that I'm not sure you're going to like."

While Oliver looked curious at the statement, Sanders' stance and expression hardened, making Marcus all the more nervous.

"I'll explain everything later properly, but for now it's probably easier to just show you." Taking a few steps back, Marcus called on his beast. His body shimmered for a moment and then morphed into his new form.

Both Oliver and Sanders took a giant step backwards in surprise, and every other man there stopped what they were doing and turned to stare as well.

"What the fuck!" Sanders exclaimed. The sentiment being repeated loudly by everyone else.

"You've definitely got some explaining to do, son," Oliver said.

Marcus snorted, dipping his head subserviently.

"At least I know how you were able to cause so much carnage here." Alaric told him, an impressed smirk on his face. After more than two millennia on Earth, not much surprised him anymore, but this…this was definitely one for the books.

Marcus crouched down on his haunches and waited for Brin to climb up onto his back. Tentatively he tested his wings with the extra weight, hoping and praying silently that he wouldn't accidently tip her off in his effort to take off. Fortunately however, he managed to lift off relatively smoothly, eager to get Brin back to the manor where they could finally have that talk he'd planned before their rescue.

Brin took in the scene on the bridge from her higher vantage on Marcus' back, and was very grateful that he was on their side, because what he did to those men and the Scree demon, looked like the aftermath of that movie, The Texas Chainsaw Massacre.

As Marcus rose higher into the night sky, Brin shifted her attention to the beast beneath her, running her fingers through the soft mane of fur about his neck, tracing the transition point to his dragon body. Marcus' whole body shivered beneath her with delight, so she did it again and chuckled when he put more power into his wings to get her home faster.

26

The flight back to Havenswood Manor took only minutes. For Marcus however, it felt like every beat of his wings was a lifetime.

Brin sat astride the warm ridge of muscle and scales between his shoulder blades, fingers curled through the dense mane of fur at the top of his neck. Every time her fingers stroked down to where fur became scale, Marcus' entire body shuddered beneath her in pleasure. So, she did it again and then again, delighting in how he purred beneath her, the vibration echoing through her core and stoking her own arousal.

They soared over the neighbouring farms, the pinprick glow of house lights flickering like fireflies far beneath them. The night was cool and crisp, carrying the faint scent of pine and woodsmoke. Brin's breath puffed out in soft clouds.

Marcus angled his wings, banking left as he spotted the familiar tree line of Savernake Forest bordering the manor's land.

As they descended, the first thing either of them saw was…more carnage. This time however, there weren't any dismembered bodies.

Most of the lawn appeared decimated, the rear garden was torn to shreds and deep claw marks gouged through flower beds which the gardeners had spent hours tending. A shattered outdoor dining table lying on its side and hellhound-sized pawprints were everywhere.

Marcus' thoughts flashed sharp and bewildered. *What the hell happened here?*

Brin startled at the clarity of the words she heard in her mind. A voice that was Marcus, and yet deeper, resonant, edged with wyvern-like timbre.

She didn't think. She just…answered.

"*It was the hellhounds*", she told him back, the words forming instinctively, sliding across the new thread connecting them. "*Cujo lost it when Tilly went into labour. The pack tried to storm the house. It looks like they nearly succeeded.*"

Marcus' wings faltered for half a beat. She *heard* his thoughts?

His beast rumbled with a satisfied purr.

Brin's breath caught, her heart thudding so hard she pressed a hand to her chest. Only if she was his true *mate,* would she be able to hear his thoughts in his beast form. Every wyvern knew that, it was basic wyvern lore.

And Marcus…She heard him as clearly as if he'd spoken out loud directly into her ear, she realised.

The truth struck with calm efficiency, shattering the fragile wall she'd tried to build around her heart.

He really had chosen her. She was his *mate*.

That kiss on the bridge certainly proved he felt a strong emotional pull toward her, but that could easily have been the result of adrenaline. Even his words about only wanting his *mate*, she'd played down in her mind. She wanted to believe he'd meant her, but there had still been a glimmer of doubt in the back of her mind. But this…This was undeniable proof.

Brin didn't know whether to laugh or cry from the welling emotion bursting to be free.

Marcus descended toward one of the few intact patches of lawn, talons sinking into the soft earth, his wings flaring out to soften their landing. He crouched low so Brin could slide off.

Her legs trembled as her feet hit the ground, partly from adrenaline and partly from the realisation that was settling inside her.

Marcus shimmered, fur, scale and bone withdrawing, and once again the man stood in the beast's place, bare-chested, powerful, breathing hard, eyes still glowing faintly gold with slitted pupils that slowly rounded back to normal.

They exchanged a long, charged look.

He held out a hand. "Come on. I think we need to have a talk."

All Brin could do was nod, and took his outstretched hand in hers and followed his steps toward the manor as they picked their way between divots and around shredded plants. Brin pushed open the patio door into the lounge room where warm firelight filled the room, along with the soft muttering of voices.

The scene inside was the complete opposite of the battlefield outside.

All the women and children in the manor were gathered around Tilly by the fireplace. The new mum lay on a thick pile of blankets, tail thumping weakly, looking both exhausted and contented. Four wriggling black pups nursed greedily at her belly while Cujo hovered over her like an anxious, proud dad.

As soon as the door clicked shut behind Marcus and Brin, a chorus of greetings erupted.

"Marcus! Brin! Come and meet the babies!" Cassie waved to them.

"Look how cute they are!" Grace gushed.

"They look just like their daddy, poor things." Abby chuckled.

"What took you so long to come and see them?" Grace asked curiously.

Marcus hesitated for a millisecond.

Brin blinked.

They all looked…normal. Cheerful. Completely oblivious to the fact that she had been kidnapped, nearly killed, and rescued by a dragon-wolf hybrid all within the last half hour.

Brin whispered to Marcus out of the side of her mouth, "I don't think anyone noticed I left."

"Wasn't that your plan?" Marcus muttered back in an accusing tone.

Brin turned to him with a frown. Right. That had been her plan, and her forgettable charm made everyone else forget about her once she was out of sight. She'd nearly died, *would have* died, and no one would've had any idea what happened to her. The irony wasn't lost on her.

Brin was such an idiotic fool. Well, lesson learned. She never planned to do anything like that again.

Grace bounded toward them, her grin lighting her whole face.

"Come on! You *have* to meet them!" She grabbed Brin's wrist, tugging her forward. "Look! Three boys and a girl!"

Tilly raised her head proudly, giving Brin a slobbery hello lick.

"And I've already named them," Grace continued.

Cassie groaned. "Grace…"

"Devil," Grace declared, pointing to the biggest pup. "This one's Lucifer." She pointed to another. "And this one's, Hades." She patted the smallest boy. "And this little lady is called, Lady."

Marcus barked out a laugh. "Original. They're going to live up to every one of those names." Except maybe Lady, he thought, but held back the comment.

Even Jocelyn, sitting stiffly on a sofa near the fireplace, arms crossed, allowed the corners of her mouth to twitch.

"Well," she said flippantly, "Let's just hope they don't inherit Cujo's table manners."

Quiet laughter rippled through the room.

Marcus didn't join in. He was too busy glaring at his mother.

Brin squeezed his hand discreetly. *Later,* she told him silently with a pointed look. His answering exhale acknowledged it, but tension still bristled off him in waves.

Grace held up one of the pups and turned it so Brin could see its squished little hellhound face.

"Ohmygod," Brin whispered. "It's so adorable."

"Aren't they." Grace said proudly.

Marcus chuckled, his hand drifting to Brin's lower back like it belonged there, thumb brushing slow circles that made her pulse skip.

She leaned subtly into him.

Cassie noticed and raised an eyebrow, a smile curving the corners of her mouth.

Brin immediately gave her the same pointed look she'd just given Marcus.

"Um," she said quickly, "We should…ah…go. Marcus and I need to, um…talk."

Several faces turned their way. Some smirked. Others just nodded knowingly.

Jocelyn stiffened.

Fortunately, for once, the women were far too distracted by puppies to pry into potentially juicy gossip. They'd drag it out of her tomorrow, Brin knew. And if she didn't willingly divulge every detail,

Abby would just pluck it from her mind and share it with the other women on her behalf.

“Alright, love,” Mrs P said, waving absently. “Go on, then. We’ll see you in the morning.”

“Enjoy,” Abby added with a meaningful wink.

Brin felt her cheeks heat.

Marcus didn’t bother hiding his smug half-smile as he placed a hand about her waist and guided her toward the door.

As the lounge room disappeared behind them, Brin’s heart thudded louder with each step.

They were finally alone. They both knew exactly what conversation was coming. What truths had to be discussed. What feelings could no longer be shoved into dark corners to be ignored.

Marcus leaned down, voice low and rough. “Your room’s on the second floor, isn’t it?”

She nodded with a sly smile. “I’m pretty sure you know exactly which room is mine.”

It was Marcus’ turn to offer her a sly smile as he led her up the stairs and along the corridor, each step humming with anticipation, fear, desire, and the unavoidable gravity of destiny finally catching up to them.

Brin opened the door and Marcus followed her into her room, closing the door behind them with a soft click that seemed to echo far louder than it should have.

Her room was dim, the only light coming from a small lamp on the side table near the sofa by the window. It cast a gentle amber glow across the room, softening the edges of the furniture and throwing shadows along the walls. The air held the faint chill of evening, the windows must’ve been cracked open earlier, she thought, and she rubbed her arms unconsciously, not from cold but from pure, vibrating nerves.

Marcus felt it too. The tension. The tight coil of anticipation. The unspoken words finally pushing their way to the surface.

He ushered her gently toward the sofa. “Sit,” he said quietly.

She did, perching on the edge, hands clasped in her lap, looking both ready to bolt and ready to hear every word he had to say.

Marcus didn’t trust himself to sit yet. His body was too wound up with nervous energy. He could still taste the fear of losing her, still smell the faint traces of demon blood in his mouth, still feel the pounding echo of his wings beneath his skin.

So, he paced. One step. Another. Dragging a hand through his hair. Trying, and failing, to figure out where to start.

Finally, he exhaled shakily and faced her.

"Okay. I guess…um…I should start at the beginning."

Her eyes lifted to watch him. Soft. Open. Patient.

"The day we met," he began, voice low and rough, "I was an asshole, I know I was."

Brin huffed a short laugh. "Understatement of the century."

He crossed his arms over his chest, then uncrossed them when it felt too defensive.

"You need to understand…Kaitlyn's mating pheromones had me completely messed up that day. I'd never been around a lycan female in mating heat before. It scrambled every rational thought I had. I had no control of what I did or said. And then I saw you…" He shook his head. "You were the most beautiful woman I'd ever seen, and under the influence of those damned mating pheromones, I reacted like an idiot." Embarrassment rippled across his expression.

"I hated myself for the way I acted toward you. And I hated that the attraction I felt didn't go away when the pheromones were gone. I didn't know if what I felt was real or a lingering influence. So, I avoided you. And picked a fight with you. And I continued to act like a complete bastard. Deliberately acting out to keep space between us."

Brin's lips tightened, but she didn't interrupt.

Marcus' voice deepened with something darker. "Then…a couple of days later, when I was injured in the battle against Bordan's army…"

She swallowed, remembering that day too.

"When you healed me," he continued softly, "Something happened. When my blood was absorbed into your palms…Brin, it felt like something inside me opened up. Like a door that had been locked, suddenly swung wide. I felt you. Not just the healing, I mean *you*. Your soul."

Brin nodded. She'd felt it too.

"And then Nathaniel mentioned the prophecy involving you." His jaw flexed. "And I knew. I knew it was me. I don't know how, I just…knew. The dragon mark, the bond, our shared destiny…all of it. And it terrified the hell out of me."

He dragged a hand down his face.

"Why?" she asked softly.

"Because I didn't want my life mapped out for me. I didn't want fate telling me who to love or how to live. I didn't want to lose my independence or my free will. So, I pushed you away. As hard and as far as I could." He told her, a tinge of regret in his words.

"And yet…you were always there. In my head. In my senses. My wolf went insane every time you were near. Every damn time someone said your name."

Her breath hitched at that.

"When I was told about the mission to Canada," he continued, pacing again, "I knew something big was coming. I felt it in my bones, like destiny was catching up with me and I'd finally run out of places to hide."

He stopped, turning toward her fully.

"And then the serpent armband bit me."

Reflexively, Brin raised her hand, her fingers tracing the hard outline of the armband beneath her top.

"You were right," he said, voice low. "Something was wrong. Over the next few days, I developed a fever and a rash on my wrist, with black lines under my skin that shifted and moved…And, I lost my connection to my wolf, Brin. Completely. I couldn't shift. Couldn't call it up. It was like losing a limb."

"Ohmygod! Marcus…"

He took a step closer, holding up a finger to stop her from saying anything further.

"Please Brin, I have to get this out."

Her mouth opened and then closed again.

"But when I was near you…I felt better. My wolf calmed. My fever eased. You were the only thing that anchored me. Then…we had sex," he said softly, reverently, "And something inside me shifted, like everything snapped back into place. Not just with my wolf. Me, all of me. My strength. My senses. My instincts."

His voice turned rough with emotion.

"And in that moment, I realised…I wasn't afraid anymore. I wasn't resisting my destiny. I *wanted* it. I wanted you. I knew I'd always wanted you. Then tonight, when those bastards took you…I nearly lost my sanity." His voice lowered to a whisper, his body trembled, as did hers, he realised.

He stood there, chest heaving, heart slamming, waiting, *fearing* her response.

"Marcus…"

Marcus swallowed hard.

"What about all those women you went out with, you must have felt something for them?"

That was not a question he saw coming, but if he was going to pour out his heart to her, he might as well lay everything out on the table, he figured.

"In hindsight, I've realised that every female I've gone out with, I chose because they had some quality that reminded me of you."

"Oh, and what qualities of mine, did Candy have?" she asked.

Marcus took a seat beside her, his hand moved to touch her cheek, cherishing the feel of her. "She was tall like you, she has red hair like you, and…she has big boobs like you." He told her, cupping his hands in front of him as though weighing them in his palms.

"I gather you like big boobs?" Brin managed to keep her expression neutral as she spoke, cupping her own breasts and massaging them slowly. She watched as his eyes snapped to her breasts like they were magnetised. She was teasing him, but she couldn't help herself.

"Yeah, I do. Although, Candy's are fake, not like yours…full, firm and the perfect handful." He said, subconsciously licking his lips at the sight of her pert nipples outlined beneath her top.

"I'm sorry, was that too much information?" He asked. He was trying his best to make a good impression, but sometimes his mouth spouted out words before checking in with his brain.

"No." She chuckled. "I like how you don't hold anything back. I always know where I stand with you. And for the record, I would never hold it against you for having a life."

"I'm assuming there have been a few men in your life too over the past few years?"

Brin shifted on the seat a little to look at him more directly.

"Yes, and no. You've heard the saying: *If you can't be with the one you love, love the one you're with.* Well, I've had a long-term relationship with BOB, also affectionately known as BOSS or BEAST."

Marcus blinked, a muscle at the corner of his eye twitching. "Oh."

The cogs in his brain churned over the idea that she hadn't pined over him, and he was desperately trying to come to terms with it, but it didn't come as easily for him as it seemed to for her, to accept that she'd had previous cuddle buddies. It wasn't that he had double standards, he'd never begrudge her some happiness. It was just her words, *long term relationship*, had caught him off guard.

Brin lifted his chin to get his attention, a cheeky smile lighting her face. "I can introduce you to him, if you'd like. Maybe we could have a threesome?"

Marcus swallowed, hard. He didn't know what to say to that. Before he had a chance to say anything, Brin stood up and walked toward her bed, opening a drawer of the side table, she pulled something out and walked back to the sofa. Taking one of his hands so his palm was face upwards, she took the item from behind her back and placed it in his hand.

"Marcus, meet BOB."

Marcus stared down at what she'd placed in his hand and began to laugh so hard his sides developed a stitch. "BOB, as in Battery Operated Boyfriend?"

"Yep, also known as BOSS, Battery Operated Satisfaction System, and BEAST, Battery Enhanced Arousal Satisfaction Tool," she told him.

Wiping away the tears, he finally composed himself. "Hell yeah, I think the three of us could have some fun together."

"But you know…" Brin began more seriously, gaining his attention again. "There were times when BOB just wasn't enough. I needed the contact of another person, to be touched and feel like I mattered, even if it was just for an hour or two. So, a few times I took the liberty of having a romp between the sheets with one of the guards at the citadel."

"Anyone in particular?"

"No. Just whoever happened to be roaming the halls at the time. They were just a means to an end. The truth is, it didn't matter who they were, I always imagined it was you with me, not them." she told him.

"And here was me, thinking that you hated me all these years."

"Marcus," she whispered, her voice thick, "I've never hated you. I hated how you acted," she corrected. "I hated the walls you put up. And I hated that you made me feel like I wasn't worth your attention."

He closed his eyes in shame.

"But you?" Her fingers brushed lightly over the dragon mark on his wrist. "I never hated you."

He opened his eyes, stunned by the softness in her gaze.

"I was…attracted to you right from the beginning too. I kept trying to push aside my feelings because you made it very clear you wanted nothing to do with me." A soft, self-conscious laugh escaped her. "I thought I was wasting my energy on someone who despised me."

His heart splintered.

Brin swallowed. "Regardless, I still hoped that one day you'd look at me and actually, see me."

He reached for her hand, but she lifted her other hand, touching his cheek gently.

"And tonight…when I heard your thoughts in my head…I knew without a doubt that you'd chosen me."

"So, just to make things perfectly clear. You're telling me that you don't hold it against me that I've behaved like a fucking moron?" He asked.

"Yes, you foolish man. That's exactly what I'm saying."

Marcus' shoulders sagged with absolute relief.

Then she added, her voice dropping to a saucy whisper. "And to avoid any misunderstandings or confusion, your new beastly form is *ridiculously* sexy. That purring growl you make when I stroke your neck…it causes a vibration between my thighs." She bit her lip. "Let's just say it's a huge turn-on."

Heat slammed into him like a tidal wave.

Her breath hitched when his pupils snapped into reptilian slits. The beast inside him pushed hard at the surface, hungry for his *mate*.

Marcus' voice was a growl of molten heat. "And…do you accept me as your *mate*?"

Brin didn't answer with words.

She gripped his face between her hands, pulling him closer and kissed him.

The kiss was full of fire and urgency, years of pent-up longing unleashed at once. There was no holding back. Not this time. Marcus groaned into her mouth, his hands sliding to her waist, pulling her flush against him, her body melting into his.

Her fingers tangled in his hair. His lips devoured hers and their breaths mingled, hot and desperate.

The taste of her undid him.

When they finally broke apart, panting, Marcus' eyes glowed gold again, pupils sharp and reptilian, his beast was practically vibrating just beneath his skin.

Brin's knees trembled.

"Marcus…" she whispered, voice thick with desire.

He cupped her face, brushing his thumb over her swollen lower lip.

"Say it," he murmured. "I need to hear it."

She held his gaze, her heart in her eyes.

"I love you," she whispered. "I always have."

His body shuddered with relief and delight.

Then his mouth was on hers again, hungrier, more demanding, claiming her lips with a heat that made her melt and gasp, her hands gripping his shoulders to ground herself in the intensity.

Marcus picked her up and carried her toward the bed, still kissing her fiercely, breathlessly, her lips swollen beneath his, her pulse racing with anticipation.

As they reached the edge of the bed, Marcus broke the kiss long enough to rest his forehead against hers, his breath ragged.

"You have no idea," he whispered, voice gravelly with emotion and lust, "What you do to me."

Brin's smile was slow and sultry.

"I think I'm starting to."

Outside, the wind rattled the windowpane. Inside, the lamp cast soft gold over their entwined bodies as they fell onto the mattress together. And the room, once chillingly quiet, now thrummed with heat, chemistry, and the inevitability of a bond sealed by both fate…and choice.

Tonight, he would claim his *mate*!

As that thought whispered through his mind, a sudden shiver of anticipation struck the thick ridge of his erection rising inside his pants.

With economical movement, Marcus kicked off his shoes and swiftly shed his jeans and boxers, leaving them where they landed on the floor.

Fully naked, she took in the sight of him. He took her breath away. His chest was broad, his abs flat and muscular. Long powerful legs rippled with muscle as he climbed back onto the bed. Between his thighs jutted his erection, thick and heavy. A vein pulsed along its length, feeding the dark head as it jerked from the lust surging through him.

As she watched, Marcus moved closer, pulling her into his arms, his lips covering hers in an explosion of pure hunger, her arms wrapping around his bare back, feeling the warmth of his skin and traced his muscles as they rippled beneath her touch with every movement.

Breaking the kiss, Brin breathed heavily, dragging much needed oxygen into her lungs. Pulling back from him, she needed more than to catch her breath, she needed to remove the barrier of her own clothes between them.

Sliding off the bed, she unfastened her jeans and pulled her top over her head, tossing both haphazardly to the floor, all the while watching Marcus' hungry expression as his eyes followed her. Slowly, she unfastened her bra, but didn't let it fall immediately, she held it in place with a hand, slipping her free hand beneath the lacy material to pinch and massage a nipple.

Marcus growled, his eyes flashing with gold, his whole body appearing to become more sensually primal as his beast rose closer to the surface. Reaching for her, he drew her once again onto the bed to kneel before him. Those pert rosy buds, level with his hungry mouth. Pulling her to him, he latched onto one proud, taut nipple, his tongue lashing at it, his teeth nipping and his mouth sucking at it. All the while he kneaded the other gently, skilfully, drawing a moan from her lips.

Releasing his hold to switch to her other breast, Brin's head fell back in pleasure as she sank down to straddle his hips, locking his hard erection between their bodies. Flexing her pelvis back and forth, she drew the broad crest of his iron-hard flesh against her heated core, caressing his length over her sensitive clit. Every pass pushed his need higher, every nip and suck of her breasts set her core on fire.

Marcus gripped her hips to switch their positions, pulling Brin beneath him on the bed, but she was anticipating the move and would have none of it, slapping away his hands and nipping at his shoulder.

"Not yet," she told him in a sultry tone. "There's something else I want first."

"Anything. Name it. What can I do for you?" he asked, his hands still trying to pull her back to him.

"It's not what you can do for me, it's what I can do for you," she purred seductively, placing a hand on his shaft and closed her fingers around it, revelling in the way Marcus' body jerked in pleasure and his breath caught and quickened. She slid her hand slowly up and down, massaging its length, adding a twist at the flushed head, circling a fingertip over the moistened slit at the tip with each pass.

"Sweetheart, this isn't fair, I should be the one…to pleasure you," he protested weakly, his words stalling when she stroked down his length, reaching beneath his balls and the sensitive strip behind them. "Holy hell woman, you're going to burn me alive." Regardless, he willingly gave into her dominance, giving her free reign.

"Not like this I'm not. But, maybe I will by doing this…"

Marcus lifted his head from the pillow, intent on asking her what she meant, but quickly fell back again with a tortured groan of pleasure, parting his legs to give her better access to any part of his body she wanted, when she replaced her tactile manipulation of his cock with her tongue, lathing it, stroking it from base to tip.

Brin parted her lips over the engorged tip of his hardened flesh, sending Marcus' pulse rocketing and his heart hammering against his chest wall. His fingers threaded themselves through the long tendrils of her hair, he couldn't help it. He tried to keep his hands to himself, he really did, but giving over total control wasn't in his DNA.

Brin's gaze lifted to his, locking the breath in his chest. She was so goddamned beautiful and sexy as hell. He watched her tongue curl around the tip, her lips slowly closing over the end of his cock, slowly, very slowly, sliding down until the entire head was enclosed, wet heat sucking him, and all the while her eyes locked with his.

Oh, sweet Jesus!

A second later that wet stalk slid back out, her tongue stroking the length of his shaft. Delving lower to the full sac beneath, Brin teased them, drawing one into her mouth and sucking. Hard. All the while her fist pumped his shaft. Her tongue traced a throbbing vein back to the hooded crest, nipping, licking and sucking, and his hips pumped rhythmically into her touch of their own accord.

A growl tore from his lips. He desperately wanted to hold back the orgasm he was rocketing toward too, but her lips tightened around him. Her tongue stroked faster, lashing against the sensitive nerve endings, sending his senses racing. She was pushing him toward the brink he couldn't return from.

Sensing Marcus' body tensing further, the rhythm of his pumping hips changing, Brin pulled back, blowing a stream of warm air over the dark pink, mushroomed head.

Marcus cried out at the loss of suction on his cock, his hands reflexively tried to draw her back. He was so close, he could feel the tingle in his balls and at the base of his spine.

"No," she scolded him. "I want you inside me when you come."

Leaning over her he managed to say, "Your wish is my command." How he'd managed to spark enough life in his brain cells to speak at all, he didn't know, especially since every drop of blood was currently pumping through his more primitive, southern brain between his legs.

With quick efficiency, he flipped their positions, removing her panties with one swift tug, bringing his tall, hard body over hers, kissing her shoulders and her neck. Grinding himself against the soft mound between her thighs, his lips took hers once again. There was no escaping the low moan that escaped.

His hand slid between them as he positioned his hardened shaft at her entrance. His other sliding about her waist to hold her in place as he slid between her swollen wet folds.

No other woman made him feel so desperate, so hungry.

As soon as the blunt head of his erection was at her entrance, she thrust her pelvis up, taking the tip inside her. She was already wet and tight, and he felt like he would come before he even finished his first stroke inside her. He was so ready, both man and beast had waited too long for this day to come.

"Marcus," she whimpered. He answered by sliding inside her a little more.

"Fuck me, damn you. Before I die from the need," she begged, lifting her hips to impale herself more deeply on his hard shaft, but he pulled back and she let out a small whimper. He loved that growl of annoyance she gave when he taunted her. It made him even harder.

"Fuck me!" she demanded, gripping the tight globes of his backside with her nails. The sharp sting forcing him to instinctively thrust his pelvis forward and pushing the head of his cock inside her further.

Marcus groaned and stilled. She was so damned tight.

Gently he pushed between her tight inner walls, each time going deeper, feeling the compression around him become tighter, until he was buried to the hilt, thrusting inside her like a piston, picking up the pace in equal response to her elicit enthusiastic cries. Every nerve ending in his body sparking with every stroke. He became lost in the sensation building inside him as they moved together at just the right rhythm.

The feeling of him filling her was like a drug. That little bit of him was not nearly enough. Planting her feet on the bed she thrust her pelvis up, sinking his length further within her tight channel.

Marcus' eyes almost rolled back into his head with pleasure as her tight walls gripped him firmly and drew him deeper.

"You're so perfect," he hissed as his slammed home within her. His speed ramped up to something that should have torn her apart, an unstoppable frenzy that cancelled out her power of speech and rational thought.

The explosive orgasm detonated through her, Marcus following only a second later with a possessive roar.

As Marcus reared back, his features seemed to shimmer and morph, his face distorting as his inner beast surged forward, his teeth extending to become long, sharp points. There were no thoughts, only instinct, biting down into the soft flesh between Brin's neck and shoulder. Marking her, claiming her as his.

Pulling his fangs from her flesh, he flung his head back and shouted in pure ecstasy. His mating hormone combining with years of unrealised desire, poured through his body, backloading his orgasm with staggering force, as though a bolt of lightning had sheared his balls in two and exploded the top of his cock off. Gasping for breath, his hips locked into the V of her thighs as he pumped his hot seed into the depths of her body, the convulsions in her womb milking him of every last drop.

Brin felt like she was tumbling down a rabbit hole as wave after wave of pleasure rolled through her, leaving her feet feeling as though she was wearing fuzzy socks and her whole body tingled.

Marcus collapsed onto her, rolling onto his side, pulling her with him, their bodies still locked together as the aftershocks of their orgasms rolled through them.

"Are you alright?" he asked breathlessly, his gaze flicking between her pleasure filled eyes and the puncture wounds, that even now were closing at an accelerated rate.

"I've never been better," she replied, equally as breathlessly, wrapping an arm about his waist to pull herself closer to him.

They stayed like that, entwined in each other's arms until Brin's breathing slowed to become an even rhythm of sleep. Even then, Marcus just lay there holding her, gently stroking her hair, marvelling at how lucky he was.

There were three things he knew for certain:

He loved her more than life itself.

The Guild would never stop trying to find her, they wanted the serpent armband…and they wanted her dead.

And, until his last breath left his lungs, and last flicker of life left his body, he would protect her and keep her safe.

In that moment Marcus realised something. According to the prophecy, he was destined to live for as long as she does, and as a wyvern, her normal lifespan was around three thousand years. Which meant, that he too would now live for the same length of time. At least, he assumed so. That was a puzzle to solve another day, he thought sleepily.

Pulling the blankets up over them both more tightly, he snuggled closer to her and closed his eyes, drifting into the first truly peaceful sleep he'd had in more than a decade..

27

The underground lab at the Alliance's Ukraine base had a way of distorting time.

Down here there were no windows to measure daylight by, only fluorescent strips that flickered faintly overhead, the sharp tang of disinfectant, and the steady mechanical hum of equipment that never slept.

Which was probably why the last twenty-four hours had felt like a month.

Owen sat on the edge of a stool at the bench with his sleeve already rolled up, and a foot tapping incessantly like it was trying to drill through the floor. Eytan leaned against the bench opposite him, arms folded, eyes fixed on Alex with an intensity that highlighted the stress of waiting.

Teagan stood just behind Alex's shoulder, one hand resting lightly between his shoulder blades, as though the contact would somehow keep her nerves from shaking loose. While Elise hovered in the doorway to the corridor housing the three motionless men, still lying in stasis beyond it. The first infected lycan soldier, Klaus and the girls' father, Gustav.

All three lay so still. Not quite alive, but not dead either, caught somewhere in limbo.

Alex finally turned away from the microscope and the mess of vials and notes spread across the bench, resembling an explosion of controlled chaos. His eyes were bright, glittering with luminescent flecks that revealed his heightened emotional state.

He held up two printouts.

"Okay," he said, voice deliberately calm. Which meant he was barely containing his excitement.

Owen's tapping stopped. "Don't do that. Don't say *'okay'*, like you're about to tell me I'm about to grow a second arse."

"It would be an improvement," Alex muttered automatically.

Owen shot him a dark look which Alex ignored. He slapped the papers down on the bench and dragged a gloved finger across the columns. "This is Owen's blood post-injection antibody profile. And here…" he tapped the second sheet, "Are the antibodies from the original virus sample."

Eytan leaned forward. "And?"

Alex grinned. Slow. Triumphant.

"They match."

For half a heartbeat no one moved, as though their bodies didn't trust the words enough to react.

Eytan exhaled a tightly held breath. "Are you saying we have a cure?"

Alex nodded. "Yep, we do."

"Alex, you're a genius." Teagan's eyes became glassy. Her composure fracturing from raw relief, a burst of nervous laughter breaking free.

"Was that ever in question?" Alex asked with smug satisfaction. "And now that we have a base sample, I can synthesise enough to stabilize and immunize every lycan and wyvern…eventually. It's not going to be instant mass production, but the cure is solid."

"Just so I'm certain, nothing you've injected me with over the last few days is going to make me mutate, sprout horns or start barking at the moon, right?" Owen asked Alex pointedly.

"Alex tipped his head. "Too early to rule out barking."

Owen stared at him.

Alex's smile widened. "I'm kidding…mostly."

Owen sagged back on the stool, rubbing his hand over his face. "You are kidding, yeah?"

"Absolutely." Alex replied, sounding offended. Even so, his expression suggested he wasn't so certain.

Eytan's eyes slid toward the cells again, and the room sobered, not with dread this time, but with something like stunned gratitude.

Elise moved first. She walked into the corridor as though pulled by a magnet, staring through the bars at her father's still form. Gustav lay on his cot, hands folded on his chest. His face was pale, but there was no thrashing. No rabid snapping. No wild, yellowed eyes.

Just…peaceful slumber.

"Don't worry dad, you'll be back to normal in no time," she told him quietly, not knowing whether he could actually hear her or not.

Teagan stepped beside her and laced their fingers together. "Before you know it, he'll be barking orders again and driving us all crazy," she chuckled, giving her sister a nudge.

"I didn't realise how stressed I was, I've been hoping for a cure but at the same time I've been bracing myself for the possibility that we wouldn't find one."

"I know," Teagan said softly, pressing her forehead to Elise's temple for a moment. "Me too."

Behind them, Alex was already moving, gloved hands flicking from vial to vial. The celebration in him took the shape of action. Now that he had a cure, he wasted no time in producing the first batch of the vaccine.

His phone buzzed once on the bench, which he ignored.

A moment after Alex's phone stopped, Teagan's phone began ringing.

"Alaric," she said the moment the call connected, pacing a tight circle through the lab. "We've got good news. Alex has found the cure. He's working on making the vaccine right now." Teagan told him.

Elise listened to Teagan's half of the conversation for a few moments until she passed the phone over to Alex and was quickly distracted when her own phone buzzed sharply in her pocket.

Pulling it out, she read the message. Her shoulders slumped on a groan.

"What's up?" Eytan asked.

Elise held up the phone. "It's the restaurant upstairs. There's an early morning customer. With most of the staff having been sent away because of the virus, I'm covering the morning shift."

Alex, still on the phone with Alaric, flicked through notes on his desk before continuing talking. "Yes, yes, I know. Although, I don't have the production capacity here that we'll need. We'll have to use external resources. Maybe a large pharmaceutical company. I haven't tested it on the infected men yet, but I'm confident it's going to work. One step at a time though."

Elise put her phone back in her pocket and forced a breath. "I'll be back shortly."

Eytan pushed himself from the bench. "I'll come with you."

Elise shook her head with a half-hearted smile. "No, it's okay. I've got it."

Eytan frowned. "Elise…"

"I said, I've got it." She repeated, giving him a friendly punch in the arm, letting out a tiny huff that might have been a laugh, then turned and headed toward the lift.

The doors closed behind her with a soft hiss.

Upstairs, the restaurant was fairly quiet, just the usual noise of pots and pans in the kitchen. The first thing Elise noticed was the smell, warm bread, coffee, and the family comfort of garlic and onions sweating in a pan. The chef moved about the kitchen like a man who'd done it all before, a thousand times. And he had. He'd been here since the first day the place opened, over twenty years ago, and Elise had always suspected he could run the restaurant single handedly, while blindfolded.

He glanced up. "Morning Elise."

"Morning," she replied. Then she hesitated. "Are you okay?"

He gave a noncommittal grunt and turned back to his chopping. "Busy."

Elise's frown tugged at her brows. He'd been…quieter lately. Less prone to complaining and cursing under his breath. But, the last week had been a slow-motion nightmare and stress had a way of making people behave strangely, she surmised, and pushed the thought aside.

Grabbing a notepad and pen, she stepped out into the dining area.

The restaurant was empty except for a single customer who sat in a booth near the back, broad shoulders beneath a dark, heavy coat, his posture casual enough…Except, Elise's skin prickled the moment she saw him.

A creeping sensation crawled over her senses like ants. The air around him felt…wrong, like a palpable darkness surrounded him.

Without meaning to, Elise slowed. Her heartbeat began to pick up, pounding hard in her chest and her mouth went dry.

Still, she kept walking, forcing herself to hold her head high and her spine straight.

Because fear was like blood in the water, attracting predators, and she suspected whoever sat in that booth would enjoy the scent of her fear.

Elise reached the table and stopped, holding her pen and notepad up ready to take his order.

"Good morning," she said in a professional tone. "What can I…"

The man turned his body to face her, lifting his chin to look her in the eyes when he spoke.

Elise's blood went instantly cold.

Recognition hit her like a slap.

She didn't move. Didn't flinch. She refused to give him the satisfaction of seeing just how much he affected her.

But her fingers tightened around the notepad so hard the paper creased.

"Scorpion," she addressed him with a contemptuous sneer. "What are you doing here, and where's your psychotic fuck buddy? I thought she had you on a tight leash."

Scorpion's mouth curved, slow and satisfied, like he'd come here purely for the pleasure of watching her unravel.

"Morganna sends her regrets," he told her.

Elise's throat worked hard at swallowing the lump that had formed, although she kept her expression hard. "How unfortunate for all of us."

His eyes flicked over her face as if cataloguing every micro expression. "She would have enjoyed catching up. Reminiscing."

Elise leaned a fraction closer, her voice low. "If you're here to threaten me, do it properly. Don't waste my time with theatrics."

Scorpion's smile sharpened. "Ah. Still the brave little one."

Elise's jaw tightened. "Why are you here?"

He rose from the booth, unhurried, and Elise had to fight the instinct to step back. His presence pressed on her senses with nauseating malevolence.

"Oh, I'm simply here to offer my condolences," he said lightly. "I heard your father is quite ill."

Everything inside Elise went still. Her heart didn't just pound…it stuttered.

The pen in her hand trembled.

"How do you know that?" she demanded, the words biting out before she could temper them.

Scorpion's gaze gleamed with amusement. "I have eyes and ears everywhere."

Elise swallowed hard. "This base is in lockdown, only a handful of people know who's sick."

"And yet," he said, stepping past her, "I know."

Elise's body stayed rigid as he walked away, her mind screaming *move, move, MOVE*, but her pride held her in place.

At the entrance, Scorpion paused just long enough to glance back.

"Morganna is looking forward to seeing you again." He said softly.

Then he was gone. The door closed behind him with a quiet chime.

And Elise's knees almost gave out. Stumbling to the nearest chair she collapsed into it, the notepad and pen slipping from her fingers, landing on the floor. Her hands shook uncontrollably.

She bent forward with her elbows on her knees, her head dropping between her shoulders as she fought for air. Inhale. Exhale. Inhale…

Her lungs wouldn't cooperate. Her vision tunnelled.

The chef called from the kitchen, "Elise?"

"I'm fine," she rasped. She forced herself to sit upright, swallowing hard until the nausea eased.

Then she stood. And ran for the lift.

She stabbed the lift button once, twice. Then repeatedly until the elevator light on the wall lit up.

When the doors finally opened, Elise practically launched herself inside and hammered the basement level button until the doors closed again.

As the lift descended, her heartbeat continued to pound hard enough to break a rib.

How did he know about Dad? Only her extended family knew.

And now Scorpion was casually offering condolences like it was common knowledge.

The doors slid open.

Elise sprinted down the corridor.

The lab was still alive with cheerful celebration, and Alex was still on the phone. Owen and Eytan bantering between themselves and Teagan sat more at ease than she had in days.

They all stopped the moment Elise appeared, her face as pale as a sheet.

Teagan moved first. "Elise…?"

Elise grabbed the doorframe to steady herself. "He was here," she said, voice shaking. "Upstairs. In the restaurant."

Owen's carefree attitude vanished instantly. "Who was here?"

Elise's eyes snapped to Alex, then to Teagan. "Scorpion."

Alex dropped the phone away from his mouth, the conversation forgotten in an instant. "What?"

"*He* was the customer in the restaurant," she told them, her words tumbling out quickly. "He knows dad is sick. He said he came to pass on his condolences, and that Morganna is looking forward to seeing us again."

Eytan went rigid, every muscle in him tightening as if he was bracing for impact.

Teagan's hands were already on Elise's shoulders, guiding her toward a stool. "Just breathe. Slowly. Now, tell us exactly what he said."

Elise did as instructed, taking in a couple of slow breaths, before repeating the conversation, every syllable, verbatim.

Alex didn't wait, he shoved past them, bypassing the slow moving lift, he took the stairs, fury radiating off him like heat.

Owen looked at Teagan. Should I go…"

"No," Teagan said, a little more harshly than she intended, then more softly, "No doubt Scorpion is long gone, but if he is still here, Alex is the best one to deal with him. Trust me."

Time ticked by at a monotonous rate, as they waited for Alex to return.

Owen stood to attention at the end of the corridor by the lift, weapons in hand and ready to use them.

Finally, Alex returned, his eyes as hard as shards of flint. "Nothing," he bit out. There's no sign of him," he announced, as he walked at a clipped pace along the corridor, Owen only a step behind.

"I want to know how he found out about Gustav." Eytan said, stepping aside to let the other two men enter the lab.

Silence fell.

Not the quiet from relief this time. The quiet of something sharpening.

Alex's voice was low. "Gustav wasn't showing any symptoms when he cleared out the base. Besides us, the only people who know are at the manor…And Emil Wagstaff."

Owen's jaw clenched. "Emil, the guy who's working as a double agent inside the Guild, yeah?"

"That's him." Alex nodded.

"Maybe he changed sides?"

"Not likely. He despises the Guild as much as we do." Alex's gaze snapped up, the pieces connecting with ugly inevitability. "Either we've got a leak…"

"…or Emil has been compromised," Teagan finished.

Elise's throat tightened. "Scorpion said he has eyes and ears everywhere."

"That's not a boast. That's a warning." Eytan's eyes darkened.

The lab felt colder suddenly, the harsh fluorescent lighting accentuating the discomfort in the room.

Owen dragged a hand through his hair, agitation spiking. "We have a vaccine. We should be celebrating. And instead…"

"Instead, we've been reminded," Alex said, his voice steady and dangerous, "That winning one battle doesn't end the war."

Elise looked past them toward the cells where her father lay in stasis. "No, it doesn't. But, the vaccine has only just been discovered. Which means neither Scorpion nor his spy knows about it yet. And we need to keep it that way."

"Pretend we're still working on it, you mean?" Eytan queried.

"Exactly. With any luck we can make enough vaccine in secret before the Guild can compromise it." Elise added.

Teagan lifted her chin. "Alright, she said calmly. "First, we need to let Alaric know, then I think we should probably do a bit of house cleaning. Look for any devices that might be hidden about, mics, cameras. Check for spyware on our phones and computers, and look into anyone who might have come on base in the last few days. And, until we can find the culprit, we should avoid talking about anything to do with the vaccine."

Alex's mouth curved into something grim. "Whoever the fucking maggot is who's backing the Guild, is going to wish they'd never been born."

He reached for his phone to call Alaric, not thinking to rein in his anger or the resultant electromagnetic energy. There was the sound of a snap, and sizzle, and a moment later the smell of burning electrical components filled the air.

"Fuck!" he grumbled. "Teagan, can I borrow yours?" he asked brusquely, pissed off that he'd fried another phone.

"Fine. But if you kill my phone, I'll kill you!"

Alex rolled his eyes at the threat, took her phone and dialed Alaric.

Behind them, in the stillness of the corridor, the three infected men slept on, peaceful for now, while everyone else braced for whatever came next.

28

Brin woke slowly, wrapped in the warmth of thick blankets and the memory of last night.

Instinctively, she reached out a hand for Marcus, only to find the space beside her empty, the sheets cool where his body had been. Instead of disappointment, a soft smile curved her lips.

Of course he was gone, Marcus never slept long once daylight crept in. Duty and instinct were stitched into his nature. Still, she turned onto her side and slid her hand across the mattress where he'd been, fingers brushing the faint impression he'd left behind, drawing his pillow closer to bury her nose in it, breathing in his scent.

Her chest filled with a quiet, bone-deep happiness she hadn't felt in…ever.

Stretching languidly, she rolled onto her back, sunlight spilling through the window in pale gold bands. The light caught on the serpent armband, glinting against her skin. For a moment, she studied it, this ancient, dangerous thing now bound to her.

Maybe it was permanent. Maybe it wasn't. Either way, she found she didn't resent it.

If the serpent hadn't bitten Marcus…if fate hadn't forced its hand so decisively…they would likely still be locked in their mutually torturous behaviour, pretending they didn't feel the pull of attraction.

She brushed her thumb over the warm gold and smiled softly.

After dressing, she slipped quietly from her room and headed downstairs, following the low murmur of voices drifting up from below.

As she rounded the corner near the sitting room, the voices grew louder, their heated tone charged with unmistakable anger.

Marcus and Jocelyn…again.

Brin froze.

Not wanting to intrude, she stayed just out of sight, her heart thudding as their argument unfolded.

"So, you've claimed *her* as your *mate*, have you?" Jocelyn's voice was sharp, disbelieving.

"My *mate* has a name. Brin." Marcus' reply was clipped, controlled and dangerous.

"Well, at least she's better than that street walker, whatever her name was."

Brin's jaw tightened instinctively.

"Candy isn't a whore, she's a model. And she's a very nice person, no matter what you thought of her." His voice held no affection, only fairness.

"You could've fooled me," Jocelyn scoffed. "And no doubt *Brin*," she over-emphasised the name like it tasted sour, "Isn't any better for you than the street…model. You're setting yourself up for an unhappy life with her, mark my words. You wouldn't have fought with her all these years if she was truly right for you."

Marcus exhaled slowly.

"Let me make something very clear to you, mum. Yes, I avoided Brin. And yes, we argued. But I had my reasons."

"Yes, yes, the prophecy," Jocelyn drawled. "I've heard."

"That's the excuse I told myself," Marcus said quietly. "But the truth is a lot closer to home than you'd like."

Jocelyn lifted her chin and a sculpted eyebrow in unison, simultaneously portraying both curiosity and haughty superiority. "Oh?"

"You," he said flatly. "You're the reason I avoided her."

"That's ridiculous." She scoffed. "You've never bothered about my opinion before, why would it matter to you what I think of your choice of *mate*, now?"

"I don't care about your opinion, " Marcus shot back. "But growing up, you were my role model for relationships. I watched how you treated my father, how cold and cruel you were. I watched how you drove him away."

"That's not true," Jocelyn snapped. "You were too young to understand. You didn't see…"

"Oh, Holly and I saw everything. We might have been young, but we weren't stupid." Marcus cut in, years of pent-up anger towards his mother started pouring out in a torrent. "Then you found your true *mate*, and you're just as cruel and uncaring towards him. Why do you think he goes away on hunting trips so often, he needs distance from you."

"That's a lie."

"No mother, that's survival," Marcus said harshly. "I was terrified of becoming like you, of waking up one day and realising I'd destroyed the person I loved most."

"How *dare* you speak to me like that," Jocelyn hissed. "I'm your mother, you need to show me some respect."

"If you'd ever behaved like one," Marcus replied, his voice shaking with restrained anger, "I'd gladly give you that respect. But the only person you've ever cared about is yourself. Gran and Alaric raised me, not you. You were too busy with getting your nails and hair done, or hobnobbing with your society friends. You never gave a damn about Holly or me. We just cramped your style, just like your husbands."

"That's rubbish."

"Suck it up mother, it's the truth," he said flatly. "And I'm done pretending otherwise."

"You're just like your father. Cruel and nasty. And you'll end up just as alone and miserable." She spat out venomously

Marcus straightened, unflinching.

"That's where you're wrong, mother. In all the years I've known Brin, we've seen each other at our worst, but never once has she been cruel or vindictive like you. She has more kindness and compassion in her little finger than you have in your entire being."

His voice softened, not weakening, but resolute.

"And I intend to spend every day for the rest of my life, showing her just how grateful I am that she chose me as her *mate.*"

"You ungrateful, spiteful…"

"Go home mother. You're not wanted here anymore." He told her, cutting off her rant before she got started.

"You don't speak for your sister or your grandmother," Jocelyn protested. "I will stay as long as I like."

"Actually, Marcus is speaking for us too." Holly told her, stepping into view from a nearby room, beside her was their Gran. Their expressions were solemn but resolute, mirroring Marcus.

Jocelyn stared at them, stunned.

"What? Surely you don't mean that." Jocelyn looked between her daughter and mother in disbelief, her expression shifting back to haughty superiority again when they wouldn't recant their words.

"Jocelyn dear, I love you," Gran said gently, "But Marcus and Holly are right. It's time for you to go home."

Jocelyn's lips thinned. "Fine. I know when I'm not wanted." With that, Jocelyn stormed past them, up the stairs to her bedroom to pack her things without a single glance back.

Silence settled as the tension dissipated.

Marcus exhaled slowly, his shoulders sagging. "Do you think I was too harsh with her?"

"Hell no. She's had that coming for a long time. I'm surprised you didn't say more." Holly told him.

Marcus shrugged. A week ago, he just might have. However, he doubted his mother would change her attitude, no matter how severely a dose of reality was dished out to her. Nor did he feel the same level of bitterness toward her that he used to, not now that he had a far different future to the one he'd feared all his life. In fact, he couldn't wait to start his new life with his *mate*.

Brin stepped from the hallway, her heart swelling with fierce, quiet certainty.

No prophecy had forced this.

He had chosen her.

And she was choosing him right back.

"Brin, how much of that did you hear?" he asked, drawing her into his arms with a kiss.

"All of it. I'm sorry." She told him sympathetically.

"I'm not. It actually felt good to get all that off my chest," he smiled.

"Speaking of getting things off your chest, we weren't deliberately eavesdropping either, we were on our way to find you. Raif and Seth are here to see the pair of you." Holly told them with a sly grin. "And, before anyone else gets a chance…Congratulations! We've been waiting for years for you two to come to your senses." She told them, hugging them in turn, the gesture repeated enthusiastically by their Gran.

"Seriously, how many people thought we were supposed to be a couple?" he asked dumbfounded.

"Everyone." Holly and Gran replied in unison with a laugh.

"My brothers are here? Do you think they know I was kidnapped last night?" she asked sheepishly.

"I'd say so love, they both have faces like thunder. And, once they've had their say, you're likely to get the same speech from everyone else in the family too for slipping out the way you did," Gran told her firmly but sympathetically.

Brin scrunched up her nose, cringing at the thought. Regardless, she had to take responsibility for her actions. She only wished she didn't have such a large extended family who would each want to express their disappointment in her. Oh, this was going to be a very long day, she thought.

"You're not getting off Scott free either my boy," Gran told him, poking her finger into his chest. "I believe you have some explaining to do too."

"Gary's already in Alaric's office, and Oliver's on his way over. They want to talk to you after you've spoken with Raif and Seth." Holly told him.

Marcus' shoulders slumped with a sigh. Yeah, he had this coming too. No doubt his brother-in-law, a.k.a commanding officer, Gary Sanders, Oliver and Alaric, had some cruel and unusual punishment lined up for him.

"I don't suppose we could put everyone in a room together and get this over with in one go?" he suggested.

"Hell no. Not that I'd mind being there to watch you having your arse handed to you, but the women of the house want more intimate details that neither of you are going to share with the men around, isn't that right Gran?" Holly grinned, enjoying Marcus' discomfort.

"Accept it love, nothing happens in this house without everyone knowing about it. And now that the two of you are a couple, you're just going to have to get used to that. Whether you like it or not, the pair of you live here now." Gran told him, giving his cheeks a smoosh.

He hadn't considered that. He'd spent the last fourteen years living in the barracks, but the manor was where he was raised, and this was the place that felt like home. It was only fitting that he would return here with his *mate.*

"You're going to have to move to a bigger suite though. Your room is far too small for the two of you…or more, down the track," Holly winked.

Marcus cleared his throat uncomfortably. "Right. Ah…On that note, I think we'll go and get the first round of lectures out of the way. Coming my dear?" he said, offering Brin the crook of his arm regally to escort her arm in arm toward the drawing room where her brothers waited.

"Ahhh, they make such a cute couple, don't they." Holly grinned, offering Gran her arm in a similar way, heading in the opposite direction toward the kitchen.

Opening the door, the drawing room had a faint, charged stillness to it. Brin felt it the moment she stepped inside, her gaze falling towards her brothers.

Raif stood near the tall windows, arms folded, broad shoulders blocking out the morning light. Seth lounged against the fireplace mantel, one ankle crossed over the other, his expression deceptively relaxed, but his eyes were sharp, assessing every movement they made.

Marcus stiffened beside her.

Brin resisted the urge to squeeze his hand, though the impulse was strong. Instead, she lifted her chin and walked in with him, shoulders back, contrite but unflinching. There was no point pretending innocence here.

"Well," Raif said at last, his voice calm in the way that meant he was anything but calm. "Brin, do you have something to tell me?" Raif asked.

"Maybe. Maybe not." That was not one of her better comebacks, she thought wincing slightly. "I gather you've heard."

Raif's eyebrow lifted. "Oh, we heard."

"Every detail," Seth added lightly. "You snuck out regardless of the danger, and then managed to get yourself kidnapped by the Guild and a Scree demon…" His gaze slid to Marcus. "And we've heard about you apparently sprouting wings and deciding gravity was optional."

Marcus cleared his throat. "Right."

Raif's attention shifted fully to Brin now, and the temperature in the room dropped a few degrees.

"I assume you have a good reason why you thought it was acceptable to leave the manor?" he asked evenly.

Brin opened her mouth. Then closed it again. "Well, duh…" Another badass comeback for the record books. It was right up there with *yeah, nah.*

"Would you care to share?" Seth asked, prompting her with a hand gesture.

"Ah…No." she said quietly. "Because there isn't one. Not a good one."

That seemed to catch them off guard.

Raif studied her for a long moment, then exhaled slowly. "At least you're honest."

Seth tilted his head. "Frankly, your *reason* doesn't require much imagination." His eyes flicked pointedly to Marcus. "The two of you have just spent a week together, and last night he went out with another woman. You were jealous. But since the two of you have now bonded, I'm assuming you've been on an emotional rollercoaster."

Brin flushed. "How do you know we've bonded?"

Raif looked at her incredulously, as though he thought she suddenly halved her IQ. "His scent is all over you. That's only possible if you've bonded," he told her, spearing his gaze toward Marcus.

Marcus looked faintly like he wanted the floor to open up and swallow him and silently prepared himself for a punch to the gut or an uppercut to his jaw from her protective brothers.

"We're not thrilled about your poor judgment to leave the manor," Raif continued. "Although, we understand the *why*, it doesn't make it acceptable."

"It was stupid and reckless," Seth added.

"I totally agree," Brin muttered.

Raif's sternness softened just a fraction. "You terrified us."

Brin swallowed. "I know, and I'm really sorry." She told them, her eyes cast downwards, unable to meet her brothers' disappointed gaze.

The silence shifted, not heavy anymore, but curious.

"Okay, moving on," Seth said at last, pushing off the mantel. "Let's talk about *you*, Marcus."

Marcus straightened instinctively.

Raif's eyes gleamed. "Would you mind showing us the mark?"

Marcus hesitated, then rolled up his sleeve. Beneath his skin, the unmistakable dark outline of a dragon's form protruded beneath flesh.

Seth let out a low whistle. "Impressive."

Raif nodded slowly. "Fascinating."

"So, when do we get a demonstration of your new beast?" Seth asked.

Marcus huffed. "Later. I've got…other meetings to get to this morning."

Raif's lips twitched. "Alaric?"

"And Oliver," Marcus muttered. "…And Sanders."

"Oh," Seth said with mock sympathy. "Good luck with that."

"Yeah, thanks." They were enjoying his discomfort far too much for his liking.

Raif's gaze sharpened, looking again at the dragon mark on his wrist, drawing Marcus' attention back to it too.

"I'm hoping you could clarify something about the prophecy for me." Marcus said.

"Sure, if we can." Raif told him.

"There's a line," Marcus said slowly, "I don't fully understand. *Together they live, apart they die.* And the part about living as long as Brin does." His jaw tightened. "Does that mean my lifespan has changed from five hundred years as a lycan to three thousand, the same as Brin?"

Raif and Seth exchanged a look.

Then Raif spoke carefully. "Grandfather explained this once. Many years ago."

Seth picked up the thread. "As long as Brin lives, you're effectively immortal. Nothing can kill you."

Marcus listened intently.

"But when she dies," Raif finished quietly, "So do you. No matter what her age is when that happens."

Their words landed hard and Marcus swallowed. "So…what you're telling me is that if I hadn't reached her last night, and the Guild had killed her…"

"You would've died too," Seth said plainly.

Marcus looked toward Brin. Really looked at her. There was no fear in his eyes, only something fierce and certain.

"Good," he said softly.

Brin's breath caught. "Marcus…"

"If I ever lose you," he continued, brushing his thumb over her cheek, "I wouldn't want to keep living anyway."

Raif watched them for a long moment, then nodded once, satisfied.

"Well," he said, straightening. "You've scared us half to death. And you're grounded indefinitely."

Brin chuckled, looking at Marcus. "I will gratefully accept any punishment my *mate* decides is fair."

"Don't worry, I have many hours of *retribution* lined up for her," Marcus told them, a very salacious lilt to his tone and expression. "I can give you in-depth detail if you'd like."

"Umm…Thanks, but no thanks. We're her brothers, we've already heard enough." Seth cringed uncomfortably.

"No doubt I'll hear all about it later from my *mate* anyway." Raif muttered under his breath with a huff.

Satisfied, the brothers began to move toward the door.

"I need to find Kaitlyn and Finn, and head home," Raif said. "Any idea where I'll find them?"

"I'd try the kitchen." Brin told him.

"Ah, of course. It's the only room with a coffee machine."

"Seth, are you returning to Fey too?" Marcus asked.

"No." Seth answered lightly, "I'm heading back to London. I love you all dearly, but I need a break from the relentless happiness." He joked.

Brin frowned. "Seth…?"

He waved away her half spoken question. "Don't. I'm fine. Just…outnumbered."

They parted ways in the hall, Raif and Seth toward the kitchen, and Marcus and Brin headed for Alaric's study.

Marcus squeezed Brin's hand. "Ready for round two?"

She grimaced. "No."

"Me too. Let's just get this over with."

The moment the study door opened, the temperature seemed to drop several degrees, and the stern facial expressions of everyone in the room, warned of trouble. Naturally, Marcus assumed that they were the cause, and almost did a backstep out again.

Alaric stood behind his desk, his hands braced against the polished wood as though the weight of the world was on his shoulders, and maybe it was. Oliver stood off to one side, arms folded, his expression calm, but razor-focused. Sanders stood rigidly still nearby, his eyes sharp beneath a carefully neutral expression.

No one was sitting.

"I'm sorry," Marcus said, clearing his throat, forcing steadiness into his voice. "We can come back if this is a bad time."

Alaric's gaze lifted, sharp but not unkind.

"No," he said evenly. "Come in, both of you. We have things to discuss."

The door closed behind them with a solid, click.

For a brief moment, the tension eased.

Alaric straightened, the severity in his expression easing just a little. "First," he said, "Congratulations. To both of you."

Oliver's mouth twitched into a small smile. "Yes, congratulations. Brin, you've got yourself a good *mate.*"

Sanders inclined his head with a sly smirk. "He's also an arsehole, my condolences to you Brin." Clapping his brother-in-law on the back and giving his soon-to-be sister-in-law a kiss on the cheek.

Brin let out a tight breath as she too relaxed a little. "Thanks," she said, as both a question and a statement at the mixed versions of compliments.

Then Alaric gestured toward the chairs opposite his desk.

"Sit."

The word wasn't harsh, but it was absolute.

They obeyed.

Alaric folded his hands in front of him on the desk, his gaze settling squarely on Marcus. "Your debriefing report from Canada was…incomplete."

Marcus grimaced. "Yes, sir."

"I'd like you to fill in the parts you omitted," Alaric continued. "Specifically, the serpent armband."

Marcus nodded once. "Understood."

He explained, succinctly, deliberately, how the armband had bitten him in the cave, how the rash and fever had followed, how his connection to his wolf had weakened and then vanished entirely. Once again however, he omitted the other events in the cabin with Brin.

Brin watched the other men closely as he spoke. They listened without interruption.

When Marcus finished, Alaric's gaze shifted toward her. "Brin, what happened last night?"

Brin swallowed. "I'm really sorry, I know I shouldn't have gone, but I…"

She looked like she was about the break down in tears so Alaric changed tact, he didn't have the time or the inclination to deal with female water works today.

"More specifically, what about the events outside the restaurant?"

Brin took a deep breath but didn't relax. "Marcus told me to wait for him. He said he'd take me home."

Marcus' jaw tightened.

"I was embarrassed that I'd followed him there." she admitted quietly. "I felt foolish. I just wanted to disappear." Her fingers curled in her lap. "I was sure nothing was going to happen to me, that I was safe…but I didn't even make it three metres from the door. The van pulled up beside me, and they grabbed me."

Marcus gripped her hand for support, as the memories replayed in her mind, still terrifyingly fresh.

"I went after them immediately. I called my wolf forward to shift." Marcus told them. His mouth pulled tight at the memory. "That's when I realised my wolf wasn't…my wolf anymore."

Oliver's brow lifted slightly. "So last night was the first time you've shifted since you were bitten? You had no idea anything had changed before then."

"Yes, Sir."

The moment of silence stretched until Sanders exhaled slowly, something like approval in the sound. "You adapted quickly."

"I didn't really have a choice."

"No," Sanders agreed. "I suppose you didn't."

There was a brief pause, then Sanders straightened. "We'll need to have a more in-depth discussion later about what this means for your future role in the lycan military."

Marcus nodded without hesitation. "I'll accept whatever you decide."

Oliver's gaze sharpened with something close to respect.

"Your shift in public did create a minor issue," Oliver said mildly. "One of the shops caught your transformation on CCTV."

Marcus winced. "Fuck! I'm sorry. And…I'm sorry for the mess on the bridge."

Sanders barked out a laugh. "It was worth it."

Marcus blinked. "Sir?"

Sanders grinned. "The cleanup was a pain in the arse, but seeing your new form? That was worth it."

Marcus huffed. "Thanks. I think."

Alaric turned to Brin. "The armband, are you still wearing it?"

She lifted her sleeve. The gold serpent glinted in the morning light. "It won't come off," she said simply.

Alaric studied it for a long moment without attempting to touch it, then nodded. "If it can defend you, that may be for the best."

His gaze returned to Marcus. "Which brings us to the Scree demon."

Marcus stiffened slightly. "I killed it."

"Yes," Oliver said dryly. "We saw that. The question is, how?"

"I bit it," Marcus replied. "And whatever venom is in my bite now, seems to be the same as the serpent armband's, the Scree died the same way as it did back in Canada, only faster."

Sanders nodded. "Impressive."

Marcus had the unsettling realisation that instead of being sidelined from his military position, he'd just become far more valuable.

He cleared his throat. "Are we still needed here?"

Alaric exchanged a look with Oliver, then said, "Not both of you. Marcus if you could stay." He turned his attention to Brin. "You're free to join the women in the kitchen if you like, I'm sure they're all dying to talk to you. And, if you ask the others to come down here, please." The others, meaning the men who were part of the Alliance.

She hesitated. Marcus met her gaze and gave a small nod, squeezing his fingers once more and slipped from the room.

Moments later, voices filtered in from the hall as the other men filed through the door, including Raif and Seth.

"What's going on?" Narayan asked.

"I have good news," he said. "And not-so-good news."

Every man in the room went quiet.

"The good news," Alaric continued, "Is that Alex has found a cure for the virus."

A ripple moved through the room, not cheers, but a quiet celebration of relief.

"And the bad news?" Oliver asked quietly.

"Scorpion paid the Ukraine base a visit earlier this morning."

The temperature in the room shifted from cool to boiling in an instant, metaphorically, from the combined anger and foul curses that echoed around the room.

"What the fuck was he doing there?" Seb asked.

"He offered condolences to Elise for Gustav's illness," Alaric said. "And informed her, quite arrogantly, that he has eyes and ears everywhere."

"He just walked in there?" Philippe demanded.

"Yes," Alaric said grimly. "Which tells us two things. One, he was fully aware the base is currently unmanned and vulnerable. And two, he and Morganna are up to something."

Sanders crossed his arms. "Clearly, we've got a leak."

"Or Emil has been compromised," Oliver added.

"Alex and the others are sweeping the base now," Alaric continued. "Phones, computer systems, every corner and crevice of the place. I've notified Emil of the breach and he's going to lay low for a while. Until we identify the source, we have to assume no communication is secure."

No one argued.

"Until then," Alaric finished, "We take extreme precautions with any information. Everything is need-to-know only. If Scorpion and Morganna are personally getting involved, we can't take any chances."

His gaze swept the room. One by one, heads nodded in agreement.

What really pissed him off, was that they always seemed to be playing catch-up with whatever evil plot the pair and their corrupt organisation came up with.

Not forever. One day, hopefully soon, the tide of fate was going to turn in their favour.

Epilogue

One week later:

The Ukraine base was still in lockdown, but the atmosphere had changed.

Where there had been dread and anxiety, there was now something else threading through the concrete corridors.

Relief. Cautious, controlled relief, because nobody here trusted hope unless it came in the form of test results.

Alex's vaccine worked. The first doses had been administered only hours after Alex confirmed his results after a second round of testing, and Teagan removed the stasis spell on the infected men. Then they watched and waited, logging every change in temperature, behaviour, heartbeat, respiration. Every twitch.

Within hours the difference had been unmistakable.

Klaus, who'd been spiralling toward the feral edge of madness, began to stabilise. His aggression dulled. That rabid flicker behind the eyes replaced with something human again, confused and exhausted, but very much alive.

Gustav's recovery was much faster. His mental state improved in tandem with his fever subsiding and was back to normal within a day.

The first lycan infected, his recovery was different.

He wasn't getting worse, not anymore, but to say he was "better", wasn't quite accurate. His body responded to the vaccine, yes. His fever broke, his muscles unclenched. He stopped thrashing against invisible enemies and stopped snarling at shadows.

And yet when he opened his eyes, there was something…missing.

The cognitive injury was obvious in the way he stared past people instead of at them, the way comprehension arrived late or not at all. He reacted to touch and sound like a man detached from reality.

That virus had ravaged him the longest. But they still held out hope for him. He was lycan after all. If he could manage to shift, his wolf could help heal what the vaccine couldn't.

Only time would tell if he made a full recovery, or he remained as he was now.

In the meantime, the cure remained a tightly kept secret. No announcements. No celebrations beyond the locked lab doors. No triumphant phone calls that could be intercepted. Nothing that might reach the Guild's ears and alert them to their "priority one" virus having been neutralised.

The Bunker Restaurant above, had also been closed. A sign hung on the front door: *Closed For Refurbishment.*

Technically that wasn't a lie. More to the point, a restaurant can't open without a chef.

The man who'd been there since the day the place opened twenty years earlier, the one Elise had always sworn could run the kitchen single-handedly…was dead.

They found him when they searched the building for the source of the leak. Starting in the basement, they worked their way upward. The restaurant being last on their list.

They found him in the freezer. By the state of him, he'd been in there for days.

Which meant the man who'd been cooking in the kitchen, had been an imposter.

Going over CCTV recordings of the restaurant for the past couple of weeks, they watched hours of footage of regular restaurant activity. And then, a man entered the restaurant, walking with purpose toward the kitchen.

And he never left.

Eytan leaned closer to the screen, face hardening into something cold and dangerous.

"I know him," he said flatly. The name landed like a curse. "Oran."

He was one of the rephaim imprisoned in the Valley of Vardin. One of the handful who had never reformed, never softened, never let the passage of fifteen centuries scrape Morganna's poison out of his bones.

And Oran, worst of all, was a skinwalker. Able to duplicate a person so completely in appearance, voice and mannerisms, it was almost impossible to tell him apart from the original. A skinwalker didn't just copy person on a superficial level, they absorbed their very essence, right down to their earliest memories. In the process, their victim died, a very painful death. Eytan should know, he was also a skinwalker.

Even so, Elise had noticed something off about their chef. It was nothing in his manner other than how unusually quiet he had been, but in hindsight it was now quite obvious. His cooking wasn't quite up to his usual standard. It wasn't bad, not enough to raise alarms. It seemed Oran could mimic the chef's identity, but he couldn't mimic decades of artful cooking skills.

By the time they discovered the truth, Oran was gone. Although, hopefully not for long.

Eytan had been born in the Valley, and after Morganna escaped, he became their leader, and leaders survived by knowing exactly who their enemies were, and how to deal with them. Oran had been high on that list, which meant Eytan had a pretty good idea of how to find him. And when he did, he planned to capture him and interrogate him. But, if that proved too difficult, Eytan had no problems with simply killing the bastard.

The revelation of the Skinwalker thankfully ruled out the possibility that Emil had been compromised. Even so, extra precautions were put into place to keep him safe.

Two months later:

Secrecy had its place. But so did humiliation, according to Alex, who excelled at both, unfortunately for anyone who crossed him.

The Alliance arranged for a pharmaceutical company to mass produce the vaccine, with Alex overseeing its production. Of course, the company employees believed it was for a new strain of flu, thanks to his very effective use of vampiric mind compulsion.

The vaccine was produced, packaged and delivered to all wyverns throughout Fey, and lycan communities across Earth. It was administered quietly and efficiently.

The Guild's virus was now effectively dead, only the Guild didn't know it yet.

And the Alliance liked it that way.

The only snag in the whole production was of course, Alex.

Not known for having a great attention span, or a conscience, Alex had clashed with the company's pompous CEO, who lied as easily as he breathed, taking credit for his employee's achievements and blaming them for his own short falls.

Alex tolerated him for a while. Then, in a moment of inspiration, he compelled the man to cluck like a chicken every time he lied. That was amusing for about three days.

Long enough for the board to begin watching him with concern, also long enough for staff morale to begin to improve, and long enough too for Alex to decide the joke needed escalation.

So, Alex being Alex, he scaled up the punishment.

Every time the CEO lied, he was compelled to drop his pants.

It didn't take long for the CEO to be removed from his position, pending psychiatric evaluation and a couple of sexual harassment charges.

Alex, naturally, was delighted. He considered it a public service, and the staff tended to agree.

Having produced, distributed and administered the vaccine, there was no need to keep the Ukraine base on lockdown and it returned to full operation. Which meant the Ukraine base could finally re-open. The restaurant too re-opened, refurbished with a new menu and a new chef.

And back at Havenswood Manor, life had shifted into a different kind of chaos.

Tilly and Cujo's hellhound pups had grown fast. At two months old, each of them was the size of a full-grown Labrador, and growing bigger every day.

Except, while a Labrador pup tended to destroy shoes and carpets by chewing alone, the hellhound's acidic slobber made a much more thorough job of it. Much to Alaric's dismay. Regardless, the household adapted.

And now, at two months of age, it was time to re-home all four pups.

Grace and Riley, predictably, had wanted to keep one each. And of course, Alaric refused. Repeatedly. Right up until Cassie delivered the only bargaining chip that ever truly worked. She promised to cut off *all sex privileges* for the next decade if he didn't agree.

Begrudgingly, Alaric caved.

Grace kept Lady, and Riley chose Devil. Except Riley decided Devil's name should be changed to Marcus, because in Riley's eyes Marcus' new beastly form had become the single coolest thing ever, and felt his new pet should be named after him. Convincing him otherwise, hadn't been easy, but he finally understood the confusion that was likely to occur with the real Marcus living under the same roof now too. So, he settled on the name Spike. Not very original, but the hellhound seemed to like it.

The other two pups went to family as well, because once two kids were allowed to keep hellhound pups, their cousins also wanted to own a demonic dog.

Lucifer went to Finn at the citadel in Avengard, while Hades went to Dray's daughter in Oxford.

In both cases, the wives made the negotiations simple. Give in or give up sex for the next decade.

And because hellhounds were four times the size of a normal dog, the druid sisters crafted special collars, the same as those worn by the hellhounds who wandered through Savernake Forest, allowing the pups to *appear* like normal, large dogs.

Life had basically returned to normal, except for one difference.

While they had deleted the shop footage of Marcus shifting into his beastly form, they weren't so lucky with footage taken of the wyvern brothers flying over Canada, which had gone viral.

Dozens of videos flooded social media and even made it to mainstream news, and with it, previous footage of Wade on top of the Jefferson Tower in Birmingham, Alabama several years prior, plus more. Videos began to surface of vampires, wolves and also demons lurking about city streets at night.

The supernatural world had worked very hard for millennia to keep their existence secret, but it now seemed that they were becoming common knowledge, and there was nothing they could do to put that genie back in the bottle and make it all go away.

Alaric stood by the lounge room window, hands folded behind his back, staring out at the manor's grounds.

The lawns and gardens were slowly coming back to life with the help of the gardener's hard work and spring's warmth. It wasn't the first time the grounds had been destroyed, nor would it be the last.

Otherwise, life had returned to something close to normal, slipping back into a comfortable routine of daily life, but how long that was going to last was anyone's guess.

They still had several artefacts to find, and Morganna and Scorpion were clearly working on a new plan.

He could only hope they were ready for whatever was coming next.

About the Author:

K.G. Inglis is the author of the Eternal series. When not writing about the sexy vampires and alpha lycans and dragons, she can be found reading about them and spending time with her family. Native to Australia, she lives in a beach town on the Southern Coast which many call a holiday destination. If you like your men hot and the action steamy, mixed with a heavy dose of humour, then the Eternal series will find a space in your 'must read again' collection.

Follow her for updates at:

www.kginglis.com/

facebook.com/kginglis.official/#

instagram.com/KGInglis

twitter.com/KG_Inglis

bookbub.com/authors/k-g-inglis

goodreads.com/author/show/17230080.K_G_Inglis

www.ingramcontent.com/pod-product-compliance
Lightning Source LLC
LaVergne TN
LVHW010600100826
845148LV00014B/2789

* 9 7 8 1 7 6 3 5 0 6 1 2 1 *